JOHN CONNOLLY

The White Road

HODDER

First published in Great Britain in 2002 Hodder & Stoughton
An Hachette UK company

This paperback edition published in 2015

7

A CIP catalogue record for this title is available from the British Library

ISBN 978 1 444 704716

Typeset in Plantin Light by Hewer Text UK Ltd, Edinburgh
Printed and bound by Clays Ltd, St Ives plc

Hodder & Stoughton policy is to use papers that are natural, renewable and recyclable products and made from wood grown in sustainable forests. The logging and manufacturing processes are expected to conform to the environmental regulations of the country of origin.

Hodder & Stoughton Ltd
338 Euston Road
London NW1 3BH

www.hodder.co.uk

For Darley Anderson

Grateful acknowledgement is made for permission to reprint from the following copyrighted works:

Extract from 'The Waste Land' reprinted by permission of Faber & Faber Ltd, 3 Queen Square, London WC1N 3AU

Pinetop Seven: lines from 'Mission District' (lyrics: Darren Richard) from *Bringing Home the Last Great Strike* (Self-Help/Truckstop Records, 2000). © Darren Richard, reprinted by permission of Darren Richard and Truckstop Audio Recording Company.
www.pinetopseven.com

Grateful acknowledgement is made for permission to reprint from the following copyrighted works:

Extract from 'The Waste Land' and reprinted by permission of Faber & Faber Ltd, 3 Queen Square London WC1N 3AU

Pinetop Seven lines from 'Mission District' (lyrics Darren Richard) from *Bringing Home the Last Great Strike* (Self-Help/Truckstop Records, 2000) © Darren Richard. Reprinted by permission of Darren Richard and Truckstop Audio Recording Company.
www.pinetopseven.com

INTRODUCTION

I'm always surprised when a reader cites *The White Road* as a particular favourite among my novels – not because I'm in any way ashamed of it, but because it's dark, and pretty relentless, and it was hard both to write and research.

Its genesis came from an exhibition of lynching photography that I attended in New York in 2000. As I write this, I have beside me the exhibition catalogue, entitled *No Sanctuary: Lynching Photography in America.* After I published *The White Road*, someone sent me an actual postcard from a lynching, dating from the end of the 19th century. It features a man hanging from a bridge, surrounded by onlookers. Below it, the text – handwritten, and then reproduced – reads 'Nickolas Foley Aged 26. Hanged by lynchers June 22nd 1889, 7 ½ miles South of Oakdale at Palmer's Bridge. Murdered Mrs Clark night of June 19th, 1889.'

It's not clear if Foley was black or white, but the law of averages would suggest that he was black. Thousands of black men and women in the United States were subjected to this form of summary justice, often accompanied by torture and brutalization before the final act. What I found so troubling was that these lynchings were not secret, shameful acts but forms of public entertainment, often attended by whole families in an atmosphere of carnival-like joviality. The lynching of Sam Hose near the town of Newman, Georgia in 1899 was attended by more than 2000 white Georgians. A special excursion train from Atlanta was organized for the event. Hose had killed his white employer, Alfred Cranford, after Cranford drew a pistol and threatened to kill him in a dispute over wages. Hose's fate was particularly awful: he was stripped, chained to a tree, soaked with oil, mutilated, and then burned alive.

I knew that, at some point in my fiction, I'd have to tackle the issue of race. I was probably already half aware of this when I introduced the character of Louis back in *Every Dead Thing*, and the opening of *The White Road* gives us some clue to the rage underpinning him, and to a personal history that would be examined more deeply in *The Reapers*. The book also picks up on the events of *The Killing Kind*, the novel that preceded it, so it's the closest thing to a sequel in the Parker series. If you're glancing through this introduction in a bookstore, and you haven't read *The Killing Kind*, then you can still read this book, but you'll probably get more out of it if you read *The Killing Kind* first.

I decided on South Carolina as a setting because the state was in the news at the time, as the South Carolina State Senate had finally passed a bill to remove the Confederate flag from the top of the State House in Columbia. (A more traditional version of the battle flag still flies in front of the building, despite a 2005 poll that showed almost 75 per cent of African-Americans surveyed wanted it removed from the grounds entirely.) I then began looking into the history and mechanics of rice cultivation, as it was rice and indigo, not cotton, which were farmed by slaves in South Carolina, and generated much of the state's wealth.

Researching the book was a miserable experience, and only in part because of the nature of the research itself. I made two trips to South Carolina to work on the book, basing myself in Charleston on each occasion. The first visit went okay, apart from backing my rental car into a tree somewhere out by the Congaree Swamp, but the second was awful. I arrived in Charleston shortly after 9/11, intending to spend a week or so there before going on to a conference in Washington DC. To get to the conference required booking a one-way flight from Charleston to Washington, which I duly tried to do over the phone with a Charleston travel agency, only to be told that they'd have to call me back. I was subsequently visited at my hotel by an agent of the FBI, who had been informed by the travel agent that someone with a foreign accent was trying to book a one-way flight to DC. (My outraged response was 'I'm not foreign, I'm Irish!')

I then decided to attend the South Carolina State Fair in Columbia, never having been to a state fair anywhere. Parking was a pain, so I found a space in a lot near the fairgrounds that was being operated for charity by a number of elderly men. I paid one of them the fee – I think it was $10 – and went off to look around the fair. When I returned, I was surrounded by a group of angry pensioners who accused me of not paying to park my car. I pointed out the guy to whom I'd given my money, and he flat-out denied ever having received a penny from me. I could almost *see* my folded ten-dollar bill in his pocket, but, like Peter denying Christ, he would only shake his head and say that he had never even spoken to me. Southern hospitality quickly went out the window, and it all grew very unpleasant and heated. I think I finally told them to call the cops if they felt so strongly about it, at which point they decided that it wasn't worth the effort, and I went on my less-than-merry way. (As I recall, 'Go on, git out of here' were the final words spoken to me in farewell.)

So it may be that my personal experiences coloured the narrative somewhat, although some years later I ended up back in Charleston when the film of my short story 'The New Daughter' was being made nearby. On that occasion a horde of hungry mosquitoes descended on me when I was filming an interview for the DVD of the movie. South Carolina may just not be my state. Responses to the book from native South Carolinians were divided: younger readers tended to identify with it more than older ones, although it was by no means an even split.

The events surrounding publication of the book weren't significantly happier. I received a letter from someone claiming to represent Charlotte/Douglas International Airport in North Carolina, objecting to my depiction of this fine aviation facility in the book and informing me, in no uncertain terms, that it would be a sorry day indeed when my literary works ever found themselves on sale there. I've passed through it since, and it's improved a lot (it has a nice tree-lined atrium), but it was pretty grim on the day I caught my connection to South Carolina. One could still smoke in the airport at that time, which might explain a lot: as a non-smoker, waiting for a flight in a packed terminal building surrounded by a fug of second-hand smoke is not conducive to happy memories.

The White Road also provided me with my least successful signing event ever. I was booked into a bookshop in a Californian city, but when I arrived it appeared that the store specialized in black literature, which made *The White Road* sound like some kind of weird self-help book for black people who wanted to be more Caucasian, with advice on buying Perry Como records or loud sweaters. One of the staff members silently lined up six chairs (6) in front of a basement podium, sat on one of the chairs (1), and waited with me while nobody (0) came to hear me speak. I stood at the podium, feeling a bit awkward, until eventually the staff member stood, put away the chairs, and went off to do something more useful instead.

Working on *The White Road* left me drained, which might explain why, after finishing it, I took time off from the series to write *Bad Men* and *Nocturnes*. It remains one of my most difficult writing experiences, but I'm proud of the book that resulted from it. I admit that this may be my creeping Catholicism at work, and the belief that, if something comes too easily, then it probably has no value. I'll leave it for you to decide.

PART ONE

Who is the third who walks always beside you?
When I count, there are only you and I together
But when I look ahead up the white road
There is always another one walking beside you
Gliding wrapt in a brown mantle, hooded
I do not know whether a man or a woman
– But who is that on the other side of you?

T. S. Eliot, 'The Waste Land'

PROLOGUE

They are coming.

They are coming in their trucks and their cars, plumes of blue smoke following them through the clear night air like stains upon the soul. They are coming with their wives and their children, with their lovers and their sweethearts, talking of crops and animals and journeys they will make; of church bells and Sunday schools; of wedding dresses and the names of children yet unborn; of who said this and who said that, things small and great, the lifeblood of a thousand small towns no different from their own.

They are coming with food and drink, and the smell of fried chicken and fresh-baked pies makes their mouths water. They are coming with dirt beneath their nails and beer on their breath. They are coming in pressed shirts and patterned dresses, hair combed and hair wild. They are coming with joy in their hearts and vengeance on their minds and excitement curling like a snake in the hollow of their bellies.

They are coming to see the burning man.

The two men stopped at Cebert Yaken's gas station, 'The Friendliest Little Gas Station in the South,' close by the banks of the Ogeechee River on the road to Caina. Cebert had painted the sign himself in 1968 in bright yellows and reds, and every year since then he had climbed onto the flat roof on the first day of April to freshen the colors, so that the sun would never take its toll upon the sign and cause the welcome to fade. Each day, the sign cast its shadow on the clean lot, on the flowers in their boxes, on the shining gas pumps, and on the buckets filled with water so that drivers could wipe the remains of bugs from their windshields. Beyond lay untilled fields, and in the early September heat the shimmer rising from the road made the sassafras dance in the still air. The butterflies mixed with the falling leaves, sleepy oranges and checkered whites and eastern tailed blues bouncing upward in the wake of passing vehicles like the sails of brightly colored ships tossing on a wild sea.

From his stool by the window, Cebert would look out on the arriving cars, checking for out-of-state tags so that he could prepare a good old Southern welcome, maybe sell some coffee and doughnuts or shift some of the tourist maps, the yellowing of their covers in the sunlight signaling the approaching end of their usefulness.

Cebert dressed the part: he wore blue overalls with his name sewn on the left breast, and a Co-Op Beef Feeds cap sat way back on his head like an afterthought. His hair was white and he had a long mustache that curled exotically over his upper lip, the two ends almost meeting on his chin. Behind his back folks said that it made Cebert look like a bird had just flown up his nose, but they didn't mean nothing by it. Cebert's family had lived in these parts for generations and Cebert was one of their own. He advertised bake sales and picnics in the windows of his gas station and donated to every good cause that came his way. If dressing and acting like Grandpa Walton helped him sell a little more gas and a couple of extra candy bars, then good luck to Cebert.

Above the wooden counter, behind which Cebert sat day in, day out, seven days each week, sharing the duties with his wife and his boy, was a bulletin board headed: 'Look Who Dropped By!' Pinned to it were hundreds of business cards. There were more cards on the walls and the window frames, and on the door that led into Cebert's little back office. Thousands of Abe B. Normals or Bob R. Averages, passing through Georgia on their way to sell more photocopy ink or hair-care products, had handed old Cebert their cards so that they could leave a reminder of their visit to the Friendliest Little Gas Station in the South. Cebert never took them down, so that card had piled upon card in a process of accretion, layering like rock. True, some had fallen over the years, or slipped behind the coolers, but for the most part if the Abe B.'s or Bob R.'s passed through again in years to come, with a little Abe or Bob in tow, there was a pretty good chance that they would find their cards buried beneath a hundred others, like a relic of the lives that they had once enjoyed and of the men that they had once been.

But the two men who paid for a full tank and put water in the steaming engine of their piece-of-shit Taurus just before five that afternoon weren't the kind who left their business cards. Cebert saw that straight off, felt it as something gave in his belly when they glanced at him. They carried themselves in a way that suggested barely suppressed menace and a potential for lethality that was as definite as a cocked gun or an unsheathed blade. Cebert barely nodded at them when they entered and he sure as hell didn't ask them for a card. These men didn't want to be remembered, and if, like Cebert, you were smart, then you'd pretty much do your best to forget them as soon as they'd paid for their gas (in cash, of course) and the last dust from their car had settled back on the ground.

Because if at some later date you did decide to remember them, maybe when the cops came asking and flashing descriptions, then, well, they might hear about it and decide to remember you too. And the next time someone dropped by to see old Cebert they'd be carrying flowers and old Cebert wouldn't get to shoot the breeze or sell them a fading tourist map because old Cebert would be dead and long past worrying about yellowing stock and peeling paint.

So Cebert took their money and watched as the shorter one, the little white guy who had topped up the water when they pulled into the gas station, flicked through the cheap CDs and the small stock of paperbacks that Cebert kept on a rack by the door. The other man, the tall black one with the black shirt and the designer jeans, was looking casually at the corners of the ceiling and the shelves behind the counter loaded high with cigarettes. When he was satisfied that there was no camera, he removed his wallet and, using leather-gloved fingers, counted out two tens to pay for the gas and two sodas, then waited quietly while Cebert made change. Their car was the only one at the pumps. It had New York plates and both the plates and the car were kind of dirty, so Cebert couldn't see much except for the make and the color and Miss Liberty peering through the murk.

'You need a map?' asked Cebert, hopefully. 'Tourist guide, maybe?'

'No, thank you,' said the black man.

Cebert fumbled in the register. For some reason, his hands had started to shake. Nervous, he found himself making just the kind of inane conversation that he had vowed to avoid. He seemed to be standing outside himself, watching while an old fool with a drooping mustache talked himself into an early grave.

'You staying around here?'

'No.'

'Guess we won't be seeing you again, then.'

'Maybe you won't.'

There was a tone in the man's voice that made Cebert look up from the register. Cebert's palms were sweating. He flicked a quarter up with his index finger and felt it slide around in a loop in the hollow of his right hand before rattling back into the register drawer. The black man was still standing relaxed on the other side of the counter but there was a tightness around Cebert's throat that he could not explain. It was as if the visitor were two people, one in black jeans and a black shirt with a soft Southern twang to his voice and the other an unseen presence that had found its way behind the counter and was now slowly constricting Cebert's airways.

'Or maybe we might pass through again, sometime,' he continued. 'You still be here?'

'I hope so,' croaked Cebert.

'You think you'll remember us?'

The question was spoken lightly, with what might have been the hint of a smile, but there was no mistaking its meaning.

Cebert swallowed. 'Mister,' he said. 'I've forgotten you already.'

With that, the black man nodded and he and his companion left, and Cebert didn't release his breath until their car was gone from sight and the shadow of the sign cast itself, once again, on an empty lot.

And when the cops came asking about the men a day or two later, Cebert shook his head and told them that he didn't know nothing about them, couldn't recall if two guys like them had passed through that week. Hell, lot of people passed through here on the way to 301 or the interstate, kept the place going like a turnstile at Disney World. And anyway, all them black fellers look alike, you know how it is. He gave the cops free coffee and Twinkies and sent them on their way and had to remind himself, for the second time that week, to release his breath.

He looked around at the business cards arrayed on every previously blank stretch of wall, then leaned over and blew some dust from the nearest bunch. The name Edward Boatner was revealed. According to his card, Edward sold machine parts for a company out of Hattiesburg, Mississippi. Well, if Edward came through here again, he could take a look at his card. It would still be there, because Edward wanted to be remembered.

But Cebert didn't remember nobody that didn't want to be remembered.

He might have been friendly, but he wasn't dumb.

A black oak stands on a slope at the northern edge of a green field, its branches like bones set against the moonlit sky. It is an old, old tree; its bark is thick and gray, deeply furrowed with regular vertical ridges, a fossilized relic stranded by a long-departed tide. In places, the orange inner bark has been exposed, exuding a bitter, unpleasant scent. The shiny green leaves are thick upon it: ugly leaves, deep and narrow, with bristle-tipped teeth at the ends of the lobes.

But this is not the true smell of the black oak that stands at the edge of Ada's Field. On warm nights when the world is quieted, hand-on-mouth, and the moonlight shines palely on the scorched earth beneath its crown, the black oak discharges a different odor, alien to its kind yet as much a part of this solitary tree as the leaves on its branches and the roots in its soil. It is the smell of gasoline and burning flesh, of human waste and singeing hair, of rubber melting and cotton igniting. It is the smell of painful death, of fear and despair, of final moments lived in the laughter and jeering of onlookers.

Step closer, and the lower parts of its branches are blackened and charred. Look, see there, on the trunk: a cloven groove deep in the wood, now faded but once bright, where the bark was suddenly, violently breached. The man who made that mark, the final mark he left upon this world, was born Will Embree, and he had a wife and a child and a job in a grocery store that paid him a dollar an hour. His wife was Lila Embree, or Lila Richardson that was, and her husband's body – after the ending of the final, desperate struggle that caused his booted foot to strike so hard against the trunk of the tree that he tore the bark from it and left a pit deep in its flesh – was never returned to her. Instead his remains were burned and the crowd took souvenirs of the blackened bones from his fingers and toes, then sent her a photograph of her dead husband that Jack Morton of Nashville had printed up in batches of five hundred to be used as postcards, Will Embree's features twisted and swollen, the figure standing at his feet grinning as the flames from the torch leap toward the legs of the man Lila loved. His corpse was dumped in a swamp and the fish stripped the last of the charred flesh from his bones until they came apart and were scattered across the mud on the bottom. The bark never reclaimed the breach made by Will Embree and it remained exposed for ever after. The illiterate man had left his mark on the sole monument to his passing as surely as if it had been carved in stone.

There are places on this old tree where no leaves ever grow. Butterflies do not rest upon it, and birds do not nest in its branches.

When its acorns fall to the ground, fringed with brown hairy scales, they are left to decay. Even the crows turn their black eyes from the rotting fruit.

Around the trunk, a vine weaves. Its leaves are broad, and from each node springs a cluster of small green flowers. The flowers smell as if they are decomposing, festering, and in daylight they are black with flies drawn by the stench. This is Smilax herbacea, *the carrion flower. There is not another one like it for a hundred miles in any direction. Like the black oak itself, it is alone of its kind. Here, in Ada's Field, the two entities coexist, parasite and saprophyte: the one fueled by the lifeblood of the tree, the other drawing its existence from the lost and the dead.*

And the song the wind sings in its branches is one of misery and regret, of pain and passing. It calls over untilled fields and one-room shacks, across acres of corn and mists of cotton. It calls to the living and the dead, and old ghosts linger in its shade.

Now there are lights on the horizon and cars on the road. It is July 17, 1964 and they are coming.

They are coming to see the burning man.

Virgil Gossard stepped into the parking lot beside Little Tom's Tavern and belched loudly. A cloudless night sky stretched above him, dominated by a yellow killer moon. To the northwest, the tail of the constellation Draco was visible, Ursa Minor below it, Hercules above, but Virgil was not a man to take time to look at the stars, not when he might miss a nickel on the ground in the process, and so the shapes that the stars had taken were lost on him. From the trees and the bushes the last of the field crickets sounded, undisturbed by traffic or people, for this was a quiet stretch of road, with few houses and fewer folk, most having abandoned their homes for more promising surroundings many years before. The cicadas were already gone and soon the woods would prepare for the winter quiet. Virgil would be glad when it came. He didn't like bugs. Earlier that day, a piece of what looked like greenish lint had moved across his hand while he lay in bed and he had felt the brief sting as the masked hunter, scouring Virgil's filthy sheets for bedbugs, bit into him. The thing was dead a second later, but the bite was still itching. That was how Virgil was able to tell the cops what time it was when the men came. He had seen the green numerals on his watch glowing as he scratched at the bug bite: 9:15 P.M.

There were only four cars in the lot, four cars for four men. The others were still in the bar, watching a rerun of a classic hockey game on Little Tom's crappy TV, but Virgil Gossard had never been much for hockey. His eyesight wasn't so good and the puck moved too fast for him to follow it. But then everything moved too fast for Virgil Gossard to follow. That was just the way of things. Virgil wasn't too smart, though at least he knew it, which maybe made him smarter than he thought. There were plenty of other fellas thought they were Alfred Einstein or Bob Gates, but not Virgil. Virgil knew he was dumb, so he kept his mouth shut and his eyes open, best he could, and just tried to get by.

He felt an ache at his bladder and sighed. He knew he should have gone before he left the bar but Little Tom's bathroom smelled worse than Little Tom himself, and that was saying something, seeing as how little Tom smelled like he was dying from the inside out, and dying hard. Hell, everybody was dying, inside out, outside in, but most folks took a bath once in a while to keep the flies off. Not Little Tom Rudge, though: if Little Tom tried to take a bath, the water would leave the tub in protest.

Virgil tugged at his groin and shifted uncomfortably from his right foot to his left, then back again. He didn't want to go back inside, but if Little Tom caught him pissing on his lot, then Virgil would be going home with Little Tom's boot stuck up his ass, and Virgil had enough troubles down there without adding a damn leather enema to his burdens. He could take a leak by the side of the road farther on down the way; but the more he thought about it the more he wanted to go now. He could feel it burning inside of him: if he waited any longer . . .

Well, hell, he wasn't going to wait. He pulled down his zipper, reached inside his pants, and waddled over to the side wall of Little Tom's Tavern just in time to sign his name, which was about as far as Virgil's education extended. He breathed out deeply as the pressure eased and his eyes fluttered closed in a brief ecstasy.

Something cold touched him behind his left ear and his eyes quickly opened wide again. He didn't move. His attention was focused on the feel of the metal on his skin, the sound of liquid on wood and stone, and the presence of a large figure behind his back. Then the voice spoke:

'I'm warnin' you, cracker: you get one drop of your sorry-ass piss on my shoes and they gonna be fittin' you up for a new skull before they put you in that box.'

Virgil gulped.

'I can't stop it.'

'I ain't askin' you to stop. I ain't askin' you nothin'. I am *tellin'* you: do not get one drop of your rotgut urine on my shoes.'

Virgil let out a little sob and tried to move the flow to the right. He'd only had three beers but it seemed like he was peeing out the Mississippi. Please stop, he thought. He glanced a little to his left and saw a black gun held in a black hand. The hand emerged from a black coat sleeve. At the end of the black coat sleeve was a black shoulder, a black lapel, a black shirt and the edge of a black face.

The gun nudged his skull hard, warning him to keep his eyes straight ahead, but Virgil still felt a sudden rush of indignation. It was a nigger with a gun, in the parking lot of Little Tom's Tavern. There weren't too many subjects upon which Virgil Gossard had strong, fully formed opinions, but one of them was niggers with guns. The whole trouble with this country wasn't that there were too many guns, it was that too many of those guns were in the hands of the wrong people, and absolutely and positively the wrong people to be carrying guns were niggers. The way Virgil figured it, white people needed guns to protect themselves from all the niggers with guns while all the niggers had guns to shoot other niggers with and, when the mood took them, white folks too. So the solution was to take away the guns from the niggers and then you'd have fewer white folks with guns because they wouldn't have so much to be scared about, plus there'd be fewer niggers shooting other niggers so there'd be less crime too. It was that simple: niggers were the wrong people to be handing out guns to. Now, near as Virgil could figure it, one of those selfsame wrong people was currently pointing one of those misplaced guns into Virgil's skull, and Virgil didn't like it one little bit. It just proved his point. Niggers shouldn't have guns and—

The gun in question tapped Virgil hard behind the ear and the voice said:

'Hey, you know you talkin' out loud, right?'

'Shit,' said Virgil, and this time he heard himself.

The first of the cars turns into the field and pulls up, its headlights shining on the old oak so that its shadow grows and creeps up the slope behind it like dark blood spilling and spreading itself across the land. A man climbs out on the driver's side, then walks around the front of the car and opens the door for the woman. They are both in their forties, hard-faced people wearing cheap clothes and shoes that have been mended so often that the original leather is little more than a faded memory glimpsed through patches and stitching. The man takes a straw basket from the trunk, a faded red check napkin carefully tucked in to cover its contents. He hands the basket to the woman, then retrieves a tattered bedsheet from behind the spare tire and spreads it on the ground. The woman sits, tucking her legs in beneath her, and whips away the napkin. Lying in the basket are four pieces of fried chicken, four buttermilk rolls, a tub of coleslaw, and two glass bottles of homemade lemonade, with two plates and two forks tucked in beside them. She removes the plates, dusts them carefully with the napkin, then lays them on the bedsheet. The man eases himself down beside her and removes his hat. It is a warm evening and already the mosquitoes have begun to bite. He slaps at one and examines its remains upon his hand.

'Sum'bitch,' he says.

'You watch your mouth, Esau,' says the woman primly, carefully dividing up the food, making sure that her husband gets the breast piece because he is a good, hardworking man despite his language and he needs his food.

'Beg pardon,' says Esau as she hands him a plate of chicken and coleslaw, shaking her head at the ways of the man she has married.

Behind and beside them, more vehicles are pulling up. There are couples, and old folks, and young boys of fifteen and sixteen. Some are driving trucks, their neighbors sitting in back fanning themselves with their hats. Others arrive in big Buick Roadmasters, Dodge Royal hardtops, Ford Mainlines, even a big old Kaiser Manhattan, no car younger than seven or eight years old. They share food, or lean against the hoods of their cars and drink beer from bottles. Handshakes are exchanged and backs are slapped. Soon there are forty cars and trucks, maybe more, in and around Ada's Field, their lights shining on the black oak. There are easily one hundred people gathered, waiting, and more arriving every minute.

The opportunities to meet up in this way don't come along so often now. The great years of the Negro barbecue have been and gone, and the old laws are buckling under the pressures imposed from without. There are some folks here who can remember the lynching of Sam Hose down in Newman in 1899, when special excursion trains were laid on so that more than two thousand people from far and wide could come see how the people of Georgia dealt with nigger rapists and killers. It didn't matter none that Sam Hose hadn't raped anyone and that he'd only killed the planter Cranford in self-defense. His death would serve as an object lesson to the others, and so they castrated him, cut off his fingers and his ears, then skinned his face before applying the oil and the torch. The crowd fought for fragments of his bones and kept them as tokens. Sam Hose, one of five thousand victims of mob lynchings in less than a century: rapists some, or so they said; killers others. And then there were those who just talked big, or made idle threats when they should have known better than to shoot their mouths off. Talk like that risked getting all sorts of folks riled up and causing no end of trouble. That kind of talk had to be stifled before it became a shout, and there was no surer way of quieting a man or a woman than a noose and a torch.

Great days, great days.

It is about 9:30 P.M. when they hear the sound of the three trucks approaching, and an excited buzz spreads through the crowd. Their heads turn as the headlights scour the field. There are at least six men in each vehicle. The middle truck is a red Ford, and in the bed a black man sits hunched, his hands tied behind his back. He is big, six seven or more, and the muscles in his shoulders and back are hard and bunched like melons in a sack. There is blood on his head and face, and one eye is swollen closed.

He is here.

The burning man is here.

Virgil was certain that he was about to die. His big mouth had just helped him into a heap of trouble, maybe the last trouble he'd ever have to endure. But the good Lord was smiling upon Virgil, even if He wasn't smiling so hard as to make the n—, beg pardon, the gunman, go away. Instead, he could feel his breath on his cheek and could smell his aftershave as he spoke. It smelled expensive.

'You say that word again and you better enjoy that leak, 'cause it *will* be the last one you ever take.'

'Sorry,' said Virgil. He tried to force the offending word from his brain, but it came back each time with renewed force. He began to sweat.

'Sorry,' he said again.

'Well, that's all right. You finished down there?'

Virgil nodded.

'Then put it away. An owl might figure it for a worm and carry it off.'

Virgil had a vague suspicion that he'd just been insulted, but he quickly tucked his manhood into his fly just in case and wiped his hands on his trousers.

'You carrying a gun?'

'Nope.'

'Bet you wish you were.'

'Yep,' admitted Virgil, in a burst of sudden and possibly ill-advised honesty.

He felt hands on him, patting him down, but the gun stayed where it was, pressed hard against his skin. There was more than one of them, Virgil figured. Hell, there could be half of Harlem at his back. He felt a pressure on his wrists as his hands were cuffed tightly behind him.

'Now turn to your right.'

Virgil did as he was told. He was facing out onto the open country behind the bar, all green as far as the river.

'You answer my questions, I let you walk away into those fields. Understand?'

Virgil nodded dumbly.

'Thomas Rudge, Willard Hoag, Clyde Benson. They in there?'

Virgil was the kind of guy who instinctively lied about everything, even if there didn't seem to be any percentage in not telling the truth. Better to lie and cover your ass later than tell the truth and find yourself in trouble from the start.

Virgil, true to character, shook his head.

'You sure?'

Virgil nodded and opened his mouth to embellish the lie. Instead, the clicking of the spittle in his mouth coincided perfectly with the impact of his head against the wall as the gun pushed firmly into the base of his skull.

'See,' whispered the voice, 'we goin' in there anyhow. If we go in and they ain't there, then you got nothin' to worry about, least until we come lookin' for you to start askin' you again where they at. But we go in there and they sittin' up at the bar, suckin' on some cold ones, then there are dead folks got a better chance of bein' alive tomorrow than you do. You understand me?'

Virgil understood.

'They're in there,' he confirmed.

'How many others?'

'Nobody, just them three.'

The black man, as Virgil had at last begun to think of him, removed the gun from Virgil's head and patted him on the shoulder with his hand.

'Thank you . . . ' he said. 'I'm sorry, I didn't catch your name.'

'Virgil,' said Virgil.

'Well, thank you, Virgil,' said the man, then brought the butt of the gun down hard on Virgil's skull. 'You been great.'

Beneath the black oak, an old Lincoln has been driven into place. The red truck pulls up beside it and three hooded men climb from the bed, pushing the black man onto the ground before them. He lands on his stomach, his face in the dirt. Strong hands yank him to his feet and he stares into the dark holes of the pillowcases, crudely burnt into the fabric with matches and cigarettes. He can smell cheap liquor.

Cheap liquor and gasoline.

His name is Errol Rich, although no stone or cross with that name upon it will ever mark his final resting place. From the moment he was taken from his momma's house, his sister and his momma screaming, Errol had ceased to exist. Now all traces of his physical presence are about to be erased from this earth, leaving only the memory of his life with those who have loved him, and the memory of his dying with those gathered here this night.

And why is he here? Errol Rich is about to burn for refusing to buckle, for refusing to bend his knee, for disrespecting his betters.

Errol Rich is about to die for breaking a window.

He was driving his truck, his old truck with its cracked windshield and its flaking paint, when he heard the shout.

'Hey, nigger!'

Then the glass exploded in on top of him, cutting his face and hands, and something hit him hard between the eyes. He braked suddenly, and smelled it upon himself. In his lap, the cracked pitcher dumped the remains of its contents on his seat and on his pants.

Urine. They had filled a pitcher between them and thrown it through his windshield. He wiped the liquid from his face, his sleeve coming away wet and bloody, and looked at the three men standing by the roadside, a few steps away from the entrance to the bar.

'Who threw that?' he asked. Nobody answered, but secretly, they were afraid. Errol Rich was a strong, powerful man. They had expected him to wipe his face and drive on, not to stop and confront them.

'You throw that, Little Tom?' Errol stood before Little Tom Rudge, the owner of the bar, but Little Tom wouldn't meet his eyes. ''Cause if you did, you better tell me now, else I'm gonna burn your shit heap down to the ground.'

But still there was no reply, so Errol Rich, who always did have a temper on him, signed his death warrant by taking a length of timber from the bed of his truck and turning to the men. They backed off, waiting for him to come at them, but instead he threw the timber, all three feet of it, through the front window of Little Tom Rudge's bar, then climbed back in his truck and drove away.

Now Errol Rich is about to die for a pane of cheap glass, and a whole town has come to watch it happen. He looks out on them, these God-fearing people, these sons and daughters of the land, and he feels the heat of their hatred upon him, a foretaste of the burning that is to come.

I fixed things, *he thinks.* I took what was broken and made it good again.

The thought seems to have come to him almost out of nowhere. He tries to shake it away, but instead, it persists.

I had a gift. I could take an engine, a radio, even a television, and I could repair it. I never read a manual, never had no formal training. It was a gift, a gift that I had, and soon it will be gone.

He looks out at the crowd, at the expectant faces. He sees a boy, fourteen or fifteen, his eyes bright with excitement. He recognizes him, recognizes too the man with his hand on the boy's shoulder. He had brought his radio to Errol, hoping to have it fixed in time for the Santa Anita because he liked to listen to the horse races. And Errol had repaired it, replacing the busted speaker cone, and the man had thanked him and paid him a dollar extra for coming through for him.

The man sees Errol looking at him, and his eyes flick away. There will be no help for him, no mercy from any of these people. He is about to die for a broken window, and they will find someone else to repair their engines and their radios, although not as well, and not as cheaply.

His legs tied, Errol is forced to hop to the Lincoln. They drag him onto the roof, these masked men, and they put the rope around his neck while he kneels. He sees the tattoo on the arm of the largest man: the word 'Kathleen' spelled out on a banner held by angels. The hand tightens the rope. The gasoline is poured over his head, and he shivers.

Then Errol looks up and says the last words anyone will ever hear from him on this earth.

'Don't burn me,' he asks. He has accepted the fact of his death, the inevitability of his passing on this night, but he does not want to burn.

Please Lord, don't let them burn me.

The tattooed man splashes the last of the gasoline into Errol Rich's eyes, blinding him, then climbs down to the ground.

Errol Rich starts to pray.

The small white man entered the bar first. A smell of stale, spilled beer hung in the air. On the floor, dust and cigarette butts formed drifts around the counter, where they had been swept but not cleaned up. There were blackened circles on the wood where soles had stamped out thousands of embers, and the orange paint on the walls had blistered and burst like infected skin. There were no pictures to be seen, just generic beer company signs that had been used to cover the worst of the damage.

The bar wasn't too big, certainly no more than thirty feet in length and fifteen across. The counter itself was on the left and shaped like the blade of an ice skate, the curved end nearest the door. At its other extreme there was a small office and storage area. The toilets were beyond the bar, beside the back door. Four booths stood against the wall to the right, a pair of round tables to the left.

There were two men sitting at the counter, and one other man behind the bar. All three were probably in their sixties. The two at the bar wore baseball caps, faded T-shirts beneath even more faded cotton shirts, and cheap jeans. One of them had a long knife on his belt. The other had a gun concealed beneath his shirt.

The man behind the bar looked like he might have been strong and fit once, a long time ago. There was bulk on his shoulders, chest, and arms that was now masked by a thick layer of fat, and his breasts were pendulous as those of an old woman. There were old yellow sweat stains beneath the arms of his white short-sleeved shirt, and his trousers hung low on his hips in a way that might have been fashionable on a sixteen year old but was ridiculous on a man fifty years older than that. His hair was yellow-white but still thick, and his face was partially obscured by a week's growth of scraggly beard.

All three men were watching the hockey game on the old TV above the bar, but their heads turned in unison as the new arrival entered. He was unshaven, wearing dirty sneakers, a loud Hawaiian shirt, and creased chinos. He didn't look like he belonged anywhere above Christopher Street, not that anybody in this bar knew where Christopher Street was, exactly. But they knew this man's type, yes they did. They could smell it on him. Didn't matter how unshaven he was, how shabbily he dressed; this boy had 'fag' written all over him.

'Can I get a beer?' he asked, stepping up to the bar.

The bartender didn't make any move for at least a full minute, then took a Bud from the cooler and placed it on the bar.

The small man picked up the beer and looked at it as if seeing a bottle of Bud for the first time.

'You got anything else?'

'We got Bud Light.'

'Wow, both kinds.'

The bartender gave him unimpressed.

'Two-fifty.' This wasn't the kind of place that ran a tab.

He counted out three bills from a thick roll, then added another fifty cents in change to bring the tip up to a dollar. The eyes of the three men remained fixed on his slim, delicate hands as he replaced the money in his pocket, then they returned their gazes to the hockey game. The small man took a booth behind the two drinkers, leaned into the corner, then put his feet up and directed his face toward the TV. All four men remained in those positions for about five minutes, until the door again opened softly and another man entered the bar, an unlit Cohiba in his mouth. He was so quiet that nobody even noticed him until he was four feet from the counter, at which point one of the men looked to his left, saw him, and said:

'Little Tom, there's a colored in your bar.'

Little Tom and the second man dragged themselves away from the TV to examine the black man who had now taken a stool at the lower end of the L-shaped bar.

'Whiskey, please,' he said.

Little Tom didn't move. First a fag, now a nigger. This was turning into quite a night. His eyes moved from the man's face to his expensive shirt, his neatly pressed black jeans, and his double-breasted overcoat.

'You from out of town, boy?'

'You could say that.' He didn't even blink at the second insult in less than thirty seconds.

'There's a coon place couple of miles down the road,' said Little Tom. 'You'll get a drink there.'

'I like it here.'

'Well, I don't like *you* here. Get your ass out, boy, before I start takin' it personal.'

'So I don't get a drink?' The man sounded unsurprised.

'No, you don't. Now you going to leave, or am I gonna have to make you leave?'

To his left, the two men shifted on their stools in preparation for the beating that they hoped to deliver. Instead, the object of their attention reached into his pocket, produced a bottle of whiskey in a brown paper bag, and twisted the cap. Little Tom reached under the counter with his right hand. It emerged holding a Louisville Slugger.

'You can't drink that in here, boy,' he warned.

'Shame,' said the black man. 'And don't call me "boy." The name is Louis.'

Then he tipped the bottle upside down and watched as its contents flowed along the bar. It made a neat turn at the elbow of the counter, the raised lip preventing the liquid from overflowing onto the floor, and seeped past the three men. They looked at Louis in surprise as he lit his cigar with a brass Zippo.

Louis stood and took a long puff on his Cohiba.

'Heads up, crackers,' he said, and dropped the flaming lighter into the whiskey.

The man with the tattoo raps sharply on the roof of the Lincoln. The engine roars and the car bucks once or twice like a steer on a rope before shooting away in a cloud of dirt, dead leaves, and exhaust fumes. Errol Rich seems to hang frozen for a moment in midair before his body uncurls. His long legs descend toward the ground but do not reach it, his feet kicking impotently at the air. A spluttering noise comes from his lips, and his eyes bulge as the rope draws tighter and tighter around his neck. His face becomes congested with blood and he begins to convulse, red drops now speckling his chin and chest. A minute goes by and still Errol struggles.

Below him, the tattooed man takes a branch wrapped in linen doused with gasoline, lights it with a match, then steps forward. He holds the torch up so Errol can see it, then touches it to Errol's legs.

Errol ignites with a roar, and somehow, despite the constriction at his throat, he screams, a high, ululating thing filled with terrible agony. It is followed by a second, and then the flames enter his mouth and his vocal cords begin to burn. He kicks again and again as the smell of roasting meat fills the air, until at last the kicking stops.

The burning man is dead.

The bar flared, a small wall of flame shooting up to scorch beards, eyebrows, hair. The man with the gun at his belt leaped back, his left arm covering his eyes while his right reached for his weapon.

'Ah-ah,' said a voice. A Glock 19 was inches from his face, held firm in the grip of the man in the bright shirt. The other's hand stopped instantly, the gun already uncovered. The small man, whose name was Angel, yanked it from its holster and held it up so that he now had two guns inches from the barfly's face. Near the door, Louis's hand now contained a SIG, trained on the man with the knife in his belt. Behind the bar, Little Tom was dousing the last of the flames with water. His face was red and he was breathing hard.

'The fuck you do that for?' He was looking at the black man, and at the SIG that had now moved to level itself at the center of his chest. A change of expression flickered in Little Tom's face, a brief candle-flame of fear that was quickly snuffed out by his natural belligerence.

'Why, you got a problem with it?' asked Louis.

'*I* got a problem with it.'

It was the man with the knife at his belt, brave now that the gun was no longer aimed at him. He had strange, sunken features: a weak chin that lost itself in his thin, stringy neck, blue eyes buried deep in their sockets, and cheekbones that looked like they had been broken and flattened by some old, almost forgotten impact. Those dim eyes regarded the black man impassively while his hands remained raised – away from his knife, but not too far away. It seemed like a good idea to make him get rid of it. A man who carries a knife like that knows how to use it, and use it fast. One of the two guns now held by Angel made an arc through the air and came to rest on him.

'Unclasp your belt,' said Louis.

The knife man paused for a moment, then did as he was told.

'Now pull it out.'

He grasped it and pulled. The belt caught once or twice before it freed the scabbard and the knife fell to the floor.

'That's good enough.'

'I still got a problem.'

'Sorry to hear that,' Louis replied. 'You Willard Hoag?'

The sunken eyes betrayed nothing. They remained fixed on the interloper's face, unblinking.

'I know you?'

'No, you don't know me.'

Something danced in Willard's eyes. 'You niggers all look the same to me anyways.'

'Guessed you'd take that point of view, Willard. Man behind you is Clyde Benson. And you—' The SIG lifted slightly in front of the bartender. 'You're Little Tom Rudge.'

The redness in Little Tom's face was due only partly to the heat of the burning liquor. There was fury building in him. It was there in the trembling of his lips, in the way his fingers were clasping and unclasping. The action made the tattoo on his arm move, as if the angels were slowly waving the banner with the name 'Kathleen.'

And all of that anger was directed at the black man now threatening him in his own bar.

'You want to tell me what's happening here?' asked Little Tom.

Louis smiled.

'Atonement, that's what's happening here.'

It is ten after ten when the woman stands. They call her Grandma Lucy, although she is not yet fifty and still a beautiful woman with youth in her eyes and few lines on her dark skin. At her feet sits a boy, seven or eight years old, but already tall for his age. A radio plays Bessie Smith's 'Weeping Willow Blues'.

The woman called Grandma Lucy wears only a nightdress and shawl, and her feet are bare, yet she rises and walks through the doorway, descending the steps into the yard with careful, measured strides. Behind her walks the little boy, her grandson. He calls to her – 'Grandma Lucy, what's the matter?' – but she does not reply. Later she will tell him about the worlds within worlds, about the places where the membrane separating the living from the dead is so thin that they can see one another, touch one another. She will tell him of the difference between daywalkers and nightwalkers, of the claims that the dead make upon those left behind.

And she will talk of the road that we all walk, and that we all share, the living and the dead alike.

But for now she just gathers her shawl closer to her and continues toward the edge of the forest, where she stops and waits in the moonless night. There is a light among the trees, as if a meteor has descended from the heavens and is now traveling close to the ground, flaming and yet not flaming, burning and yet not burning. There is no heat, but something is ablaze at the heart of that light.

And when the boy looks into her eyes, he sees the burning man.

'You recall Errol Rich?' said Louis.

Nobody responded, but a muscle spasmed in Clyde Benson's face.

'I said, do you recall Errol Rich?'

'We don't know what you're talking about, boy,' said Hoag. 'You got the wrong men.'

The gun swiveled, then bucked in Louis's hand. Willard Hoag's chest spat blood through the hole in his left breast. He stumbled backward, taking a stool with him, then landed heavily on his back. His left hand scrambled at something unseen on the floor, and then he was still.

Clyde Benson started to cry, and then it all went down.

Little Tom dived to the floor of the bar, his hands seeking the shotgun beneath the sink. Clyde Benson kicked a stool at Angel, then ran for the door. He got as far as the men's room before his shirt puffed twice at the shoulder. He stumbled through the back door and disappeared, bleeding, into the darkness. Angel, who had fired the shots, went after him.

The crickets had grown suddenly quiet and the silence in the night had a strange anticipatory quality, as though the natural world awaited the inevitable outcome of the events in the bar. Benson, unarmed and bleeding, had almost made it to the edge of the parking lot when the gunman caught up with him. His feet were swept from under him and he landed painfully in the dirt, blood flecking the ground before him. He began to crawl toward the long grass, as if by reaching its cover he might somehow be safe. A boot caught him under the chest, skewering him with white hot pain as he was forced onto his back, his eyes squeezing shut involuntarily. When they opened again, the man in the loud shirt was standing over him and his gun was pointed at Clyde Benson's head.

'Don't do this,' said Benson. 'Please.'

The younger man's face was impassive.

'Please,' said Benson. He was sobbing. 'I repented of my sins. I found Jesus.'

The finger tightened on the trigger, and the man named Angel said:

'Then you got nothing to worry about.'

In the darkness of her pupils the burning man stands, the flames shooting from his head and arms, his eyes and mouth. There is no skin, no hair, no clothing. There is only fire shaped like man, and pain shaped like fire.

'You poor boy,' whispers the woman. 'You poor, poor boy.'

The tears begin to well up in her eyes and fall softly onto her cheeks. The flames start to flicker and waver. The burning man's mouth opens and the lipless gap forms words that only the woman can hear. The fire dies, fading from white to yellow until at last there is only the silhouette of him, black on black, and then there is nothing but the trees and the tears and the feel of the woman's hand upon the boy's own – 'Come, Louis.' – as she guides him back to the house.

The burning man is at peace.

Little Tom rose up with the shotgun to find the room empty and a dead man on the floor. He swallowed once, then moved to his left, making for the end of the counter. He got three steps when the wood splintered at the level of his thigh and the bullets ripped through him, shattering his left femur and his right shin. He collapsed and screamed as his wounded legs impacted on the floor, but still managed to empty both barrels through the cheap wood of the bar. It exploded in a shower of shot and splinters and shattering glass. He could smell blood and powder and spilled whiskey. His ears rang as the noise faded, leaving only the sound of dripping liquid and falling timber.

And footsteps.

He looked to his left to see Louis standing above him. The barrel of the SIG was pointing at Little Tom's chest. He found some spittle in his mouth and swallowed. Blood was fountaining from the ruptured artery in his thigh. He tried to stop it with his hand but it sprayed through his fingers.

'Who are you?' asked Little Tom. From outside came the sound of two shots as Clyde Benson died in the dirt.

'Last time: you recall a man named Errol Rich?'

Little Tom shook his head. 'Shit, I don't know . . . '

'You burned him. You ought to know.'

Louis aimed the SIG at the bridge of the bartender's nose. Little Tom raised his right arm and covered his face.

'*I remember! I remember!* Jesus. Yes, I was there. I saw what they did.'

'What you did.'

Little Tom shook his head furiously.

'No, you're wrong. I was there, but I didn't hurt him.'

'You're lying. Don't lie to me, just tell me the truth. They say confession is good for the soul.'

Louis lowered the gun and fired. The top of Little Tom's right foot disappeared in a blur of leather and blood. He shrieked then as the gun moved toward his left foot, the words erupting from his gut like old bile.

'Stop, please. Jesus, it hurts. You're right, we did it. I'm sorry for what we did to him. We were younger then, we didn't know no better. It was a terrible thing we did, I know it was.' His eyes pleaded with Louis. His whole face was bathed in sweat, like that of a man melting. 'You think a day don't go by when I don't think about him, about what we did to him? You think I don't live with that guilt every day?'

'No,' said Louis. 'I don't.'

'Don't do this,' said Little Tom. A hand reached out in supplication. 'I'll find a way to make up for what I did. Please.'

'I got a way that you can make up for it,' said Louis.

And then Little Tom Rudge was dead.

In the car they disassembled the guns, wiping every piece down with clean rags. They scattered the remains of the weapons in fields and streams as they drove, but no words were exchanged until they were many miles from the bar.

'How do you feel?' asked Louis.

'Numb,' Angel replied. 'Except in my back. My back hurts.'

'How about Benson?'

'He was the wrong man, but I killed him anyway.'

'They deserved what they got.'

Angel waved his assurance away as a thing without substance or meaning.

'Don't get me wrong. I got no problem with what we just did back there, but killing him didn't make me feel any better, if that's what you're asking. It wasn't him I wanted to kill. When I pulled that trigger, I didn't even see Clyde Benson. I saw the preacher. I saw Faulkner.'

There was silence for a time. Dark fields went by, the hollow shapes of brokeback houses visible against the horizon.

It was Angel who spoke again.

'Bird should have killed him when he had the chance.'

'Maybe.'

'There's no maybe about it. He should have burned him.'

'He's not like us. He feels too much, thinks too much.'

Angel sighed deeply. 'Feeling and thinking ain't the same thing. That old fuck isn't going away. As long as he's alive, he's a threat to all of us.'

Beside him, Louis nodded silently in the darkness.

'And he cut me, and I swore that no one would ever cut me again. No one.'

After a time, his companion spoke softly to him.

'We have to wait.'

'For what?'

'For the right time, the right opportunity.'

'And if it doesn't come?'

'It will come.'

'Don't give me that,' said Angel, before repeating his question. 'What if it doesn't come?'

Louis reached out and touched his partner's face gently.

'Then we will make it ourselves.'

Shortly after, they drove across the state line into South Carolina just below Allendale, and nobody stopped them. They left behind the semiconscious form of Virgil Gossard and the bodies of Little Tom Rudge, Clyde Benson, and Willard Hoag, the three men who had taunted Errol Rich, who had taken him from his home, and who had hanged him from a tree to die.

And out on Ada's Field, at the northern edge where the ground sloped upward, a black oak burned, its leaves curling to brown, the sap hissing and spitting as it burst from the trunk, its branches like the bones of a flaming hand set against the star-sprinkled blackness of the night sky.

I

Bear said that he had seen the dead girl.

It was one week earlier, one week before the descent on Caina that would leave three men dead. The sunlight had fallen prey to predatory clouds, filthy and gray like the smoke from a garbage fire. There was a stillness that presaged rain. Outside, the Blythes' mongrel dog lay uneasily on the lawn, its body flat, its head resting between its front paws, its eyes open and troubled. The Blythes lived on Dartmouth Street in Portland, overlooking Back Cove and the waters of Casco Bay. Usually, there were birds around – seagulls, ducks, plovers – but nothing flew that day. It was a world painted on glass, waiting to be shattered by unseen forces.

We sat in silence in the small living room. Bear, listless, glanced out of the window, as if waiting for the first drops of rain to fall and confirm some unspoken fear. No shadows moved on the polished oak floors, not even our own. I could hear the ticking of the china clock on the mantel, surrounded by photographs from happier times. I found myself staring at an image of Cassie Blythe clutching a mortarboard to her head as the wind tried to make off with it, its tassel raised and spread like the plumage of an alarmed bird. She had frizzy black hair and lips that were slightly too big for her face, and her smile was a little uncertain, but her brown eyes were peaceful and untouched by sadness.

Bear tore himself away from the daylight and tried to meet the gaze of Irving Blythe and his wife, but failed and looked instead to his feet. His eyes had avoided mine from the beginning, refusing even to acknowledge my presence in the room.

He was a big man, wearing worn blue jeans, a green T-shirt, and a leather vest that was now too small to comfortably accommodate his bulk. His beard had grown long and straggly in prison, and his shoulder-length hair was greasy and unkempt. He had acquired some jailhouse tattoos in the years since I had last seen him: a poorly executed figure of a woman on his right forearm and a dagger beneath his left ear. His eyes were blue and sleepy, and sometimes he had trouble remembering the details of his story. He seemed a pathetic figure, a man whose future was all behind him.

When his pauses grew too long, his companion would touch Bear's big arm and speak for him, nudging the tale gently along until Bear found his way back onto the winding path of his recollection. Bear's escort wore a powder blue suit over a white shirt and the knot on his red tie was so large it looked like a growth erupting from his throat. He had silver hair and a year-round tan. His name was Arnold Sundquist and he was a private investigator. Sundquist had been dealing with the Cassie Blythe case, until a friend of the Blythes had suggested that they should talk to me instead. Unofficially, and probably unprofessionally, I had advised them to dispense with the services of Arnold Sundquist, to whom they were paying a retainer of $1,500 per month, ostensibly to look for their daughter. She had disappeared six years earlier, shortly after her graduation, and had not been heard from since. Sundquist was the second private investigator that the Blythes had hired to look into the circumstances of Cassie's disappearance and he couldn't have looked more like a parasite if there had been hooks on his mouth. Sundquist was so slick that when he took a swim in the sea, birds farther down the coast got oil on their feathers. I figured that he had managed to bilk them out of maybe thirty grand in the two years that he had supposedly been working on their behalf. Steady earners like the Blythes are hard to come by in Portland. No wonder he was now trying to regain their trust, and their money.

Ruth Blythe had called me barely an hour earlier to tell me that Sundquist was coming over, claiming to have news about Cassie. I had been chopping maple and birch as firewood for the coming winter when she called and didn't have time to change. There was sap on my hands, on my tattered jeans, and on my 'Arm the Lonely' T-shirt. Now here was Bear, fresh out of Mule Creek State Pen, his pockets rattling with cheap pharmaceuticals bought from flyblown drugstores in Tijuana, his parole transferred home, telling us how he had seen the dead girl.

Because Cassie Blythe was dead. I knew it, and I suspected that her parents knew it too. I think maybe they had felt it at the very moment of her death, some tearing or wrenching in their hearts, and had understood instinctively that something had happened to their only child, that she would never be returning home to them, though they kept her room clean, dusting carefully once each week, changing the bedclothes twice each month so that they would be fresh for her in case she eventually appeared at their door, bearing with her fantastic stories to explain away six years of silence. Until they learned otherwise, there was always the chance that Cassie might still be alive, even as the clock on the mantel tolled softly the knowledge of her passing.

Bear had pulled three years in California for receiving stolen goods. Bear was kind of dumb that way. He was so dumb he would steal stuff he already owned. Bear was too dumb to know Cassie Blythe from a Dumpster, but still he ran through the details of the story again, stumbling occasionally, his face contorted with the effort of recalling the details that I was sure he had been forced to learn from Sundquist: how he had traveled down to Mexico after his release from Mule Creek to stock up on cheap drugs for his nerves; how he had come across Cassie Blythe drinking with an older Mexican in a bar on the Boulevard Agua Caliente, close by the racetrack; how he'd spoken to her when the guy went to the john and had heard the Mainer in her; how the guy had come back and told Bear to mind his own business before hustling Cassie into a waiting car. Somebody at the bar said the man's name was Hector, and he had a place down in Rosarito Beach. Bear didn't have any money to follow them, but he was sure that the woman he had seen was Cassie Blythe. He remembered her photograph from the newspapers that his sister used to send to him to pass the time while he was in jail, even though Bear couldn't read a parking meter, let alone a newspaper. She had even looked over her shoulder at him when he called her name. He didn't think that she looked unhappy or that she was being held against her will. Still, when he got back to Portland the first thing he did was to contact Mr. Sundquist, because Mr. Sundquist was the private detective named in the newspaper reports. Mr. Sundquist had told Bear that he was no longer involved in the case, that a new PI had taken over. But Bear would only work with Mr. Sundquist. He trusted him. He'd heard good things about him. No, if the Blythes wanted Bear's help in Mexico, then Bear wanted Mr. Sundquist back on the case. Sundquist, nodding along gently beside Bear, straightened up at this point in Bear's narrative and looked disapprovingly at me.

'Hell, Bear here is uneasy just having this other guy in the room,' Sundquist confirmed. 'Mr. Parker has a reputation for violence.' Bear, all six three and three hundred pounds of him, tried his best to make it look like he was troubled by my presence. He was, although not for any reason to do with the Blythes or the unlikely possibility that I could inflict some physical harm upon him.

My gaze upon him was unflinching.

I know you, Bear, and I don't believe a word you're saying. Don't do this. Stop it now before it goes too far.

Bear, having finished up his story for the second time, released a relieved breath. Sundquist patted him softly on the back and arranged his features into the best expression of concern that they could muster. Sundquist had been around for about fifteen years and his reputation had been okay, if not exactly great, for much of that, but lately he'd suffered some reverses: a divorce, rumors of gambling problems. The Blythes were a cash cow that he couldn't afford to lose.

Irving Blythe remained quiet when Bear had finished. It was his wife, Ruth, who was the first to speak. She reached out and touched her husband's arm.

'Irving,' she said. 'I think—'

But he raised his hand and she stopped talking immediately. I had mixed feelings about Irving Blythe. He was old school, and sometimes treated his wife like she was a second-class citizen. He had been a senior manager at the International Paper company in Jay, facing down the United Paper Workers International Union when it sought to organize labor in the north woods in the 1980s. The seventeen-month-long walkout at International during 1987 and 1988 was one of the bitterest strikes in the state's history, with over one thousand workers replaced in the course of the action. Irv Blythe had been a staunch opponent of compromise, and the company had sweetened his retirement package considerably as a mark of its appreciation when he eventually called it a day and moved back to Portland. But that didn't mean that he didn't love his daughter, or that her disappearance hadn't aged him in the last six years, the weight falling from his body like water from melting ice. His white shirt hung limply from his arms and his chest, and the gap between its collar and his neck could have accommodated my fist. His trousers were cinched tightly at the waist, billowing out emptily where once they would have been filled by his ass and his thighs. Everything about him spoke of absence and loss.

'I think you and I should talk, Mr. Blythe.' It was Sundquist. 'In private,' he added, with a meaningful look at Ruth Blythe in the process, a look that said that this was men's talk, not to be obstructed or diverted by the emotions of women, no matter how sincerely felt they might be.

Blythe rose and Sundquist followed him into the kitchen, leaving his wife seated on the sofa. Bear stood and removed a pack of Marlboros from his vest pocket.

'I'll step outside to smoke, ma'am,' he said.

Ruth Blythe just nodded and watched Bear's departing bulk, her clenched right fist close to her mouth, tensing to defend herself from a blow that she had already received. It was Mrs. Blythe that had encouraged her husband to dispense with the services of Sundquist. He had acceded only because of Sundquist's proven lack of progress, but I got the feeling that he didn't like me very much. His wife was a small woman, but small the way terriers are small, her size masking her energy and tenacity. I recalled the news reports of Cassie Blythe's disappearance, Irving and Ruth seated together at a table, Ellis Howard, the Portland PD's deputy chief, beside them, a picture of Cassie clasped tightly in Ruth Blythe's hands. She had given me the tapes of the press conference to look at when I had agreed to review the case, along with news cuttings, photographs, and increasingly slim progress reports from Sundquist. Six years ago, I would have said that Cassie Blythe resembled her father more than her mother, but as the years had gone by, it seemed to me more and more that it was Ruth to whom Cassie bore the greatest resemblance. The expression in her eyes, her smile, even her hair now seemed more like Cassie's than ever before. In a strange way, it was almost as if Ruth Blythe were somehow transforming herself, acquiring facets of her daughter's appearance, so that by doing so she might become both daughter and wife to her husband, keeping some part of Cassie alive even as the shadow of her loss grew longer and longer upon them.

'He's lying, isn't he?' she asked me when Bear was gone.

For a moment, I was about to lie in turn, to tell her that I wasn't sure, that nothing could be ruled out, but I couldn't say those things to her. She deserved better than to be lied to; but then, she deserved better than to be told that there was no hope, and that her daughter would never return to her.

'I think so,' I said.

'Why would he do that? Why would he try to hurt us like this?'

'I don't think he is trying to hurt you, Mrs. Blythe, not Bear. He's just easily led.'

'It's Sundquist, isn't it?'

This time, I didn't reply.

'Let me go talk to Bear,' I said. I stood and moved toward the front door. In the window, I saw Ruth Blythe reflected, the torment clear on her face as she struggled between her desire to grasp the slim hope offered by Bear and her knowledge that it would come apart like ash in her hand if she tried.

Outside, I found Bear puffing on a cigarette and trying to entice the Blythes' dog over to play with him. The dog was ignoring him.

'Hey, Bear.'

I recalled Bear from my youth, when he had been only slightly smaller and marginally dumber. He had lived in a small house on Acorn, off Spurwink Road, with his mother, his two older sisters, and his stepfather. They were decent people: his mother worked at the Woolworth and his stepfather drove a delivery van for a soda company. They were dead now, but his sisters still lived close by, one in East Buxton and the other in South Windham, which was convenient for visiting when Bear spent three months in the Windham Correctional Facility for assault at the age of twenty. It was Bear's first taste of jail and he was lucky not to serve more in the years that followed. He did a little driving for some guys out of Riverton then departed for California following a territorial dispute that left one man dead and another crippled for life. Bear wasn't involved but scores were about to be settled and his sisters encouraged him to go away. Far away. He'd picked up some kitchen cleaning work in L.A., had once again drifted into bad company and had ended up in Mule Creek. There was no real malice in Bear, although that didn't make him any less dangerous. He was a weapon to be wielded by others, open to promises of money, work, or maybe just companionship. Bear saw the world only through bewildered eyes. Now he had come home, but he seemed as lost and out of place as ever.

'I can't talk to you,' he said, as I stood beside him.

'Why not?'

'Mr. Sundquist told me not to. He said you'd just fuck things up.'

'What things?'

Bear smiled and wagged a finger at me. 'Uh-uh. I ain't that dumb.'

I took a step onto the grass and squatted down, my palms out. Immediately, the dog rose up and approached me slowly, its tail wagging. When it reached me, it sniffed my fingers then buried its muzzle in the palms of my hands as I scratched its ears.

'How come he wouldn't do that for me?' asked Bear. He sounded hurt.

'Maybe you scared him,' I replied, then felt bad as I saw the regret on his face. 'Could be he smells my own dog on me, though. Yeah, you scared of big Bear, fella? He's not so scary.'

Bear squatted down beside me, moving as slowly and unthreateningly as his bulk permitted, then brushed his huge fingers against the hair on the dog's skull. Its eyes flicked toward him in mild alarm and I felt it tense, until slowly it began to relax as it realized the big man meant it no harm. Its eyes closed in pleasure beneath the joint pressure of our fingers.

'This was Cassie Blythe's dog, Bear,' I said, and watched as Bear's hand paused momentarily in its exploration of the animal's fur.

'It's a nice dog,' he said.

'Yes, it is. Bear, why are you doing this?'

He didn't respond, but I saw the guilt flicker in the depths of his eyes, like a small stray fish sensing the approach of a predator. He tried to take his hand away, but the dog lifted its muzzle and pressed at his fingers until he went back to petting it. I left him to it.

'I know you don't want to hurt anybody, Bear. You remember my grandfather?' My grandfather had been a Cumberland County sheriff's deputy.

Bear nodded silently.

'He once told me that he saw gentleness in you, even if you didn't always recognize it in yourself. He thought you had the potential to be a good man.'

Bear looked at me, seemingly uncomprehendingly, but I persevered.

'What you're doing today is not gentle, Bear, and it's not good. These people are going to get hurt. They've lost their daughter, and they desperately want her to be alive in Mexico. They want her to be alive, period. But you and I, Bear, we know that's not the case. We know she's not down there.'

Bear said nothing for a time, as if hoping that I might somehow disappear and stop tormenting him.

'What did he offer you?'

Bear's shoulders sagged slightly, but he seemed almost relieved to be confessing.

'He said he'd give me five hundred dollars, and maybe put some work my way. I needed the money. Need the work too. It's hard to get work when you've been in trouble. He said you were no good for them, that if I told them the story I'd be helping them in the long run.'

I felt the tension ease between my shoulders, but I also felt a tug of regret, a tiny fraction of the pain the Blythes would feel when I confirmed that Bear and Sundquist had lied to them about their daughter. Yet I couldn't find it in myself to blame Bear.

'I have some friends that might be able to give you some work,' I said. 'I hear they're looking for someone to help out down at the Pine Point Co-op. I can put in a word for you.'

He looked at me. 'You'd do that?'

'Can I tell the Blythes that their daughter isn't in Mexico?'

He swallowed. 'I'm sorry,' he said. 'I wish she was in Mexico. I wish I had seen her. Will you tell them that?' He was like a big child, incapable of understanding the great hurt that he had caused them.

I didn't answer. Instead, I patted him once on the shoulder in thanks. 'I'll call you at your sister's, Bear, tell you about that job. You need money for a cab?'

'Nah, I'll just walk into town. Ain't far.'

He gave the dog an extra vigorous rub, then started toward the road. The dog followed him, probing at his hands, until Bear reached the sidewalk, then it lay down on the ground again and watched him depart.

Inside the house, Ruth Blythe had not moved from her position on the sofa. She looked up at me and I glimpsed the tiny light in her eyes that I was about to extinguish.

I shook my head, then left the room as she rose and walked to the kitchen.

I was sitting on the hood of Sundquist's Plymouth when he emerged. The knot on his tie was slightly askew and there was a red mark on his cheek where Ruth Blythe's open hand had connected. He paused at the edge of the lawn and watched me nervously.

'What are you going to do?' he asked.

'Now? Nothing. I'm not going to lay a finger on you.'

He visibly relaxed.

'But you're finished as a private investigator. I'll make sure of that. Those people deserve better.'

Sundquist almost laughed.

'What, they deserve you? You know, Parker, a lot of people around here don't like you. They don't think you're such a big shot. You should have stayed in New York, because you don't belong in Maine.'

He walked around the car and opened the door.

'I'm tired of this fucking life anyway. Tell you the truth, I'll be happy to be out of it. I'm moving to Florida. You can stay here and freeze for all I care.'

I stepped away from the car.

'Florida?'

'Yeah, Florida.'

I nodded and headed for my Mustang. The first drops of rain began to fall from the clouds, speckling the mass of twisted wire and metal that lay on the curb and the oil seeping slowly into the road as Sundquist's key turned uselessly in the ignition.

'Well,' I said, 'you sure won't be driving there.'

I passed Bear on the road and gave him a ride to Congress Street. He strode off in the direction of the Old Port, crowds of tourists parting before him like earth before the plow. I thought of what my grandfather had said about Bear, and the way the dog had followed him to the verge of the lawn, sniffing hopefully at his hand. There was a gentleness to him, even a kindness, but his weakness and stupidity left him open to manipulation and perversion. Bear was a man in the balance, and there was no way of knowing how the scales would tip, not then.

I made the call to Pine Point the next morning, and Bear began working shortly after. I never saw him again, and I wonder now if my intervention cost him his life. And yet I sense, somehow, that deep down inside him, in the great gentleness that even he did not fully recognize, Bear would not have had it any other way.

When I look out on the Scarborough marsh from the windows of my house and see the channels cutting through the grass, interlinking with one another, each subject to the same floods, the same cycles of the moon, yet each finding its own route to the sea, I understand something about the nature of this world, about the way in which seemingly disparate lives are inextricably inter-twined. At night, in the light of the full moon, the channels shine silver and white, thin roads feeding into the great glittering plain beyond, and I imagine myself upon them, walking on the white road, listening to the voices that sound in the rushes as I am carried into the new world waiting.

2

There were twelve snakes in all, common garters. They had taken up residence in an abandoned shack at the edge of my property, secure among the fallen boards and rotting timbers. I spotted one of them slipping through a hole beneath the ruined porch steps, probably on its way home from a morning spent hunting for prey. When I ripped away the floorboards with a crowbar I found the rest. The smallest looked to be about a foot long, the largest closer to three. They coiled over one another as the sunlight shone upon them, the yellowish stripes on their dorsa glowing like strips of neon in the semidarkness. Some had already begun to flatten their bodies, the better to display their colors as a warning. I poked at the nearest with the end of the crowbar and heard it hiss. A sweetish, unpleasant odor began to rise from the hole as the snakes released their musk from the glands at the base of their tails. Beside me Walter, my eight-month-old golden Labrador retriever, drew back, his nose quivering. He barked in confusion. I patted him behind the ear and he looked at me for reassurance; this was his first encounter with snakes and he didn't seem too sure about what was expected of him.

'Best to keep your nose out of there, Walt,' I told him, 'or else you'll be wearing one of them on the end of it.'

We get a lot of garters in Maine. They're tough reptiles, capable of surviving sub zero temperatures for up to one month, or of submerging themselves in water during the winter, aided by stable thermals. Then, usually in mid-March when the sun begins to warm the rocks, they emerge from their hibernation and start searching for mates. By June or July they're breeding. Mostly, you get ten or twelve young in a nest. Sometimes there are as few as three. The record is eighty-five, which is a lot of garter snakes no matter what way you look at it. These snakes had probably chosen to make their home in the shack because of the comparative sparsity of conifers on this part of my land. Conifers make the soil acidic, which is bad for night crawlers, and night crawlers are a garter's favorite snack.

I replaced the boards and stepped back out into the sunlight, Walter at my heels. Garters are unpredictable creatures. Some of them will take food from your hand while others will bite and keep biting until they get tired or bored or killed. Here, in this old shack, they were unlikely to harm anyone, and the local population of skunks, raccoons, foxes, and cats would sniff them out soon enough. I decided to let them be unless circumstances forced me to do otherwise. As for Walter, well, he'd just have to learn to mind his own business.

Below me and through the trees, the salt marsh gleamed in the morning sun and wild birds moved on the waters, their shapes visible through the swaying grasses and rushes. The Native Americans had named this place Owascoag, the Land of Many Grasses, but they were long gone, and to the people that lived here now it was simply 'the marsh,' the place where the Dunstan and Nonesuch Rivers came together as they approached the sea. The mallards, year-round residents, had been joined for the summer by wood ducks, pintails, black ducks, and teal, but the visitors would soon be leaving to escape the harsh Maine winter. Their whistles and cries carried on the breeze, joining with the buzz of the insects in a gentle clamor of feeding and mating, hunting and fleeing. I watched a swallow make an arcing dive toward the mud and alight upon a rotting log. It had been a dry season and the swallows in particular had enjoyed good eating. Those that lived close to the marsh were grateful to them, for they kept down not only the mosquitoes but the far nastier greenheads, with their strong-toothed jaws that tore through the skin with the force of a razor cut.

Scarborough is an old community, one of the first colonies established on the northern New England coast that was not simply a transient fishing station but a settlement that would become a permanent home for the families who lived within its boundaries. Many were English settlers, my mother's ancestors among them; others came from Massachusetts and New Hampshire, attracted by the promise of good farmland. The first governor of Maine, William King, was born in Scarborough, although he left there at the age of nineteen when it became clear that it didn't have too much to offer in the way of wealth and opportunity. Battles have been fought here – like most of the towns on the coastline, Scarborough has been dipped in blood – and the community has been blighted by the ugliness of Route 1, but through it all the Scarborough salt marsh has survived, and its waters glow like molten lava in the setting sun. The marsh was protected, although the continuing development of Scarborough meant that new housing – not all of it pretty, and some of it unquestionably ugly – had grown up close to the marsh's high-water mark, attracted both by its beauty and by the presence of older, preexisting populations. The big, black-gabled house in which I now lived dated from the 1930s and was mostly sheltered from the road and the marsh by a stand of trees. From my porch, I could look out upon the water and sometimes find a kind of peace that I hadn't felt in a long, long time.

But that kind of peace is fleeting, an escape from reality that ends as soon as you tear your eyes away and your attention returns to the matters in hand: to those whom you love and who depend upon you to be there for them; to those who want something from you but for whom you feel little or nothing in return; and to those who would hurt you and those close to you, if given the opportunity. Right now, I had enough to be getting along with in all three categories.

Rachel and I had moved to this house only four weeks previously, after I had sold my grandfather's old home and adjoining land on Mussey Road, about two miles away, to the U.S. Postal Service. A huge new mail depot was being built in the Scarborough area and I had been paid a considerable amount of money to vacate my land so that it could be used as a maintenance area for the mail fleet.

I had felt a twinge of sorrow when the sale was finally agreed. After all, this was the house to which my mother and I had come from New York after my father's death, the house in which I had spent my teenage years, and the house to which I, in turn, had returned after the death of my own wife and child. Now, two and a half years later, I was starting again. Rachel had only just begun to show, and it seemed somehow apt that we would begin our life as a couple in earnest in a new home, one that we had chosen together, furnished and decorated together, and in which, I hoped, we would live and grow old together. In addition, as my ex-neighbor Sam Evans had pointed out to me as the sale was nearing completion and as he himself was about to depart for his new place in the South, only a crazy person would want to live in close proximity to thousands of postal workers, all of them little ticking time bombs of frustration waiting to explode in an orgy of gun-related violence.

'I'm not sure that they're really that dangerous,' I suggested to him.

He looked skeptical. Sam had been the first to sell when the offers were made, and the last of his possessions were now in a U-Haul truck ready to head for Virginia. My hands were dusty from helping him carry the boxes from the house.

'You ever see that film *The Postman*?' he asked.

'No. I heard it kind of sucked.'

'It sucked sperm whales. Kevin Costner should have been stripped naked, soaked in honey, and staked out over an anthill for it, but that's not the point. What's *The Postman* about?'

'A postman?'

'An *armed* postman,' he corrected. 'In fact, lots of armed postmen. Now, I bet you fifty bucks that if you accessed the records of shitty video stores in any city in America, you know what you'd find?'

'Porn?'

'I wouldn't know about that,' he lied. 'You'd find that the only people who rented *The Postman* more than once were other postmen. I swear it. Check the records. *The Postman* is like a call to arms for these guys. I mean, it's a vision of an America in which postal workers are heroes and still get to blow away anyone who pisses them off. It's like porno for postals. They probably sit around in circles jerking off at their favorite parts.'

I discreetly took a step away from him. He wagged a finger at me.

'You mark my words. What Marilyn Manson is to crazy high schoolers, *The Postman* is to postal workers. You just wait until the killings start, then you'll say to yourself that old Sam was right all along.'

That, or old Sam was crazy all along. I still wasn't sure how serious he was. I had visions of him holed up in a farmhouse in Virginia, waiting for the postal apocalypse to come. He shook my hand and walked to the truck. His wife and children had already gone on ahead of him, and he was looking forward to the peace of the road. He paused at the door of the truck and winked.

'Don't let the crazy bastards get you, Parker.'

'They haven't succeeded yet,' I replied.

For a moment, the smile departed from his face, and the undercurrent to his comments rippled his surface good humor.

'That don't mean they'll stop trying.'

'I know.'

He nodded.

'If you're ever in Virginia . . . '

'I'll keep driving.'

He gave me a final wave and then he was gone, his middle finger raised in a last farewell to the future home of the U.S. Mail.

From the porch of the house, Rachel called my name and waved the cordless phone at me. I raised a hand in acknowledgment and watched Walt tear away from me at full speed to join her. Rachel's red hair burned in the sunlight, and once again I felt a tightening in my belly at the sight of her. My feelings for her coiled and twisted inside me, so that for a moment I found it hard to isolate any single emotion. There was love – that much I knew for certain – but there was also gratitude, and longing, and fear: fear for us, a fear that I would somehow let her down and force her away from me; fear for our unborn child, for I had lost a child before, had watched again and again in my uneasy sleep as she slipped away from me and disappeared into the darkness, her mother by her side, their passing wreathed in rage and pain; and fear for Rachel, a terror that I might somehow fail to protect her, that some harm might befall her when my back was turned, my attention distracted, and she too would be torn away from me.

And then I would die, for I would not be able to take such pain again.

'It's Elliot Norton,' she said as I reached her, her hand over the mouthpiece. 'He says he's an old friend.'

I nodded, then patted Rachel's butt as I took the phone. She swatted me playfully on the ear in response. At least, I think it was meant to be playful. I watched her head back into the house to continue her work. She was still traveling down to Boston twice weekly to hold her psychology tutorials, but she now did most of her research work in the small office we had set up for her in one of the spare bedrooms, her left hand resting gently on her belly while she wrote. She looked over her shoulder at me as she headed into the kitchen and wiggled her rump provocatively.

'Hussy,' I muttered at her. She stuck her tongue out and disappeared.

'Excuse me?' said Elliot's voice from the phone. His Southern accent was stronger than I remembered.

'I said "hussy". It's not how I usually greet lawyers. For them I use "whore", or "leech" if I want to get away from the whole sexual arena.'

'Uh-huh. You don't make any exceptions?'

'Not usually. By the way, I found a nest of your peers at the bottom of my garden this morning.'

'I won't even ask. How you doing, Charlie?'

'I'm good. It's been a while, Elliot.'

Elliot Norton had been an assistant attorney in the homicide bureau of the Brooklyn D.A.'s office when I was a detective. We had managed to get on pretty well together both professionally and personally on those occasions when our paths crossed, until he got married and moved back home to South Carolina, where he was now practicing law in Charleston. I still received a Christmas card from him each year. I'd met him the previous September for dinner in Boston when he was dealing with the sale of some property in the White Mountains, and had stayed in his house some years before when Susan, my late wife, and I were passing through South Carolina during the early months of our marriage. He was in his late thirties now, prematurely gray and divorced from his wife, a woman named Alicia who was pretty enough to stop traffic on rainy days. I didn't know anything about the circumstances of the breakup, although I figured Elliot for the kind of guy who might have strayed from the marital fold on occasion. When we'd had dinner, at Sonsi on Newbury, the girls in their summer dresses passing by the open doors, his eyes had practically been out on stalks, like those of a character in a Tex Avery cartoon.

'Well, we Southern folks tend to keep ourselves pretty much to ourselves,' he drawled. 'Plus we're kinda busy, what with keeping the coloreds in check and all.'

'It's good to have a hobby.'

'That it is. You still private detecting?'

The small talk had come to a pretty sudden end, I thought.

'Some,' I confirmed.

'You in the market for work?'

'Depends upon the kind.'

'I have a client due for trial. I could do with some help.'

'Maine is a long way from South Carolina, Elliot.'

'That's why I'm calling you. This isn't something that the local snoops are too interested in.'

'Why?'

'Because it's bad.'

'How bad?'

'Nineteen-year-old male accused of raping his girlfriend, then beating her to death. His name is Atys Jones. He's black. His girlfriend was white, and wealthy.'

'That's pretty bad.'

'He says he didn't do it.'

'And you believe him?'

'And I believe him.'

'With respect, Elliot, the jails are full of guys who say they didn't do it.'

'I know. I helped to put some of them away, and I *know* they did it. But this one's different. He's innocent. I've bet the homestead on it. Literally: my house is security on his bail.'

'What do you want from me?'

'I need somebody to help me move him to a safe house then look around, check witness statements; someone who isn't from around here and isn't likely to be scared off too easy. It's a week's work, maybe a day or two more. Look, Charlie, this kid had a death sentence passed on him before he even set foot in a courtroom. As things stand, he may not live to see his trial.'

'Where is he now?'

'Richland County lock up, but I can't leave him in there for too much longer. I took over the case from the public defender and now rumor is that some lowlifes from the Skinhead Riviera may try to make a name for themselves by shanking the kid in case I get him off. That's why I've arranged bail. Atys Jones is a sitting duck in Richland.'

I leaned back against the rail of my porch. Walter came out with a rubber bone in his mouth and pressed it into my hand. He wanted to play. I knew how he felt. It was a bright autumn day, my girlfriend was radiant with the knowledge that our first child was slowly growing inside her, and we were pretty comfortable financially. That kind of situation encourages you to kick back for a time and enjoy it while it lasts. I needed Elliot Norton's client like I needed scorpions in my shoes.

'I don't know, Elliot. Every time you open your mouth, you give me another good reason to close my ears.'

'Well, while I have your attention you may as well hear the worst of it. The girl's name was Marianne Larousse. She was Earl Larousse's daughter.'

With the mention of his name, I recalled some details of the case. Earl Larousse was just about the biggest industrialist from the Carolinas to the Mississippi; he owned tobacco plantations, oil wells, mining operations, factories. He even owned most of Grace Falls, the town in which Elliot had grown up, except you didn't read about Earl Larousse in the society pages or the business sections, or see him standing beside presidential candidates or dullard congressmen. He employed PR companies to keep his name out of the public domain and to stonewall journalists and anybody else who tried to poke around in his affairs. Earl Larousse liked his privacy, and he was prepared to pay a lot of money to protect it, but the death of his daughter had thrust his family unwillingly into the limelight. His wife had died a few years back, and he had a son, Earl Jr., older than Marianne by a couple of years, but none of the surviving members of the Larousse clan had made any public comment on the death of Marianne or the impending trial of her killer.

Now Elliot Norton was defending the man accused of raping and murdering Earl Larousse's daughter, and that was a course of action likely to make him the second most unpopular person in the state of South Carolina, after his client. Anybody drawn into the maelstrom surrounding the case was going to suffer; there was no question about it. Even if Earl himself didn't decide to take the law into his own hands there were plenty of other people who would because Earl was one of their own, because he paid their wages, and because maybe Earl would smile upon whoever did him the favor of punishing the man he believed had killed his little girl.

'I'm sorry, Elliot,' I said. 'This isn't something I want to get involved with right now.'

There was silence at the other end of the line.

'I'm desperate, Charlie,' he said at last, and I could hear it in his voice: the tiredness, the fear, the frustration. 'My secretary is quitting at the end of the week because she doesn't approve of my client list and pretty soon I'll have to drive to Georgia to buy food because nobody around here will sell me jackshit.' His voice rose. 'So don't fucking tell me that this is something you don't want to get involved with like you're running for fucking Congress or something, because my house and maybe my life are on the line and . . .'

He didn't finish the sentence. After all, what more was there to say?

I heard him exhale a deep breath.

'I'm sorry,' he whispered. 'I don't know why I said that.'

'It's okay,' I replied, but it wasn't, not for him and not for me.

'I hear you're about to become a father,' he said. 'That's good, after all that's happened. If I was you, maybe I'd stay up there in Maine too and forget that some asshole called you up out of the blue to join in his crusade. Yeah, I think that would be what I'd do, if I was you. You take care now, Charlie Parker. Look after that little lady.'

'I will.'

'Yeah.'

Then he hung up. I tossed the phone on one of the chairs and dragged my hands over my face. The dog now lay curled at my feet, his bone clasped between his front paws as he tugged at it with his sharp teeth. The sun still shone on the marsh and birds still moved slowly on the waters, calling to one another as they glided between the cattails, but now the transient, fragile nature of what I was witnessing seemed to weigh heavily upon me. I found myself looking toward the ruined shack where the garter snakes lay, waiting for rodents and small birds to stumble into their path. You could walk away from them, pretend to yourself that they weren't doing you any harm and that you had no cause to go interfering with them. If you were right, then you might never have to face them again, or maybe creatures bigger and stronger than they would do you a favor and deal with them for you.

But, someday, you might go back to that cabin and lift up those same floorboards, and where once there were a dozen snakes there would now be hundreds and no collection of old boards and decaying timbers would be enough to contain them. Because ignoring them or forgetting them doesn't make them go away.

It just makes it easier for them to breed.

That afternoon, I left Rachel working in her office and headed into Portland. My trainers and sweats were in the trunk of the car, and I had intended to go into One City Center and do a couple of circuits, but instead I ended up walking the streets, browsing in Carlson & Turner's antiquarian bookstore up on Congress Street and Bullmoose Music down in the Old Port. I picked up the new Pinetop Seven album, *Bringing Home the Last Great Strike*, an advance copy of Ryan Adams's *Heartbreaker*, and *Leisure and Other Songs* by a group called Spokane, because they were led by Rick Alverson, who used to head up Drunk and who made the kind of music you wanted to listen to when old friends let you down or you caught a glimpse of a former lover on a city street, her fingers entwined with those of another, looking at him in a way that reminded you of how she had once looked at you. There were still crowds of tourists around, the last of the summer wave. Soon the leaves would start to turn in earnest and then the next wave would arrive, to watch the trees burn like fire as far north as the Canadian border.

I was angry with Elliot and more angry with myself. It sounded like a difficult case but difficult cases were part of the job. If I sat around waiting for easy ones, then I'd starve or go crazy. Two years ago, I'd have headed down to South Carolina to help him out without a second thought, but now I had Rachel and I was about to become a father again. I had been given a second chance, and I didn't want to endanger it in any way.

I found myself back at my car. This time, I took my kit from the trunk and spent an hour pushing myself as hard as I had ever pushed myself in the gym, working until my muscles burned and I had to sit on a bench with my head down before the worst of the nausea had passed. But I still felt ill as I drove back to Scarborough, and the sweat that dripped from my face was the sweat of the sickbed.

Rachel and I didn't talk properly about the call until dinner that evening. We had been together as a couple for about nineteen months, although we had only been living under the same roof for less than two. There were those who looked at me differently now, as if wondering how a man who had lost his wife and daughter under such terrible circumstances less than three years before could bring himself to begin again, could create another child and attempt to find a place for it in a world that had spawned a killer capable of tearing a daughter and her mother apart.

But if I had not tried, if I had not reached out to another person and made some small, halting connection to her in the hope that it might one day bring us closer together, then the Traveling Man, the creature that had taken them away from me, would have won. I could not change the fact that we had all suffered at his hands, but I refused to be his victim for the rest of my life.

And this woman was, in her quiet way, extraordinary. She had seen in me something worthy of love, of salvation, and had set about recovering that thing from the deep place to which it had retreated in order to protect itself from further harm. She was not so naive as to believe that she could save me: rather, she made me want to save myself.

Rachel had been shocked when she discovered that she was pregnant. We both were, a little, in the beginning, but it seemed even then that there was a rightness to it, an appropriateness, that allowed us to face our new future with a kind of quiet confidence. It sometimes felt like the decision to have a child had been made for us by some higher power, and all we could do now was hang on and enjoy the ride. Well, maybe Rachel wouldn't have used the word 'enjoy': after all, it was she who had felt a strange heaviness to all her actions from the moment the test had proved positive; she who stared at her figure in alarm as she began to put on weight in strange places; she whom I found crying at the kitchen table in the dead of one August night, overcome by feelings of dread and sadness and exhaustion; she who threw up every morning with all the certainty of sunrise; and she who would sit, her hand upon her belly, listening to the spaces between her heartbeats with both fear and wonder, as if she could hear the little bundle of cells slowly growing within her. The first trimester had been especially difficult for her. Now, in her second, she had found new reserves of energy initiated for her by the child's first kicks, by the confirmation that what lay inside her was no longer potential but had become actual.

While I watched her quietly, Rachel tore into a piece of beef so rare she had to hold it down with her fork to keep it from making a break for the door. Beside it, potatoes and carrots and zucchini lay heaped in little mountains.

'Why aren't you eating?' she asked, when she came up briefly for air.

I curled my arm protectively around my plate. 'Back,' I said. 'Bad dog.'

To my left, Walt's head spun toward me, a brief flash of confusion visible in his eyes. 'Not you,' I reassured him, and his tail wagged.

Rachel finished chewing, then jabbed her momentarily empty fork at me. 'It was that call today. Am I right?'

I nodded and toyed with my food, then told her Elliot's story. 'He's in trouble,' I concluded. 'And anyone who sides with him against Earl Larousse is going to be in trouble too.'

'Have you ever met Larousse?'

'No. The only reason I know about him is because Elliot has told me things in the past.'

'Bad things?'

'Nothing worse than you'd expect from a man with more money than ninety-nine point-nine percent of the people in the state: intimidation, bribery, crooked land deals, brushes with the EPA over polluted rivers and poisoned fields, the usual stuff. Throw a stone in Washington when Congress is in session and you'll hit apologists for any one of a hundred people like him. But that doesn't make the loss of his daughter any less painful for him.'

An image of Irv Blythe flashed briefly in my mind. I swatted the thought away like a fly.

'And Norton is certain that his client didn't kill her?'

'Seems that way. After all, he took over the case from the original lawyer and then stood bail for the guy, and Elliot isn't the kind of man who risks his money or his reputation on a losing prospect. Then again, a black man accused of the murder of a rich white girl could be at risk among the general population, assuming somebody got it into his head to make a name for himself with the grieving family. According to Elliot, he either bailed his client or he buried him. Those were the options.'

'When is the trial?'

'Soon.' I had gone through the newspaper reports of the murder on the Internet, and it was clear that the case had been fast-tracked from the beginning. Marianne Larousse had been dead for only a few months, but the case would be tried early in the new year. The law didn't like to keep people like Earl Larousse waiting.

We stared at each other across the table.

'We don't need the money,' said Rachel. 'Not that badly.'

'I know.'

'And you don't want to go down there.'

'No, I sure don't.'

'Well, then.'

'Well, then.'

'Eat your dinner, before I do.'

I did as I was told. I even tasted some of it.

It tasted like ash.

After dinner, we drove out to Len Libby's on Route 1 and sat on a bench outside to eat our ice cream. Len Libby's used to be on Spurwink Road, on the way to Higgins Beach, with tables inside where people sat and shot the breeze. It had moved out to its new location, on the highway, a few years back, and while the ice cream was still good, eating it while looking out at four lanes of traffic wasn't quite the same. Instead, there was now a life-size chocolate moose beside the ice cream counter, which probably counted as some form of progress.

Rachel and I didn't speak. The sun set behind us, our shadows growing longer before us, stretching away ahead of us like our hopes and fears for the future.

'You see the paper today?' she asked.

'No, I didn't get a chance.'

She picked up her bag and rummaged through it until she found the piece she had kept from the *Press Herald*, then handed it to me. 'I don't know why I tore it out,' she said. 'I knew you'd have to see it sometime, but part of me didn't want you to have to read about him again. I'm tired of seeing his name.'

I unfolded the paper.

THOMASTON – The Rev. Aaron Faulkner will remain at Thomaston State Prison until his trial, a Department of Corrections spokesman said yesterday. Faulkner, indicted earlier this year on charges of conspiracy and murder, was transferred to Thomaston from the state supermax facility a month ago, following what appeared to be a failed suicide attempt.

Faulkner was arrested in Lubec in May of this year following a confrontation with Scarborough-based private detective Charlie Parker, during which two people, a male calling himself Elias Pudd and an unnamed female, were killed. DNA tests revealed that the dead man was in fact Faulkner's son, Leonard. The woman was identified as Muriel Faulkner, the preacher's daughter.

Faulkner was formally indicted in May for the murders of the Aroostook Baptists, the religious group headed by the preacher that disappeared from its settlement at Eagle Lake in January 1964, and conspiracy to murder at least four other named individuals, among them the industrialist Jack Mercier.

The remains of the Aroostook Baptists were uncovered close by Eagle Lake last April. Officials in Minnesota, New York and Massachusetts may also be examining unsolved cases in which Faulkner and his family were allegedly involved, although no attempt has yet been made to charge Faulkner outside Maine.

According to sources within the Maine attorney general's office, both the Bureau of Alcohol, Tobacco and Firearms and the FBI are examining Faulkner's case, with a view to trying him on federal charges.

Faulkner's attorney, James Grimes, told reporters yesterday he remained concerned for the health and well-being of his client and was considering appealing to the State Supreme Court following the decision of a Washington County Superior Court to refuse bail. Faulkner has said he is innocent of all charges and was kept a virtual prisoner by his family for almost forty years.

Meanwhile, the consultant entomologist employed by investigators to catalogue the collection of insects and spiders found at the Lubec compound occupied by the Rev. Aaron Faulkner and his family told the *Press Herald* yesterday that he had almost completed his work. According to a state police spokesman, the collection is believed to have been assembled by Leonard Faulkner, alias Elias Pudd, over many years.

'So far we've identified about 200 different species of spider, as well as about 50 other species of insect,' Dr. Martin Lee Howard said. He said the collection contained some very rare species, including a number that his team had so far failed to identify.

'One of them seems to be some form of extremely nasty cave spider,' said Dr. Howard. 'It's certainly not a native of the United States.' Asked if there were any patterns emerging from his research, Dr. Howard said that the only common factor uniting the various species at this point was their 'general unpleasantness. I mean, insects and spiders are my life's work and even I have to admit that there are a lot of these guys and gals I wouldn't like to find in my bed at night.'

Dr. Howard added: 'But we did discover a lot of recluse spiders, and when I say a lot, I mean a lot. Whoever assembled this collection had a real affection for recluses, and that's not something you're going to find too often. Affection is pretty much the last thing the average person is going to feel for a recluse.'

I refolded the paper, then threw it in the trash can. The possibility of a bail appeal was troubling. The attorney general's office had gone straight to a grand jury after Faulkner's apprehension, common practice in a case which looked set to deal with matters that had gone unsolved for a long time. A 23-member grand jury had been specially convened at Calais, in Washington County, twenty-four hours after Faulkner was found, and an arrest warrant had been issued upon his indictment on charges of murder, conspiracy to murder and accomplice liability in the murder of others. The state had then asked for a 'Harnish hearing' to decide upon the issue of bail. In the past, when the death penalty had still existed in the state of Maine, those accused of capital offenses were not entitled to bail. After the abolition of the death penalty, the constitution was amended to deny bail for formerly capital offenses as long as there was 'proof evident and presumption great' in the alleged guilt of the accused. In order for that proof and presumption to be established, the state could request a Harnish hearing, conducted before a judge with both sides entitled to present arguments.

Both Rachel and I had given evidence before the hearing, as had the primary detective from the state police responsible for the investigation into the deaths of Faulkner's flock and the murder of four people in Scarborough, allegedly on Faulkner's orders. The deputy AG, Bobby Andrus, had argued that Faulkner was both a flight risk and a potential threat to the state's witnesses. Jim Grimes did his best to pick holes in the prosecutor's arguments but barely six days had elapsed since Faulkner's apprehension and Grimes was still playing catch-up. Altogether it was enough for the judge to deny bail, but only just. There was, as yet, little hard evidence to link Faulkner to the crimes of which he was accused, and the Harnish hearing had forced the state to demonstrate the comparative paucity of its case. That Jim Grimes was now talking publicly about an appeal indicated that he believed a judge in the state's highest court might reach a different conclusion on the bail issue. I didn't want to think about what might happen if Faulkner was released.

'We could take the long view and look at it as free publicity,' I said, but the joke sounded hollow. 'There's no getting away from it, not until they put him away permanently, and maybe not even then.'

'I guess it's your defining moment.' She sighed.

I put on my best earnest romantic look and clasped her hand. 'No,' I told her, as dramatically as I could. '*You* define me.'

She mimed sticking her finger down her throat, but she smiled and the shadow of Faulkner passed from us for a time. I reached out and held her hand, and she raised my fingers to her mouth and licked the last of the ice cream from the tips.

'Come on,' she said, and her eyes shone with a new hunger. 'Let's go home.'

But there was a car standing in the driveway of the house when we arrived. I recognized it as soon as I glimpsed it through the trees: Irving Blythe's Lincoln. When we pulled up he opened his door and stepped out, the sound of classical music from NPR flowing like honey into the still evening air. Rachel said hi and headed into the house. I watched as the lights went on in our bedroom and the shades came down. Irv Blythe had picked his moment perfectly if he was trying to come between me and an active love life.

'How can I help you, Mr. Blythe?' I asked, my tone betraying the fact that right now helping him was pretty low down on my list of priorities.

His hands were deep in the pockets of his trousers, his short-sleeved shirt tucked tightly into the elastic waistband. His pants were shucked up high over what remained of his paunch, making his legs look too long for his body. We had spoken little since I had agreed to look into the circumstances of his daughter's disappearance. Instead, I dealt mostly with his wife. I had gone back over the police reports, begun to speak again to those who had seen Cassie in the days before she disappeared, and retraced her movements in those final days; but too much time had elapsed for those who recalled her to remember anything new. In some cases, they had trouble remembering anything at all. I had come up with nothing remarkable so far, but I had declined the offer of a retainer similar to that enjoyed for so long by Sundquist. I told the Blythes that I would bill them for my time, nothing more. Yet if Irv Blythe wasn't openly hostile toward me, he still left me with the sense that he would have preferred it if I had not become involved in the investigation. I was not sure how the events of the previous day would affect our relationship. As it turned out, it was Blythe who brought them up.

'Yesterday, at the house . . . ,' he began, then stopped.

I waited.

'My wife thinks I owe you an apology.' His face was very red.

'What do you think?'

He was nothing if not blunt.

'I think I wanted to believe Sundquist and that man he brought with him. I resented you for taking away the hope they brought with them.'

'It was false hope, Mr. Blythe.'

'Mr. Parker, until now we've had no hope at all.'

He removed his hands from his pockets and started to dig at the skin in the center of his palms, hoping to locate the source of his pain there and remove it like a splinter. I noticed half-healed sores on the back of his hand and the exposed patches of his scalp, where he had torn at himself in his hurt and frustration.

It was time to clear the air between us.

'I get the sense that you don't like me very much,' I said.

His right hand stopped digging and flailed loosely at the air, as if he were trying to grasp his feelings toward me, to snatch them from the air so he could display them on his wrinkled, gouged palm instead of being forced to put them into words.

'It's not that,' he began. 'I'm sure that you're very good at what you do. It's just that I know about you. I've read the newspaper reports. I know that you solve difficult cases, that you've found out the truth about people who've been missing for years, longer even than Cassie. The trouble is, Mr. Parker, that those people are usually dead when you find them.' The final words came out in a rush, and left him with a tremble in his voice. 'I want my daughter back alive.'

'And you think that hiring me is like an admission that she's gone forever?'

'Something like that.'

Irv Blythe's words seemed to open wounds inside me that, like his own exposed sores, were only half healed. There were those whom I had failed to save, that was true, and there were others who were long gone before I had even begun to understand the nature of what had been visited upon them. But I had made an accommodation with my past, a recognition that although I had failed to protect individuals, had even failed to protect my own wife and child, I was not entirely responsible for what had happened to them. Susan and Jennifer had been taken by another, and even had I sat with them twenty-four hours a day for ninety-nine days, he would have waited until the hundredth day for me to turn my back briefly before he came for them at last. Now I spanned two worlds, the worlds of the living and the dead, and to both I tried to bring some measure of peace. It was all that I could do in reparation. But I would not have my failings judged by Irving Blythe, not now.

I opened his car door for him. 'It's getting late, Mr. Blythe. I'm sorry that I can't offer you the reassurance that you want. All I can say is that I'll keep asking questions. I'll keep trying.'

He nodded and looked out over the marsh, but made no move to get into his car. The moonlight shone on the waters, and the sight of the gleaming channels seemed to jolt him into some final form of self-examination

'I know she's dead, Mr. Parker,' he said softly. 'I know that she's not coming home to us alive. All I want is to put her to rest somewhere pretty and quiet where she can be at peace. I don't believe in closure. I don't believe that this thing will ever be closed to us. I just want to lay her down, and to be able to go to her with my wife and place flowers at her feet. You understand?'

I almost reached out and touched him, but Irving Blythe was not a man for such gestures between men. Instead, I spoke to him as gently as I could.

'I understand, Mr. Blythe. Drive carefully. I'll be in touch.'

He climbed into his car and didn't look at me until he had turned it toward the road. Then I saw his eyes in the rearview, and caught the hatred in them for the words that I had somehow forced him to speak, the admission that I had drawn from deep inside him.

I didn't join Rachel, not for some time. I sat on my porch and watched the passing lights of solitary cars until the biting of the insects forced me inside. By then, Rachel was asleep, and yet she smiled as she felt me close beside her.

Beside both of them.

That night a car drew up outside Elliot Norton's house on the outskirts of Grace Falls. Elliot heard the car door opening, then footsteps running across the grass of his yard. He was already reaching for the gun on his nightstand when the window of his bedroom exploded inward and the room erupted into flame. The burning gasoline splashed his arms and chest and set fire to his hair. He was still burning when he staggered down the stairs, through his front door, and onto his lawn, where he rolled in the damp grass to quench the fire.

He lay on his back in the moonlight and watched his house burn.

And as Elliot Norton's house flamed far to the south, I awoke to the sound of a car idling on Old County Road. Rachel was asleep beside me, something clicking inside her air passages as she breathed, a soft noise as regular as the ticking of a metronome. Gently, I slipped from beneath the covers and walked to the window.

In the moonlight, an old black Cadillac Coupe de Ville stood on the bridge that crossed the marshes. Even from a distance, I could see the dents and scratches on the paintwork, the broken-limb curve of the damaged front bumper, and the spiderweb tracery of cracked glass in the corner of the windshield. I could hear its engine rumbling but no smoke came from the exhaust;

and though the moon was bright that night I could not glimpse the interior of the car through the dark glass of the windows.

I had seen such a car before. It had been driven by a being named Stritch, a foul creature, pale and deformed. But Stritch was dead, a hole torn in his chest, and the car had been destroyed.

Then the rear door of the Cadillac opened. I waited for someone to emerge, but no one did. Instead the car just stood, its door wide open, for a minute or two until an unseen hand pulled the door closed, the coffin-lid thud coming to me across water and grass, and the car moved away, executing a U-turn to head northwest toward Oak Hill and Route 1.

I heard movement from the bed.

'What is it?' asked Rachel.

I turned to her and saw the shadows drifting across the room, clouds chased by moonlight, until they reached her and, slowly, began to devour her paleness.

'What is it?' asked Rachel.

I was back in bed, except now I was sitting bolt upright and I had pushed the sheets away from me with my feet. Her hand was warm upon me, flat against my chest.

'There was a car,' I said.

'Where?'

'Outside. There was a car.'

I stepped naked from the bed and walked to the window. I pulled back the curtain, but there was nothing there, only the road, quiet, and the silver threads of the water on the marsh.

'There was a car,' I said, for the last time.

And I saw the marks of my fingertips against the window, left there as I reached out to the car, just as they, reflected in the glass, now reached out for me.

'Come back to bed,' she said.

I went to her and I held her, spoonlike, as she slipped softly into sleep.

And I watched over her until morning came.

3

Elliot Norton called me again the morning after the arson attack. He had first-degree burns to his face and arms. He considered himself pretty lucky, all told. The fire had destroyed three rooms on the second floor of his house and left a big hole in his roof. No local contractor would touch the work and he'd engaged some guys from Martinez, just across the Georgia state line, to fix up the damage.

'You talk to the cops?' I asked him.

'Yeah, they were out here first thing. They got no shortage of suspects, but if they can make a case I'll retire from law and become a monk. They know it's linked to the Larousse case and I know it's linked to the Larousse case, so we're all in agreement. Just lucky I'm not paying them for their opinion.'

'Any suspects?'

'They'll round up some of the local assholes, but it won't do much good, not unless someone saw or heard something and is willing to stand up and say it. A lot of folks will take the view that I shouldn't have expected anything less for taking this on.'

There was a pause. I could feel him waiting for me to fill the silence. In the end I did, and felt my feet start to slide as the inevitability of my involvement became clear.

'What are you going to do?'

'What can I do? Cut the kid loose? He's my client, Charlie. I can't do that. I can't let them intimidate me out of this case.'

He was turning the guilt screws on me and he knew it. I didn't like it, but maybe he felt that he had no other option.

Yet it wasn't only his willingness to use our friendship that made me uneasy. Elliot Norton was a very good lawyer, but I'd never before seen the milk of human kindness flow from him in his professional dealings. Now he had put his house and possibly his life on the line for a young man he couldn't have known too well, and that didn't sound like the Elliot Norton I knew. I wasn't sure that I could turn my back on him any longer, even with my doubts, but the least I could do was to try and get some answers that satisfied me.

'Why are you doing this, Elliot?'

'Doing what, being a lawyer?'

'No, being this kid's lawyer.'

I waited for the speech about a man sometimes having to do what a man has to do, about how nobody else would stand up for the kid and how Elliot had been unable to stand by and watch while he was strapped to a gurney and injected with poisons until his heart stopped. Instead, he surprised me. Perhaps it was tiredness, or the events of the previous night, but when he spoke there was a bitterness in his voice that I had not heard before.

'You know, part of me always hated this place. I hated the attitudes, the small-town mentality. The guys I saw around me, they didn't want to be princes of industry, or politicians, or judges. They didn't want to change the world. They wanted to drink beer and screw women, and a thousand a month working in a gas station would allow them to do that. They were never going to leave, but if they weren't, then I sure as hell was.'

'So you became a lawyer.'

'That's right: a noble profession, whatever you might think.'

'And you went to New York.'

'I went to New York, but I hated New York even more than I hated here, and maybe I still had something to prove.'

'So now you're going to represent this kid as a way of getting back at them all?'

'Something like that. I have a gut feeling, Charlie: this kid didn't kill Marianne Larousse. He may be lacking in some of the social graces, but a rapist and a murderer he ain't. There's no way that I can stand by and watch them execute him for a crime he didn't commit.'

I let it sink in. Maybe it wasn't for me to question another's crusade. After all, I'd been accused of being a crusader myself often enough in the past.

'I'll call you tomorrow,' I said. 'Try to stay out of trouble until then.'

He breathed out deeply at what he saw as a crack of light in the darkness. 'Thanks, I'd appreciate that.'

When I hung up the phone, Rachel was leaning against the doorjamb watching me.

'You're going down there, aren't you?'

It wasn't an accusation, just a question.

I shrugged. 'Maybe.'

'You seem to feel some debt of loyalty to him.'

'No, not to him in particular.' I wasn't sure that I could put my reasons into words, but I felt like I had to try, to explain it to myself as much as to Rachel.

'When I've been in trouble, when I've taken on cases that were difficult, and worse than difficult, I've had people who were willing to stand alongside me: you, Angel, Louis, others too, and some of those people didn't survive their involvement. Now I have someone asking me for help and I'm not sure that I can turn away so easily.'

'"What goes around comes around?"'

'I guess so. But if I go down, there are things that need to be taken care of first.'

'Such as?'

I didn't reply.

'You mean me.' Invisible fingers traced thin lines of irritation on her forehead. 'We've talked about this before.'

'No, I've talked about it. You just block your ears.'

I heard my voice rising, and took a deep breath before I spoke again.

'Look, you won't carry a gun, and—'

'I'm not listening to this,' she said. She stormed up the stairs. Seconds later, I heard the door to her office slam shut.

I met Detective Sergeant Wallace MacArthur of the Scarborough PD in the Panera Bread Company over by the Maine Mall. I'd had a run-in with MacArthur during the events leading up to Faulkner's capture but we'd settled our differences over a meal at the Back Bay Grill. Admittedly, the meal had cost me the best part of two hundred bucks, including the wine MacArthur drank, although it was worth it to have him back on my side.

I ordered a coffee and joined him at a booth. He was tearing apart a warm cinnamon roll with his fingers, the frosting reduced to the consistency of melted butter, and leaving stains on the personal ads in the latest issue of the *Casco Bay Weekly*. The personals in the *CBW* tended to be pretty heavy on women who wanted to cuddle in front of fires, go hiking in the depths of winter, or join experimental dance classes. None of them seemed like candidates for MacArthur, who was about as cuddly as a holly bush and didn't like any physical activity that involved getting out of bed. Aided by the metabolism of a greyhound and his bachelor lifestyle, he had reached his late forties without being forced into the potential pitfalls of good eating and regular exercise. MacArthur's idea of exercise was using alternate fingers to push the remote.

'Found anyone you like?' I asked.

MacArthur chewed reflectively on a chunk of roll.

'How come all these women claim they're "attractive" and "cute" and "easygoing"?' he replied. 'I mean, I'm single. I'm out there, looking around, and I never meet women like these. I meet unattractive. I meet noncute. I meet hard-going. If they're so good looking and happy-go-lucky, how come they're advertising at the back of the *Casco Bay Weekly*? I tell you, I think some of these women are telling lies.'

'Maybe you should try the ads farther on.'

MacArthur's eyebrows gave a startled leap.

'The freaks? Are you kidding? I don't even know what some of that stuff means.' He flicked discreetly to the back pages, then gave the tables nearby a quick scan to make sure no one was watching. His voice dropped to a whisper. 'There's a woman in here looking for "a male replacement for her shower". I mean, what the hell is that? I wouldn't even know what she wanted me to do. Does she want me to fix her shower, or what?'

I looked at him. He looked back. For a man who had been a cop for over twenty years, MacArthur could come across as a little sheltered.

'What?' he asked.

'Nothing.'

'No, say it.'

'No, I just don't think that woman's for you, that's all.'

'You're telling me. I don't know what's worse: understanding what these people are looking for, or not understanding. Jesus, all I want is a normal, straightforward relationship. That's got to exist somewhere, right?'

I wasn't sure that there was such a thing as a normal, straightforward relationship, but I understood what he meant. He meant that Detective Wallace Mac Arthur wasn't going to be anybody's shower replacement.

'Last I heard you were helping Al Buxton's widow overcome her grief.' Al Buxton had been a York County deputy until he contracted some weird degenerative disease that made him look like a mummy without its bandages. His passing was mourned by pretty much nobody. Al Buxton was so unpleasant he made shingles look good.

'It didn't last. I don't think she had too much grief to overcome. Y'know, she told me once that she fucked his embalmer. I don't think he even got to wash his hands, she was on him so fast.'

'Maybe she was grateful for the nice job he'd done. Al looked a whole lot better dead than he did alive. Better company, too.'

MacArthur laughed, but the action seemed to irritate his eyes. It was only then that I saw how red and swollen they were. He looked like he'd been crying. Maybe the whole single thing was getting to him more than I thought.

'What's wrong with you? You look like Bambi's mother just died.'

He instinctively raised his right hand to wipe at his eyes, which had begun to tear, then seemed to think better of it.

'I got Maced this morning.'

'No way. Who did it?'

'Jeff Wexler.'

'*Detective* Jeff Wexler? What did you do, try to ask him out? You know, that guy in the Village People wasn't really a cop. You shouldn't use him as a role model.'

MacArthur looked seriously unimpressed.

'You about done? I got Maced because it's department regs: you want to carry Mace, you got to experience what it feels like to get Maced, just so you won't be too hasty about doing it to somebody else.'

'Really? Does it work?'

'Like hell. I just want to get out there and blast some bastard in the face so I can feel better about myself. That stuff *stings*.'

Shocker. Mace stings. Who'd have thought?

'Someone told me you're working for the Blythes,' said MacArthur. 'That's a pretty cold case.'

'They haven't given up, even if the cops have.'

'That's not fair, Charlie, and you know it.'

I raised a hand in apology. 'I had Irv Blythe out at my house last night. I had to tell his wife and him that their first lead in years was false. I didn't feel good about it. They're in pain, Wallace: six years on and they're still in pain every day. They've been forgotten. I know it's not the cops' fault. I know the case is cold. It's just not cold for the Blythes.'

'You think she's dead?' His tone told me that he had already reached his own conclusion.

'I hope she's not.'

'There's always hope, I guess.' He smiled crookedly. 'I wouldn't be looking at the personals if I didn't believe that.'

'I said I was hopeful, not insanely optimistic.'

MacArthur gave me the finger. 'So, you wanted to see me? Plus you got here late so I had to buy my own cinnamon roll, and these things are kind of expensive.'

'Sorry. Look, I may have to leave town for a week. Rachel doesn't like me being overprotective and she won't carry a gun.'

'You need someone to drop by, keep an eye on her?'

'Just until I get back.'

'It's done.'

'Thanks.'

'This about Faulkner?'

I shrugged. 'I guess.'

'His people are gone, Parker. It's just him.'

'Maybe.'

'Anything happen to make you think otherwise?'

I shook my head. There was nothing but a feeling of unease and a belief that Faulkner would not let the annihilation of his brood slide.

'You lead a charmed life, Parker, you know that? The order from the attorney general's office was strictly hands off: you weren't to be pursued for obstructing the investigation, no charges against you or your buddy for the deaths in Lubec. I mean, it's not like you killed aid workers or nothing, but still.'

'I know,' I said sharply. I wanted the subject dropped. 'So, you'll have someone stop by?'

'Sure, no problem. I'll do it myself, when I can. You think she'd agree to a panic button?'

I thought about it. It would probably require UN-level diplomatic skills, but I figured Rachel might eventually come around. 'Probably. You got someone in mind to install it?'

'I know a guy. Give me a call when you've talked to her.'

I thanked him and rose to leave. I got about three steps when his voice stopped me.

'Hey, she doesn't have any single friends, does she?'

'Yeah, I think so,' I replied, just before the ground crumbled beneath my feet and I realized what I had let myself in for. MacArthur's face brightened as mine fell.

'Oh, no. What am I, a dating agency?'

'Hey, come on, it's the least you can do.'

I shook my head. 'I'll ask. I can't promise anything.'

I left MacArthur with a smile on his face.

A smile, and lots of frosting.

For the rest of the morning and part of the afternoon I did some wrap-ups on outstanding paperwork, billed two clients, then went over my meagre notes on Cassie Blythe. I had spoken to her ex-boyfriend, her closest friends, and her work colleagues, as well as to the recruitment company she had gone to visit in Bangor on the day that she had disappeared. Her car was being serviced so she had taken the bus to Bangor, leaving the Greyhound depot at the corner of Congress and St John at about 8 A.M. According to the police reports and Sundquist's follow-ups, the driver recalled her and remembered exchanging a few words with her. She had spent an hour with the recruitment company in its offices at West Market Square, before browsing in Book Marcs bookstore. One of the staff remembered her asking about signed Stephen King books.

Then Cassie Blythe had disappeared. The return portion of her ticket was unused and there was no record of her using any other bus company or taking one of the commuter flights south. Her credit card and ATM card had not been used since the date of her disappearance. I was running out of people to chase down and I was getting nowhere.

It seemed like I wasn't going to find Cassie Blythe, alive or dead.

The black Lexus pulled up outside the house shortly after three. I was upstairs at my computer, printing off the stories on Marianne Larousse's murder. Most of them were pretty uninformative, except for one short piece in the *State* detailing the fact that Elliot Norton had taken over the defense of Atys Jones from the assistant public defender appointed to his case, a man named Laird Rhine. There had been no motion for substitution filed, which meant that Rhine had agreed with Elliot to step aside. In a short comment, Elliot told the journalist that, while Rhine was a fine lawyer, Jones stood a better chance with his own attorney than a time-pressed public defender. Rhine gave no comment. The piece was a couple of weeks old. I was printing it off just as the Lexus arrived.

The man who stepped from the passenger seat wore paint-stained Reebok sneakers, paint-stained blue jeans, and just to complete the ensemble, a paint-stained denim shirt. He looked like the runway model for a decorators' convention, assuming that the decorators' tastes veered toward five-six semiretired gay burglars. Now that I thought of it, when I lived in the East Village there were any number of decorators whose tastes veered in that direction.

The driver of the car was at least a foot taller than his partner and was getting the last wear out of his summer wardrobe of oxblood loafers and a tan linen suit. His black skin shone in the sunlight, obscured only by the faintest growth of hair on his scalp and a circular beard around his pursed lips.

'Now, this place is a whole lot nicer than that other dump you called home,' said Louis when I went down to greet them.

'If you hated it so much, why did you bother visiting?'

''Cause it got you pissed.'

I reached out to shake Louis's hand and found a piece of Louis Vuitton luggage thrust into my palm.

'I don't tip,' he said.

'I guessed that when I saw you were too cheap to fly up for the weekend.'

His eyebrow raised itself a fraction. 'Hey, I work for you for free, I bring my own guns, and I pay for my own bullets. I can't afford to take no plane up here.'

'You still carrying an arsenal in the trunk of your car?'

'Why, you need something?'

'No, but if your car is hit by lightning I'll know where my lawn went.'

'Can't be too careful. It's a mean old world out there.'

'You know, there's a name for people who believe the world is out to get them: paranoid.'

'Yeah, and there's a name for people who don't: dead.'

He swept past me to where Rachel waited and hugged her gently. Rachel was the only person Louis ever showed any real affection toward. I could only assume that he occasionally patted Angel on the head. After all, they'd been together for almost six years.

Angel appeared beside me. 'I think he's getting more charming as he gets older,' I told him.

'He was any less charming he'd have claws, eight legs, and a sting on the end of his tail,' he replied.

'Wow, and he's all yours.'

'Yeah, ain't I the lucky one?'

Angel seemed to have grown suddenly older in the months since I had last seen him. There were pronounced lines around his eyes and mouth, and his black hair was now iced with gray. He even walked more slowly, as if afraid of the consequences of putting a foot wrong. I knew from Louis that he still endured a lot of pain with his back, where the preacher, Faulkner, had cut away a square of skin from between his shoulder blades and left him to bleed into an old tub. The transplants were taking but the scars hurt every time he moved. In addition, the two men had endured a period of enforced separation. Angel's direct involvement in the events leading up to Faulkner's capture had inevitably drawn the attention of the law to him. He was now living in an apartment ten blocks away from Louis so that his partner did not fall within the ambit of their enquiries, since Louis's past did not bear close examination by the forces of law and order.

They were taking a chance even coming up here together, but it was Louis who had suggested it, and I was not about to argue with him. Maybe he felt that it would do Angel some good to be around other people who cared about him.

Angel guessed what I was thinking, because he smiled ruefully. 'Not looking so good, am I?'

I smiled back. 'You never looked good.'

'Oh yeah, I forgot. Let's go inside. You're making me feel like an invalid.'

I watched Rachel kiss him softly on the cheek and whisper something in his ear. For the first time since he had arrived, he laughed.

But when she looked over his shoulder at me, Rachel's eyes were filled with sorrow for him.

We ate dinner in Katahdin, at the junction of Spring and High in Portland. Katahdin has mismatched furniture, eccentric decor, and feels like eating in somebody's living room. Rachel and I love it. Unfortunately, so do a lot of other people, so we had to wait for a while at the cozy bar, listening to the locals who regularly eat there gossiping and chatting. Angel and Louis ordered a bottle of Kendall-Jackson chardonnay and I allowed myself a half glass. For a long time after the deaths of Jennifer and Susan I hadn't touched alcohol. I had been in a bar on the night they died and had found a whole series of ways to torment myself for not being there when they needed me. Now I took an occasional beer and, on very special occasions, a glass of Flagstone wine at home. I didn't miss drinking. My taste for alcohol had largely disappeared.

We eventually got a table in a corner and started in on Katahdin's excellent buttermilk rolls. We talked about Rachel's pregnancy, dissed my furniture, and caught up on New York gossip over their seafood and my London broil.

'Man, your house is full of old shit,' said Louis.

'Antiques,' I corrected him. 'They were my grandfather's.'

'I don't care they were Moses's, they just old shit. You like one of them e-Bay motherfuckers, peddling trash on the Web. When you gonna make him buy some new furniture, girl?'

Rachel raised her hands in an I'm-staying-out-of-it gesture, just as the hostess stepped up to make sure everything was okay. She smiled at Louis, who was slightly nonplussed to find that she wasn't intimidated by him. Most people tended to find Louis intimidating at the very least, but the hostess at Katahdin was a strong, attractive woman who didn't do intimidated, thank you for asking. Instead, she fed him more buttermilk rolls and gave him the kind of look a dog might give a particularly juicy bone.

'I think she likes you,' said Rachel, radiating innocence.

'I'm gay, not blind.'

'But then, she doesn't know you like we do,' I added. 'Still, you'd better eat up. You'll need all your strength for running away.'

Louis scowled. Angel remained quiet, as he had for much of the day. He cheered up a little when talk turned to Willie Brew, who ran the auto shop in Queens that had supplied my Boss 302, and in which Angel and Louis were silent partners.

'His son got some girl pregnant,' he told me.

'Which son, Leo?'

'No, the other one, Nicky. The one who's like an idiot savant, minus the savant.'

'Is he going to do the right thing?'

'Already has. He ran away to Canada. Girl's father is seriously pissed. Guy's name is Pete Drakonis, but everybody calls him Jersey Pete. You know, you don't fuck with guys who've got a state as part of their names, except maybe Vermont. The guy's got Vermont in his name, the only thing he's gonna try to make you do is save the whales and drink chai tea.'

Over coffee I told them about Elliot Norton and his client. Angel shook his head wearily. 'South Carolina,' he said, 'is not my favorite place.'

'An official Gay Pride Day march is some way off,' I admitted.

'Where'd you say this guy's from?' asked Louis.

'A town called Grace Falls. It's up by—'

'I know where it's at,' he replied.

There was something in his voice that made me stop talking. Even Angel gave him a look, but didn't press the point. We just watched as Louis fragmented a piece of discarded roll between his thumb and forefinger.

'When you planning on leavin'?' he asked me.

'Sunday.' Rachel and I had discussed it and agreed that my conscience was unlikely to rest unless I went down for a couple of days at least. At the risk of developing a roughly Rachel-shaped hole in my body where she had gone through me for a short cut, I had raised the subject of my earlier conversation with MacArthur. To my surprise, she had agreed to both regular drop-bys and panic buttons in the kitchen and main bedroom.

Incidentally, she had also agreed to find Mac Arthur a date.

Louis appeared to consult some kind of mental calendar.

'Meet you down there,' he said.

'*We'll* meet you down there,' corrected Angel.

Louis glanced at him. 'I got something I got to do first,' he said. 'Along the way.'

Angel flicked at a crumb. 'I got nothing else planned,' he replied. His voice was studiedly neutral.

The conversation seemed to have taken a turn down a strange road, and I wasn't about to ask for a map. Instead, I called for the check.

'You want to hazard a guess as to what that was about?' Rachel asked as we walked to my car, Angel and Louis ahead of us, unspeaking.

'No,' I answered. 'But I get the feeling that somebody is going to be very unhappy that those two ever left New York.'

I just hoped that it wouldn't be me.

That night, I awoke to a noise from downstairs. I left Rachel sleeping, pulled on a robe, and went down to find the front door slightly ajar. Outside, Angel sat on the porch seat, dressed in sweatpants and an old Doonesbury T-shirt, his bare feet stretched out before him. He had a glass of milk in his hand as he looked out over the moonlit marsh. From the west came the cry of a screech owl, rising and falling in pitch. There was a pair nesting in the Black Point Cemetery. Sometimes, at night, the headlights of the car would catch them ascending toward the treetops, a vole or mouse still struggling in their claws.

'Owls keeping you awake?'

He glanced over his shoulder at me, and there was a little of the old Angel in his smile. 'The silence is keeping me awake. The hell do you sleep in all this quiet?'

'I can go beep my horn and swear in Arabic if you think it will help.'

'Gee, would you?'

Around us, mosquitoes danced, waiting for their chance to descend. I took some matches from the windowsill and lit a mosquito coil, then sat down beside him. He offered me his glass.

'Milk?'

'No thanks. I'm trying to give it up.'

'You're right. That calcium'll kill ya.'

He sipped his milk.

'You worried about her?'

'Who, Rachel?'

'Yeah, Rachel. Who'd you think I was asking about, Chelsea Clinton?'

'She's fine. But I hear Chelsea's doing well in college, so that's good too.'

A smile fluttered at his lips, like the brief beating of butterfly wings.

'You know what I mean.'

'I know. Sometimes, yes, I'm afraid. I get so scared that I come out here in the darkness and I look down on the marsh and I pray. I pray that nothing happens to Rachel and our child. Frankly, I think I've done my share of suffering. We all have. I was kind of hoping the book was closed for a while.'

'Place like this, on a night like tonight, maybe lets you believe that could happen,' he said. 'It's pretty here. Peaceful too.'

'You thinking of retiring here? If you are, I'll have to move again.'

'Nah, I like the city too much. But this is kind of restful, for a change.'

'I have snakes in my woodshed.'

'Don't we all? What are you going to do about them?'

'Leave them alone. Hope they go away, or that something else kills them for me.'

'And if they don't?'

'Then I'll have to deal with them myself. You want to tell me why you're out here?'

'My back hurts,' he said simply. 'Places on my thighs where they took the skin from, they hurt too.'

In his eyes I could see the night shapes reflected so clearly that it was as if they were a part of him, the elements of a darker world that had somehow entered and colonized his soul.

'I still see them, you know, that fucking preacher and his son, holding me down while they cut away at me. He whispered to me, you know that? That fucking Pudd, he whispered to me, rubbed my brow, told me that it was all okay, while his old man cut me. Every time I stand or stretch, I feel that blade on my skin and I hear him whispering and it brings me back. And when that happens, the hate comes flooding back with it. I've never felt hate like it before.'

'It fades,' I said quietly.

'Does it?'

'Yes.'

'But it doesn't go away.'

'No. It's yours. You do with it what you have to do.'

'I want to kill someone.' He said it without feeling, in level tones, the way somebody might announce that they were going to take a cold shower on a warm day.

Louis was the killer, I thought. It didn't matter that he killed for motives that went beyond money or politics or power; that he was no longer morally neutral; that whatever he might have done in the past, those he now chose to destroy went largely unmourned. Louis had it in him to take a life and not lose a moment's sleep over it.

Angel was different. When he'd been placed in situations where it was kill or be killed, then he had taken lives. It troubled him to do it, but better to be troubled above ground than to be untroubled below, and I had personal reasons to be thankful for his actions. Now Faulkner had destroyed something inside Angel, some small dam that he had constructed for himself behind which was contained all of his sorrow and hurt and rage at the things that had been done to him throughout his life. I knew only fragments of it – abuse, starvation, rejection, violence – but I was now beginning to realize the consequences of its release.

'But you still won't testify against him, if they ask,' I said.

I knew the deputy DA was debating the wisdom of calling Angel for the trial, particularly given the fact that they would have to subpoena him to do it. Angel wasn't one for making voluntary visits to courtrooms.

'I wouldn't make such a great witness.'

This was true but I didn't know how much I should tell him about the case against Faulkner, about how weak it was and how there were fears that it might collapse entirely without more hard evidence. As the newspaper report had pointed out, Faulkner was claiming that he had been a virtual prisoner of his son and daughter for four decades; that they alone were responsible for the deaths of his flock and a series of attacks against groups and individuals whose beliefs differed from their own; and that they had brought skin and bone from their victims to him and forced him to preserve them as relics. It was the classic defense of 'The dead guys done it'.

'You know where Caina is?' asked Angel.

'Nope.'

'It's in Georgia. Louis was born near there. On our way to South Carolina, we're going to make a stop in Caina. Just so you know.'

There was something in his eyes as he spoke, a fierce burning. I recognized it instantly, for I had seen it in my own eyes in the past. He rose and turned his face from me to hide the evidence of the pain, then walked to the screen door.

'It won't solve anything,' I said.

He paused.

'Who cares?'

The next morning Angel hardly spoke at breakfast, and the little that he did say was not directed at me. Our conversation on the porch had not brought us any closer. Instead, it had confirmed the existence of a growing divide between us, an estrangement acknowledged by Louis before they departed.

'You two talk last night?' he asked.

'A little.'

'He thinks you should have killed the preacher when you had the chance.'

We were watching Rachel talking quietly to Angel. Angel's head was down, and he nodded occasionally, but I could feel the restlessness coming from him in waves. The time for talking, for reasoning, was gone.

'Does he blame me?'

'It ain't that simple for him.'

'Do you?'

'No, I don't. Angel would be dead twice over, you hadn't done the things you done for him. There ain't no quarrel between us, you and me. Angel, he just troubled.'

Angel leaned over and kissed Rachel gently but quickly on the cheek, then headed for their car. He looked over at us, nodded once to me, then climbed in.

'I'm going up there today,' I said.

Louis seemed to tighten beside me. 'To the prison?'

'That's right.'

'I ask why?'

'Faulkner requested my presence.'

'And you agreed to see him?'

'They need all the help they can get, and Faulkner is giving them nothing. They don't think it can hurt.'

'They wrong.'

I didn't respond.

'They may still subpoena Angel.'

'They have to find him first.'

'If he testifies, maybe he can help keep Faulkner behind bars until he dies.'

Louis was already moving away.

'Maybe we don't want him behind bars,' he said. 'Maybe we want him out in the open, where we can get at him.'

I watched their car as it drove down Black Point Road, across the bridge and onto Old County, until they were lost from sight. Rachel stood next to me, holding my hand.

'You know,' she said, 'I wish you'd never heard from Elliot Norton. Ever since he called, nothing has felt the same.'

I squeezed her hand tightly, a gesture that seemed equal parts reassurance and agreement. She was right. Somehow, our lives had become tainted by events of which we had no part. Walking away from them wouldn't help, not now.

And we stood there together, she and I, as, in a Carolina swamp, a man reached out to his darkness mirrored, and was consumed by it.

4

The man named Landron Mobley stopped and listened, his finger resting outside the trigger guard of his hunting rifle. Above his head, rainwater dripped from the leaves of a cottonwood, staining the massive gray trunk of the tree. The deep, resonant calls of bullfrogs came from the undergrowth to his right while a reddish brown centipede worked its way around the toe of his left boot, hunting for spiders and insects, the pill bugs feeding nearby seemingly unaware of the approaching threat. For a few seconds Mobley followed its progress, watching in amusement as the centipede put on a sudden burst of speed, its legs and antennae little more than a blur, the pill bugs scattering or rolling themselves into gray, plated balls to protect themselves. The centipede curled itself around one of the little crustaceans and began working at the point where its head and metallic lower body now met, seeking a vulnerable spot into which to inject its venom. The struggle was short, ending fatally for the pill bug, and Mobley returned his full attention to the matter in hand.

He shifted the walnut stock of the Voere against his shoulder, blinked once to clear the sweat from his eyes, then placed his right eye close to the aperture of the telescopic sight, the blued finish of the rifle gleaming dully in the late afternoon light. From his right, the rustling sound came again, followed by a shrill *clee-clee-clee*. He sighted, pivoting the gun slightly until it came to rest on a tangle of sweet gum, elm, and sycamore from which dead vines hung like the discarded skins of snakes. He took a single deep breath, then released it slowly just as the kite burst from cover, its long black tail forking behind it, its white underparts and head strangely ghostlike against the blackness of its wing tips, as if a dark shadow had fallen over the hunting bird, a foretelling of the death that was to come.

Its breast exploded in a flurry of blood and feathers and the kite seemed to bounce in midair as the .308 slug tore through it, the bird tumbling to the ground seconds later and coming to rest in a clump of alder. Mobley eased the stock away from his shoulder and released the now-empty five-round magazine. With the kite added, that meant that his five bullets had accounted for a raccoon, a Virginia opossum, a song sparrow, and a snapping turtle, the latter beheaded with a single shot as it lay sunning itself on a log not twenty feet from where Mobley had been standing.

He walked to the alders and poked around until the corpse of the bird was revealed, its beak slightly open and the hole at the center of its being gleaming black and red. He felt a satisfaction that had not come to him in the earlier kills, an almost sexual thrill bound up in the transgressive nature of the act he had just committed, the ending not merely of a small life but the removal of a little grace and beauty from the world it had inhabited. Mobley touched the bird with the muzzle of the rifle and its warm body yielded to the pressure, the feathers bending slightly in upon themselves as if they might somehow close up the wound, time running in reverse as the tissue fused, the blood flowed backward into the body, the breast, now sunken, suddenly became full again, and the kite soared back into the air, its body reconstituting itself as it rose until the moment of impact became an instant not of destruction but of creation.

Mobley squatted down and carefully reloaded the magazine, then sat on the trunk of a fallen beech tree and removed a Miller High Life from his knapsack. He popped the cap, took a long pull, and belched once, his eyes fixed on the spot where the dead kite had come to rest as if he did indeed expect it to come to life, to ascend bloodied from the earth and take once again to the skies. In some dark place inside him, Landron Mobley secretly wished that the kite wasn't dead but merely injured; that he had pushed back the leaves and found the bird thrashing on the ground, its wings beating vainly at the dirt, blood spreading from the hole in its underside. Then Mobley could have knelt down, placed his left hand against the bird's neck, and inserted his finger into the bullet hole, twisting against the flesh while the creature struggled, feeling the warmth of it against him, the meat tearing as his finger probed, until finally it shuddered and died; Mobley, in his way, becoming almost like a bullet himself, exploring its body as both the instrument and the agent of the kite's destruction.

He opened his eyes.

There was blood on his fingers. When he looked down, the kite had been ripped apart, the feathers scattered across the ground, the sightless eyes reflecting the movements of clouds in the skies above. Mobley absently touched his fingers to his lips and tasted the kite with his tongue, then blinked hard and wiped himself clean on his pants, both embarrassed yet aroused by this sudden conflation of act and desire. They came to him so quickly, these red moments, that they were often upon him before he could even register their approach and over before he could enjoy their consummation.

For a time, he had found an outlet for his cravings in his work. He could take one of the women from her cell and let his fingers explore her flesh, his hand over her mouth as he forced her legs apart; but those days were gone. Landron Mobley was one of fifty-one guards and prison staff who had been fired that year by the South Carolina Corrections Department for having 'improper relationships' with inmates. Improper relationships: Mobley almost smiled. That was what the department told the media in an effort to cloud the reality of what took place. Sure, there were inmates who participated willingly, sometimes out of loneliness or pure horniness, or so they could get hold of a couple of packs of cigarettes, some pot, maybe even something a little stronger. It was whoring, nothing more than that, no matter what they told themselves, and Landron Mobley wasn't above taking a little pussy as a thank-you for a good deed done, no sir. In fact, Landron Mobley wasn't above taking pussy, period, and there were inmates at the Women's Correctional Institution on Columbia's Broad River Road who had reason to look at Landron Mobley with more than a little respect and, yes sir, fear after he had shown them what they could expect if they crossed good old Landron. Landron, with his bleak, empty eyes seeking to fill their void with the reflected emotions of another, her lips drawn back in pleasure or pain, Landron making no distinction between the two extremes, the feelings of the other inconsequential to him but his preference, truth be told, lying in resistance and struggle and forced surrender. Landron, roving from cell to cell, probing for weaknesses in the curled forms beneath the blankets. Landron, filled with venom, leaning over a slim, dark shape, working at the head, drawing it away from the woman's chest, paralyzing her with his weight as he descended upon her. Landron, amid the water dropping from the leaves and the calling of the bullfrogs, the blood of the kite still warm upon his fingers, growing hard at the memory.

Then one of the local rags revealed that a female inmate named Myrna Chitty had been assaulted while serving a six-month sentence for purse snatching, and an investigation had commenced. And damn if Myrna Chitty hadn't told the investigators about Landron's occasional visits to her cell and how Landron had forced her over her bunk and how she had heard the sound of his belt unbuckling and then the pain, oh Jesus, the pain. The next day Landron was off the payroll and the following week he was pink-slipped, but it wasn't going to stop there. There was a hearing of the Corrections and Penology Committee scheduled for September 3 and there was talk of rape charges being pressed against Landron and a couple of other guards who might have let their enthusiasm get the better of them. It was a major embarrassment all round and Mobley knew that if they had their way, he was going to be hung out to dry.

One thing was for certain: Myrna Chitty wouldn't be testifying at no rape trial. He knew what happened to prison guards who ended up doing hard time, knew that what he had visited on the women in his charge would be returned one-hundredfold upon him, and Landron Mobley didn't plan on pulling no train or sifting through his food for glass fragments. Myrna Chitty's testimony, if it was heard in court, would be the passing of a virtual death sentence on Landron Mobley, one that would eventually be carried out with a shank or a broom handle. She was scheduled for release on September 5, her sentence reduced in return for her cooperation with the investigation, and Landron would be waiting for her when she got her white trash tail back to her shitty little house. Then Landron and Myrna were going to have a little talk, and maybe he would have to remind her of what she was missing now that she didn't have old Landron to drop by her cell or take her down to the showers to search her for contraband. No, Myrna Chitty wouldn't be putting her hand on no Bible and calling Landron Mobley a rapist. Myrna Chitty would learn to keep her mouth shut unless Landron told her otherwise, or else Myrna Chitty would be dead.

He took another long drink and kicked at the dirt with the toe of his boot. Landron Mobley didn't have too many friends. He was a mean drunk, although, to his credit, he was mean sober, so no one could claim that he'd misled them into a false sense of security. That had always been the way with him. He was an outsider, despised for his lack of education, for his taste for violence, and for the miasma of debased sexuality that hung around him like a polluted fog. Yet his capacities had drawn others to him, who recognized in Mobley a creature that might enable them to dabble in depravity without losing themselves to it totally, using Mobley's absolute corruption as a means of indulging their own appetites without consequence.

But there were always consequences, for Mobley was like a pitcher plant, attracting victims with the promise of sweet juices, then thriving as they slowly drowned in an abundance of that which they had sought. Mobley's corruption could be passed on in a word, a gesture, a promise, exploiting weakness as water exploits a crack in concrete, widening it, extending itself deeper and deeper, until the structures were ruined beyond salvation.

He had a wife once. Her name was Lynnette. She wasn't beautiful, not even smart, but she was a wife nonetheless, and he'd worn her down as he'd worn down so many others over the years. One day, he came back from the prison and she was gone. She didn't take much, apart from a suitcase of mangy old clothes and some cash that Landron kept in a cracked coffee-pot for emergencies, but Landron could still recall the surge of anger that he'd felt, the sense of abandonment and betrayal as his voice echoed emptily around their tidy home.

He'd found her, though. He'd warned her about what would happen if she ever tried to leave him, and Landron was a man of his word, when it counted. He'd tracked her down to a dingy motel room on the outskirts of Macon, Georgia, and then she and Landron, they'd had themselves a time. Least of all, Landron had had himself a time. He couldn't speak for Lynnette. When he'd finished with her she couldn't speak for herself either, and it would be a long time before a man looked at Lynnette Mobley and didn't want to puke at the sight of her face.

For a time, Landron descended into his own private fantasy world: a world in which the Lynnettes knew their place and didn't go running off when a man's back was turned; a world in which he still wore his uniform and could still pick the weakest ones to take for his amusement; a world in which Myrna Chitty was trying to run from him and he was gaining, gaining, until at last he caught her and turned her to him, those brown eyes full of fear as she was forced down, down . . .

Around him, the Congaree Swamp seemed to recede, blurring at the edges, becoming a haze of gray and black and green, with only the dripping of water and the calling of birds to distract him. Soon, even that was lost to Landron as he moved to his own, private rhythm in his own red world.

But Landron Mobley had not left the Congaree.

Landron Mobley would never leave the Congaree.

The Congaree Swamp is old, very old. It was old when the prehistoric foragers hunted its reaches, old when Hernando de Soto passed through in 1540, old when the Congaree Indians were annihilated by smallpox in 1698. The English settlers used the inland waterways as part of their ferry system in the 1740s, but it wasn't until 1786 that Isaac Huger began construction of a formal ferry system to cross the Congaree. At its northwestern and southwestern boundaries, the bodies of workers are buried beneath the mud and silt, left where they died during the construction of dikes by James Adams and others in the 1800s.

At the end of that century, logging began on land owned by Francis Beidler's Santee River Cypress Lumber Company, ceasing in 1915, only to recommence half a century later. In 1969, logging interest was renewed and clearcutting commenced in 1974, leading to the growth of a movement among local people to save the land, some of which had never been logged and represented the last significant old-growth of river-bottom hardwood forest in this part of the country. There were now close to 22,000 acres designated as a national monument, half of them old-growth hardwood forest, stretching from the junction of Myers Creek and the Old Bluff Road to the northwest, down to the borders of Richland and Calhoun Counties to the southeast, close by the railroad line. Only one small section of land, measuring about two miles by half a mile, remained in private hands. It was close to this tract that Landron Mobley now sat, lost in dreams of women's tears. The Congaree was his place. The things he had done here in the past, among the trees and in the mud, never troubled him. Instead, he luxuriated in them, the memory of them enriching the poverty of his current existence. Here, time became meaningless and he lived once again in remembered pleasures. Landron Mobley was never closer to himself than he was in the Congaree.

Mobley's eyes flicked open suddenly, but he remained very still. Slowly, almost imperceptibly, he turned his head to his left and his gaze alighted on the soft brown eyes of a white-tailed deer. It was reddish brown and about five feet in height, with white rings at its nose, eyes, and throat. Its tail flicked back and forth in mild agitation, displaying its white underside. Mobley had guessed that there were deer around. He had come across their split heart tracks a mile or so back toward the river and had followed the trail of their pellets, of the raggedly browsed vegetation and the worn tree trunks where the males had rubbed the bark off with their antlers, but had eventually lost it in the thick undergrowth. He had almost given up hope of killing a deer on this trip; now here was a fine doe staring at him from beneath a loblolly pine. Keeping his eyes on the deer, Mobley reached out with his right hand for his rifle.

His hand clutched empty air. Puzzled, he looked to his right. The Voere was gone, a slight depression in the soft earth the only indication that it had ever been there. He stood quickly and heard the deer give a loud whistling snort of alarm before padding into the cover of the trees, its tail erect. Mobley barely noticed its flight. The Voere was just about his most prized possession and now somebody had taken it while Mobley had been daydreaming with his dick in his hand. He spit furiously on the ground and checked for tracks. There were footprints a couple of feet to his right, but the bushes were thick beyond them and he could find no further trace of the thief. The soles were thick with a zigzag pattern, the tread seemingly heavy.

'Fuck you,' he hissed. Then, louder: 'Fuck you! *Fuck!*'

He looked at the footprints again and his anger began to fade, to be replaced by the first gnawings of fear. He was out in the Congaree without a gun. Maybe the thief had headed back into the swamp with his prize, or maybe he was still close by, watching to see how Landron would react. He scanned the trees and the undergrowth, but could catch no sign of another human being. Hurriedly, and as silently as he could, he picked up his knapsack and began to walk toward the river.

The journey back to where he had left his boat took almost twenty minutes, the speed of his progress diminished by his reluctance to make more noise than was necessary and his decision to pause at regular intervals to search for signs that he was being shadowed. Once or twice, he thought that he caught glimpses of a figure among the trees, but when he stopped he could detect no signs of movement and the only sounds came from the soft drip of water from leaves and branches. But it was not the false sightings that increased Mobley's fear.

The birds had stopped singing.

As he neared the river, he increased his pace, his boots making a soft sucking noise as they lifted from the mud. He found himself in a dwarf forest of cypress knees, bordered by downed logs and the gray remains of standing dead trees now home to woodpeckers and small mammals. Some of this destruction was a relic of hurricane Hugo, which had decimated the park in 1989 but had, in turn, stimulated new growth. Beyond some rising saplings Mobley could see the dark waters of the Congaree River itself, fed by the spills of the Piedmont. He burst through the last low wall of vegetation and found himself on the bank, Spanish moss hanging low from a cypress branch almost tickling the nape of his neck as he stood close to the spot where he had tied up his boat.

His boat, too, was now gone.

But there was something else in its place.

There was a woman.

Her back was to Mobley so he couldn't see her face, and a white sheet covered her from head to toe like a hooded robe. She stood in the shallows, the ends of the material swirling in the current. While Mobley watched, she lowered herself down and gathered water in her hands, then raised her face and allowed the water to splash onto her skin. Mobley could see that she was naked beneath the white robe. The woman was heavy and the dark cleft of her buttocks had pressed itself against the material as she squatted down, her skin like chocolate beneath the frosting of her garment. Mobley was almost aroused, except—

Except he wasn't sure that what was beneath the cloth could actually be called skin. It seemed broken all over, as if the woman were scaled or plated. Some kind of substance had either been released from her skin or smeared upon it, causing the material of her cloak to adhere to it in places. It was almost reptilian and lent the woman a predatory aspect that caused Mobley to back away slightly. He tried to glimpse her hands but they were now beneath the water. Slowly, the woman bent down farther, submerging her arms first to the wrists, then the elbows, until finally she was almost hunched over. He heard her exhale, as if in pleasure. It was the first sound he had heard from her, and her silence unnerved, then angered, him. He had made more noise than the frightened deer as he tramped heavily toward the bank when the river came in sight, but the woman appeared not to have noticed, or had chosen not to recognize his presence. Mobley, despite his unease, decided to put an end to that.

'Hey!' he called.

The woman didn't respond, but he thought he saw her back stiffen slightly.

'Hey!' he repeated. 'I'm talking to you.'

This time, the woman rose to her full height, but she did not look around. Mobley advanced slightly, until his feet were almost at the water's edge.

'I'm looking for a boat. You seen it?'

The woman was now completely still. Her head, thought Mobley, looked like it was too small for her body until he realised that she was completely bald. Beneath the robe, he could see traces of the scaling on her skull. He reached out a hand to touch her.

'I said—'

Mobley felt a huge pressure on the side of his left leg, and then it collapsed beneath his weight as he registered the gunshot. He toppled sideways, coming to rest half in, half out of the water, and stared down at the remains of his knee. The bullet had blown away his kneecap, and what lay inside was white and red. Already his blood was flowing into the Congaree. Mobley's gritted teeth separated, and he howled in agony. He looked around for the shooter and a second bullet tore into the small of his back, nicking his spine on its way through his body. Mobley pitched sideways and lay on the ground, watching as a black pool spread around his legs. He found himself paralyzed, yet still capable of feeling the hurt that was colonizing every cell of his being.

Mobley heard footsteps approaching and swiveled his eyes. He opened his mouth to speak but something sharp entered his flesh below the chin, the hook cutting through the soft tissue and piercing his tongue and upper palate. The pain was beyond belief, an agony that superseded the burning in his lower body and leg. He tried to scream, but the hook now held his mouth closed and all he emitted was a harsh, croaking noise. The pressure increased as his head was jerked back and, slowly, he was pulled toward the forest. He could see the steel of the hook in front of his face, could taste it on his tongue and feel it against his teeth. He tried to raise a hand to grasp it, but he was already growing weak and his fingers could only brush the metal before falling down to his side. A gleaming trail of blood was being laid on the leaves and dirt. Above him, the canopy appeared like a black shroud across the sky. The forest gathered around him, and he stared for the last time toward the river as the woman dropped the sheet from her body and turned, naked, to look at him.

And deep inside himself, in the dark place where all that was truly Landron Mobley dreamed of visiting pain on others, a host of scaled women fell upon him, and he began to scream.

PART TWO

'He gave no comfort, saved no one
Adrift he moves by guilty moons'

Darren Richard, Pinetop Seven,
'Mission District'

5

Looking back, I see a pattern in all that took place: a strange joining of disparate occurrences, a series of links between seemingly unconnected events stretching back into the past. I recall the honeycomb created by the imperfect layering of history, the proximity of what has gone before to that which now pertains, and I begin to understand. We are trapped not only by our own history but by the histories of all those with whom we choose to share our lives. Angel and Louis brought their pasts with them, as did Elliot Norton, as did I, and so it should have come as no surprise that just as current lives became interwoven, impacting on one another, so too pasts began to exert their pull, dragging innocent and guilty alike down beneath the earth, drowning them in brackish water, tearing them apart among the swollen buttresses of the Congaree.

And in Thomaston, the first link lay waiting to be uncovered.

The maximum security facility at Thomaston, Maine, looked reassuringly like a prison; at least, it looked reassuring as long as you weren't a prisoner there. Anyone arriving in Thomaston with the prospect of long-term incarceration in his future was likely to feel his spirits sink at his first sight of the jail. It had high, imposing walls and the kind of solidity that came from being burned down and rebuilt a couple of times since it was first opened, in the 1820s. Thomaston had been selected as the site for the state prison since it was roughly halfway up the coast and accessible by boat for the transportation of inmates, but it was now nearing the end of its working life. A Supermax facility known as the MCI, or Maine Correctional Institution, had been opened some miles away in 1992. It was designed to house the worst offenders in a state of near-permanent lockdown, along with those prisoners with serious behavioral problems, and the new state prison would eventually be added on an adjoining tract of land. Until then, Thomaston was still home to about four hundred men, one of whom, since his suicide attempt, was now the preacher, Aaron Faulkner.

I recalled Rachel's response when she heard that Faulkner had apparently tried to take his own life.

'It doesn't fit,' she said. 'He's not that type.'

'So why did he do it? It's hardly a cry for help.'

She chewed at her lip. 'If he did it, he did it to further some aim. According to the newspaper reports, the wounds in his arms were deep, but not so deep that he was in immediate danger. He cut veins, not arteries. That's not the action of a man who really wants to die. For some reason, he wanted out of supermax. The question is, why?'

Now it seemed that I might have the opportunity to pose that question to the man himself.

I drove up to Thomaston after Angel and Louis had left for New York. I parked in a visitor's space outside the main gate, then entered the reception area and gave my name to the sergeant of the guards at the desk. Behind him, and beyond the metal detector, was a wall of tinted toughened glass concealing the main control room for the prison, where alarms, video cameras and visitors were constantly monitored. The control room looked down on the visitation room to which, under ordinary circumstances, I would have been led for a face-to-face meeting with any of the men incarcerated in the facility.

Except these were not ordinary circumstances, and the Reverend Aaron Faulkner was far from being an ordinary prisoner.

Another guard arrived to escort me. I passed through the metal detector, attached my pass to my jacket, and was led to the elevator and the administration level on the third floor. This section of the prison was termed 'soft side': no prisoners were permitted here without escort, and it was separated from 'hard side' by a system of dual air-locking doors that could not be opened simultaneously, so that even if a prisoner managed to get through the first door, the second would remain closed.

The colonel of the guards and the prison warden were both waiting for me in the warden's office. The prison had swung between various regimes over the past thirty years: from strict discipline, rigidly enforced, through an ill-fated campaign of liberalism, disliked by the longer-serving guards, until finally it had settled at a midpoint that erred on the side of conservatism. In other words, the prisoners no longer spit at visitors and it was safe to walk through the general population, which was fine by me.

A bugle call sounded, indicating the end of rec time, and through the windows I could see blue-garbed prisoners begin to move across the yards toward their cells. Thomaston enclosed an area of eight or nine acres, including Haller Field, the prison's playing field, its walls carved out of sheer rock. Unmarked, in a far corner beneath the walls, was the old execution site.

The warden offered me coffee, then played nervously with his own cup, spinning it around the table by its handle. The colonel of the guards, who was almost as imposing as the prison itself, remained standing and silent. If he was as uneasy as the warden, then he didn't show it. His name was Joe Long and his face displayed all the emotion of a cigar store Indian.

'You understand that this is highly unusual, Mr. Parker,' the warden began. 'Visits are usually conducted in the visiting area, not through the bars of a cell. And we rarely have the attorney general's office calling to request that we facilitate alternative arrangements.' He stopped talking and waited for me to respond.

'The truth is, I'd prefer not to be here myself,' I said. 'I don't want to face Faulkner again, not until the trial.'

The two men exchanged a look. 'Rumor is that this trial has all the makings of a disaster,' said the warden. He seemed tired and vaguely disgusted.

I didn't answer, so he spoke to fill the silence.

'Which, I guess, is why the prosecutor is so anxious that you should talk to Faulkner,' he concluded. 'You think he'll give anything away?' The expression on his face told me that he already knew the answer but I gave him the echo he expected anyway.

'He's too smart for that,' he said.

'Then why are you here, Mr. Parker?' asked the colonel.

It was my turn to sigh.

'Frankly, colonel, I don't know.'

The colonel didn't speak as he, along with a sergeant, led me through 7 Dorm, past the infirmary, where old men in wheelchairs were given the drugs they needed to maximize their life sentences; 5 and 7 Dorms housed the older, sicker prisoners, who shared multibed rooms decorated with hand-lettered signs ('Get Use To It,' 'Ed's Bed'). In the past, older special prisoners like Faulkner might have been housed here, or placed in administrative segregation in a cell among the general population, their movements restricted, until a decision was made about them. But the main segregation unit was now at the Supermax facility, which did not have the capacity to offer psychiatric services to prisoners, and Faulkner's attempts to injure himself appeared to require some form of psychiatric investigation. A suggestion that Faulkner be transferred to the Augusta Mental Health Institute had been rejected by the attorney general's office, which did not want to prejudice any future jurors into making a pretrial association between Faulkner and insanity, and by Faulkner's own lawyers, who feared that the state might use the opportunity to discreetly place their client under more elaborate observation than was possible elsewhere. Since the state regarded the county jail as unsuitable for holding Faulkner, Thomaston became the compromise solution.

Faulkner had attempted to cut his wrists with a slim ceramic blade that he had concealed in the spine of his Bible before his transfer to the MCI. He had kept it, unused, until almost three months into his incarceration. A guard on routine night rounds had spotted him and called for help just as Faulkner appeared to be losing consciousness. The result was Faulkner's transfer to the mental health stabilization unit at the western end of Thomaston prison, where he was initially placed in the acute corridor. His clothing was taken away and he was given instead a nylon smock. He was placed under constant camera watch, as well as being monitored by a prison guard who noted any movement or conversation in a logbook. In addition, all communication was recorded electronically. After five days in acute, Faulkner was transferred to sub-acute, where he was allowed state blues to replace his smock, hygiene products (but no razors), hot meals, showers, and access to a telephone. He had commenced one-on-one counseling with a prison psychologist and had been examined by psychiatrists nominated by his legal team, but had remained unresponsive. Then he had demanded a telephone call, contacted his lawyers, and asked that he be allowed to speak to me. His request that the interview should be conducted from his cell was, perhaps surprisingly, met with approval.

When I arrived in the MHSU, the guards were finishing off some chicken burgers left over from the prisoners' lunches. In the unit's main recreation area, the inmates stopped what they were doing and stared at me. One, a stocky, hunched man, barely five feet tall with lank dark hair, approached the bars and appraised me silently. I caught his eye, didn't like what I felt, then looked away again. The colonel and the sergeant sat on the edge of a desk and watched as one of the unit's guards led me down the corridor to Faulkner's cell.

I felt the chill while I was still ten feet away from him. At first, I thought it was brought on by my own reluctance to face the old man, until I felt the guard beside me shiver slightly.

'What happened to the heating?' I asked.

'Heating's on full blast,' he replied. 'This place leaks heat like it's blowing through a sieve, but never like this.'

He stopped while we were still out of sight of the cell's occupant, and his voice dropped. 'It's him. The preacher. His cell is freezing. We've tried installing two heaters outside, but they short out every time.' He shifted uneasily on his feet. 'It's something to do with Faulkner. He just brings the temperature right down somehow. His lawyers are screaming a blue fit about the conditions, but there's nothing we can do.'

As he concluded, something white moved to my right. The bars of the cell were almost flush with my line of sight, so that the hand that emerged appeared to have passed through a solid wall of steel. The long white fingers probed at the air, twitching and turning, as if they were gifted with the sense not only of touch, but of sight and sound as well.

And then the voice came, like iron filings falling on paper.

'Parker,' it said. 'You've come.'

Slowly, I walked toward the cell and saw the moisture on the walls. The droplets glittered in the artificial light, gleaming like thousands of small silver eyes. A smell of damp arose from the cell and from the man who stood before me.

He was smaller than I remembered him, and his long white hair had been cut back close to his skull, but the eyes still burned with that same strange intensity. He remained horribly thin: he had not put on weight, as some inmates do when they switch to a diet of prison food. It took me a moment to realize why.

Despite the cold in the cell, Faulkner was giving off waves of heat. He should have been burning up, his face feverish, his body wracked with tremors, but instead there was no trace of sweat on his face, and no sign of discomfort. His skin was dry as paper, so that it seemed he was on the verge of igniting from within, and the flames that emerged would consume him and leave him as burnt ash.

'Come closer,' he said.

Beside me, the guard shook his head.

'I'm good,' I replied.

'Are you afraid of me, sinner?'

'Not unless you can pass through steel.' My words brought back that image of the hand seemingly materializing in the air and I heard myself swallow hard.

'No,' said the old man. 'I have no need of parlor tricks. I'll be out of here, soon enough.'

'You think?'

He leaned forward and pressed his face against the cold bars. 'I *know*.'

He smiled and his pale tongue emerged from his mouth and licked at his dry lips.

'What do you want?'

'To talk.'

'About what?'

'Life. Death. Life after death; or, if you prefer, the death after life. Do they still come to you, Parker? The lost ones, the dead, do you still see them? I do. They come to me.' He smiled and drew in a long breath that seemed to catch in his throat, as if he were in the early stages of sexual excitement. 'So *many* of them. They ask after you, the ones whom you have despatched. They want to know when you're going to join them. They have plans for you. I tell them: soon. He'll be with you real soon.'

I didn't respond to the taunts. Instead, I asked him why he had cut himself. He held his scarred arms up before me and looked at them, almost in surprise.

'Perhaps I wanted to cheat them of their vengeance,' he replied.

'You didn't do a very good job.'

'That's a matter of opinion. I'm no longer in that *place*, that modern hell. I have contact with others.' His eyes shone brightly. 'I may even be able to save some lost souls.'

'You have anyone in mind?'

Faulkner laughed softly. 'Not you, sinner, that is a certainty. You are beyond salvation.'

'Yet you asked to see me.'

The smile faded, then died.

'I have an offer for you.'

'You've got nothing to bargain with.'

'I have your woman,' came that low, parched voice. 'I can bargain with her.'

I made no move toward him, yet he stepped back suddenly from the bars, as if the force of my stare had forced him to do so, like a shove to the chest.

'What did you say?'

'I'm offering you the safety of your woman, and your unborn child. I'm offering you a life untroubled by fear of retribution.'

'Old man, your fight now is with the state. You'd better save your bargains for the court. And if you mention those close to me again, I'll—'

'You'll what?' he mocked. 'Kill me? You had your chance, and it won't come again. And my fight is not only with the state. Don't you remember: you killed my children, my family, you and your deviant colleague. What did you do to the man who killed your child, Parker? Didn't you hunt him down? Didn't you kill him like a mad dog? Why should you expect me to respond any differently to the death of my children? Or is there one rule for you, and another for the rest of humanity?' He sighed theatrically. 'But I am not like you. I am not a killer.'

'What do you want, old man?'

'I want you to withdraw from the trial.'

I waited a heartbeat.

'And if I don't?'

He shrugged. 'Then I can't be held responsible for the actions that may be taken against you, or them. Not by me, of course: despite my natural animosity toward you, I have no intention of inflicting harm upon you or those close to you. I have never hurt anybody in my life and have no intention of starting now. But there may be others who would take up my cause, unless it was made clear to them that I wished no such thing.'

I turned to the guard. 'You hearing this?'

He nodded, but Faulkner merely turned his gaze impassively upon the guard. 'I am merely offering to plead for no retaliation against you, but in any case Mr. Anson here is hardly in a position to be of assistance. He's fucking a little whore behind his wife's back. Worse, behind her parents' back. What is she, Mr. Anson, fifteen? The law frowns upon rapists, statutory or otherwise.'

'You fuck!' Anson surged toward the bars, but I caught his arm. He spun at me, and I thought for a moment he was about to strike me, but he restrained himself and shook my hand off. I looked to my right and saw Anson's colleagues approaching. He raised his hand to let them know that he was okay, and they stopped in their tracks.

'I thought you didn't go in for parlor tricks,' I said.

'Who knows what evil lurks in the hearts of men?' he whispered. 'The Shadow knows!' He laughed softly. 'Let me go, sinner. Walk away, and I will do likewise. I am innocent of the accusations leveled against me.'

'This meeting is over.'

'No, it has only just begun. Do you remember what our mutual friend said before he died, sinner? Do you remember the words that the Traveling Man spoke?'

I didn't reply. There was much about Faulkner that I despised, and much that I did not understand, but his awareness of events about which he could not possibly know disturbed me more than anything else. Somehow, in some way that I was unable to recognize, he had inspired the man who killed Susan and Jennifer, confirming him on the path that he had chosen, a path that had led him at last to our door.

'Didn't he tell you about hell? That this was hell, and we were in it? He was misguided in many ways, a flawed, unhappy man, but about that much he was correct. This is hell. When the rebel angels fell, this was the place to which they were consigned. They were blighted, their beauty taken away, and left to wander here. Don't you fear the dark angels, Parker? You should. They know of you, and soon they will start to move against you. What you've faced until now is as nothing compared to what is approaching. Before them I am insignificant, a foot soldier sent ahead to prepare the way. The things that are coming for you are not even *human*.'

'You're insane.'

'No,' whispered Faulkner. 'I am damned for failure, but you will be damned alongside me for your complicity in that failure. They will damn you. Already they wait.'

I shook my head. Anson, the other guards, even the prison bars and walls seemed to melt away. There was only the old man and I, suspended. There was sweat on my face, a product of the heat he exuded. It was as if I had caught some terrible fever from him.

'Don't you want to know what he said to me when he came? Don't you care about the discussions that led to the deaths of your wife and your little girl? Somewhere deep inside of yourself, don't you want to know of what we spoke?'

I cleared my throat. The words, when they came, felt coated in nails.

'You didn't even know them.'

He laughed. 'I didn't need to know them. But you . . . Oh, we spoke of you. Through him, I came to understand you in ways that you didn't even understand yourself. I am glad, in a way, that we had this opportunity to meet, although . . .'

His face darkened.

'We have both paid a high price for the inter-twining of our lives. Divorce yourself now, from all of this, and there will be no more conflict between us. But continue on this road and I will be unable to stop what may occur.'

'Good-bye.'

I moved to walk away, but my struggle with Anson had brought me within Faulkner's reach. His hand reached out and clasped my jacket and then, while I was off balance, pulled me closer to him. I turned my head instinctively, my lips apart to cry out a warning.

And Faulkner spit in my mouth.

It took me a moment to realize what had happened, and then I was striking out at him, Anson now pulling me away as I reached for the old man. The other guards came running toward us and I was hauled away, expelling the taste of Faulkner from my mouth even as he continued to howl out at me from his cell.

'Take it as a gift, Parker,' he called. 'My gift to you, that you might see as I see.'

I pushed the guards away and wiped my mouth, then kept my head down as I walked past the recreation area, where those deemed to be no danger to themselves or others watched me from behind their bars. Had my head been raised, and my attention been focused elsewhere than on the preacher and what he had just done to me, then perhaps I might have seen the stooped, dark-haired man watching me more closely than the rest.

And as I left, the man named Cyrus Nairn smiled, his arms outstretched, his fingers forming a constant flow of words, until a guard looked his way and he stopped, his arms withdrawing back toward his body.

The guard knew what Cyrus was doing, but he paid him no heed. After all, Cyrus was a mute and that was what mutes did. They signed.

I was almost at my car when I heard the sound of footsteps on the gravel behind me. It was Anson. He shifted uneasily.

'You okay?'

I nodded. I had washed my mouth out in the guards' quarters with borrowed mouthwash, but I still felt as if some element of Faulkner was coursing through me, infecting me.

'What you heard in there—,' he began.

I interrupted him. 'Your private life is your own affair. It's nothing to do with me.'

'What he said, it's not like it seems.'

'It never is.'

A red glow began at his neck and spread into his features as if drawn by osmosis.

'Are you being smart with me?'

'Like I said, it's your business. I do have one question. If you're worried, you can check me for a wire.'

He considered the offer for a moment, then motioned to me to continue.

'Is what the preacher said true? I don't care about the law or about why you're doing it. All I want to know is: was he correct in the details?'

Anson didn't reply. He just looked at his feet and nodded.

'Could one of the other guards have let it slip?'

'No. Nobody knows about it.'

'A prisoner, maybe? Somebody local who might have been in a position to spread a little jailhouse gossip?'

'No, I don't believe so.'

I opened the car door. Anson seemed to feel the need to make some final macho comment. As in other things, he didn't appear to be a man who believed in restraining his urges.

'If anyone finds out about this, you'll be in a world of shit,' he warned. It sounded hollow, even to himself. I could see it in the mottling of his skin and the way in which he had to concentrate on straining the muscles in his neck so that they bulged over the collar of his shirt. I let him retrieve whatever dignity he thought he could salvage from the situation, then watched as he slowly padded back to the main door, seemingly reluctant to place himself in proximity to Faulkner once again.

A shadow fell across him, as if a huge winged bird had descended and were slowly circling above him. Over the prison walls, more birds seemed to hover. They were big and black, moving in lazy, drifting loops, but there was in their movements something unnatural. They glided with none of the grace or beauty of birds, for their thin bodies seemed almost to be at odds with their enormous wings, as though struggling with the pull of gravity, the torso always threatening to plummet toward the ground, the wings allowing the slide for a time before beating wildly to draw them back to the safety of the air.

Then one broke from the flock, growing larger and larger as it descended in a spiral, coming to rest at last on the top of one of the guard towers, and I could see that this was no bird, and I knew it for what it was.

The dark angel's body was emaciated, its arms black mummified skin over slim bones, its face elongated and predatory, its eyes dark and knowing. It rested a clawed hand on the glass and its great wings, feathered in darkness, beat a low cadence against the air. Slowly, it was joined by others, each silently taking up a position on the walls and the towers, until it seemed at last that the prison was black with them. They made no move toward me but I sensed their hostility, and something more: their sense of betrayal, as if I were somehow one of them and had turned my back upon them.

'Ravens,' said a voice at my side. It was an elderly woman. She carried a brown paper bag in her hand, filled with some small items for one of the inmates: a son, perhaps, or a husband among the old men in 7 Dorm. 'Never seen so many before, or so big.'

And now they *were* ravens: two feet tall at least, the fingered wing tips clearly visible as they moved upon the walls, calling softly to one another.

'I didn't think they came together in those numbers,' I said.

'They don't,' she said. 'Not normally, nohow, but who's to say what's normal these days?'

She continued walking. I got in my car and began to drive away, but in the rearview mirror the black birds did not seem to decrease in size as I left them behind. Instead, they seemed to grow larger even as the prison receded, taking on new forms.

And I felt their eyes upon me as the preacher's saliva colonized my body like a cancer.

My gift to you, that you might see as I see.

* * *

Apart from the prison and the prison craft shop there isn't a whole lot to keep a casual visitor in Thomaston, but the town has a pretty good diner at its northern end, with homemade pies and bread pudding served piping hot to locals and those who come to talk after meeting their loved ones across a table or through a screen farther up the road. I bought another bottle of mouthwash at the drugstore and sluiced my mouth out in the parking lot before heading into the diner.

The small eating area with its mismatched furniture was largely empty, with the exception of two old men who sat quietly, side by side, watching the traffic go by, and a younger man in an expensively tailored suit who sat in a wooden booth by the wall, his overcoat folded neatly beside him, a fork resting among the cream and crumbs on his plate, a copy of *USA Today* beside it. I ordered a coffee and took a seat across from him.

'You don't look so good,' said the man.

I felt my gaze drawn toward the window. I could not see the prison from where I sat. I shook my head, clearing it of visions of dark creatures crowding on prison walls, waiting. They were not real. They were just ravens. I was ill, nauseated by Faulkner's assault.

They were not real.

'Stan,' I said, to distract myself. 'Nice suit.'

He turned the jacket to show me the label inside. 'Armani. Bought it in an outlet store. I keep the receipt in the inside pocket, just in case I get accused of corruption.'

My coffee arrived, and the waitress retreated behind the counter to read a magazine. Somewhere, a radio played sickly MOR. The Rush revival begins here.

Stan Ornstead was an assistant district attorney, part of the team assembled to prosecute the Faulkner case. It was Ornstead who had convinced me to face Faulkner, with the full knowledge of deputy DA Andrus, and who had arranged for the interview to be conducted at the cell so that I could see the conditions that he appeared to have created for himself. Stan was only a few years younger than I was and was considered a hot prospect for the future. He was going places; he just wasn't going there fast enough for him. Faulkner, he had hoped, might have changed that situation, except, as the warden had indicated, the Faulkner case was turning into something very bad indeed, something that threatened to drag everyone involved down with it.

'You look kind of shaken up,' Stan said, after I'd taken a couple of fortifying sips from my coffee.

'He has that effect on people.'

'He didn't give too much away.'

I froze, and he raised his palms in a what-you-gonna-do? gesture.

'They mike sub-acute cells?' I asked.

'*They* don't, if you mean the prison authorities.'

'But somebody else has taken up the slack.'

'The cell has been lojacked. Officially, we know nothing about it.' Lojacking was the term used to describe a surveillance operation not endorsed by a court. More particularly, it was the term used by the FBI to describe any such operation.

'The Feebs?'

'The trenchcoats don't have too much faith in us. They're worried that Faulkner may walk on our beef so they want to get as much as they can, while they can, in case of federal charges or a double prosecution. All conversations with his lawyers, his doctors, his shrink, even his nemesis – that's you, in case you didn't know – are being recorded. The hope is that, at the very least, he'll give something away that might lead them to others like him, or even give them a lead to other crimes he might have committed. All inadmissible, of course, but useful if it works.'

'And will he walk?'

Ornstead shrugged.

'You know what he's claiming: he was kept a virtual prisoner for decades and had no part in, or knowledge of, any crimes committed by the Fellowship or those associated with it. There's nothing to link him directly to any of the killings, and that underground nest of rooms he lived in had bolts on the outside.'

'He was at my house when they tried to kill me.'

'You say, but you were woozy. You told me yourself you couldn't see straight.'

'Rachel saw him.'

'Yes, she did, but she'd just been hit on the head and had blood in her eyes. She herself admits that she can't remember a lot of what was said, and he wasn't there for what followed.'

'There's a hole in the ground at Eagle Lake where seventeen bodies were found, the remains of his flock.'

'He says fighting broke out between the families. They turned on each other, then on his own family. They killed his wife. His children responded in kind. He claims he was over in Presque Isle on the day they were killed.'

'He assaulted Angel.'

'Faulkner denies it, says his kids did it and forced him to watch. Anyway, your friend says he won't testify and even if we subpoena him any lawyer worth more than a dollar an hour would tear him apart. A credible witness he is not. And, with respect, you're hardly an ideal witness either.'

'Why would that be?'

'You've been pretty free with that cannon of yours, but just because charges have been let slide doesn't mean that they've disappeared off everybody's radar. You can be damn sure that Faulkner's legal team knows all about you. They'll push the angle that you came tearing in there, shooting the place up, and the old man was lucky to escape with his life.'

I pushed my coffee cup away. 'Is that why you brought me here, to rip my story to shreds?'

'Do it here, do it in court, makes no difference. We're in trouble. And maybe we have other worries.'

I waited.

'His lawyers have confirmed that they're going to petition for a Supreme Court review of the bail decision within the next ten days. We think that the available judge may be Wilton Cooper, and that's not good news.'

Wilton Cooper was only a few months shy of retirement, but he would continue to be a thorn in the side of the AG's office until then. He was obstinate, unpredictable, and had a personal animosity toward the AG, the source of which was lost in the mists of time. He had also spoken out in the past against preventive bail and was quite capable of defending the rights of the accused at the cost of the rights of society in general.

'If Cooper takes the review, it could go either way,' said Ornstead. 'Faulkner's claims are bullshit, but we need time to amass the evidence to undermine them and it could be years before a trial. And you've seen his cell: we could keep him at the bottom of a volcano and it would still be cold. His lawyers have got independent experts who will claim that Faulkner's continued incarceration is endangering his health, and that he will die if he remains in custody. If we move him to Augusta we could shoot ourselves in the foot in the event of an insanity plea. We don't have the facilities for him at the supermax, and where do we put him if we move him out of Thomaston? County? I don't think so. So what we have right now is an upcoming trial with no reliable witnesses, insufficient evidence to make the case watertight, and a defendant who may be dead before we can even get him on the stand. Cooper would just be the icing on the cake.'

I found that I was clutching the handle of my coffee cup so tightly that it had left a mark on the palm of my hand. I released my grip and watched the blood flow back into the white areas. 'If he's bailed, he'll flee,' I said. 'He won't wait around for a trial.'

'We don't know that.'

'Yes, we do.'

We were both hunched over the table, and we both seemed to realize it simultaneously. Over near the window, the two old men had turned to watch us, their attention attracted by the tension between us. I leaned back, then looked at them. They returned to watching the traffic.

'Anyway,' said Ornstead, 'even Cooper won't set a bail below seven figures and we don't believe that Faulkner has access to that level of funds.'

All of the Fellowship's assets had been frozen and the AG's office was trying to follow the paper trail that might lead to other accounts undiscovered so far. But somebody was paying Faulkner's lawyers, and a defense fund had been opened into which dispiriting numbers of right-wing crazies and religious nuts were pouring money.

'Do we know who's organizing the defense fund?' I asked. Officially, the fund was the responsibility of a firm of lawyers, Muren & Associates, in Savannah, Georgia, but it was a pretty low-rent operation. There had to be more to it than a bunch of Southern shysters working out of an office with plastic chairs. Faulkner's own legal team, led by Grim Jim Grimes, was separate from it. Stone features apart, Jim Grimes was one of the best lawyers in New England. He could talk his way out of cancer, and he didn't come cheap.

Ornstead blew out a large breath. It smelled of coffee and nicotine.

'That's the rest of the bad news. Muren had a visitor a couple of days back, a guy by the name of Edward Carlyle. Phone records show that the two of them have been in daily contact since this thing started, and Carlyle is a co-signatory on the fund checking account.'

I shrugged. 'Name doesn't ring a bell.'

Ornstead tapped his fingers lightly on the table in a delicate cadence.

'Edward Carlyle is Roger Bowen's right-hand man. And Roger Bowen is—'

'A creep,' I finished. 'And a racist.'

'And a neo-Nazi,' added Ornstead. 'Yup, clock stopped sometime around nineteen thirty-nine for Bowen. He's quite a guy. Probably has shares in gas ovens in the hope that things might pick up again on the old "final solution" front. As far as we can tell, Bowen is the one behind the defense fund. He's been keeping a low profile these last few years but something has drawn him out from under his rock. He's making speeches, appearing at rallies, passing around the collection plate. Seems to me like he wants Faulkner back on the streets pretty bad.'

'Why?'

'Well, that's what we're trying to find out.'

'Bowen's base is in South Carolina, isn't it?'

'He moves between South Carolina and Georgia, but spends most of his time somewhere up by the Chattooga river. Why, you planning on visiting down there?'

'Maybe.'

'I ask why?'

'A friend in need.'

'The worst kind. Well, while you're down there you could always ask Bowen why Faulkner is so important to him, though I wouldn't recommend it. I don't imagine you're top of his wish list of friends he hasn't met yet.'

'I'm not top of anybody's wish list.'

Ornstead stood and patted me on the shoulder.

'You're breaking my heart.'

I walked with him to the door. His car was parked right outside.

'You heard everything, right?' I asked. I assumed that Stan had been listening in to all that had passed between Faulkner and me.

'Yeah. We talking about the guard?'

'Anson.'

'Doesn't concern me. You?'

'She's underage. I don't believe that Anson is going to be an influence for the better in her life.'

'No, I guess not. We can get someone to look into it.'

'I'd appreciate it.'

'Done. Now I got a question for you. What happened in there? Sounded like there was a scuffle.'

Despite the coffee, I could still taste the mouthwash.

'Faulkner spit in my mouth.'

'Shit. You going to need a test?'

'I doubt it, but I feel like swallowing battery acid to burn it out of my mouth and insides.'

'Why'd he do it? To get you pissed at him?'

I shook my head.

'No, he told me it was a gift, to help me see more clearly.'

'See what?'

I didn't answer, but I knew.

He wanted me to see what was waiting for him, and what was coming for me.

He wanted me to see his kind.

6

The militant racist movement has never been particularly significant in terms of size. Its hard-core membership is probably 25,000 at most, augmented by maybe a further 150,000 active sympathizers and possibly another 400,000 fly-by-nighters, who offer neither money nor manpower but will tell you all about the threat to the white race posed by the coloreds and the Jews if you loosen them up with enough booze. More than half of the hard core comprises Klan members, with the remainder consisting of skinheads and assorted Nazis, and the level of cooperation between the groups is pretty minimal, sometimes descending into a competitiveness bordering on outright aggression. Membership is rarely constant: people move in and out of the groups on a regular basis, depending on the requirements of employers, enemies, or the courts.

But at the head of each group is a cadre of lifelong activists, and even as the names of their movements change, even as they fight amongst themselves and shatter into smaller and smaller splinters, those leaders remain. They are missionaries, zealots, proselytizers for the cause, spreading the gospel of intolerance at state fairs, rallies, and conferences, through newsletters and pamphlets and late night radio shows.

Of these men, Roger Bowen was one of the longest serving, and also one of the most dangerous. Born to a Baptist family in Gaffney, South Carolina, by the foothills of the Blue Ridge, he had passed through the ranks of any number of far-right organizations, including some of the most notorious neo-Nazi groups of the past twenty years. In 1983, at the age of twenty-four,

Bowen had been one of three young men questioned without charge about their involvement in the Order, the secret society formed by the racist Robert Matthews and linked to Aryan Nations. During 1983 and 1984 the Order carried out a series of armored car and bank robberies to fund its operations, which included assorted arson attacks, bombings, and counterfeiting efforts. The Order was also responsible for the murders of the Denver talk show host Alan Berg and a man named Walter West, a member of the Order who was suspected of betraying its secrets. Eventually, all members of the Order were apprehended, with the exception of Matthews himself, who was killed during a shoot-out with FBI agents in 1984. Since there was no evidence to link Bowen to its activities he escaped prosecution, and the truth about the extent of Bowen's involvement in the Order died with Matthews. Despite its comparatively small force of activists, the FBI's operations against the Order had consumed one quarter of the bureau's total manpower resources. The Order's size had worked in its favor, making it difficult to infiltrate by outsiders and informers, the unfortunate Walter West excepted. It was a lesson that Bowen never forgot.

Bowen then drifted for a time before finding a home of sorts in the Klan movement, although by then it had been largely defanged by the activities of the FBI's Counterintelligence Program: klaverns had folded, its prestige had plummeted, and its average age had begun to drop as older members left or died. The result was that the Klan's traditionally uneasy relationship with the trappings of neo-Nazism became less ambiguous, the new bloods being less fussy about such matters than the more senior members. Bowen joined Bill Wilkinson's Invisible Empire, Knights of the Ku Klux Klan, but by the time the Invisible Empire disbanded in 1993, following an expensive lawsuit, Bowen had already established his own Klan, the White Confederates.

Except Bowen didn't go recruiting members like the other Klans and even the Klan name was little more than a flag of convenience for him. The White Confederates never numbered more than a dozen individuals, but they wielded power and influence beyond their size and contributed significantly to the ongoing Nazification of the Klan in the 1980s, further blurring the traditional lines between the Klansmen and the neo-Nazis.

Bowen wasn't a Holocaust denier either: he *liked* the idea of the Holocaust, the possibility of a force capable of murder on a previously unthought of scale, murder with a sense of order and planning behind it. It was this, more than any moral qualms, that had led Bowen to distance himself from the casual outrages, the sporadic outbursts of violence, that were endemic to the movement. At the annual Stone Mountain rally in Georgia he had even publicly condemned one incident, the beating to death of a middle-aged black man named Bill Perce in North Carolina by a group of drunken klavern rejects, only to hear himself booed off the platform. Since then, Bowen had avoided Stone Mountain. They didn't understand him and he didn't need them, although he continued to work behind the scenes, supporting occasional Klan marches in small towns on the Georgia–South Carolina border. Even if, as frequently occurred, only a handful of men took part, the threat of a march still gained newspaper coverage and bleats of outrage from liberal sheep, and contributed to the atmosphere of intimidation and distrust that Bowen needed for his work to continue. The White Confederates was largely a front, a piece of theater akin to the waves of a magician's wand before a trick is performed. The real trickery was being performed out of sight, and the movement of the wand was not only unconnected with the illusion but largely immaterial to it.

For it was Bowen who was trying to heal the old enmities; Bowen who was building bridges over the divides between the Christian Patriots and the Aryans, the skinheads and the Klans; Bowen who was reaching out to the more vocal, and extreme, members of the Christian right; Bowen who understood the importance of unity, of intercommunication, of extending the funding base; and Bowen who now felt that, by bringing

Faulkner under his protection, he could convince those who believed the preacher's story to redirect their money toward him. The Fellowship had pulled in more than $500,000 in the year before Faulkner's arrest. It was small beans compared to the kind of cash flow enjoyed by the better-known televangelists, but it represented serious income to Bowen and his kind. Bowen had watched the money flowing into Faulkner's appeal fund: there was already enough to meet 10 percent of a low seven-figure bail and then some, and it was still coming in, but no bondsman would be crazy enough to cover Faulkner's bail in the event of a review finding in his favor. Bowen had other plans, other irons in the fire. If they played it right, Faulkner could be out and vanished before the end of the month, and if rumors persisted that Bowen had squirreled him away to safety, then so much the better for Bowen. In fact, it wouldn't much matter after that if the preacher lived or died. It would be enough that he remained unseen, and he could do that just as easily below ground as above it.

But Bowen also felt an admiration for what the old preacher and his Fellowship had achieved. Without resorting to the bank jobs that had undermined the Order, and with manpower never numbering more than four or five persons, he had carried out a campaign of murder and intimidation against soft targets for the best part of three decades and had covered his tracks brilliantly. Even the FBI and the ATF were still having problems connecting the Fellowship to the deaths of abortion doctors, outspoken homosexuals, Jewish leaders, and the other bugbears of the far right whose annihilation Faulkner was believed to have authorized.

It was strange, but Bowen had barely considered the possibility of allying himself to Faulkner's cause until Kittim had reappeared. Kittim was a legend among the extreme right, a folk hero. He had come to Bowen shortly after Faulkner's arrest, and from there, the idea of involving himself with the case had just come naturally to Bowen. And if he couldn't remember exactly what Kittim was reputed to have done, or even where he had come from, well, that hardly mattered. That was the way with folk heroes, wasn't it? They were only partly real, but with Kittim beside him, Bowen felt a new sense of purpose, of near invincibility.

It was so strong that he hardly noticed the fear that he felt in the man's presence.

Bowen's admiration, spurred into action by Kittim's arrival, had apparently appealed to Faulkner's ego, for through his lawyers the preacher had agreed to nail his colors to Bowen's mast, had even offered up funds from hidden accounts, untraceable by his persecutors, if Bowen could arrange his disappearance. More than anything else, the old man did not want to die in jail; he would rather be hunted for the remainder of his life than rot behind bars while awaiting trial. Faulkner had asked for just one further favor. Bowen had been kind of annoyed at this, given the fact that he was already offering to hide Faulkner from the law, but when Faulkner told him what he wanted Bowen had relaxed. It was just a small favor, after all, and would give Bowen almost as much pleasure as it would give Faulkner.

Bowen believed that, in Kittim, he had found just the man for the job, but he was wrong.

In truth, the man had found him.

Bowen's truck pulled into the small clearing before the hut, just across the South Carolina state line in eastern Tennessee. The building was dark wood, four rough-hewn steps leading to a porch, two narrow windows on either side. It looked like a blockhouse, designed with defense in mind.

A man sat on a rocking chair to the right of the door, smoking a cigarette. This was Carlyle. He had short curly hair that had begun to recede when he was in his early twenties but had mysteriously arrested its retreat in his thirties, leaving him with a clown wig of fair hair around his domed skull. He was in good condition, like most of those whom Bowen kept close. He drank little, and Bowen couldn't remember ever having seen him smoke before. He looked tired and ill. Bowen noticed the smell as he approached: vomit.

'You okay?' asked Bowen.

Carlyle wiped his lips with his fingers and examined the tips for any detritus. 'Why? I got shit on me?'

'No, but you smell bad.'

Carlyle took a last drag on the cigarette, then carefully extinguished the butt on the sole of his boot. When he was satisfied that it was cold, he tore it to shreds and let the breeze carry the remains away.

'Where did we get this guy, Roger?' he asked when he was done.

'Who? Kittim?'

'Yeah, Kittim.'

'He's a legend,' said Bowen. It had the sound of a mantra about it.

Carlyle ran a hand over his bare pate. 'I know that. I mean, I think I know.' His features collapsed into uncertainty, then rebuilt themselves into an expression of disgust. 'Anyway, wherever he came from, he's a freak.'

'We need him.'

'We got by okay without him until now.'

'This is different. Did you get anything out of the guy?'

Carlyle shook his head.

'He doesn't know anything. He's just muscle.'

'You sure?'

'Believe me, if he knew anything he'd have told us by now. But that sick fuck keeps at him.'

Bowen wasn't a great believer in Jewish conspiracies. Sure, there were wealthy Jews with power and influence, but they were pretty scattered when you looked at the big picture. Still, if Faulkner was to be believed, some old Jews in New York had tried to have him killed, and had dispatched a man to do it. That man was now dead, but Faulkner wanted to know who had sent him so that, when the time came, he could revenge himself upon them, and Bowen was of the opinion that it couldn't hurt to know what they were up against. That was why they had taken the kid, pulled him from the streets of Greenville when he drew attention to himself by asking the wrong questions in the wrong places. After that, he had been driven up here, gagged and bound in the trunk of a car, and handed over to Kittim.

'Where is he?'

'Out back.'

As Bowen moved to pass him, Carlyle extended an arm to block his way.

'You eaten yet?'

'Not much.'

'Lucky you.'

The arm dropped. Bowen continued on around the side of the house until he came to an enclosed pen that had once been used to hold pigs. The stench of them still hung around it, thought Bowen, until he saw what lay on the bare ground at the center of the pen and realized that what he was smelling was not animal, but human.

The young man was naked and staked out in the sun. He had a short, neatly-trimmed beard, and his black hair was pasted to his skull with sweat and mud. A leather belt had been tied around his head. His teeth were visible, gritted against it, as the wounds he had suffered were widened and probed. The man stooped over him wore coveralls and gloves as he worked on the body, his fingers exploring the new cavities and apertures he had created with his blade, pausing occasionally as the staked man tensed and made soft mewling sounds from behind the gag before continuing his work. Bowen didn't know how he had kept the kid on the ground alive, let alone conscious, but then Kittim was a man of many talents. He rose at the sound of Bowen's approach, his body unfolding like that of a disturbed insect, and turned to face him.

Kittim was tall, six two or six three. The cap and glasses that he habitually wore almost obscured his features, intentionally so because there was something wrong with Kittim's skin. Bowen didn't know precisely what it was, and he had never worked up the courage to ask, but Kittim's face was a pinkish purple color, with wispy clumps of hair attached to the flaking skull. He reminded Bowen of a marabou stork, built to feed on the dead and the dying. His eyes, when he chose to reveal them, were a very dark green, like a cat's eyes. Beneath the coveralls his body was hard and slim, almost emaciated. His nails were neatly trimmed, and he was clean shaven. He smelled vaguely of meat and Polo aftershave.

And sometimes of burning oil.

Bowen looked beyond him to where the young man lay, then returned his attention to Kittim. Carlyle was right, of course: Kittim was a freak, and of Bowen's small retinue only Landron Mobley, who was himself little better than a mad dog, appeared to feel any kind of affinity for him. It was not merely the torments being visited on the Jew that disgusted Bowen, but the sense of carnality that accompanied them. Kittim was aroused. Bowen could see it straining against the coveralls. For a moment, it caused anger to overcome Bowen's underlying fear of the man.

'You enjoying yourself?' asked Bowen.

Kittim shrugged. 'You asked me to find out what he knew.' His voice was like a broom sweeping across a dusty stone floor.

'Carlyle says he knows nothing.'

'Carlyle isn't in charge here.'

'That's right. I am, and I'm asking you if you've found out anything useful from him.'

Kittim stared at him from behind his shades, then turned his back on Bowen.

'Leave me,' he said, as he knelt to recommence his exploration of the young man. 'I have not finished.'

Instead of departing, Bowen drew his gun from its holster. His thoughts were once again concentrated on this strange deformed man and the wraithlike nature of him and his past. It was as if they had conjured him up, he thought, as if he were a personification of all their hatreds and fears, an abstraction made flesh. He had come to Bowen, offering his services, and the knowledge of him had begun to seep into Bowen like gas into a room, half-remembered tales assuming a new substance around him, and Bowen had been unable to turn him away. What was it Carlyle had said? He was a legend, but why? What had he done?

And he didn't seem interested in the cause, in the niggers and the faggots and the kikes whose very existence gave most of his kind the fuel they needed for their hatred. Instead, Kittim seemed distant from such matters, even while he was inflicting torments on a naked victim. Now Kittim was trying to tell him what to do, ordering him to leave his presence like Bowen was just some house nigger with a tray. It was about time that Bowen regained control of this situation and showed everybody who was boss. He stepped lightly around Kittim, then raised the gun and pointed it at the young man on the ground.

'No,' said Kittim softly.

Bowen looked over and—

And Kittim shimmered.

A sudden wave of intense heat seemed to pass over him, causing him to ripple behind its passage, and for an instant he was both Kittim and something else, something dark and winged, with eyes like those of a dead bird, reflecting the world without revealing any life within. His skin was loose and withered, the bones visible beneath it, the legs slightly bent, the feet elongated. The smell of oil grew stronger and, for an instant, Bowen understood. By doubting him, by allowing his own feelings of anger to break through, he had somehow permitted his mind to register an aspect of Kittim, the truth of him, that had remained hidden until now.

He's old, thought Bowen, older than he looks, older than any of us could have imagined. He has to concentrate to hold himself together.

That's why his skin is the way it is, why he walks so slowly, why he keeps himself apart. He has to struggle to maintain this form. He's not human. He is—

Bowen took a step back as the figure reconstituted itself, until once again he was staring at a man in coveralls with blood on his gloved hands.

'What's wrong?' asked Kittim.

Even in his confusion and fear Bowen knew better than to answer truthfully. In fact, he couldn't have told the truth even if he wanted to because his mind was doing some pretty rapid work to shore up his threatened sanity, and now he wasn't sure what the truth was. Kittim couldn't have shimmered. He couldn't have changed. He couldn't be what Bowen had thought, for an instant, he might be: a thing dark and winged, like a foul, mutated bird.

'It's nothing,' said Bowen. He stared dumbly at the gun in his hand, then put it away.

'Then let me get back to work,' said Kittim, and the last thing Bowen saw was the fading hope in the eyes of the young man on the ground before Kittim's thin form blocked him from view.

Bowen brushed past Carlyle on his way back to the car.

'Hey!' Carlyle reached out to grasp him, then drew back and allowed his hand to fall as he saw Bowen's face.

'Your eyes,' he said. 'What happened to your eyes?'

But Bowen didn't reply. Later, he would tell Carlyle what he had seen, or what he thought he had seen, and in the aftermath of what was to come Carlyle would tell the investigators. But for now Bowen kept it to himself and his face registered no emotion as he drove away, not even when he stared into the rearview mirror and saw that the capillaries in his eyeballs had burst, his pupils now black holes at the center of red pools of blood.

Far to the north, Cyrus Nairn retreated back into the darkness of his cell. He was happier here than outside, mingling with the others. They didn't understand him, couldn't understand him.

Dumb: that was the word a whole lot of people had used about Cyrus throughout his life. Dumb. Dummy. Mute. Schizo. Cyrus didn't care too much about what they said. He knew that he was smart. He also, deep down inside, suspected that he was crazy.

Cyrus had been abandoned by his mother at nine and tormented by his stepfather until he was finally incarcerated for the first time, at the age of seventeen. He could still recall some details about his mother: not love or tenderness – no, never that – but the look in her eyes as she grew to despise what she had brought into the world in the course of a difficult, complicated birth had remained with him. The boy was born hunched, unable to stand fully upright, his knees buckled as if he were laboring constantly beneath some unseen weight. His forehead was too large, overshadowing dark eyes, the irises nearly black. He had a flattened nose with elongated nostrils, and a small, rounded chin. His mouth was very full, the upper lip overhanging the lower, and it remained slightly open even in repose, making Cyrus appear always to be on the verge of biting.

And he was strong. There was thick muscle on his arms and shoulders and chest, tapering down to a narrow waist before exploding again at his buttocks and thighs. His strength had been his salvation; had he been weaker, prison would have broken him long before now.

The first sentence was handed down for aggravated burglary after he had entered the house of a woman in Houlton, armed with a homemade knife. The woman had locked herself in her room and called the cops, and they'd caught Cyrus as he tried to escape through a bathroom window. Through signing, Cyrus had told them that he was just looking for money to buy beer, and they'd believed him. He'd still pulled three years, though, and served eighteen months.

It was in the course of an examination by the prison psychiatrist that he was first diagnosed as schizophrenic, exhibiting what the psychiatrist told him were classic 'positive' symptoms: hallucinations, delusions, strange patterns of thinking and self-expression, hearing voices. Cyrus had nodded along as all of this was explained to him through a signer, although he could hear perfectly well. He simply chose not to reveal the fact, much as it seemed that he had chosen, one night a long, long time before, no longer to speak.

Or perhaps the choice had been made for him. Cyrus was never entirely sure.

He was prescribed medication, the so-called first gener ation antipsychotics, but he hated their debilitating side effects and quickly learned to disguise the fact that he was no longer taking them. But more than the side effects, Cyrus hated the loneliness that came with the drugs. He despised the silence. When the voices resumed, he embraced them and welcomed them as old friends now returned from some faraway place with strange new tales to tell. When he was eventually released, he could barely hear the standard patter of the guard processing him over the clamor of the voices, excited at the prospect of freedom and the resumption of the plans they had so carefully rehearsed for so long.

Because for Cyrus, the Houlton affair had been a failure on two accounts: In the first place, he'd been caught. In the second, he hadn't gone into the house for money.

He'd gone in for the woman.

Cyrus Nairn lived in a small cabin on a patch of land that his mother's family had owned, close by the Androscoggin River, about ten miles south of Wilton. In the old days, people used to store fruit and vegetables in hollows dug into the bank, where the temperature would keep them fresh long after they'd been plucked or dug up. Cyrus had found these old hollows and strengthened them, then disguised the entrances using bushes and timber. The hollows had served as his retreat from the world when he was a boy. Sometimes, it almost seemed to him that he had been created to fit into them, that they were his natural home. The curvature of his spine; the short, thick neck; his legs, slightly bent at the knees: all seemed expressly designed to enable him to fit into those places beneath the riverbank. Now the cold hollows hid other things, and even during the summer, the natural refrigeration meant that he had to go down on his hands and knees and sniff the earth before he could catch a hint of what lay beneath.

After Houlton, Cyrus had learned to be more careful. Each knife he made was used only once, then burned, and the blade buried far from his own property. In the beginning, he could go for a year, maybe more, without taking one, satisfying himself by crouching in the cool silence of the hollows, before the voices got too loud and he had to go a-hunting once more. Then, as he grew older, the voices became more insistent, their demands coming closer and closer together, until he tried to take the woman in Dexter, and she screamed and the men came and beat him. He got five years for that, but now the end was in sight. The parole board had been presented with the results of Cyrus's Hare PCL-R evaluation, the test developed by a professor of psychology at the University of British Columbia that was now widely regarded as the standard indicator of recidivism, violence, and the subject's response to therapeutic intervention, and the board's reaction had been positive. Within days Cyrus would be free to go, free to return to the river and his beloved hollows. That was why he liked the cell, the darkness of it, especially at night when he could close his eyes and imagine himself there once again, among the women and the girls, the perfumed girls.

He owed his release in part to his natural intelligence, for Cyrus, had the prison psychiatric services studied him further, would have provided some support for the theory that the genetic factors that contributed to his condition had also endowed him with a creative brilliance. But Cyrus had also received help in recent weeks from an unexpected source.

The old man had arrived in the MHSU, had watched Cyrus from behind his bars, and his fingers had begun to move.

Hello.

It had been so long since Cyrus had signed to another person other than a head doctor that he had almost forgotten how to converse, but slowly, then faster, he began to sign in return.

Hello. My name is—

Cyrus. I know your name.

How do you know my name?

I know all about you, Cyrus. You, and your little larder.

Cyrus had pulled back then and returned to his cell, where he lay huddled in the corner for the rest of the day while the voices shouted and argued over one another. But the next day he returned to the edge of the recreation unit, and the old man was waiting for him. He knew. He knew that Cyrus would come back to him.

Cyrus began to sign.

What do you want?

I have something to give you, Cyrus.

What?

The old man paused, then made the sign, the one that Cyrus made to himself in the darkness, when it all threatened to become too much for him and he needed some hope, something to cling to, something for which to yearn.

A woman, Cyrus. I'm going to give you a woman.

Barely yards away from where Cyrus lay, Faulkner knelt in his cell and prayed for success. He knew that by coming here he would find one that he could use. The ones in the other prison were no good to him; they were long-term prisoners, and Faulkner was not interested in long-termers. So he had injured himself, necessitating the transfer to the mental health stabilization unit and access to a more suitable population. He had expected it to be more difficult, but he had spotted Nairn instantly and had felt his pain. Faulkner tightened his fingers together, and the whispering of his prayers increased in volume.

The guard Anson approached the cell quietly, then paused as he stared down at the kneeling figure. His hand flicked in a neat, practiced movement and the ligature passed over the head of the praying man. Then, with a swift glance over his shoulder, Anson tugged and Faulkner was dragged, retching and clawing, to the bars. Anson pulled him up, then reached through the bars and gripped the old man's chin.

'You fuck!' hissed Anson, keeping his voice low, for he had seen the men in Faulkner's cell before the preacher was moved and suspected that some form of monitoring was in progress. Already, he had spoken to Marie and warned her to say nothing of their relationship in case his suspicions were correct. 'You ever open your mouth about me again and I'll finish what you started, you understand?' His fingers dug into Faulkner's dry, hot skin and felt the bone beneath, fragile and waiting to be broken. He released his grip, then allowed the rubber cord to slacken before he jerked it back again, banging the old man's head painfully against the bars.

'And you better watch what you eat, you old cocksucker, because I'm gonna be playing with your food before you get it, y'hear?' Then he slipped the cord over Faulkner's head and allowed him to fall to the ground. The preacher raised himself slowly and staggered to his bunk, drawing deep ragged breaths and touching the indentation on his neck. He listened as the guard's footsteps faded away, then, remaining seated and keeping his distance from the bars, he returned to his prayers.

As he sat, something on the floor seemed to draw his attention and his head turned to follow its movements. He watched it for a time then brought his foot down hard and firm upon it, before scraping the remains of the spider from his shoe.

'Boy,' he whispered, 'I warned you. I warned you to keep your pets under control.'

From close by came a sound that might have been the hissing of steam or an exhalation of barely restrained rage.

And in his own cell, half asleep, the remembered smell of damp earth flooding his senses, Cyrus Nairn stirred as another voice was added to the chorus in his head. This one had been coming to him more and more regularly in the previous weeks, ever since he and the preacher had begun to communicate and share the details of their lives. Cyrus now welcomed the stranger's arrival, feeling him stretch searching tendrils through his mind, establishing his presence and silencing the others.

Hello, said Cyrus, hearing in his head his own voice, the one no one else had heard in so many years, and signing his words by habit with his fingers.

Hello Cyrus, the visitor responded.

Cyrus smiled. He wasn't sure what to call the visitor, because the visitor had lots of names, old names that Cyrus had never heard spoken before. But there were two that he used more than others.

Sometimes he called himself Leonard.

Mostly he called himself Pudd.

7

That night Rachel watched me, unspeaking, while I undressed.

'Are you going to tell me what happened?' she asked at last.

I lay down beside her and felt her move in close to me, her belly touching my upper thigh. I placed my hand upon her and tried to sense the life inside.

'How are you feeling?' I asked.

'Great. Only puked a little this morning.' She grinned and poked me. 'But then I came in and kissed ya!'

'Lovely. It's a testament to your personal hygiene that I didn't notice it being any more unpleasant than usual.'

Rachel pinched me hard at the waist, then raised her hand so that she could run it through my hair. 'Well? You still haven't answered my question.'

'He said that he wanted me – us, I guess, since you'll be called too – to withdraw from the case and refuse to testify. In return, he promised to let us be.'

'Do you believe him?'

'No, and even if I did, it wouldn't change anything. Stan Ornstead has doubts about my suitability as a witness, but I think he's just edgy and those doubts really don't extend to you anyway. We'll be testifying whether we want to or not, but I got the feeling that Faulkner didn't really care about our testimony and that he was pretty certain of making bail after the review. I don't understand why he called me to him except to taunt me. Maybe he's so bored in prison that he thought I'd provide some amusement.'

'And did you?'

'A little, but he's kind of easily amused. There were other things too: his cell is freezing, Rachel. It's almost as if his body is drawing all the warmth from its surroundings. And he baited one of the guards about a relationship with a young girl.'

'Gossip?'

'No. The guard reacted like he'd been struck in the face. I don't think he'd shared that information with anybody. According to Faulkner, the girl is underage, and the guard confirmed as much to me later.'

'What are you going to do?'

'About the girl? I asked Stan Ornstead to set something in motion. That's all I can do.'

'So what's your conclusion about Faulkner? That he's psychic?'

'No, not psychic. I don't think there's a word for what Faulkner is. Before I left him, he spit at me. Actually, he spit into my mouth.'

I felt her stiffen.

'Yeah, that's kind of how I feel about it too. There isn't enough mouthwash in the world to take that one away.'

'Why would he do that?'

'He told me it would help me to see better.'

'See what better?'

This was delicate ground. I almost told her then: about the black car, about the things on the prison walls, about the visions of lost children that I'd had in the past, about Susan and Jennifer visiting me from some place beyond. I so badly wanted to tell her, but I could not, and I did not understand why this should be. She sensed some of it, I thought, but chose not to ask. And if she had asked, how could I have explained it to her? I was still unsure myself about the nature of the gift that I had. I did not like to think that something in me drew these lost souls to me. It was easier, sometimes, to try to believe that it was a psychological disturbance, not a psychic one.

I was tempted, too, to call Elliot Norton and tell him that his troubles were his own, that I wanted no part of them, but I had made a promise to him. And as long as Faulkner remained behind bars, awaiting a decision on his bail, I believed that Rachel would be safe. Faulkner, I felt certain, would do nothing that might endanger the possibility of his release.

The black car was another matter. It was neither a dream nor a reality. It was as if, for a brief moment, something that resided in a blind spot of my vision had drifted into sight, that a slight alteration of perception had permitted me to see that which usually existed unseen. And, for reasons that I did not fully understand, I believed that the car, real or imagined, did not represent a direct threat. Its purpose was more indistinct, its symbolism more ambiguous. Still, the thought that the Scarborough PD would be watching the house provided an added consolation, even if I thought it unlikely that police officers would be reporting sightings of a battered black Coupe de Ville.

There was also the matter of Roger Bowen. No good could come of a confrontation with him, but I was curious to see him, maybe to dig around a little and see what I could come up with. Most of all I felt a convergence of events, of which Elliot Norton's case was a distinct yet linked part. I'm not a great believer in coincidence. I have found in the past that what passes for coincidence is usually life's way of telling you that you're not paying enough attention.

'He thinks the dead talk to him,' I said at last. 'He thinks that there are deformed angels hovering above Thomaston prison. That's what he wanted me to see.'

'And did you see them?'

I looked at her. She wasn't smiling.

'I saw ravens,' I answered. 'Scores of ravens. And before you consider making me sleep in the spare room, I wasn't the only one that saw them.'

'I don't doubt you,' said Rachel. 'Nothing you could tell me about that old man would surprise me. Even locked up he gives me the creeps.'

'I don't have to go away,' I told her. 'I can stay here.'

'I don't want you to stay here,' she replied. 'That wasn't what I meant. Give it to me straight: are we at risk?'

I thought about it. 'I don't think so. In the end, nothing's going to happen until his lawyers appeal the bail decision. After that, we'll have to reconsider. For now, the Scarborough PD's guardian angel role is just a safeguard, although they may need a little unofficial backup.'

She opened her mouth to raise some fresh objection, but I covered her lips gently with my hand. Her eyes narrowed in reproach.

'Look, it's as much for my sake as yours. If it comes it won't be conspicuous or obtrusive, but I'll sleep a little easier for it.'

I lifted my hand slightly from her mouth and prepared myself for the tirade. Her lips parted and I pressed my hand down again. She let out a resigned sigh, her shoulders sagging in defeat. This time, I took my hand away completely and kissed her on the lips. She didn't respond at first, then I felt her lips part and her tongue move cautiously against mine. Her mouth opened wider, and I moved against her.

'Are you using sex to get what you want?' she asked, her breath catching a little as my hand brushed the inside of her thigh.

I raised my eyebrows in a poor imitation of hurt.

'Of course not,' I assured her. 'I'm a man. Sex *is* what I want.'

I could taste her laughter on my tongue as we gently began the slow dance together.

In blackness I awoke. There was no car waiting, yet the road seemed newly empty.

I left the bedroom and walked softly down to the kitchen. I could no longer sleep. When I reached the final steps, I saw that Walt was sitting in the doorway to the living room. His ears were erect and his tail was beating slowly on the floor. He looked at me once, then returned his attention to the room beyond. When I scratched at his ear, he didn't respond. Instead, his eyes remained fixed on a patch of darkness in the corner, denied light by the thick drapes but darker yet than it should have been, like a hole torn between worlds.

Something in that darkness had drawn the dog close to it.

I found the only weapon to hand – the letter opener on the coatstand – and palmed it, then stepped into the room, conscious of my nakedness.

'Who's there?' I asked. At my feet, Walt let out a little whine, but it was more excitement than fear. I moved closer to the darkness.

And a hand emerged.

It was a woman's hand, very white. Three horizontal wounds had been torn upon it so deeply that I could see the exposed bones in the fingers. The wounds were old, gray-brown within, and the skin had hardened around them. There was no blood. The hand extended farther, palm facing out, fingers raised,

stop

and I knew that these wounds were only the first, that she had lifted up her hands against the blade but it had made its way to her face and her body despite them, and there were more cuts like this upon her, made unto death and beyond.

please

I stopped.

Who are you?

you're looking for me

Cassie?

i felt you looking for me

Where are you?

lost

What can you see?

nothing

dark

Who did this to you? Who is he?

not one

many in one

Then I heard a whispering begin, and other voices joined with her own.

cassie let me speak let me talk to him cassie will he help us does he know cassie does he know my name cassie can he tell me my name cassie cassie can he take me away from here cassie i want to go home please i'm lost cassie please i want to go home

please

Cassie, who are they?

i don't know

i can't see them

but they're all here

he put us all here

Then, from behind me, a hand touched my bare shoulder, and Rachel was beside me, her breasts against my back, the feel of the sheets cool against my skin. The voices were fading, barely audible, yet desperate and insistent.

please

And in her sleep, Rachel's brow furrowed and she whispered softly:

'Please.'

8

I flew out of the Portland Jetport the next morning. It was early Sunday and the roads were still quiet when Rachel dropped me at the door of the terminal building. I had already called Wallace MacArthur to confirm that I was leaving and had passed on my cell phone and hotel numbers to him. Rachel had arranged a date for him with a friend of hers named Mary Mason, who lived out at Pine Point. Rachel knew her from the local Audubon Society and figured that she and Wallace would probably get along pretty well. Wallace had taken the trouble to check out her photo through the BMV and had professed himself pleased with his prospective mate.

'She looks good,' he told me.

'Yeah, well don't get too cocky. She hasn't seen you yet.'

'What's not to love?'

'You have a pretty healthy self-image, Wallace. In anyone else it would come across as smugness, but you manage to pull it off.'

There was a noticeable pause before he asked: 'Seriously?'

Rachel leaned across and kissed me on the lips. I held her head close to mine. 'You take care of yourself,' she said.

'You too. You got your cell phone?'

She dutifully raised her phone from her bag.

'And you're going to leave it on?'

She nodded.

'All the time?'

Pursed lips. Shrug. Reluctant nod.

'I'll be calling to check.'

She punched me on the arm. 'Go get on your plane. There are flight attendants waiting to be charmed.'

'Seriously?' I said, and instantly wondered if I had more in common with Wallace MacArthur than was really healthy.

She smiled. 'Yep. You need all the practice you can get.'

Louis once told me that the New South was like the Old South, except everybody was ten pounds heavier. He was probably kind of bitter, and he certainly wasn't a fan of South Carolina, often considered the most redneck state in the South after Mississippi and Alabama, although it had managed its racial affairs in a slightly more developed way. When Harvey Gantt became the first black student to go to Clemson College in South Carolina, the legislature, rather than opting for blockades and guns, grudgingly accepted that the time for change had come. Still, it was in Orangeburg, S.C., in 1968 that three black students were killed during demonstrations outside the whites-only All Star Bowling Alley; anyone over forty in South Carolina had probably gone to a segregated school; and there were still those who believed that the Confederate flag should fly over the state Capitol in Columbia. Now they were naming lakes after Strom Thurmond, as if segregation had never happened.

I flew into Charleston International via Charlotte, which seemed to be a kind of clearinghouse for the runts of evolution and a dumping ground for the worst fashion excesses of the polyester industry. Fleetwood Mac was playing on the jukebox in the Taste of Carolina saloon, where overweight men in shorts and T-shirts drank light beer in a fog of cigarette smoke, the women beside them feeding quarters into the poker machines that stood on the polished wood of the bar. A man with a tattoo of a skull in joker's regalia on his left arm gave me a hard look from where he sat, splay-legged, at a low table, the neck of his T-shirt soaked with sweat. I held his gaze until he belched and looked away with a studiedly bored expression on his face.

I checked the screens for my departure gate. There were planes flying out of Charlotte to places that nobody in his right mind would want to visit, the kind of places where the routes should have been strictly one-way, heading out of there to just about anywhere else, doesn't matter, just get me a damn ticket. We boarded on time and I sat beside a big man with a Charleston Fire Department cap on his head. He leaned across me to look out at the military vehicles and aircraft on the tarmac, and at a US Airways Express twin-prop that was taxiing toward the runway.

'Glad we're on one of these here jets and not one of them little biddy planes,' he said.

I nodded as he took in the aircraft and the buildings of the main terminal. 'I remember when Charlie was just a little old two-runway place,' he continued. 'Hell, they was still building it. That was when I was in th' army . . .'

I closed my eyes.

It was the longest short flight of my life.

Charleston International was near empty when we landed, the walkways and stores largely devoid of passengers. To the northwest, at Charleston AFB, gray-green military aircraft stood in the afternoon sun, tensed like locusts prepared for flight.

They picked me up at the baggage claim, close by the car rental desks. There were two men, one of them fat and wearing a bright hemp shirt, the other older with slicked-back dark hair, dressed in a T-shirt and vest beneath a black linen jacket. They watched me discreetly as I stood at the Hertz desk, then waited at the side door of the terminal building as I walked through the heat of the parking lot to the small marquee beneath which my Mustang was waiting. By the time I had the keys in my hand, they were sitting in a big Chevy Tahoe at the intersection with the main exit road and they stayed two cars behind me all the way to the interstate. I could have lost them, but there didn't seem to be much point. I knew they were there, and that was what mattered.

The new Mustang I had rented didn't drive like my Boss 302. When I put my foot to the floor nothing happened for about a second while the engine woke up, stretched, and scratched itself before eventually getting around to accelerating. Still, it had a CD player so I was able to listen to the Jayhawks as I drove along the neobrutalist stretch of I-26, 'I'd Run Away' blaring as I took the North Meeting Street exit for Charleston, until the ambiguity of the lyrics made me turn it off in favor of the radio, the words of the bridge still echoing in my head.

So, we had a little baby boy,
knew it wouldn't last too long.
Kind of what I had in mind,
but what I had in mind was strong.

Meeting Street is one of the main arteries into Charleston, leading straight into the heart of the business and tourist district, but its upper reaches are pretty unsavory. A black man sold watermelons by the side of the road from the back of a pickup, the fruit piled up neatly in rows, a sign advertising the Diamonds Gentleman's Club rising up above him. The Mustang juddered over railroad tracks, past boarded-up warehouses and abandoned strip malls, drawing glances from kids shooting hoop on overgrown green lots and old men in porch chairs, the paint peeling from the fronts of the houses and weeds bursting through the cracks in the steps in a mockery of fruition. The only building that looked clean and new was the housing authority's modern glass-and-red-brick office. It seemed to be inviting those who lived by its gift to storm it and steal all of the furniture and fittings. The Chevy stayed behind me the whole way. I slowed down once or twice, and did a full circle from Meeting, through Calhoun and Hutson and back on to Meeting again, just to bug the two men. They maintained their distance until I reached the courtyard of the Charleston Place Hotel, then moved slowly away.

In the hotel lobby, wealthy blacks and whites dressed in their Sunday best stood talking and laughing in their postservice ease. Occasionally, calls were made for parties to head to the dining room, Charleston Place's Sunday brunch being a tradition for some. I left them to it and headed up the stairs to my room. It had a pair of queen-size beds and a view of the ATM at the bank across the street. I sat on the bed nearest the window and called Elliot Norton to let him know that I'd arrived. He let out a long sigh of relief.

'The hotel okay for you?'

'Sure,' I said, noncommitally. Charleston Place was certainly luxurious, but the bigger the hotel, the easier it is for strangers to gain access to the rooms. I hadn't noticed anybody who looked particularly like hotel security, although security was probably deliberately discreet here, and the hallway had been empty apart from a chambermaid pushing a cart loaded with towels and toiletries. She hadn't even looked at me.

'It's the best hotel in Charleston,' said Elliot. 'It's got a gym, a pool. You prefer, I can book you in someplace where the roaches will keep you company.'

'I got followed from the airport,' I told him.

'Uh-huh.'

He didn't sound surprised.

'You think they could be listening in on your calls?'

'I guess. I never bothered to have the place swept. Didn't see the need. But it's hard to keep a lid on anything in this town. Also, like I told you, my secretary left this week and she made it pretty clear that she didn't approve none of some of my clients. Her last act was to make your hotel booking. Could be she let something slip.'

I wasn't too concerned about the tail. People involved in the case were going to know I was here soon enough anyway. I was more worried about the possibility that somebody might find out our plans for Atys Jones and take action against him.

'Okay, just in case: no more calls to or from the hotel, your office, or your home. We'll need clean cells for routine business.

I'll pick them up this evening. Anything sensitive can wait until we see each other in person.' Cells weren't an ideal solution, but if we didn't sign contracts, kept the numbers to ourselves, and used them carefully we would probably get away with it. Elliot gave me directions to his house again, which was about eighty miles northwest of Charleston, and I told him I'd be there later that afternoon. Before he hung up, he added: 'I had another reason for checking you into the CP, apart from your comfort.'

I waited.

'The Larousses go there for Sunday brunch most weeks, catch up on gossip and business. You go down there now, you'll probably see them: Earl, Earl Jr., maybe some cousins, business associates. Thought you might like to get a feel for them discreetly, but if someone tailed you from the airport, then I figure they may be checking you out as much as you're checking on them. Sorry, bud. I fucked up there.'

I let it go.

Before I headed down to the lobby I checked the yellow pages and called a company named Loomis Car Rental. I arranged to have an anonymous Neon delivered to the parking garage within the hour. My guess was that anyone who was keeping tabs on me would be looking out for the Mustang, and I wasn't about to make life too easy for a potential tail.

I spotted the Larousse group as it was coming out of the dining room. Earl Larousse, instantly identifiable from the newspaper photos I'd seen, wore his trademark white suit and a black silk tie, like a mourner at a Chinese funeral. He was about five eight, bald, and heavily built. Beside him stood a younger, slimmer version of himself, although there was a slight effeminacy to the son that was absent from the father. Earl Jr.'s slim frame was concealed beneath a billowing white shirt and a pair of black trousers that were too tight around the ass and thighs, making him look like a flamenco dancer on his day off. He had very fair hair, which rendered his eyebrows almost invisible, and I reckoned he had to shave about once a month. Five other people – three men, two women – were talking with them as they left the room. The party was quickly joined by an eighth person, the man with the slicked-back hair, who walked up to Earl Jr. and whispered discreetly in his ear before moving on. Immediately, Earl Jr. looked over at me. He said something to his father, then detached himself from the group and came over to me. I wasn't sure what to expect but it certainly wasn't to see his hand outstretched and a regretful smile on his face as he reached me.

'Mr. Parker?' he said. 'Let me introduce myself: Earl Larousse Jr.'

I took his hand and shook it. 'You usually have people followed from the airport?'

The smile wavered then resumed its post, this time the regret more pronounced.

'I'm sorry,' he said. 'We were curious to see what you looked like.'

'I don't understand.'

'We know why you're here, Mr. Parker. We don't necessarily approve, but we understand. We don't want there to be problems between us. We understand you have a job to do. Our concern is that whoever is responsible for my sister's death is punished with the full force of the law. For the moment, we believe that person to be Atys Jones. If that proves not to be the case, then we'll accept it. We've made our statements to the police, and told them all we know. All we ask of you is that you respect our privacy and leave us in peace. We have nothing to add to what has already been said.'

It had the air of a rehearsed speech about it. More than that, I sensed a detachment about Earl Jr. Although he sounded sincere, if mechanical, his eyes were both mocking and slightly fearful. He wore a mask, although I didn't yet know what lay behind it. Farther back, his father watched us, and in his face I saw hostility. For some unknown reason, it seemed to be directed at his son as much as at me. Earl Jr. turned and walked back to the group, and a shroud fell across his father's anger as they made their way out of the lobby and into their waiting cars.

With nothing else to do I returned to my room, showered, ate a club sandwich, and waited for the car rental guy to arrive. When the call came from the desk I went down, signed the paperwork, and entered the parking garage. I put on my sunglasses and headed out, the sunlight gleaming off the windshield, but there was no sign of the Chevy and nobody seemed interested in me or the car. On the way out of town I stopped at a big mall and bought two new cell phones.

Elliot Norton lived about two miles outside Grace Falls in a modest white faux-Colonial with two pillars at its front door and a big porch running the full length of the first floor. It looked like the kind of place where the mint juleps would still have the julep mix dissolving in the glass. The large sheet of industrial plastic covering the hole in the roof did nothing to add an air of authenticity. I found Elliot round back, talking to a pair of men in coveralls who leaned against a van, smoking. The legend on the side of the van indicated that the two men were roofers from Dave's Construction and Roofing out of Martinez, Georgia ('Want To Save? Call Dave!'). To their left was a pile of scaffolding, ready to be put in place so that work could commence the following morning. One of the men was idly tossing a piece of burnt, blackened slate from hand to hand. As I approached, he stopped and jutted his chin in my direction. Elliot turned a little too quickly, then left the two workmen and stretched out his hand to me.

'Man, am I glad to see you!' He smiled. Some of his hair had been scorched away on the left side of his head. What remained had been cut back in an effort to disguise the damage. There was gauze over his left ear and burn marks glistened along his cheek, chin, and neck. His left hand, where it was visible beneath a white tube bandage, was blistered.

'Don't take this wrong, Elliot,' I said, 'but you don't look so good.'

'I know. Fire took out most of my wardrobe. Come on.' He reached behind my back and guided me toward the house. 'I'll buy you an iced tea.'

Inside, the house smelled badly of smoke and damp. Water had penetrated the floors above and damaged the plasterwork in the downstairs rooms, brown clouds now sweeping across the white skies of the ceilings. Some of the wallpaper had already begun to peel and I reckoned there was a good chance that Elliot would be forced to replace most of the timbers in the hallway. In the living room was an unmade sofa bed, and clothes hung from the curtain rod or splayed themselves across the backs of chairs.

'You're still living here?' I asked.

'Yup,' he replied, as he washed some ash from a pair of glass tumblers.

'You might be safer in a hotel.'

'I might be, but then the folks who did this to my house would probably come back and finish the job.'

'They could come back anyway.'

He shook his head. 'Nah, they're done, for now. Murder isn't their style. If they'd wanted to kill me, they'd have done a better job first time round.'

He took a jug of iced tea from the refrigerator and filled the tumblers. I stood by the window and stared out at Elliot's yard and the land beyond. The skies were empty of birds and the woods surrounding Elliot's property were almost silent. Along the coast, the migrants were already in flight, the wood ducks joining the terns, the hawks and warblers and sparrows soon to follow. Here, farther inland, there was less evidence of their departure, and even the permanent residents were not as obvious as they formerly were, their spring mating songs ended and their bright summer plumage slowly fading to the mourning cloaks of winter. As if to make up for the absence of the birds and their colors, the wildflowers had begun to bloom now that the worst of the summer heat had departed. There were asters and sunflowers and goldenrods, and butterflies flocked to them, attracted by the predominance of yellows and purples. Beneath the leaves, the field spiders would be waiting for them.

'So when do I get to meet Atys Jones?' I asked.

'Be easiest if you talk to him after we get him out of county. We pick him up from the Richland County Detention Center late tomorrow, then switch him to a second car out back of Campbell's Country Corner to lose anyone with an interest in where we might be taking him. From there, I'll drive him to the safe house in Charleston.'

'Who's the second driver?'

'Son of the old guy who's gonna be taking care of him. He's okay, knows what he's doing.'

'Why not stash him closer to Columbia?'

'We got a better chance of keeping him safe down in Charleston, believe me. He'll be over on the east side, in the heart of a black neighborhood. Anybody comes asking questions and we'll hear about it in plenty of time to move him again if we have to. Anyhow, it's a purely temporary arrangement. Could be that we'll have to stash him somewhere more secure, maybe hire private security. We'll see.'

'So what's his story?' I asked.

Elliot shook his head and rubbed his eyes with dirty fingers. 'His story is that he and Marianne Larousse had a thing going.'

'They were lovers?'

'Occasional lovers. Atys thinks she was using him to get back at her brother and her daddy, and he was pretty happy to go along with that.' He made a clicking noise with his tongue against his teeth. 'I got to tell you, Charlie, my client ain't exactly nature's own charmer, if you catch my drift. He's one hundred and thirty pounds of attitude with a mouth at one end and an asshole at the other, and most of the time I can't tell which end is which. According to him, the night Marianne died they'd been screwing around in the front of his Grand Am. They had a fight, she ran off into the trees. He went after her, thought he'd lost her somewhere in the forest, then found her with her head beaten to a pulp.'

'Weapon?'

'Weapon of convenience: a ten-pound rock. Police arrested Atys with blood on his hands and clothes and fragments of rock and dust matching the weapon. He admits he touched her head and body when he found her and rolled the rock away from her skull. He'd smeared some blood on his face as well, but there was nothing consistent with the kind of blood splash you get from beating on someone with a rock. No traces of semen inside her, although they did pick up lubricant from a condom – Trojan – matching the ones found in Atys's wallet. It looks like it was consensual sex but a good prosecutor might still be able to argue rape. You know, they get excited, then she tries to back off and he doesn't take it so good. I don't think it will hold up but they'll be trying to bolster their case anyway they can.'

'You think there's enough there to sow seeds of doubt in a jury?'

'Maybe. I'm looking for an expert witness to testify on the blood splashes. The prosecution will probably find one who'll say the exact opposite. This is a black man accused of killing a white girl from the Larousse clan. It's all uphill on this one. Prosecutor will be looking at loading the jury with middle-income, middle-aged-to-elderly whites who'll see in Jones the black bogeyman. Best we can hope to do is dilute it, but . . .'

I waited. There's always a 'but'. There wouldn't be a story without one.

'There's local history behind all this; the worst kind of local history.'

He flicked through the pile of files that lay on the kitchen table. I glimpsed police reports, witness statements, transcripts of the interviews conducted with Atys Jones by the police, even crime scene photographs. But I could also see photocopied pages from history books, cuttings from old newspapers, and books on slavery and rice cultivation.

'What you got here,' said Elliot, 'is a regular blood feud.'

9

The first files were blue and contained witness statements and other material assembled by the police in the aftermath of Marianne Larousse's death. The historical file was green. Beside it was a slim white file. I opened it, saw more clearly the photographs that lay within, then closed it carefully. I was not yet ready to deal with the reports on Marianne Larousse's body.

I had taken on a little defense work in Maine in the past, so I had a pretty good idea of what was ahead of me. Atys Jones would be the most important element, of course, at least to begin with. Defendants will often tell an investigator things that they haven't even told their attorney, sometimes out of sheer forgetfulness or the stress surrounding their arrest, other times because they trust the investigator more than their lawyer, especially if their lawyer is a hard-pressed public defender already overwhelmed by his or her caseload. The rule of thumb is that any additional information is passed on to the attorney, whether favorable or prejudicial to the case. Elliot had already received some statements and testimonials from those who knew Jones, including schoolteachers and former employers, in an effort to form a favorable profile of his client that could be presented to the jury, so that was a little less donkey work for me to do.

I'd have to go over the police reports with Jones as these would provide the basis for the charges against him, but also because he might pick up on mistakes made or witnesses that had not been contacted. The police reports would also be useful to me in checking statements, since they usually contained the addresses and phone numbers of those to whom the police had spoken. After that, the real legwork would begin: all of those witnesses would have to be reinterviewed because the early police reports were rarely in-depth, the cops preferring to leave the detailed interviewing for the prosecutor's investigators or the primary detective. Signed statements would have to be obtained, and while most witnesses would be willing to talk, fewer would be willing to sign their names to a summary of their comments without a struggle. In addition, it was likely that the prosecutor's investigators had spoken to them already, and they often had a way of intimating to witnesses that they should not talk to the defendant's investigator, placing another barrier in the way. All things considered, I had a busy time ahead of me, and I might be able to do little more than scratch the surface of the case before I had to return to Maine.

I pulled the green file toward me and flipped it open. Some of the material inside dated back to the seventeenth century and the earliest origins of Charleston. The most recent cutting came from 1981.

'Somewhere in here may be part of the reason why Marianne Larousse died, and why Atys Jones is going to be tried for her murder,' said Elliot. 'This is the weight that they carried with them, whether they knew it or not. This is what destroyed their lives.'

He had been rummaging in his kitchen cabinets as he spoke, and he now returned to the table with his right fist tightly closed.

'But in a way,' said Elliot softly, 'this is really why we're here today.'

And he opened his fist to let a stream of yellow rice cascade onto the tabletop.

Amy Jones
Age 98 when interviewed by Henry Calder in Red Bank, S.C. *From The Age of Slavery: Interviews with Former North and South Carolina Slaves*, ed. Judy and Nancy Buckingham (New Era, 1989).

I was born a slave in Colleton County. My pappy name Andrew and my mammy name Violet. They belong to the Larousse family. Marster Adgar was a good marster to his slaves. Him had about sixty families of slaves before the Yankees come and made a mess out of their lives.

Old Missus tell all the colored people to run. She come to us with a bagful of silver all sew up in a blanket, 'cause the Yankees apt to take all they valuables. She tell us that she couldn't protect us no longer. They broke in the rice barn and share the rice out, but they not enough rice there to feed all the colored people. Worst nigger men and women follow the army, but us stay and watch the other chillun die.

Us wasn't ready for what come. Us had no education, no land, no cow, no chicken. Yankees come and take all us had away, left us with freedom. They give us to understand us as free as our marster was. Couldn't write, so us just had to touch the pen and tell what name us wanted to go in. After the war, Marster Adgar give us one-third of what us make, now that us free. Pappy dead just before my mammy. They stay right to plantation and dead there after they free.

But they tole me. They tole me about Old Marster, Marster Adgar's pappy. They tole me what he done . . .

To understand the crop is to understand the history, for the history is Carolina Gold.

Rice cultivation began here in the 1680s, when the rice seed reached Carolina from Madagascar. They called it Carolina Gold because of its quality and the color of its hull, and it made the families associated with it wealthy for generations. There were the Englishmen

– the Heywards, the Draytons, the Middletons, and the Alstons – and the Huguenots, among them the Ravenels, the Manigaults, and the Larousses.

The Larousses were scions of Charleston aristocracy, one of a handful of families that controlled virtually all aspects of life in the city, from membership in the St. Cecilia Society to the organization of the social season, which lasted from November to May. They valued their name and reputation above all else, and safeguarded both with money and the influence that it bought. They could not have suspected that their great wealth and security would be undermined by the actions of a single slave.

The slaves would work from first light until last, six days each week, but did not work on Sundays. A conch shell was used to call in the laborers, its tones sweeping across the fields of rice now afire in the dying rays of the setting sun, the black shapes against them like scarecrows amid the conflagration. Their backs would straighten, their heads rise and, slowly, they would begin the long walk back to the rice barn and the shacks. They would feed on molasses, peas, corn bread, sometimes home-raised meat. They would sit in their homemade clothes of copper straw and white cloth at the end of the long day, and eat and talk. When a new delivery of wooden-soled shoes came, the women would soak the rawhide leather in warm water and grease them with tallow or meat skin so the shoes would slip onto their feet, and the smell would cling to their fingers when they made love to their men, the stench of dead animals mingling with the sweat of their lovemaking.

The men did not learn how to read or write. Old Marster was strict on that. They were whipped for stealing, or for telling lies, or for looking at books. There was a dirt house out by the swamp where they used to carry those who had smallpox. Most of the slaves carried out there never returned. They kept the Pony in the rice barn, and when the time came for more serious punishments to be meted out, the man or woman would be spread-eagled upon it, strapped down, and whipped. When the Yankees burned down the rice barn, there was blood on the floor where the Pony had stood, as if the very ground itself had begun to rust.

Some of the East African slaves brought with them an understanding of rice cultivation that enabled the plantation owners to overcome the problems faced by the original English colonists, who had found its cultivation troublesome. A task system was introduced on many plantations that allowed skilled slaves to work somewhat independently, enabling them to create free time to hunt, garden, or improve the situation of their families. The produce or products created could then be bartered by the slaves to the owner, and removed some of the pressure of providing for his slaves from him.

The task system created a hierarchy among the slaves. The most important bondsman was the slave driver, who acted as the mediator between the planter and the labor force. Beneath him were the trained artisans, the blacksmiths and carpenters and bricklayers. It was these skilled workers that were the natural leaders in the slave community, and consequently they had to be watched more closely for fear that they might foment unrest or choose to run away.

But the most crucial task of all fell to the trunk minder, for the fate of the rice crop lay in his hands. The rice fields were flooded when necessary with freshwater collected in reservoirs above the fields on higher ground. Salt water flowed inland with the tide, forcing the freshwater to the surface of the coastal rivers. It was only then that the low, wide floodgates could be opened to permit the freshwater to flow into the fields, a system of subsidiary gates allowing the water to run into the adjoining fields, a drainage technique whose correct application was a direct result of the involvement of African slaves. Any breach or break in the gates would permit salt water to enter the fields, killing the rice crop, so the trunk minder, in addition to opening and closing the main gates, was required to keep the trunks, the drainage ditches, and the canals in working order.

Henry, husband of Annie, was the trunk minder for the Larousse plantation. His grandfather, now dead, had been captured in January 1764 and taken to the out-factory of Barra Kunda in upper Guinea. From there, he was transported to James Fort on the river Gambia in October 1764, the main point of embarkation for slaves bound for the New World. He arrived in Charles Town in 1765, where he was purchased by the Larousse family. He had six children and sixteen grandchildren by the time he died, of whom Henry was the eldest grandson. Henry had married his young wife, Annie, six years previously, and they now had three young children. Only one, Andrew, would survive to maturity, and he would father his own children in turn, a line that would continue until the early twenty-first century, and end with Atys Jones.

They strapped Annie, wife of Henry, to the Pony one day in 1833, and they whipped her until the whip broke. But by then the skin on her back had been torn away, so they turned her and started in again on her front with a new whip. Their intention was to punish, not to kill. Annie was too valuable a commodity to be killed. She had been tracked down by a team of men led by William Rudge, whose descendant would later hang a man named Errol Rich from a tree in front of a crowd of onlookers in northeastern Georgia, and whose own life would come to an end at the hands of a black man on a bed of spilled whiskey and sawdust. Rudge was the 'pattyroller,' the slave patroller whose job it was to hunt down those who chose to run. Annie had run after a man named Coolidge had held her over a tree stump and tried to rape her from behind when he found her out on a dirt road delivering beef from a cow that Old Marster had ordered killed the previous day. While Coolidge was tearing at her, Annie had taken a branch from the ground and stabbed him in the eye, partially blinding him. And then she had run, for nobody would care or believe that she had been defending herself, even if Coolidge had not claimed that the attack was unprovoked, that he'd found the nigger drinking stolen hooch by the side of the road. The pattyroller and his men had followed her and they took her back to Old Marster, and she was strapped to the Pony and whipped while her husband and their three children were forced to watch. But she did not survive the whipping, for she went into convulsions and died.

Three days later, Henry, husband of Annie and trusted trunk minder, flooded the Larousse plantation with salt water, destroying the entire crop.

They followed him for five days with a party of heavily armed men, for Henry had stolen a Marston pepperbox percussion pistol, and any man who was standing in the way when those six barrels discharged was likely to be meeting his maker that very day. So the riders held back and sent ahead a line of expendable Ibo slaves to track Henry, with the promise of a gold coin for the man who found their quarry.

They cornered Henry at last at the edge of the Congaree Swamp, not far from where a bar named the Swamp Rat now stands, the bar at which Marianne Larousse would be drinking on the night that she died, for the voice of the present contains the echo of the past. The slave who had found Henry lay dead on the ground, with ragged holes in his chest where the Marston had hit him at close range.

They took three metal rice samplers, hollow T-shaped devices with a sharp point on the end for digging into the ground, and they crucified Henry against a cypress tree and left him there with his balls in his mouth. But before he died, Old Marster drew up before him in a cart, and in the back of the cart sat Henry's three children. The last sight Henry saw before his eyes finally closed was his youngest boy, Andrew, being led into the bushes by Old Marster, and then the boy's cries commenced and Henry died.

That was how it began between the families of Larousse and Jones, masters and slaves. The crop was wealth. The crop was history. It had to be safeguarded. Henry's offense lived on for a time in the memory of the Larousse family and was then largely forgotten, but the sins of the Larousses were passed down from Jones to Jones. And the past was transported into each new present, and it spread through generations of lives like a virus.

The light had begun to fade. The men from Georgia were gone. From the big oak tree outside the window a bat descended, hunting mosquitoes. Some had found their way into the house and now buzzed at my ear, waiting to bite. I swatted at them with my hand. Elliot handed me some repellent and I smeared it across my exposed skin.

'But there were still members of the Jones family working for the Larousses, even after what took place?' I asked.

'Uh-huh,' said Elliot. 'Slaves died sometimes. It happened. The folks around them had lost parents, children too, but they didn't take it quite so personal. There were some members of the Jones family who felt that what was done was done, and should be left in the past. And then there were others who maybe didn't feel that way.'

The Civil War devastated the lives of the Charleston aristocracy, as it did the structures of the city itself. The Larousses were protected somewhat by their foresight (or perhaps by their treason, for they retained most of their wealth in gold and had only a small fraction tied up in Confederate bonds and currency). Still they, like many other defeated Southerners, were forced to watch as the surviving soldiers of the Fifty-fourth Massachusetts Regiment, or Shaw's Niggers as they were known, paraded through the streets of Charleston. Among them was Martin Jones, Atys Jones's great-great-grandfather.

Once again, the lives of these two families were about to collide violently.

The night riders move through the darkness, white against the black road. It will be many years before an olive-skinned man with slave marks on his legs will claim to have seen them as they will become, figures in negative, black on white, a reversal that would sicken these men were they to know of it now as they go about their business, their horses draped, guns and bullwhips banging dully against saddles.

For this is the South Carolina of the 1870s, not of the turn of a new millennium, and the night riders are the terror of these times. They roam upcountry, visiting their version of justice on poor blacks and the Republicans that support them, refusing to bow to the requirements of the Fourteenth and Fifteenth Amendments. They are a symbol of the fear felt by the whites for the blacks, and much of the white population stands behind them. Already, the Black Codes have been introduced as an antidote to reform, restricting the rights of blacks to hold arms, to hold a position above farmer or servant, even to leave their premises or entertain visitors without a permit.

In time, Congress will fight back with the Reconstruction Amendment, the Enforcement Act of 1870, the Ku Klux Klan Act of 1871. Governor Scott will form a black militia to protect voters in the 1870 election, further enraging the white population. Eventually, habeas corpus will be suspended in the nine upcountry counties, leading to the arrest of hundreds of Klan members without due process, but for the present the law rides a draped horse and brings with it vengeance, and the actions of the federal government will be too late to save thirty-eight lives, too late to prevent rapes and beatings, too late to stop the burning and destruction of farms and crops and livestock.

Too late to save Missy Jones.

Her husband, Martin, had campaigned to bring out the black vote in 1870 in the face of intimidation and violence. He had refused to repudiate the Republican Party and had earned a whipping for his troubles. Then he had lent his support and his savings to the nascent black militia, and had marched his men through the town one bright Sunday afternoon, no more than one in ten of them armed but still an act of unparalleled arrogance to those who were fighting the tide of emancipation.

It was Missy who heard the riders approaching, Missy who told her husband to run, that this time they would kill him if they found him. The night riders had not yet harmed a woman in York County and Missy, although she feared the armed men, had no reason to believe that they would commence with her.

But they did.

Four men raped Missy Jones, for if they could not harm her husband directly, then they would hurt him through his woman. The rape was without any physical violence beyond the violation itself, devoid, it seemed to the woman, even of an element of pleasure for the men who committed the act. Instead, it was as functional as the branding of a cow or the strangling of a chicken. The last man even helped her to cover herself up and gave her his arm as he escorted her to a kitchen chair.

'You tell him to behave himself, y'hear?' said the man. He was young and handsome and she saw in him something of his father and

his grandfather. He had the Larousse chin, and the fair hair common to that family. His name was William Larousse. 'We don't want to be coming back through here again,' he warned her.

Two weeks later, William Larousse and two other men were ambushed outside Delphia by a group of masked assailants armed with cudgels. William's companions fled but he remained, curled into a ball, as the blows rained down. The beating left him paralyzed, able to move only his right hand and unable to eat any food that had not been mashed to the consistency of paste.

But Missy Jones was unheeding of what had been done in her name. She had barely spoken to her husband when he returned from his hiding place, and rarely spoke again thereafter. Neither did she return to her husband's bed, but slept instead among the animals in their small barn, reduced in her own mind to their level by the men who had raped her to hurt her husband, retreating slowly and irretrievably into madness.

Elliot rose and poured the remains of his coffee into the sink.

'Like I said, there were some who wanted to forget the past, and some who never forgot it, even to this day.'

He let the last words in the air.

'You think Atys Jones might have been one of those?'

He shrugged. 'I think that some part of him liked the idea that he was fucking Earl Larousse's daughter, and fucking over Earl by extension. I don't even know if Marianne knew about the history between the two families. I guess it meant more to the Joneses than it did to the Larousses, if you catch my drift.'

'But their history is common knowledge?'

'There's been some reporting on the history of the families in the newspapers by those with the energy to go digging, but not much. Still, I'd be surprised if some of the jurors don't know about it, and it may come up at the trial. The Larousses have a name and a history that they safeguard religiously. Their reputation means everything to them. Whatever they might have done in the past, they now contribute to socially responsible causes.

They support black charities. They supported integration in schools. They don't decorate their houses with the flag of the Confederacy. They've made up for the sins of previous generations, but could be the prosecution will use old ghosts to claim that Atys Jones set out to punish them again by taking Marianne away from them.'

He stood and stretched.

'Unless, of course, we can find the person who did kill Marianne Larousse. Then we got us a whole new ball game.'

I put aside the copy of the photograph of Missy Jones, dead by her forties and lying in her cheap box coffin, and sifted through the documents on the table once again until I came to the final cutting. It was a newspaper story dated July 12, 1981, and it detailed the disappearance of two young black women who had lived near the Congaree. Their names were Addy and Melia Jones, and after that night, when they were seen drinking together in a local bar, they were never heard of again.

Addy Jones was Atys Jones's mother.

I held the cutting up for Elliot to see.

'What is this?'

He reached out and took it from me.

'This,' he said, 'is the final puzzle for you. Our client's mother and aunt disappeared nineteen years ago, and neither he nor anybody else has seen them since.'

That night, I drove back to Charleston with the radio tuned to a talk show out of Columbia, until the signal began to fade into hisses and distortion. Failed gubernatorial candidate Maurice Bessinger, the owner of the state's Piggie Park chain of barbecue restaurants, had taken to flying a Confederate flag over his outlets. He was arguing that it was a symbol of Southern heritage, and maybe it was, except that in the past, Bessinger had twice worked on George Wallace's presidential campaign, had run a group called the National Association for the Preservation of White People, and had found himself in federal court for violating the Civil Rights Act of 1964 after he refused to serve blacks in his restaurants. He even managed to win his case at trial level, only to be forced to integrate by a higher court. Since then he had apparently enjoyed a religious conversion and rejoined the Democratic Party, but old habits seemed to be dying hard.

I thought of the flag as I drove through the darkness, about the families of Jones and Larousse and the weight of history that was like a lead belt strapped to their bodies, dragging them always down to the bottom. Somewhere in that history, in the living past, was an answer to the death of Marianne Larousse.

But down here, in a place that seemed alien to me, the past assumed strange forms. The past was an old man draped in a red-and-blue flag, howling his defiance beneath the sign of a pig. The past was a dead hand on the face of the living. The past was a ghost garlanded with regrets.

The past, I would come to learn, was a woman in white with scales for skin.

PART THREE

'I seemed to move among a world of ghosts
And feel myself the shadow of a dream.'

Alfred, Lord Tennyson, 'The Princess'

10

Now at last, in the quiet of my hotel room, I opened the file on Marianne Larousse. The darkness around me was less an absence of light than a felt presence: shadows with substance. I lit the table lamp and spread across the desk the material that Elliot had given to me.

And as soon as I saw the photos I had to look away, for I felt the weight of her loss upon me, though I had not known her and would never know her now. I walked to the door and tried to banish the shadows by flooding the room with brightness, but instead they merely retreated to the spaces beneath the tables and behind the closet, waiting for the inevitable passing of the light.

And it seemed to me that my being somehow separated, that I was both here in this hotel room, with the evidence of Marianne Larousse's violent wrenching from this world, and back in the stillness of the Blythes' living room, watching Bear's mouth move to form well-meant lies, Sundquist like a ventriloquist beside him, manipulating, poisoning the atmosphere in the room with greed and malice and false hope while Cassie's eyes stared out at me from a graduation photograph, that uncertain smile hovering about her mouth like a bird unsure of the safety of alighting. I found myself trying to imagine her alive now, living a new life far from home, secure in the knowledge that her decision to abandon her former existence was the right one to make. But I was unable to do so, for when I tried to picture her there was only a shadow without a face and a hand adorned with parallel wounds.

Cassie Blythe was not alive. Everything I had learned about her told me that she was not the kind of young woman to drift away and condemn her parents to a lifetime of hurt and doubt. Someone had torn her from this world, and I did not know if I could find that person and, through that discovery, reveal at last the truth behind her disappearance.

I knew then that Irving Blythe was right, that what he had said about me was true: to invite me into their lives was to admit failure and allow death its provenance, for I was the one who arrived when all hope was gone, offering nothing but the possibility of a resolution that would bring with it more grief and pain and a knowledge that perhaps would make ignorance appear like a blessing. The only consolation in all that would occur was that some small measure of justice might begin to accrue from my involvement, that lives might continue with some small degree of certainty restored: the certainty that the physical pain of a loved one was at an end, and that somebody cared enough to try to discover why that pain had been visited on them at all.

When I was a younger man, I became a policeman. I joined the force because I felt that it was incumbent upon me to do so. My father had been a policeman, as had my grandfather, but my father had ended his career and his life in ignominy and despair. He took two lives before taking his own, for reasons that perhaps will never be known, and I, being young, felt the need to take his burdens upon myself and to try to make up for what he had done.

But I was not a good policeman. I did not have the temperament, or the discipline. True, I had other talents – a tenacity, a need to discover and understand – but those were not enough to enable me to survive in that environment. I lacked also one other crucial element: distance. I did not have the defense mechanisms in place that enabled my peers to look upon a dead body and see it only as that: not a human being, not a person, but the absence of being, the negation of life. On a superficial but ultimately necessary level, a process of dehumanization needs to occur for the police to do their job. Its hallmarks are mortuary humor and apparent detachment, enabling them to refer to a found corpse as a 'body dump' or 'trash' (except in the case of a fallen comrade, for that is so close to home as to make distance impossible), to examine wounds and mutilation without descending, weeping, into a void that makes life and death impossible to bear. Their duty is to the living, to those left behind, and to the law.

I did not have that. I have never had that. Instead, I have learned to embrace the dead, and they, in their turn, have found a way to reach out to me. Now, in this hotel room, far from home, faced with the death of another young woman, Cassie Blythe's disappearance troubled me once more. I was tempted to call the Blythes, but what would I have said? Down here I could do nothing for them, and the fact that I was thinking about their daughter would provide cold comfort for them. I wanted to be finished in South Carolina, to check the witness statements and assure myself of Atys Jones's safety, however tentative it might be, then return home. I could do no more than that for Elliot.

But now Marianne Larousse's body was beckoning me with a strange intimacy, demanding that I bear witness, that I understand the nature of that with which I was involving myself, and the possible consequences of my intervention.

I did not want to look. I was tired of looking.

Yet I looked.

The sorrow of it; the terrible, crushing sorrow of it.

It is the photographs that do it, sometimes. You never truly forget. They stay with you always. You turn a corner, drive past a boarded-up storefront, maybe a garden that's become overgrown with weeds, the house behind it rotting like a bad tooth because nobody wants to live there; because the stink of death is still in the house; because the landlord got some immigrant laborers and paid them $50 each to hose it down and they used whatever piss-poor materials they had to hand: lousy disinfectants and dirty mops that spread rather than eradicated the stench, that turned the logic of bloodstains into a chaotic smear of half-remembered violence, a swath of darkness across the white walls. Then they painted it with cheap, watery paints, running the rollers over the tainted parts two or three times more than the rest, but when the paint dried it was still there: a bloody hand that had wiped itself through the whites and creams and yellows and left the memory of its passing ingrained in the wood and plaster.

So the landlord locks the door, bars the windows, and waits until people forget or until someone too desperate or dumb to care agrees to pay a cut-price rent and he accepts it, if only to try to erase the memory of what has taken place there with the problems and worries of a new family, a kind of psychic cleansing that might succeed where the immigrants have failed.

You could go inside, if you chose. You could show your badge and explain that this was routine, that old unsolved cases are rechecked after a few years have passed in the hope that the passage of time might have revealed some previously undiscovered detail. But you don't need to go inside, because you were there on the night that they found her. You saw what was left of her on the kitchen floor, or in the garden among the shrubs, or draped across the bed. You saw how, with the last breath of air that left her body, something else had passed away too, the thing that gave her substance, a kind of inner framework wrenched somehow through her body without damaging the skin, so that now she has crumpled and faded even as she has swollen, the woman both expanding and contracting as you watch, marks already appearing on her skin where the insects have begun to feed, because the insects always get there before you do.

And then maybe you have to find a photo. Sometimes, the husband or the mother, the father or the lover, will hunt it down for you, and you're watching as their hands move across the pages of the album, through the shoe box or the purse, and you're thinking: Did they do this thing? Did they reduce this person to what I'm seeing now? Or maybe you know that they did it – you can't tell how, exactly, but you just know – and this touching of the relics of a lost life seems somehow like a second violation, one that you should stop with a sweep of your hand because you failed once and now, now you have the chance to make up for that failure.

But you don't do it, not then. You wait, and you hope that with the waiting will come the proof or the confession, and the first steps can be taken toward restoring a moral order, a balance between the needs of the living and the demands of the dead. But still, those images will come back to you later, unbidden, and if you're with someone whom you trust, you may say: 'I remember. I remember what happened. I was there. I was a witness, and later I tried to become more than that. I tried to achieve a measure of justice.'

And if you succeeded, if punishment was meted out and the file marked accordingly, you may feel a twinge of – not pleasure, not that, but of . . . peace? Relief? Maybe what you feel doesn't have a name, shouldn't have a name. Maybe it is only the silence of your conscience, because this time it isn't screaming out a name in your head and you won't have to go back and pull the file to remind yourself again of that suffering, that death, and your failure to maintain the balance that is required if life and time are not to cease forever.

Case closed: isn't that the phrase? It's been so long, it seems, since you've had call to use it, to taste the falsity of the words even as they are forming on your tongue and passing through your lips. Case closed. Except it isn't closed, for the absence continues to be felt in the lives of those left behind, in the hundred thousand tiny adjustments required to account for that absence, for the life, acknowledged or unacknowledged, that should be impacting on other lives. Irv Blythe, for all his faults, understood that. There is no closure. There are only lives continued or lives ended, with attendant consequences in each case. At least the living are no longer your concern. It is the dead that stay with you.

And maybe you spread the photos and think: I remember.

I remember you.

I have not forgotten.

You will not be forgotten.

She was lying on her back on a bed of crushed spider lilies, the dying white blooms of the plants like starburst flaws upon the print, as if the negative itself had been sullied by its exposure to this act. Marianne Larousse's skull had suffered massive damage. Her scalp had been lacerated in two places at either side of her central parting, hairs and fibrous strands crossing in the wounds. A third blow had broken through the right side of her cranium, and the autopsy had revealed fracture lines extending through the base of the skull and the upper edge of the left eye socket. Her face was completely red with blood, for the scalp is very vascular and bleeds profusely after damage, and her nose had been broken. Her eyes were tightly closed and her features contorted, wincing against the force of the blows.

I flipped forward to the autopsy report. There were no bite marks, bruises, or abrasions to Marianne Larousse's body consistent with sexual assault, but foreign hairs recovered from the victim's pubic hair were found to have come from Atys Jones. There was redness around Marianne's genitals – a result of recent sexual contact – but no internal or external bruising or laceration, although traces of lubricant were found in the vaginal canal. Jones's semen was mixed in with her pubic hair, but no semen was found inside her. Jones told the investigators, just as Elliot had told me, that they regularly used condoms during intercourse.

Tests showed fibers matching Marianne Larousse's clothes on Atys Jones's sweater and jeans, while acrylic fibers from his car seat were found in turn on her blouse and skirt, along with cotton fibers from his clothing. According to the analysis, the chances that the fibers had a different origin were remote. Over twenty matches had been found in each case. Five or six would usually be enough for relative certainty.

The evidence still didn't convince me that Marianne Larousse had been raped before she died, but then I wasn't the one that the prosecutors would be trying to convince. Her blood alcohol levels were above normal, so a good prosecutor could argue that she was probably not in a position to fend off a strong young man like Atys Jones. In addition, Jones had used a condom and lubricant, and the lubricant would have reduced the level of physical damage to his victim.

What could not be denied was that Marianne Larousse's blood had been found on Jones's face and hands when he entered the bar to call for help, and that mixed in with it were found dust fragments from the rock used to kill her. The bloodstain analysis of the area around Marianne Larousse's body revealed medium-velocity impact splatter, the blood droplets radially distributed away from the impact site both above and beyond her head and to one side where the final, fatal blow was delivered. Her assailant would have received blood splatter to the lower legs, the hands, and possibly the face and upper body. There was no apparent blood splatter on Jones's legs (although his jeans had been soaked through from kneeling in Marianne Larousse's blood, so the splatter could well have been absorbed or obscured), and the blood on his face and hands had been wiped too much to reveal traces of any original splatter pattern.

According to Jones's statement, he and Marianne Larousse had met that night at nine o'clock. She had already been drinking with friends in Columbia, then had driven to the Swamp Rat to join him. Witnesses saw them talking together, then they left side by side. One witness, a barfly named J. D. Herrin, admitted to police that he had hurled racial epithets at Jones shortly before the two young people left the bar. He timed his abuse at about ten after eleven.

Jones told police that he then proceeded to have sexual intercourse with Marianne Larousse in the passenger seat of his car, she on top, he seated beneath her. After intercourse, an argument had commenced, caused in part by a discussion of J.

D. Herrin's abuse and centering on whether or not Marianne Larousse was ashamed to be with him. Marianne had stormed off, but instead of taking her car she had run into the woods. Jones claimed that she started to laugh and called for him to follow her to the creek, but he was too angry with her to do so. Only after ten minutes had passed and she had failed to return did Jones follow her. He found her about one hundred feet down the trail. She was already dead. He claimed to have heard nothing in the intervening period: no screams, no sounds of struggle. He didn't remember touching her body, but figured that he must have since he got blood on his hands. He also admitted that he must have handled the rock, which he later recalled as lying against the side of her head. He then went back to the bar and the police were called. He was interviewed by agents from SLED, the State Law Enforcement Division, initially without the benefit of a lawyer since he had not been arrested or charged with any crime. After the interview, he was arrested on suspicion of the murder of Marianne Larousse. He was given a court-appointed lawyer, who later stepped aside in favor of Elliot Norton.

And that was where I came in.

I ran my fingers gently across her face, the indentations in the photographic paper like the pores on her skin. I'm sorry, I thought. I didn't know you. I have no way of telling if you were a good person or a bad one. If I had met you, encountered you in a bar or sat beside you in a coffee shop, would we have got on together, even if only in that small, passing way in which two lives may briefly interlock before continuing, somehow both altered yet unchanged, on their own paths, one of those small, flickering moments of contact between strangers that make this life liveable? I suspect not. We were, I think, very different. But you did not deserve to end your life in this way, and if I could, I would have intervened to stop what occurred, even at the risk of my own life, because I could not have stood by and allowed even you, a stranger, to suffer. Now I will try to retrace your steps, to understand what led you to this place, to rest at last among crushed lilies, the night insects drowning in your blood.

I'm sorry that I have to do this thing. People will be hurt by my intervention, and elements of your past may be revealed that you might have wished to remain undisclosed. All I can promise you is that whoever did this will not walk away and will not be allowed to go unpunished because of any action that I may take.

In all of this, I will remember you.

In all of this, you will not be forgotten.

11

I called the number on the Upper West Side the next morning. Louis picked up.

'You still coming down here?'

'Uh-huh. Be down in a couple of days.'

'How's Angel?'

'Quiet. How you doin'?'

'Same old same old.'

'That bad?'

I had just spoken to Rachel. Hearing her voice had made me feel alone and had renewed my concern for her now that she was so far away.

'I have a favor to ask,' I said.

'Ask away. Askin' is free.'

'You know someone who could stay with Rachel for a while, at least until I get back?'

'She ain't goin' to like it.'

'Maybe you could send someone who wouldn't care.'

There was a silence as he considered the problem. When he eventually spoke, I could almost hear him smile.

'You know, I got just the guy.'

I spent the morning making calls, then drove up to Wateree and spoke to one of the Richland County deputies who had been first on the scene the night Marianne Larousse was killed. It was a pretty short conversation. He confirmed the details in his report but it was clear that he believed Atys Jones was guilty and that I was trying to pervert the course of justice by even speaking to him about the case.

I then headed on up to Columbia and spent some time speaking with a special agent named Richard Brewer at the headquarters of SLED. It was SLED special agents that had investigated the murder, as they did all homicides committed in the state of South Carolina, with the occasional exception of those that occurred within the jurisdiction of the Charleston PD.

'They like to think of themselves as independent down there,' said Brewer. 'We call it the Republic of Charleston.'

Brewer was about my age, with straw-colored hair and a jock's build. He wore standard-issue SLED gear: green combats, a black T-shirt with 'SLED' in green letters on the back, and a Glock 40 on his belt. He was one of the team of agents that had worked the case. He was a little more forthcoming than the deputy but could add little to what I already knew. Atys Jones was virtually alone in the world, he said, with only a few distant relatives left alive. He had a job packing shelves at a Piggly Wiggly and lived in a small one-bed walk-up in Kingville that was now occupied by a family of Ukrainian immigrants.

'That boy,' he said, shaking his head. 'He had few people in this world to care about him before this, and he has a whole lot fewer now.'

'You think he did it?'

'Jury will decide that. Off the record, I don't see no other candidates on the horizon.'

'And it was you that spoke to the Larousses?' Their statements were among the material Elliot had passed on to me.

'Father and son, plus the staff at their house. They all had alibis. We're pretty professional here, Mr. Parker. We covered all the bases. I don't think you'll find too many holes in them there reports.'

I thanked him and he gave me his card in case I had any other questions.

'You got yourself a hard job, Mr. Parker,' he said as I stood to leave. 'I reckon you're going to be about as popular as shit in summertime.'

'It'll be a new experience for me.'

He raised a skeptical eyebrow.

'You know, I find that hard to believe.'

Back at my hotel, I spoke to the people at the Pine Point Co-op about Bear, and they confirmed that he had arrived on time the day before and had worked about as hard as a man could be expected to work. They still sounded a little nervous, so I asked them to put Bear on the line.

'How you doing, Bear?'

'Okay.' He reconsidered. 'Good, I'm doing good. I like it here. I get to work on boats.'

'Glad to hear it. Listen, Bear, I have to say this: you screw this up, or cause these people any trouble, and I'll personally hunt you down and drag you to the cops, you understand?'

'Sure.' He didn't sound aggrieved or hurt. I figured Bear was used to people warning him not to screw up. It was just a question of whether or not he took it in.

'Okay, then,' I said.

'I won't screw up,' he confirmed. 'I like these people.'

After I hung up on Bear, I spent an hour in the hotel gym, followed by as many lengths of the pool as I could manage without cramping and drowning. Afterward, I showered and reread those sections of the case file that Elliot and I had discussed the night before. I kept coming back to two items: the story, photocopied from an out-of-print local history, of the death of the trunk minder Henry; and the disappearance, two decades before, of Atys Jones's mother and aunt. Their pictures stared out at me from the newspaper clippings, two women forever frozen in their late teens and vanished from a world that had largely forgotten about them, until now.

As evening approached, I left the hotel and had coffee and a muffin in the Pinckney Café. While I waited for Elliot to arrive, I leafed through a copy of the *Post and Courier* that somebody had abandoned. One story in particular caught my eye: a warrant had been issued for the arrest of a former prison guard named

Landron Mobley after he had missed a hearing of the corrections committee in connection with allegations of 'improper relationships' with female prisoners. The only reason the story attracted my attention was that Landron Mobley had hired one Elliot Norton to represent him at both the hearing and what was expected to be a subsequent rape trial. I mentioned the case to Elliot when he arrived fifteen minutes later.

'Old Landron's a piece of work,' said Elliot. 'He'll turn up, eventually.'

'Doesn't seem like a high-class client,' I commented.

Elliot glanced at the story, then pushed it away, although he still seemed to feel that some further explanation was necessary.

'I knew him when I was younger, so I guess that's why he came to me. And hey, every man is entitled to representation, doesn't matter how guilty he is.'

He raised his finger to the waitress for the check, but there was something about the movement, something too hurried, that indicated Landron Mobley had just ceased to be a welcome topic of conversation between us.

'Let's go,' he said. 'Least I know where one of my clients is at.'

The Richland County Detention Center stood at the end of John Mark Dial Road, about one hundred miles northwest of Charleston, the approach marked by the offices of bondsmen and attorneys. It was a complex of low redbrick buildings surrounded by two rows of fencing topped with razor wire. Its windows were long and narrow, overlooking the parking lot and the woods beyond on one side. The inner fence was electrified.

There wasn't a great deal that we could do to prevent the knowledge of Atys Jones's impending release from reaching the media, so it wasn't too much of a surprise to find a camera crew and a handful of journalists and photographers in the parking lot, drinking coffee and smoking cigarettes. I had gone on ahead of Elliot and had been watching them for about fifteen minutes by the time Elliot's car appeared. Nothing exciting had happened to either them or me in the interim, apart from one brief flurry of domestic theater when an unhappy wife, a small, dainty woman in high heels and a blue dress, arrived to collect her husband after he'd spent some time cooling his heels in a cell. He had blood on his shirt and beer stains on his pants as he emerged blinking into the fading light of the early evening, at which point his wife slapped him once across the head and gave him the benefit of her wide and pretty profane vocabulary. He looked like he wanted to run back to jail and lock himself in his cell, especially when he saw all the cameras and thought, for one brief moment, that they'd come for him.

The media pounced on Elliot as soon as he stepped from his car, then tried to block his way again when he came out twenty minutes later through the wired tunnel that led into the jail's reception area, his arm around the shoulders of a young man with light brown skin who kept his head low and his baseball cap pulled down almost to the bridge of his nose. Elliot didn't even dignify them with a 'No comment.' Instead, he thrust the young man into the car and they drove away at speed. The more sensationalist members of the fourth estate raced to their vehicles to follow him.

I was already in place. I waited until Elliot had passed me, then kept close behind him as far as the exit road, at which point I gave the wheel a good spin and managed to block both lanes before stepping from the car. The TV van ground to a halt a few feet from my door and a cameraman in jungle fatigues opened the driver's door and started screaming at me to get out of his way.

I examined my nails. They were nice and short. I tried to keep them neat. Neatness was a very underrated virtue.

'You hear me? Get the fuck out of the way,' yelled Combat Man. His face was turning a bright shade of red. Behind his van I could see more media types congregating as they tried to figure out what all the fuss was about. A small group of young black males in low-slung jeans and Wu Wear shirts emerged from a bondsman's office and wandered down to enjoy the show.

Combat Man, tired of shouting and achieving no result, stormed toward me. He was overweight and in his late forties. His clothing looked kind of ludicrous on him. The black guys started in on him almost immediately.

'Yo, GI Joe, where the war at?'

'Vietnam over, motherfucker. You gotta let it go. You can't be livin' in the past.'

Combat Man shot them a look of pure hatred. He stopped about a foot from me and leaned in until our noses were almost touching.

'The fuck are you doing?' he asked.

'Blocking the road.'

'I can see that. Why?'

'So you can't get through.'

'Don't get smart with me. You move your car or I'll drive my van through it.'

Over his shoulder I could see some prison guards emerging from the lockup, probably on their way to see what all the fuss was about. It was time to go. By the time the reporters got on to the main road, it would be too late for them to find Elliot and Atys. Even if they did find the car, their quarry would not be in it.

'Okay,' I told Combat Man. 'You win.'

He seemed a little taken aback.

'That's it?'

'Sure.'

He shook his head in frustration.

'By the way—'

He looked up at me.

'Those kids are stealing stuff from the back of your van.'

I let the media convoy get well ahead of me, then drove along Bluff Road, past the Zion Mill Creek Baptist Church and the

United Methodist, until I reached Campbell's Country Corner at the intersection of Bluff and Pineview. The bar had a corrugated roof and barred windows and didn't look a whole lot different in principle from the county lockup, except that you could order a drink and walk away anytime you wanted. It advertised 'Cold Beer at Low Prices,' held a turkey shoot Fridays and Saturdays, and was a popular stopping-off point for those enjoying their first alcoholic taste of freedom. A hand-lettered sign warned patrons against bringing in their own beer.

I turned onto Pineview, past the side of the bar and a yellow lock-up storage garage, and saw a shack standing in the middle of an overgrown yard. Behind the shack a white GMC 4x4 was waiting, into which Elliot and Atys had been transferred before Elliot's own car, now being driven by another man, had continued on its way. It pulled out of the lot as I appeared, and I stayed a few cars behind it as it headed along Bluff toward 26. The plan was that we would drive Jones straight into Charleston and take him to the safe house. It was kind of a surprise, then, to see Elliot make a left into the lot of Betty's Diner before he even reached the highway, open the passenger door, and allow Jones to walk ahead of him into the restaurant. I parked the Neon in back then followed them inside, trying to look casual and unconcerned.

Betty's Diner was a small room with a counter to the left of the door, behind which two black women took orders while two men worked the grills. It was furnished with plastic garden tables and chairs, and the windows were obscured by both blinds and bars. Two TVs played simultaneously and the air was thick with the smell of fried foods and oil. Elliot and Jones were sitting at a table at the back of the room.

'Do you want to tell me what you're doing?' I asked when I reached them.

Elliot looked embarrassed.

'He said he needed to eat,' he stammered. 'He was cramping. Said he was going to collapse on me if he didn't eat. He even threatened to jump from the car.'

'Elliot, step outside and you can still hear the echo of his cell door closing. Any closer and he'd be eating prison food again.'

Atys Jones spoke for the first time. His voice was higher than I expected, as if it had broken only recently instead of over half a decade before.

'Fuck you, man, I got to eat,' he said.

He had a thin face, so light in color as to be almost Hispanic, and nervous, darting eyes. His head stayed low when he spoke, and he looked up at me from under his cap. Despite his bluster, his spirit had been broken. Atys Jones was about as tough as a pinãta. Hit him hard enough and candy would come out his ass. Still, it didn't make his manners any easier to take.

'You were right,' I told Elliot. 'He's quite the charmer. You couldn't have picked someone a little less irritating to save?'

'I tried, but the Little Orphan Annie case was already taken.'

'The fuck—'

Jones was about to launch into a predictable tirade. I raised a finger at him.

'Stop right now. You swear at me again and that salt shaker is as close as you'll get to a meal.'

He backed down.

'I didn't eat nothing in jail. I was scared.'

I felt a stab of guilt and shame. He was a frightened young man with a dead girlfriend and the memory of her blood on his hands. His fate was in the hands of two white men and a jury that would most likely redefine the word 'hostile.' All things considered, he was doing well just to be sitting upright with dry eyes.

'Please, man,' he said. 'Just let me eat.'

I sighed. From the window where we sat I could see the road, the 4x4, and anybody approaching on foot. Even if somebody had taken it into his mind to hurt Jones, he wasn't going to do it in Betty's Diner. Elliot and I were the only white folk in the place, and the handful of people at the other tables were very deliberately ignoring our presence. If we saw any journalists, I could take him out the back way, assuming Betty's had a back way. Maybe I was overreacting.

'Whatever,' I conceded. 'Just be quick about it.'

It was pretty obvious that Jones hadn't eaten much during his time in jail. His cheeks were hollow, his eyes sunken, and spots and boils had erupted on his face and neck. He devoured a plate of smothered porkchops with rice, green beans, and macaroni and cheese, then followed it with a slice of strawberry cream cake. Elliot nibbled at some fries while I stuck with coffee from the Mr. Coffee machine on the counter. When we were done, Elliot left Jones with me and went to pay the check.

Jones's left hand lay flat upon the table, its only adornment a cheap Timex. His right hung on the stainless steel cross around his neck. It was T-shaped, and both its vertical and horizontal shafts appeared hollow. I reached out to touch it, but he drew back and there was something in his eyes that I didn't like.

'What you doin'?'

'I just wanted to take a look at your cross.'

'It's mine. I don't want nobody else touchin' it.'

'Atys,' I said softly. 'Let me see the cross.'

He held on to it for a moment longer, then uttered a long '*Shiiiit*.' He lifted the cross from around his neck and let it fall gently into the palm of my hand. I dangled it from my fingers, then gave the shaft an experimental twist. It came loose in my hand. I let it fall to the table, exposing a two-inch length of sharpened steel. I clasped the 'T' in the palm of my hand, closed my fist and left the point sticking out between my middle and ring fingers.

'Where did you get this?'

The sunlight danced on the blade, reflecting in Jones's eyes and face. He was reluctant to answer.

'Atys,' I said, 'I don't know you, but you're already starting to bug me. Answer the question.'

He did some theatrical head shaking before he answered.

'Preacher gave it to me.'

'The chaplain?'

Jones shook his head. 'No, one of the ministers comes to the jail. Tole me he was a prisoner too, once, 'cept the Lord set him free.'

'Did he say why he was giving this to you?'

'Tole me he knowed I was in trouble, knowed there was people tryin' to kill me. Tole me that it would protect me.'

'He give you his name?'

'Tereus.'

'What did he look like?'

Jones met my eyes for the first time since I had taken the cross.

'He looked like me,' he replied, simply. 'He looked like a man seen trouble.'

I replaced the shaft, covered the blade, then after a moment's hesitation handed it back to him. He looked surprised, then nodded at me once in acknowledgment.

'If we do this right, then you won't need it,' I said. 'And if we screw up, maybe you'll be glad of it.'

With that, Elliot returned and we left. Neither of us mentioned the knife to him. This time, there were no more stops, and nobody followed us as we made our way to Charleston and the East Side.

The East Side neighborhood was one of the original developments outside the old walled city, and had always been unsegregated. Blacks and whites shared the warren of streets bordered by Meeting and East Bay to the west and east, and the Crosstown Expressway and Mary Street to the north and south, although even in the mid-nineteenth century the black population was higher than the white. Working-class blacks, whites, and immigrants continued to live together on the East Side until after World War II, when the whites moved to the suburbs west of the Ashley. From then on, the East Side became a place into which you didn't want to stray if you were white. Poverty took root, bringing with it the seeds of violence and drug abuse.

But the East Side was changing once again. Areas south of Calhoun Street and Judith Street that had once been exclusively black were now nearly all white, and wealthily so, and the wave of urban renewal and gentrification was also breaking on the southern verges of the East Side. Six years before, the average price of a house in the area was about $18,000. Now there were houses on Mary Street making $250,000; and even homes on Columbus and Amherst, close to the small park where the drug dealers congregated and within sight of the brownstone projects and yellow-and-orange public housing, were selling for two or three times what they were worth only half a decade before. But this was still, for the present, a black neighborhood, the houses painted in faded pastels, relics of the days without air-conditioning. The Piggly Wiggly grocery store at Columbia and Meeting, the yellow Money Man pawn shop across from it, the cut price liquor store nearby all spoke of lives far removed from those of the wealthy whites returning to the old streets.

The faces of the young men at the corners and the old people on their porches regarded us warily as we drove: a black man and a white man in one car, being tailed by a white man in a second car. We might not have been Five-O, but whatever we were we were still bad news. At the corner of American and Reid, on the side of a two-room house erected as some kind of art exhibit, someone had written the following lines:

'The Afro-American has been heir to the myths that it is better to be poor than rich, lower-class rather than middle or upper, easygoing rather than industrious, extravagant rather than thrifty, and athletic rather than academic.'

I didn't know the source of the quotation, and neither did Elliot when I asked him about it later. Atys had apparently just looked blankly at the words on the wall. I guess he probably already knew all that it said from experience. Around us, hydrangeas were in bloom, and heavenly bamboo grew by the front steps of a neat two-story house on Drake Street, midway between a ruined building at the junction of Drake and Amherst and the Fraser Elementary at the corner of Columbus. It was painted white with yellow trim, and there were shutters drawn on both the upper and lower floors, slatted on the top floor to let the air in. A bay window faced out onto the street from beneath the porch, with the front doorway to the right, a mass-produced carved wood pattern above it for decoration. A flight of five stone steps led up to the door.

When he was certain the street was quiet, Elliot backed the GMC into the yard to the right of the doorway. I heard the sound of the doors opening, then footsteps as Atys and Elliot entered the house from the rear. Drake seemed largely empty apart from two small kids playing ball by the railings of the school. They remained there until it began to rain, the raindrops glittering in the glow of the streetlamps that had just begun to shine, then ran for shelter. I waited ten minutes, the rain falling hard on the car, until I was certain that we hadn't been followed, before I too headed into the house.

Atys – I was forcing myself to think of him by his first name in an effort to establish some kind of connection with him – sat uncomfortably at a cheap pine kitchen table, Elliot beside him. By the sink, an elderly black woman with silver hair was pouring five glasses of lemonade. Her husband, who was a lot taller than she was, held the glasses as she poured, then passed them, one by one, to their guests. His shoulders were slightly stooped, but the strength of his deltoid and trapezius muscles was still apparent from their definition beneath his white shirt. He was well over sixty years old, but I guessed that he could have taken Atys easily in a straight fight. He could probably have taken me.

'Devil and wife fighting,' he said, as I shook the rain from my jacket. I must have looked puzzled, because he repeated himself, then pointed out the window at the rain and sunlight mingling.

'De wedduh,' he said. 'Een yah cuh, seh-down.'

Elliot grinned at the incomprehension on my face. 'Gullah,' he explained. Gullah was the term commonly used to describe the language and the people of the coastal islands, many of them the descendants of slaves who had been given island land and abandoned rice fields to settle in the aftermath of the Civil War.

'Ginnie and Albert used to live out on Yonges Island, but then Ginnie got sick and one of their sons, Samuel, the one who's taking care of my car, insisted they move back to Charleston. They've been here ten years now, and I still don't get some of what they say, but they're good people. They know what they're doing. He's asking you to come in and sit down.'

I accepted the lemonade, thanked them, then took Atys by the shoulder into the small living room. Elliot seemed like he was about to follow me, but I indicated that I wanted a minute or two alone with his client. Elliot didn't look too happy about it, but he stayed where he was.

Atys sat down on the very edge of the sofa, as if he were preparing to make a break for the door at any moment. He wouldn't meet my eye. I sat opposite him in an overstuffed armchair.

'You know why I'm here?' I asked.

He shrugged. ''Cause you bein' paid to be here.'

I smiled. 'There's that. Mostly, I'm here because Elliot doesn't believe that you killed Marianne Larousse. A lot of other people do, though, so it's going to be my job to maybe find evidence to prove them wrong. I can only do that if you help me.'

He licked his lips. There was sweat beading on his forehead. 'They goan kill me,' he said.

'Who's going to kill you?'

'Larousses. Don't matter if they do it theyselves or get the state to do it, they still goan kill me.'

'Not if we can prove them wrong.'

'Yeah, and how you goan do that?'

I hadn't figured that out yet, but talking to this young man was a first step.

'How did you meet Marianne Larousse?' I asked.

He sank back heavily into the sofa, resigned now to speaking of what had occurred.

'She was a student in Columbia.'

'I don't see you as the student type, Atys.'

'Shit, no. I sold weed to them motherfuckers. They like to score.'

'Did she know who you were?'

'No, she didn't know shit about me.'

'But you knew who she was?'

''S right.'

'You know about your past, about the problems between your family and the Larousses.'

'That's old shit.'

'But you know about it.'

'Yeah, I know.'

'She come on to you, or did you come on to her?'

He blushed and his face broke into a shit-eating grin. 'Oh man, y'know, she was smokin' and I was smokin' and, s'like, shit happened.'

'When did this start?'

'January, maybe February.'

'And you were with her all that time?'

'I was with her some. She went away in June. I didn't see her from end of May until week, maybe two weeks before . . .' His voice trailed off.

'Did her family know she was seeing you?'

'Maybe. She didn't tell them nothin', but shit gets out.'

'Why were you with her?'

He didn't answer.

'Because she was pretty? Because she was white? Because she was a Larousse?'

There was just a shrug in reply.

'Maybe all three?'

'I guess.'

'Did you like her?'

A muscle trembled in his cheek.

'Yeah, I liked her.'

I let it rest. 'What happened on the night she died?'

Atys's face seemed to fall, all of the confidence and front disappearing from it like a mask yanked away to reveal the true expression beneath. I knew then for certain that he hadn't killed her, for the pain was too real, and I guessed that what might have started out as a means of getting back at some half-sensed enemy had developed, at least on his side, into affection, and perhaps something more.

'We was screwing around in my car, out at the Swamp Rat by Congaree. Folks there don't give a shit what you do, 'long as you got money and you ain't a cop.'

'You had sex?'

'Yeah, we had sex.'

'Protected?'

'She was on the pill and, like, I been tested and shit, but yeah, she still like me to use a rubber.'

'Did that bother you?'

'What are you, man, stupid? You ever fucked with a rubber? It ain't the same. It's like . . . ' He struggled for the comparison.

'Wearing your shoes in the bathtub.'

For the first time he smiled and a little of the ice broke.

'Yeah, 'cept I ain't never had a bath that good.'

'Go on.'

'We started arguing.'

'About what?'

'About how maybe she was ashamed of me, didn't want to be seen with me. Y'know, we was always fuckin' in cars, or in my crib if she got drunk enough not to care. Rest of the time, she drift by me like I don't exist.'

'Did this argument turn violent?'

'No, I never touched her. Ever. But she start screamin' and shoutin', and next thing I know, she's runnin' away. I was goan just let her go, m'sayin, let her cool off and shit? Then I went after her, callin' her name.

'Then I found her.'

He swallowed and placed his hands behind his head. His lips narrowed. He seemed on the verge of tears.

'What did you see?'

'Her face, man, it was all busted in. Her nose . . . There was just blood. I tried to lift her, tried to brush away her hair from her face, but she was gone. There was nothin' I could do for her. She was gone.'

And now he was crying, his right knee pumping up and down like a piston with the grief and rage that he was still suppressing.

'We're nearly done,' I said.

He nodded and wiped away his tears with a sharp, embarrassed jerk of his arm.

'Did you see anybody, anyone at all, who might have done this to her?'

'No, man, nobody.'

And for the first time, he lied. I watched his eyes, saw them look up and away from me for an instant before he answered.

'You sure?'

'Yeah, I'm sure.'

'I don't believe you.'

He was about to give me outraged when I reached across and raised a finger in warning before him.

'What did you see?'

His mouth opened and closed twice without producing any sound, then: 'I thought I saw something, but I'm not sure.'

'Tell me.'

He nodded, more to himself than to me.

'I thought I saw a woman. She was all in white, and movin' away into the trees. But when I looked closer, there was nothin' there. It could have been the river, I guess, with the light shinin' on it.'

'Did you tell the police?' There had been no mention of a woman in the reports.

'They said I was lyin'.'

And he was still lying. Even now, he was holding back, but I knew I was going to get nothing more from him for the present.

I sat back in the chair, then passed him the police reports. We went through them for a time, but he could find nothing to question beyond their implicit assumption of his guilt.

He stood as I placed the reports back in their file. 'We done?'

'For now.'

He moved a couple of steps, then stopped before he reached the door.

'They took me past the death house,' he said softly.

'What?'

'When they was takin' me to Richland, they drove me to Broad River and they showed me the death house.'

The state's capital punishment facility was located at the Broad River Correctional Institution in Columbia, close by the reception and evaluation center. In a move that combined psychological torture with democracy, prisoners convicted of capital crimes prior to 1995 were allowed to choose between electrocution and lethal injection as their final punishment. All others were executed by injection, as Atys Jones would be if the state succeeded in its efforts to convict him of Marianne's murder.

'They tole me I was goan be strapped down and then they was goan inject poisons into me, and that I'd be dying inside but I wouldn't be able to move or cry out none. They tole me it be like suffocatin' slow.'

There was nothing I could say.

'I didn't kill Marianne,' he said.

'I know you didn't.'

'But they goan kill me for it anyhow.'

His resignation made me feel cold inside.

'We can stop that from happening, if you help us.'

But he just shook his head and loped back to the kitchen. Elliot entered the room seconds later.

'What do you think?' he asked in a whisper.

'He's holding something back,' I replied. 'He'll give it to us, in time.'

'We don't have that kind of time,' snapped Elliot.

As I followed him into the kitchen, I could see the muscles bunched beneath his shirt, and his hands flexing and unflexing by his sides. He turned his attention to Albert.

'You need anything?'

'Us hab 'nuff bittle,' said Albert.

'I don't mean just food. You need more money? A gun?'

The woman slammed her glass down on the table and shook her finger at Elliot.

'Don' pit mout' on us,' she said firmly.

'They think having a gun in the house will bring them bad luck,' Elliot said.

'They may be right. What do they do if there's trouble?'

'Samuel lives with them, and I suspect he has less trouble with guns than they have. I've given them all our numbers. If anything goes wrong, they'll call one of us. Just make sure you keep your phone with you.'

I thanked them both for the lemonade, then followed Elliot to the door.

'You leavin' me here?' cried Atys. 'With these two?'

'Dat boy ent hab no mannus,' scolded the old woman. 'Dat boy gwi' punish fuh'e wickitty.' She poked at Atys with his finger. 'Debblement weh dat chile lib.'

'Get off me,' he retorted, but he looked kind of worried.

'Be good, Atys,' said Elliot. 'Watch some TV, get some sleep. Mr. Parker will check on you tomorrow.'

Atys raised his eyes to mine in a last, desperate plea.

'Shit,' he said, 'by tomorrow these two probably have eaten me.'

When we left him, the old woman had just started poking him again. Outside, we passed their son, Samuel, on the way back to the house. He was a tall, handsome man, my age or a little younger, with large brown eyes. Elliot introduced us and we shook hands.

'Any trouble?' asked Elliot.

'None,' Samuel confirmed. 'I parked outside your office. Keys are on top of the right rear wheel.'

Elliot thanked him and he headed toward the house.

'You sure he'll be okay with them?' I asked Elliot.

'They're smart, like their boy, and the folks round here look out for them. Any strangers come sniffing down this street and half the young bucks will be following them before they have a chance to get their shoes dirty. As long as he's here, and no one finds out about it, he'll be safe.'

The same faces watched us leave their streets and I thought that maybe Elliot was right. Maybe they would take account of strangers coming into their neighborhood.

I just wasn't sure that it would be enough to keep Atys Jones safe from harm.

12

Elliot and I exchanged a few words outside the house, then parted. Before we did, he handed me a newspaper from the backseat of his car.

'Since you been reading the newspapers so closely, you happen to see this?'

The story was buried in the lifestyles section and headlined 'In the Midst of Tragedy, Charity.' The Larousses were hosting a charity lunch in the grounds of an old plantation house on the western shore of Lake Marion later that week, one of two large houses that the family owned. From the list of expected guests, half the grandees in the state were going to be there.

'While still mourning the death of his beloved daughter Marianne,' the report read, 'Earl Larousse, his son Earl Jr. by his side, said that "we have a duty to those less fortunate than ourselves that even the loss of Marianne cannot absolve." The charity lunch, in aid of cancer research, will be the first public engagement for the Larousse family since the murder of Marianne, 19, last July.'

I handed the paper back to Elliot.

'You can bet that there'll be judges and prosecutors there, probably the governor too,' he said. 'They should just hold the trial right there on the lawn and get done with it.'

Elliot told me he had business to conclude back at his office, and we agreed to meet again over the next day or two to discuss progress and options. I followed his car as far as Charleston Place, then peeled off and parked. I showered in my room and called Rachel. She was just about to head into South Portland for a reading at Nonesuch Books. She'd mentioned it to me a couple of days earlier, but I'd forgotten about it until now.

'An interesting thing happened today,' she said, giving me just enough time to get the word 'hi' out of my mouth. 'I opened the front door and there was a man on my doorstep. A big man. A very big, very black man.'

'Rachel—'

'You said it would be discreet. His T-shirt had the words "Klan Killer" written on the front.'

'I—'

'And do you know what he said?'

I waited.

'He handed me a note from Louis and told me he was lactose intolerant. That was it. Note. Lactose intolerant. Nothing else. He's coming to the reading with me. It was all I could do to get him to change his T-shirt. The new one reads "Black Death". I'm going to tell people it's a rap band. Do you think it's a rap band?'

I figured it was probably his occupation, but I didn't say that. Instead, I said the only thing I could think of to say.

'Maybe you'd better buy some soya milk.'

She hung up without saying good-bye.

Despite the earlier rain, it was still stiflingly warm when I left the hotel to grab a bite to eat, and I felt as if my clothes were soaked through before I'd walked more than a few blocks. I passed the site of the Confederate Museum, its exterior now surrounded by scaffolding, and headed into the residential district between East Bay and Meeting, admiring the big old houses, the lamps by their doors glowing softly. It was just after ten and the tourists had begun to throng the dive bars on East Bay that sold premixed cocktails in souvenir glasses. Young men and women cruised up and down Broad, rap and nu-metal grinding out insistent, competing beats. Fred Durst, record company vice president, proud father, and multimillionaire, was telling the kids how their parents just didn't understand his generation. There's nothing sadder than a thirty-year-old man in short pants rebelling against his mom and dad.

I was looking for somewhere to eat when I saw a familiar face at the window of Magnolia's. Elliot was sitting across from a woman with jet black hair and tight lips. He was eating, but the pained look on his face told me that he wasn't enjoying his meal, maybe because the woman was clearly unhappy with him. She was leaning across the table, her palms flat upon the cloth, and her eyes were blazing. Elliot gave up trying to feed himself and spread out his hands in a 'Be reasonable' gesture, the one that men use when they're feeling put upon by a woman. It doesn't work, mainly because there's nothing guaranteed to add fuel to the fire of a male-female argument quicker than one party suggesting to the other that she's being unreasonable. True to form, the woman stood up abruptly and walked determinedly from the restaurant. Elliot didn't follow. He sat for a moment looking after her, then shrugged resignedly, picked up his knife and fork, and resumed his meal. The woman, dressed entirely in black, got into an Explorer parked a couple of doors down from the restaurant and drove off into the night. She wasn't crying but her anger lit up the interior of the SUV like a flare. Out of little more than habit I memorized the tag number. I briefly considered joining Elliot but I didn't want him to think that I might have seen the argument, and anyway, I wanted some time alone.

I ended up on Queen Street and ate at Poogan's Porch, a Cajun and low country restaurant that was rumored to be a favorite of Paul Newman and Joanne Woodward, although the celebrity count was zero that night. Poogan's had flowered wallpaper and glass on the tables, and I pretty much had to take one of the staff hostage to keep the ice water coming fast enough to cool me down, but the Cajun duck looked good. Despite my hunger, I barely picked at my food when it arrived. It tasted wrong, but it was not the fault of the chef. A memory flashed: Faulkner spitting in my mouth, the taste of him on my tongue. I pushed the plate away.

'Is there something wrong with your food, sir?'

It was the waiter. I looked up at him but he was blurred, like a Batut photograph in which images of different individuals had been overlaid on one another to create a single composite.

'No,' I said. 'It's fine. I've just lost my appetite.'

I wanted him to go away. I couldn't look at his face. It reminded me of slow decay.

The cockroaches were clicking across the sidewalks when I left the restaurant, the remains of those that had not been quick enough to avoid human footfalls lying scattered in small dark piles, troops of ants already feeding hungrily upon them. I found myself walking down deserted streets watching the lights in the windows of the houses, catching shadow plays of the lives continuing behind the drapes. I missed Rachel and wished that she were with me. I wondered how she was getting along with the Klan Killer, now apparently aka Black Death. Trust Louis to send along the only guy who looked more conspicuous than he did, but at least I was no longer worrying as much about Rachel. I still wasn't even sure how much help I could be to Elliot down here. True, I was curious about the jailhouse preacher who had given Atys Jones the T-bar knife, but it seemed to me that I was somehow adrift from all that was happening, that I had not yet found a way to break the surface and explore the depths beneath, and I still didn't fully share Elliot's faith in the ability of the old Gullah couple and their son to handle any situation that might arise. I found a public phone and checked in with the safe house. The old man answered and confirmed that all was well.

'Mek you duh worry so?' he said. 'Dat po' creetuh, 'e rest.'

I thanked him and was about to hang up when he spoke again.

'Do boy suh'e yent kill de gel, 'e meet de gel so.'

I had to ask him to repeat himself twice before I understood.

'He told you that he didn't kill her? You've talked to him about it?'

'Uh-huh. Uh ax, 'en 'e mek ansuh suh 'e yent do'um.'

'Did he say anything else?'

''E skay'd. 'E skay-to-det.'

'Scared of what?'

'De po-lice. De 'ooman.'

'What woman?'

'De ole people b'leebe sperit walk de nighttime up de Congaree. Dat 'ooman alltime duh fludduh-fedduh.'

Again, I had to get him to repeat himself. Eventually, I managed to figure out that he was talking about spirits.

'You're telling me that there is the ghost of a woman in the Congaree?'

'Uh-huh.'

'And this is the woman Atys saw?'

'Uh yent know puhzac'ly, but uh t'ink so.'

'Do you know who she is?'

'No, suh, I cahn spessify, bud'e duh sleep tuh Gawd-acre.'

God-acre: the cemetery.

I asked him to try to get something more from Atys, because it still seemed to me that he knew more than he was telling. The old man promised to try, but said he wasn't no 'tarrygater'.

By now I was in the French Quarter between Meeting and East Bay. I could hear the sounds of distant traffic, and sometimes raised voices as revelers moved through the night, but around me there was no life.

And then, as I passed by Unity Alley, I heard singing. The voice was a child's, and very lovely. It was singing a version of an old Roba Stanley number, 'Devilish Mary,' but it sounded as if the child didn't know the whole song or else had just decided to sing her favorite part, which was the nursery-rhyme refrain at the end of each verse:

A ring-tuma-ding-tuma dairy
A ring-tuma-ding-tuma dairy
Prettiest girl I ever saw
And her name was Devilish Mary.

The singing stopped, and the girl stepped from the murk of the alleyway to be illuminated by the lamps on the adjoining houses.

'Hey, mister,' she said. 'You got a light?'

I stopped. She was thirteen or fourteen, and wore a short, tight black skirt with no stockings. Her bare legs were very white, and her midriff was exposed beneath a black cutoff T-shirt. Her face, too, was pale, smudged dark with make up around the eyes and wounded by a streak of too-red lipstick around her mouth. She wore high heels, but still stood no taller than five feet as she leaned against the brickwork. Her hair was brown and untidy, and partially obscured her face. The darkness seemed to move around her, as if she were standing beneath a moonlit tree, its branches moving slowly in an evening breeze. She seemed strangely familiar, in the way that a childhood photograph will contain traces of the woman that the child will become. I felt as though I had seen the woman first, and now was being allowed to see the child that she once was.

'I don't smoke,' I said. 'Sorry.'

I stared at her for a few seconds more, then began to move away.

'Where you going?' she said. 'You want to have some fun? I got a place we can go.' She stepped forward and I saw that she was younger even than I had thought. This girl was barely into double figures, and yet there was something about her voice. It sounded older than it should have, far older.

She opened her mouth and licked her lips. Her teeth were green where they met the gums.

'How old are you?' I asked her.

'How old would you like me to be?' She wiggled her hips in a kind of parody of lasciviousness, and the grating tone to her voice was clearer now. She gestured with her right hand toward the alleyway. 'Come on, down here. I got a place we can go.' Slowly, she placed her hand on the hem of her skirt and began to lift. 'Let me show you—'

I reached out to her and her smile broadened, then froze as I gripped her arm. 'Maybe we should get you to the police,' I told her. 'They'll find someone who can help you.' But her arm felt wrong: not firm, but liquid, like a body in the process of putrefaction. There was heat there but it was extreme, and I was reminded of the preacher in his cell, burning up from within.

The girl hissed and with a movement of surprising strength and agility wrenched herself from my grasp.

'*Don't touch me!*' she hissed. 'I'm not your daughter.'

For seconds, I couldn't move. I couldn't even speak. Then she started to run down the alleyway and I followed her. I thought I would catch her easily, but suddenly she was ten feet ahead of me, then twenty, moving yet not moving, like a film from which somebody had removed crucial frames at regular intervals. She passed by McCrady's Restaurant in a kind of blur, then paused as she neared East Bay.

The car appeared behind her as she stood waiting. It was a black Cadillac Coupe de Ville, with a battered front bumper and a star-shaped crack in the corner of the darkened windshield. The rear passenger door opened beside the girl and a kind of dark light spilled out, seeping like oil across the sidewalk.

'No!' I shouted. 'Get away from the car.'

Her head turned and she stared into the interior, then looked back at me. She smiled, her features already blurring, the gums receding, the teeth like yellowed stones.

'Come on,' she said. 'I got a place we can go.'

She climbed into the car and it pulled away from the curb, its brake lights glowing as it disappeared into the night.

But shapes had fallen from the interior of the car before the door had closed, dropping like small clods of dirt to the sidewalk. While I watched, they converged on a cockroach and began to crawl across its body, biting at its head and underside, trying to slow it down so that they could begin to consume it. I knelt and saw the distinctive violin-shaped mark on the back of one of the spiders.

Recluses. The cockroach was covered with recluses.

I felt something shudder through my system and a huge spasm wrenched at my gut. I collapsed back against the wall and wrapped my arms around myself as the nausea passed over me in waves. I could taste duck and rice in my mouth as my food threatened to come back up from my stomach. I took deep breaths and kept my head down. Then, when I could walk again, I hailed a cab on East Bay and returned to my hotel.

I drank some water in my room to try to cool myself down but my temperature was way up. I was feverish and ill. I tried to concentrate on the TV, but the colors hurt my eyes and I turned it off before the late night news bulletin came on with the first details of the killings of three men in a bar near Caina, Georgia. Instead, I lay down in bed and tried to sleep, but the heat was too much, even with the AC on full. I found myself drifting in and out of consciousness, unsure of whether I was awake or dreaming when I heard a knock at the door and saw, through the spyhole, the figure of a little girl in black waiting at my door, her lipstick smeared

hey mister, I got a place we can go

and when I tried to open the door I found that I was holding the chrome of a Coupe de Ville. I smelled the stench of rotting meat as I heard the lock release with a click.

And all was darkness within.

13

They had traveled separately to the motel, the tall black man driving there in a three-year-old Lumina, the shorter white man arriving later in a cab. They each took a standard double room on different levels, the black man on the first floor, the white man on the second. There was no communication between them, nor would there be until they departed from this place the following morning.

In his room, the white man checked his clothes carefully for traces of blood but could find none. When he was satisfied that they were clean, he tossed them on the bed and stood naked before the mirror in the small bathroom. Slowly, he turned his body, wincing a little as he did so, to reveal the scars on his back and his thighs. He stared at them for a long time, gently tracing the pattern of them against his skin. He watched himself blankly in the mirror, as if he were looking not at his own reflection but at a distinct entity, one that had suffered terribly and was now marked not only psychologically but physically as well. Yet this man in the glass was no part of him. He himself was unblemished, untouched, and as soon as the lights went out and the room grew dark, he could walk away from the mirror and leave the scarred man behind, remembering only the look in his eyes. He allowed himself the luxury of the fantasy for a few moments longer, then quietly wrapped himself in a clean towel before the glow of the television.

There had been a great many misfortunes in the life of the man named Angel. Some of them, he knew, could be attributed to his own larcenous nature, to his once strongly held belief that if an item was salable, movable, and stealable, then it was only to be expected that a transfer of ownership should occur in which he, Angel, would play a significant if fleeting part. Angel had been a good thief, but he had not been a great one. Great thieves do not end up in prison, and Angel had spent enough time behind bars to realize that the flaws in his character prevented him from becoming one of the true legends of his chosen profession. Unfortunately he was also an optimist at heart and it had taken the combined efforts of prison authorities in two different states to cloud his naturally sunny predisposition toward crime. Yet he had chosen this path, and he had taken his punishment, when possible, with a degree of equanimity.

But there were other areas of his life over which Angel had been granted little control. He had not been allowed to choose his mother, who had disappeared from his life when he was still crawling on all fours, whose name appeared on no marriage certificate, and whose past was as blank and unyielding as a prison wall. She had called herself Marta. That was all he knew of her.

Worse, he had not been able to choose his father, and his father had been a bad man: a drunk, a petty criminal, an indolent, solitary character who had kept his only son in filth, feeding him on breakfast cereals and fast food when he could remember, or work up the enthusiasm, to do so. The Bad Man. Never father, in his memories, and never dad.

Just the Bad Man.

They lived in a walk-up on Degraw Street, in the Columbia Street waterfront district of Brooklyn. At the turn of the last century it had been home to the Irish who worked the nearby piers. In the 1920s, they had been joined by the Puerto Ricans, and from then on Columbia Street had remained relatively unchanged until after World War II, but the area was already in decline when the boy was born. The opening of the Brooklyn-Queens Expressway in 1957 had sundered working-class Columbia from the wealthier districts of Cobble Hill and

Carroll Gardens, and a plan to build a commercial containerization port in the neighborhood had led many residents to sell up and move elsewhere. But the container port did not materialize; instead, the shipping industry moved to Port Elizabeth, New Jersey, with the result that there was massive unemployment in Columbia Street. The Italian bakeries and the grocery stores began to close, Puerto Rican *casitas* instead springing up in the empty lots. The solitary boy moved through this place, claiming boarded-up buildings and unroofed rooms as his own, trying always to stay out of the path of the Bad Man and his increasingly volatile moods. He had few friends and attracted the attentions of the more violent of his peers the way some dogs attract maulings from others of their kind, until their tails remain forever fastened between their legs, their ears plastered low to their heads, and it becomes impossible to tell if their attitude is a consequence of their sufferings or the very reason for them.

The Bad Man lost his delivery job in 1958 after he attacked a union activist during a drunken brawl and found himself blacklisted. Men had come to the apartment some days later and beaten him with sticks and lengths of chain. He was lucky to get away with some broken bones, for the man he had attacked was a union leader in name only and the office that bore his name was rarely troubled by his presence. A woman, one of the few who passed like unwelcome seasons through the life of the boy, trailing cheap scent and cigarette smoke behind them, nursed him through the worst of it and fed the boy on bacon and eggs fried in beef fat. She left following an altercation with the Bad Man in the night, one that drew the neighbors to their windows and the police to their door. There were no more women after her, as the Bad Man descended into despair and misery, dragging his son down with him.

The Bad Man sold Angel for the first time when he was eight years old. The man gave him a case of Wild Turkey in return for his son, then drove him home five hours later wrapped in a blanket. The boy who became Angel lay awake in his bed that night, his eyes fixed to the wall, afraid to blink in case, in that second of darkness, the man should return, afraid to move for fear of the pain he felt below.

The Bad Man had fed him Froot Loops when he returned, and a Baby Ruth bar as a special treat.

Even now, looking back, Angel could not recall properly how many days passed in this way, except that the transactions became more and more frequent, and the number of bottles involved became fewer and fewer, the handful of bills slimmer and slimmer. At the age of fourteen, after several attempts to flee had been met with severe punishment by the Bad Man, he broke into a candy store on Union Street, just a couple of blocks from the Seventy-sixth Precinct, and stole two boxes of Baby Ruth bars, then devoured them in an empty lot on Hicks Street until he vomited. When the police found him the cramps in his stomach were so severe that he could barely walk. The robbery earned him a two-month stretch in juvie because of the damage he had caused while breaking into the store and the judge's desire to make an example of someone in the face of growing youth crime in the dying neighborhood. When he was finally released the Bad Man was waiting for him at the gates, and there were two more men sitting smoking in the grubby brownstone apartment that father and son shared.

This time, there was no candy bar.

At sixteen, he left and took the bus across the river to Manhattan, and for almost four years he lived life on the margins, sleeping rough or in dingy, dangerous tenements, supporting himself through dead-end jobs and, increasingly, theft. He recalled the flash of knives and the sound of gunshots; the scream of a woman slowly fading to sobs before she drifted into sleep or eternal silence. The name Angel became a part of his escape, a shedding of his old identity just as a snake sheds its skin.

But at night he would still imagine the Bad Man coming, padding softly through the empty hallways, the windowless rooms, listening for his son's breathing, his hands filled with candy bars. When the Bad Man at last passed away, burning himself to death in a fire that consumed his apartment and those above it and on either side, a consequence of a lit cigarette left to dangle while its smoker slept, the boy-man learned about it from the newspapers, and cried without knowing why.

In a life that had not been short of misfortune, of pain and humiliation, Angel would still look back on September 8, 1971 as the day when events went from bad to very bad indeed. For on that day, a judge sentenced Angel and two accomplices to a nickel in Attica for their part in a warehouse robbery in Queens, a destination partly dictated by the fact that two of the accused had attacked a bailiff in the corridor after he had suggested that by the end of the day they would be facedown on bunks with towels stuffed in their mouths. Angel, at nineteen, was the youngest of the three to be imprisoned.

To be sent to the Attica Correctional Facility, thirty miles east of Buffalo, was bad enough. Attica was a hellhole: violent, overcrowded, and a tinderbox waiting to explode. On September 9, 1971, the day after Angel arrived in Prison Yard D, Attica did just that, and Angel's luck really started to run out. The siege at Attica that resulted from the seizure by prisoners of several parts of the facility would eventually leave forty-three men dead and eighty wounded. Most of the fatalities and injuries resulted from the decision of Governor Nelson A. Rockefeller to order the retaking of Prison Yard D using whatever force was necessary. Tear gas canisters rained down on the inmates in the yard and then the shooting began, indiscriminate firing into a crowd of over twelve hundred men followed by a wave of state troopers armed with guns and batons. When the smoke and gas had cleared, eleven guards and thirty-two prisoners were dead, and the reprisals were swift and merciless. Inmates were stripped and beaten, forced to eat mud, pelted with hot shell casings, and threatened with castration. The man named Angel, who had spent most of the siege cowering in his cell, fearful of his own fellow inmates almost as much as of the inevitable punishment that would befall all involved when the prison was retaken, was forced to crawl naked over a yard full of broken glass while the guards watched. When he stopped, unable any longer to take the pain in his stomach, hands, and legs, a guard named Hyde had walked over to him, the glass crunching beneath his heavy shoes, and had stood on Angel's back.

Almost three decades later, on August 28, 2000, federal judge Michael A. Telesca of the Federal District Court in Rochester finally divided an $8 million settlement among five hundred former Attica inmates and their relatives for what had taken place in the aftermath of the uprising and siege. The case had been delayed for eighteen years but in the end some two hundred plaintiffs got to tell their stories in open court, including one Charles B. Williams, who had been so badly beaten that his leg had to be amputated. Angel's name was not among those attached to the class action suit, for Angel was not a man who believed that reparation came from courtrooms. Other prison terms had followed his time spent in Attica, including a total of four years in Rikers. When he had emerged from what would be his final prison term, he was broke, depressed, and on the verge of suicide.

And then, one hot August night, he spotted an open window in an apartment on the Upper West Side, and he used the fire escape to gain access to the building. The apartment was luxurious, fifteen hundred square feet in size, with Persian carpets laid over bare boards, small items of African art tastefully arrayed on shelves and tables, and a collection of vinyl and compact discs that, with its almost exclusive emphasis on country music, led Angel to suspect that he had somehow wandered into Charley Pride's New York crash pad.

He went through all of the rooms and found them empty. Later, he would wonder how he had missed the guy. True, the apartment was huge, but he'd searched it. He'd opened closets, even checked under the bed, and he hadn't even found dust. But just as he was about to lift the television out onto the fire escape, a voice behind him said: 'Man, you the dumbest damn burglar since Watergate.'

Angel turned around. Standing in the doorway, wearing a blue bath towel around his waist, was the tallest black man Angel had ever seen outside a basketball court. He was at least six six and totally bald, his chest hairless, his legs smooth. His body was a series of hard curves and knots of muscle, almost entirely without fat. In his right hand he held a silenced pistol, but it wasn't the gun that scared Angel. It was the guy's eyes. They weren't psycho eyes, for Angel had seen enough of those in prison to know what they looked like. No, these eyes were intelligent and watchful, amused and yet strangely cold.

This guy was a killer.

A real killer.

'I don't want no trouble,' said Angel.

'Ain't that a shame?'

Angel swallowed.

'Suppose I told you that this isn't what it looks like.'

'It looks like you tryin' to steal my TV.'

'I know that's what it looks like, but—'

Angel stopped and decided, for the first time in his life, that honesty might at this point be the best policy.

'No, it is what it looks like,' he admitted. 'I'm trying to steal your TV.'

'Not anymore you ain't.'

Angel nodded.

'I guess I should put it down.' In truth, the TV was starting to feel kind of heavy in his arms.

The black guy thought for a moment. 'No, tell you what, why don't you hold on to it?' he said at last.

Angel's face brightened. 'You mean I can keep it?'

The gunman almost smiled. At least, Angel thought it might have been a smile; that, or some kind of spasm.

'No, I said you could hold *on to* it. You just stay there and keep holdin' my TV. Cause if you drop it' – the smile broadened – 'I'll kill you.'

Angel swallowed. Suddenly, the weight of the TV seemed to double.

'You like country music?' asked the guy, reaching for the remote control and causing the CD player to light up.

'Nope,' said Angel.

From the speakers came the sound of Gram Parsons singing 'We'll Sweep Out the Ashes in the Morning.'

'Then you shit out of luck.'

Angel sighed. 'Tell me about it.'

The seminaked man settled himself into a leather armchair, rearranged his towel carefully, and trained the gun on the hapless burglar.

'No,' he said. 'You tell me . . . '

The man named Angel thought about these things, these seemingly random events that had brought him to this place, as he sat in the semidarkness. The final words of Clyde Benson, just before Angel had killed him, replayed themselves in his memory.

I made my peace with the Lord.

Then you got nothing to worry about.

He had asked for mercy but had received none.

For so much of his life, Angel had been at the mercy of others: his father; the men who had taken him in back rooms and sweat-filled apartments; the guard Hyde in Attica; the prisoner Vance in Rikers, who had decided that Angel's continued existence was an insult that could not be tolerated, until someone else had stepped in and ensured that Vance would no longer be a danger to Angel, or to anyone else.

And then he had found this man, the man who now sat in a room below, and a new life of sorts had begun, a life in which he would no longer be the victim, in which he would no longer be at the mercy of others, and he had almost started to forget the events that had made him what he was.

Until Faulkner had chained him to a shower rail and begun to cut the skin from his back, his son and daughter holding the hanging man still, the woman licking at the sweat that broke from Angel's brow, the man hushing him softly as he screamed through the gag. He remembered the feel of the blade, the coldness of it, the pressure on his skin before it broke through and entered the flesh beneath. All of the old ghosts had come howling back then, all of the memories, all of the suffering, and he could taste candy bars in his mouth.

Blood and candy bars.

Somehow, he had survived.

But Faulkner too was still alive, and that was simply too much for Angel to bear.

For Angel to live, Faulkner had to die.

And what of this other man, the quiet, deliberate black male with the killer's eyes?

Each time he watched his partner dress and undress Louis's face remained studiedly neutral, but he felt his gut clench as the tangled scars were revealed on the back and thighs, as the other man paused to let the pain subside while pulling on a shirt or pants, sweat dotting his forehead. In the beginning, in those first weeks after he returned from the clinic, Angel had simply neglected to remove his clothes for days, preferring instead to lie, fully clothed, on his stomach until it became necessary to change his dressings. He rarely spoke of what had occurred on the preacher's island, although it consumed his days and drew out his nights.

Louis knew a great deal more about Angel's past than his partner had learned about his, Angel recognizing in his reticence a reluctance to reveal himself that went beyond mere privacy. But Louis understood, at some minor level, the sense of violation that Angel now felt. Violation, the infliction of pain upon him by someone older and more powerful, should have been left behind long ago, sealed away in a casket filled with hard hands and candy bars. Now, it was as if the seal had been broken and the past was seeping out like foul gas, polluting the present and the future.

Angel was right: Parker should have burned the preacher when he had the chance. Instead, he had chosen some alternative, less certain path, placing his faith in the force of law while a small part of him, the part of him that had killed in the past and would, Louis felt certain, kill again in the future, recognized that the law could never punish a man like Faulkner because his actions went so far beyond anything that the law could comprehend, impacting on worlds gone and worlds yet to exist.

Louis believed that he knew why Parker had acted in the way that he had, knew that he had spared the unarmed preacher's life because he believed the alternative was to reduce himself to the old man's level. He had chosen his own first faltering steps toward some form of salvation over the wishes, perhaps even the needs, of his friend, and Louis could not find it in him to blame Parker for this. Even Angel did not blame him: he merely wished that it were otherwise.

But Louis did not believe in salvation, or if he did, he lived his life knowing that its light would not shine upon him. If Parker was a man tormented by his past, then Louis was a man resigned to it, accepting the reality, if not the necessity, of all that he had done and the requirement that, inevitably, a reckoning would have to be endured. Occasionally, he would look back over his life and try to determine the point at which the path had fatally forked, the precise moment in time at which he had embraced the incandescent beauty of brutality. He would picture himself, a slim boy in a houseful of women, with their laughter, their sexual banter, their moments of prayerfulness, of worship, of peace. And then the shadow would fall, and Deber would appear, and the silence would descend.

He did not know how his mother had found such a man as Deber, still less how she had endured his presence, however inconstant, for so long. Deber was small and mean, his dark skin pitted about the cheeks, a relic of shotgun pellets discharged close to his face when he was a boy. He carried a metal whistle on a chain around his neck, and used it to call breaks for the Negro work crews that he supervised. He used it also to impose discipline in the house, to draw the family to supper, to call the boy for chores or punishment, or to summon the boy's mother to his bed. And she would stop what she was doing and, head low, follow the whistle, and the boy would close his ears to the sound of them coming through the walls.

One day, after Deber had been absent for many weeks and a kind of peace had descended upon the house, he came and took the boy's mother away, and they never saw her alive again. The last time her son saw his mother's face, they were closing the casket over her and the mortician's cosmetics were heavy on the marks beside her eyes and behind her ears. A stranger had killed her, they said, and Deber's friends had provided him with an alibi that could not be shaken. Deber stood by the casket and accepted the condolences of those too afraid not to show their faces.

But the boy knew, and the women knew. Yet Deber returned to them, a month later, and he led the boy's aunt into a bedroom that night, and the boy lay awake and listened to the moaning and swearing, the woman whimpering and, once, emitting a yell of pain that was muffled by a pillow to her mouth. And when the moon was still full, dim-shining on the waters beyond the house, he heard a door open and he stole to the window and watched as his aunt descended to the waters, then, hunched over, cleansed herself of the man who now lay sleeping in the bedroom beyond, before she sank down in the still lake and began to cry.

The next morning, when Deber was gone and the women were about their chores, he saw the tangled sheets and the blood upon them, and he made his choice. He was fifteen by then and he knew that the law was not written to protect poor black women. There was an intelligence to him beyond his years and his experience, but something else too, something that he thought Deber had begun to sense because a duller, less sophisticated version of it dwelt within himself. It was a potential for violence, the aptitude for lethality that, many years later, would cause an old man at a gas station to lie for fear of his life. The boy, despite his delicate good looks, represented a burgeoning threat to Deber, and he would have to be dealt with. Sometimes, when Deber returned from his labors and sat on the porch step, carving a stick with his knife, the boy would become conscious of his gaze upon him and, with the foolishness of youth, would hold his stare until Deber smiled and looked away, the knife still in his hand but the knuckles now white as he clenched it in his fist.

One day, the boy watched while Deber stood at the edge of the trees and beckoned to him. He had a curved filleting knife in his hand, and his fingers were red with blood. He had caught him some fish, he said, needed the boy to come help him gut them. But the boy did not go to him and he saw Deber's face harden as he backed away from him. From around his neck, the man drew his whistle to his mouth and blew. It was the summons. They had all heard it, all responded to it in their time, but on this occasion the boy recognized the finality in it and he did not respond. Instead, he ran.

That night the boy did not return to the house but slept among the trees and allowed the mosquitoes to feed upon him, even as Deber stood upon the porch and blew the whistle emptily, again and again and again, disturbing the stillness of the night with its promise of retribution.

The boy did not go to school the next day, for he was convinced that Deber would come looking for him and take him away as he had taken away his mother, and this time there would be no body to bury, no hymns by the graveside, merely a covering of grass and swamp dirt, and the calling of birds and the scrabbling of animals come to feed. Instead, he remained hidden in the woods, and waited.

* * *

Deber had been drinking. The boy smelled it as soon as he entered the house. The bedroom door was open and he could hear the sound of Deber's snoring. He could kill him now, he thought, cut his throat as he lay sleeping. But they would find him and they would punish him, perhaps punish the women as well. No, the boy thought, better to continue with what he had set out to do.

White eyes grew in the darkness and his aunt, her small breasts bare, stared at him silently. He placed his finger to his lips, then indicated the whistle that lay close by her on the bedside locker. Slowly, so as not to disturb the sleeping man, she reached across his body and gathered up the chain. It made a soft scraping sound on the wood but Deber, deep in his alcoholic sleep, did not move. The boy reached out, and the woman dropped the whistle into his hand. Then he left.

That night, he broke into the school. It was a good school by the standards of this place, unusually well equipped and supported with funds from a local man made good in the city, with a gym and a football field and a small science lab. The boy made his way quietly to the lab and set about assembling the ingredients that he needed: solid iodine crystals, concentrated ammonium hydroxide, alcohol, ether, all staples of even the most basic of school laboratories. He had learned their uses through trial and sometimes painful error, facilitated by petty theft and backed up with voracious reading. He slowly combined the iodine crystals and the ammonium hydroxide to create a brownish red precipitate, then filtered it through paper and washed it, first with alcohol and then with ether. Finally, he wrapped the substance carefully and laid it into a beaker of water. This was nitrogen tri-iodide, a simple compound he had encountered in one of the old chemistry books in the public library.

He used a steamer to separate the metal whistle into its natural halves, then, with wet hands, packed the nitrogen tri-iodide into the sides of the whistle until each was about a quarter full. He replaced the ball of the whistle with a wad of crumpled sandpaper, then carefully glued the two halves of the whistle back together again before returning to the house. His aunt was still awake. She reached out her hand for the whistle, but he shook his head and placed it carefully on the table, smelling Deber's breath upon him as he did so. As the boy walked away, he smiled to himself. There was, he thought, an aptness to what was about to occur.

The next morning Deber rose early, as he usually did, and left the house carrying the brown paper sack of food that the women always left for him. That day he drove eighty miles to start a new job and the nitrogen tri-iodide was as dry as dust when he put the whistle to his mouth for the last time and blew, the little ball of sandpaper providing the friction required to set off the primitive explosive charge.

They questioned the boy, of course, but he had cleaned the lab and washed his hands in bleach and water to remove all traces of the substances he had handled. And the boy had an alibi: God-fearing women who would swear that the boy had been with them the previous day, that he had never left the house during the night for they would surely have heard him, that Deber had in fact lost the whistle some days before and was desperate for its recovery, regarding it as a totem, a lucky charm. The police held him for a day, beat him halfheartedly to see if he would crack, then let him go, for there were disaffected workers, jealous husbands, and humiliated enemies to pursue in his place.

After all, that was a miniature bomb that had torn Deber's face apart, designed so that Deber, and Deber alone, would suffer when it exploded. That wasn't the work of a boy.

Deber died two days later.

It was, folks said, a mercy.

In his room, Louis watched impassively as the late news on cable reported on the discovery of the bodies and a bewildered Virgil Gossard enjoyed his fifteen minutes of fame, his head bandaged and his dried urine still upon his fingers. A police spokeswoman announced that they were following definite leads and a description of the old Ford was given out. Louis's brow furrowed slightly. They had set fire to the car in a field west of Allendale, then headed on north in the clean Lumina before splitting up at the edge of the city. If found and connected to the killings, the Ford would yield up no evidence, constructed as it was from the cannibalized innards of half a dozen other vehicles and kept ready for fast use and easy disposal. What bothered him was that somebody had seen them leave, in which case a description might follow. Those fears were eased somewhat, but not eradicated entirely, when the spokeswoman announced that they were seeking a black male and at least one other unidentified person in connection with what had occurred.

Virgil Gossard, thought Louis. They should have killed him when they had the chance, but if he was the only witness and all he knew was that one of the men was black then they had little to worry about, although the possibility that the police knew more than they were saying troubled him vaguely. It would be better if he and Angel separated for a time, and the decision brought his thoughts back to the man in the room above him. He lay thinking about him until the streets beyond grew quiet, then left the motel and began to walk.

The phone booth stood five blocks north, in the parking lot behind a Chinese laundry. He dropped in two dollars in quarters, dialed, and heard the phone ring three times at the other end before it was picked up.

'It's me. I got something for you to do. There's a gas station down by the Ogeechee, on sixteen out of Sparta. You can't miss it, place look like the Teletubbies decorated it. The old guy inside needs to remember to forget the two men that passed through his place yesterday. Man will know what you're talkin' about.'

He paused and listened to the voice at the other end of the line.

'No, it comes to that I'll do it myself. For now, make sure he understand the consequences if he decide to be a good citizen. Tell him the worms don't make no distinction between good and bad meat. Then find a man called Virgil Gossard, a regular local celebrity by now. Buy him a drink, see what he knows about what went down. Find out what he saw. When you're done and back you call me, then check your messages for the next week. I got something else I may need you for.'

With that, Louis hung up the phone, removed the cloth from his hand, and used it to wipe down the phone keys. Then, head low, he walked back to the motel and lay awake until the passing cars grew sparse and a stillness descended on the world.

And so these two remained in their separate rooms, apart but somehow together, barely thinking about the men who had died at their hands that night. Instead, one reached out to the other and wished him peace, and that peace was granted, temporarily, by sleep.

But true peace would require a sacrifice.

Already, Louis had some idea of how that sacrifice might be achieved.

Far to the north, Cyrus Nairn was enjoying his first night of freedom.

He had been released from Thomaston that morning, his possessions contained in a black plastic garbage bag. His clothes still fitted him no better or no worse than they ever had, for incarceration had made little impact on Cyrus's crooked body. He stood outside the walls and looked back at the prison. The voices were silent so he knew that Leonard was there with him, and he felt no fear at the sight of the things that crowded along the walls, their huge wings drawn back against their bodies, their dark eyes watchful. Instead, he reached behind his back and imagined that he felt, at either side of his curved spine, the first swellings of those great wings upon his own body.

Cyrus made his way to Thomaston's main street and ordered

a Coke and a doughnut in the diner, pointing silently at the items that he wanted. A couple at a nearby table stared at him, then looked away when he caught their eye, his demeanor giving him away as much as the black bag at his feet. He ate and drank quickly, for even a simple Coke tasted better outside those walls, then gestured for a refill and waited for the diner to empty. Presently, he found himself alone, with only the women behind the counter to cast the odd anxious glance in his direction.

Shortly after midday, a man entered and took the table next to Cyrus. He ordered a coffee, read his newspaper, then departed, leaving the newspaper behind. Cyrus reached out for it and pretended to read the front page, then dropped it back on his own table. The envelope concealed within the newspaper's folds slid into his hand with only the gentlest of jingles, and from there, into the pocket of his jacket. Cyrus left $4 for his food on the table, then walked quickly from the diner.

The car was an anonymous, two-year-old Nissan Maxima. Inside the glove compartment was a map, a piece of paper with two addresses and a telephone number written upon it, and a second envelope, containing $1,000 in used bills and a set of keys for a trailer located in a park near Westbrook. Cyrus memorized the addresses and the number, then disposed of the paper by masticating it into a wet ball and dropping it down a drain, as he had been instructed to do.

Finally, he leaned down and felt beneath the passenger seat with his hand. He ignored the gun taped into place and instead allowed his fingers to brush the blade once, twice, before he raised them to his nostrils and sniffed.

Clean, he thought. Nice and clean.

Then he turned the car and headed south, just as the voice came to him.

Happy, Cyrus?

Happy, Leonard.

Very happy.

14

I looked at myself in the mirror.

My eyes were bloodshot and there was a red rash across my neck. I felt like I'd been drinking the night before: my movements were out of sync and I kept bumping into the furniture in the room. My temperature was still above normal and my skin was clammy to the touch. I wanted to crawl back into bed and pull the covers up over my head, but I didn't have that luxury. Instead, I made coffee in my room and watched the news. When the Caina story came on, I put my head in my hands and let my coffee go cold. A long time went by before I felt certain enough of myself to start working the phone.

According to a man named Randy Burris at the South Carolina Department of Corrections, the Richland County Detention Center was one of a number of institutions participating in a scheme involving former prisoners who preached the gospel to those still incarcerated. The program, called F.A.R. (Forgiveness and Renewal) and run out of Charleston, was an outreach ministry similar to the T.H.U.G. (True Healing Under God) program that was trying to help inmates in the north of the state by using ex-offenders to convince others not to reoffend. In South Carolina, about 30 per cent of the ten thousand inmates released each year ended up back behind bars within three years, so it was in the interest of the state to support the ministry in whatever way it could. The man named Tereus – his only given name – was a recent recruit to F.A.R. and, according to one of the administrators, a woman named Irene Jakaitis, the only one of its members to opt for a ministry as far north as

Richland. The warden at Richland told me that Tereus had spent most of his time at the prison counseling Atys Jones. Tereus now had an address in a rooming house off King Street close by the Wha Cha Like gospel store. Prior to that, he had lived in one of the city's charity hostels while he searched for a job, The rooming house was about a five-minute ride from my hotel.

The tourist buses were making their way along King as I drove, and the spiel of the guides carried above the noise of passing cars. King has always been Charleston's center of commerce, and down by Charleston Place there are some pretty nice stores aimed mostly at the out-of-towners. But as you head north, the stores become more practical, the restaurants a little more homely. There are more black faces, and more weeds on the sidewalks. I passed Wha Cha Like and Honest John's TV Repair and Record Store. Three young white men in gray dress uniforms, cadets from the Citadel, marched silently along the sidewalk, their very existence a reminder of the city's past, for the Citadel owed its beginnings to the failed slave revolt of Denmark Vesey and the city's belief that a well-fortified arsenal was necessary to guard against future uprisings. I stopped to let them cross then turned left onto Morris Street and parked across from the Morris Street Baptist Church. An old black man watched me from where he sat on the steps leading up to the side porch of Tereus's home, eating what looked like peanuts from a brown paper bag. He offered the bag to me as I approached the steps.

'Goober?'

'No thanks.' Goobers were peanuts boiled in their shells. You sucked them for a time, then cracked them open to eat the nuts inside, made soft and hot by their time spent in the water.

'You allergic?'

'No.'

'You watching your weight?'

'No.'

'Then take a damn goober.'

I did as I was told, even though I didn't care much for peanuts. The nut was so hot I had to pout and suck in air in order to cool my mouth down.

'Hot,' I said.

'What you expect? I done tole you it was a goober.'

He peered at me like I was kind of slow. He might have been right.

'I'm looking for a man called Tereus.'

'He ain't home.'

'You know where I might find him?'

'Why you lookin' for him?'

I showed him my ID.

'You a long ways from home,' he said. 'Long ways.' He still hadn't told me where I might find Tereus.

'I don't mean him any harm, and I don't want to cause him trouble. He helped a young man, a client of mine. Anything Tereus can tell me might make the difference between living and dying for this kid.'

The old man eyed me up for a time. He had no teeth, and his lips made a wet sucking sound as he worked on the nut in his mouth.

'Well, living and dying, that's pretty serious,' he said, with just a hint of mockery. He was probably right to yank my chain a little. I sounded like a character from an afternoon soap.

'I sound overdramatic?'

'Some,' he nodded. 'Some.'

'Well, it's still pretty bad. It's important that I talk to Tereus.'

With that, the shell softened enough for him to bite through to the nut inside. He spit the remnants carefully into his hand.

'Tereus work down at one of them titty bars off Meeting,' he said, grinning. 'Don't take off his clothes, though.'

'That's reassuring.'

'He cleans up,' he continued. 'Man's a jizz mopper.'

He cackled and slapped his thigh, then gave me the name of the club: LapLand. I thanked him.

'Can't help but notice that you still suckin' on that goober,' he said, as I was about to leave him.

'To be honest, I don't like peanuts,' I confessed.

'I knowed that,' he said. 'I just wanted to see if you had the good manners to accept what was offered you.'

I discreetly spat the peanut into my hand and tossed it in the nearest trash can, then left him laughing to himself.

The city of Charleston's sporting fraternity had been out celebrating since the day I had arrived in the city. That weekend, the South Carolina Gamecocks had ended a twenty-one-game losing streak by beating New Mexico State 31–0 in front of almost eighty-one thousand victory-starved supporters who hadn't had a reason to cheer for more than two years, not since the Gamecocks beat Ball State 38–20. Even quarterback Phil Petty, who for the whole of last season hadn't looked like he could lead a group of old people in a conga line, headed two touchdown drives and completed ten of eighteen for eighty-seven yards. The sad cluster of strip joints and gentlemen's clubs on Pittsburg Avenue had probably made a real killing from the celebrants over the last few days. One of the clubs offered a nude car wash (hey, practical *and* fun!) while another made a hopeful play for class punters by denying access to anyone in jeans or sneakers. It didn't look like LapLand had any such scruples. Its parking lot was pitted with water-filled holes around which a handful of cars had conspired to arrange themselves without losing a wheel in the mire. The club itself was a single-story concrete slab painted in varying shades of blue – porn blue, sad stripper blue, cold skin blue – with a black steel door at its center. From inside came the muffled sound of Bachman-Turner Overdrive's 'You Ain't Seen Nothin' Yet.' BTO in a strip joint had to be a sign that the place was in trouble.

Inside it was dark as a Republican donor's motives, apart from a strip of pink light along the bar and the flashing bulbs that illuminated the small central stage, where a girl with chicken legs and orange-peel thighs waved her small breasts at a handful of rapt drunks. One of them slipped a dollar bill into her stocking, then took the opportunity to press his hand between her legs. The girl moved away from him but nobody tried to drag him outside and kick him in the head for touching the dancer. LapLand clearly encouraged a more than average amount of customer-artiste interaction.

Over by the bar, two women dressed in lace bras and G-strings sat drinking sodas through straws. As I tried to avoid tripping over a table in the gloom, the elder of the two, a black woman with heavy breasts and long legs, moved toward me.

'I'm Lorelei. Get you somethin', sugar?'

'Soda is fine. And something for yourself.'

I handed her a ten and she wiggled her hips at me as she walked away. 'I be right back,' she assured me.

True to her word, she materialized a minute later with a warm soda, her own drink, and no change.

'Expensive here,' I said. 'Who'd have thought it?'

Lorelei reached across and laid her hand on the inside of my thigh, then moved her fingers across it, allowing the back of her hand to glance against my crotch.

'You get what you pay for,' she said. 'And then some.'

'I'm looking for somebody,' I said.

'Sugar, you found her,' she breathed, in what passed for an approximation of sexy if you were paying for it by the hour, and paying cheap. It seemed like LapLand was flirting perilously with prostitution. She leaned in closer, allowing me to peer at her breasts if I chose. Like a good Boy Scout, I looked away and counted the bottles of cheap, watery liquor above the bar.

'You ain't watchin' the show,' she said.

'High blood pressure. My doctor warned me not to get overexcited.'

She smiled and dragged a fingernail across my hand. It left a white mark. I glanced up at the stage and found myself looking at the girl from an angle even her gynecologist probably hadn't explored. I left her to it.

'You like her?' Lorelei asked, indicating the dancer.

'She seems like a fun girl.'

'I can be a fun girl. You lookin' for fun, sugar?' The back of her hand pressed harder against me. I coughed and discreetly moved her hand back onto her own chair.

'No, I'm good.'

'Well, I'm *baaaad* . . . '

This was getting kind of monotonous. Lorelei seemed to be some kind of double entendre machine.

'I'm not really a fun kind of guy,' I told her. 'If you catch my drift.'

It was as if a pair of transparent shutters had descended over her eyes. There was intelligence in those eyes too: not merely the low cunning of a woman turning tricks in a dying strip joint but something clever and alive. I wondered how she kept the two sides of her character apart without one seeping into the other and poisoning it forever.

'I catch it. What are you? You're not a cop. Process server, maybe, or a debt collector. You got that look about you. I should know, I've seen it enough.'

'What look would that be?'

'The look that says you're bad news for poor folks.' She paused and reappraised me for a second. 'No, on second thoughts, I reckon you're bad news for just about everybody.'

'Like I said, I'm looking for somebody.'

'Go fuck yourself.'

'I'm a private detective.'

'Oooh, look at the bad man. Can't help you, sugar.'

She began to move away, but I gripped her wrist gently and placed two more tens on the table. She stopped and waved to the bartender, who had begun to sense trouble and was moving to alert the gorilla at the door. He went back to polishing glasses but kept a discreet eye on our table.

'Wow, two dimes,' said Lorelei. 'I be able to buy me a whole new outfit.'

'Two, if you stick with the kind you're wearing.'

I said it without sarcasm, and a small smile broke through the pack ice on her face. I showed her my license. She picked it up and examined it closely before tossing it back on the table.

'Maine. Looks like you the real deal. Congratulations.' She made a move for the bills but my hand was quicker.

'Uh-uh. Talk first, then the money.'

She glanced back at the bar, then slid reluctantly into the chair. Her eyes bored a hole through the back of my hand to the notes beneath.

'I'm not here to cause trouble. I just want to ask questions. I'm looking for a man named Tereus. You know if he's here?'

'What you lookin' him for?'

'He helped a client of mine. I wanted to thank him.'

She laughed humorlessly. 'Yeah, right. You got a reward, you give it to me. I'll pass it on. Don't fuck with me, mister. I may be sittin' here with my titties hangin' out, but don't mistake me for no fool.'

I leaned back. 'I don't think you're a fool, and Tereus did help a client of mine. He spoke to him in jail. I just want to know why.'

'He found the Lord, that's why. He even tried to convert some of the johns who come in here, till Handy Andy threatened to beat him upside the head.'

'Handy Andy?'

'He runs this place.' She made a gesture with her hand as of a man slapping someone across the back of the head. 'You get me?'

'I get you.'

'You gonna cause that man more trouble? He done had his share. He don't need no more.'

'No trouble. I just want to talk.'

'Then give me the twenty. Go outside and wait around back. He'll be out soon enough.'

For a moment I held her eyes and tried to find out if she was lying. I couldn't be sure but I still released the bills. She grabbed them, slipped them into her bra, and walked away. I saw her exchange a few words with the bartender then pass through a door marked 'Dancers and Guests Only.' I knew what was behind it: a dingy dressing room, a bathroom with a busted lock, and a couple of rooms equipped with nothing more than chairs, some rubbers, and a box of tissues. Maybe she wasn't so intelligent after all.

The dancer onstage finished her set, then picked up her discarded underwear and headed for the bar. The bartender announced the next dancer, and her place was taken by a small, dark-haired girl with sallow skin. She looked about sixteen. One of the drunks whooped with delight as Britney begged to be hit one more time.

Outside, it was beginning to rain, droplets distorting the shapes of the cars and the colors of the sky reflected in the puddles on the ground. I followed the wall around to where a Dumpster stood half full of trash next to some empty beer kegs and stacks of crated bottles. I heard footsteps behind me and turned to find a man who most certainly wasn't Tereus. This guy was six four and built like a quarterback, with a domed, shaved head and small eyes. He was probably in his late twenties. A single gold ring glittered in his left ear, and he had a wedding band on one of his big fingers. The rest of him was lost beneath a baggy blue sweatshirt and a pair of gray sweatpants.

'Whoever you are, you got ten seconds to get the fuck off my property,' he said.

I sighed. It was raining and I didn't have an umbrella. I didn't even have a coat. I was standing in the parking lot of a third-rate strip joint being threatened by a woman beater. Under the circumstances, there was only one thing to do.

'Andy,' I said. 'You don't remember me?'

His brow furrowed. I took one step forward, my hands open, and drove the toe of my right foot as hard as I could between his legs. He didn't let out a sound, apart from the rush of air and spittle that shot from his lips as he collapsed to the ground. His head touched the gravel and he started to retch.

'You won't forget me again.'

There was the bulge of a gun at his back and I removed it from his waistband. It was a stainless steel Beretta. It looked like it had never been used. I tossed it in the Dumpster, then helped Handy Andy to his feet and left him leaning against the wall, his bald head speckled with raindrops and the knees and shins of his sweatpants soaked with filthy water. When he had recovered a little, he placed his hands on his knees and glared at me.

'You want to try that again?' he whispered.

'Nope,' I answered. 'It only works once.'

'What do you do for an encore?'

I removed the big Smith 10 from its holster and let him take a good look at it.

'Encore. Curtain down. Theater closed.'

'Big man with a gun.'

'I know. Look at me.'

He tried to stand upright, thought better of it, and kept his head down instead.

'Look,' I said, 'this doesn't have to be difficult. I talk, I go away. End of story.'

He thought about what I'd said.

'Tereus?' He seemed to be having trouble speaking. I wondered if I'd kicked him too hard.

'Tereus,' I agreed.

'That's all?'

'Uh-huh.'

'Then you go away and you never come back?'

'Probably.'

He staggered away from the wall and made for the back door. He opened it, the volume of the music immediately increasing, then seemed about to disappear inside. I stopped him by whistling at him and jogging the Smith.

'Just call him,' I said, 'then take a walk.' I gestured to where Pittsburg disappeared into warehouses and green grass. 'Over there.'

'It's raining.'

'It'll stop.'

Handy Andy shook his head, then called into the darkness. 'Tereus, get your ass out here.'

He held the door as a lean man appeared on the step beside him. He had black negroid hair and dark olive skin. It was almost impossible to tell his race, but the striking combination of features marked him out as a member of one of those strange ethnic groups that seemed to proliferate in the south: Brass Ankle, maybe, or an Appalachian Melungeon, a group of 'free people of color' with a mixture of black, Native American, British, and even Portuguese blood, a dash of Turkish reputedly thrown in to confuse the issue even more. A white T-shirt hugged the long thin muscles on his arms and the curve of his pectorals. He was at least fifty years old and taller than I was, but there was no stoop to him, no sign of weakness or disintegration apart from the tinted glasses that he wore. The cuffs of his jeans had been turned up almost to the middle of his shins and he wore plastic sandals on his feet. In his hand was a mop, and I could smell it from where I stood. Even Handy Andy took a step back.

'Damn head again?'

Tereus nodded, looked from Andy to me, then back to Andy again.

'Man wants to talk to you. Don't take too long.' I stepped aside as Andy slowly walked toward me, then proceeded onto the road. He took a pack of cigarettes from his pocket and lit one as he walked gingerly away, holding the glowing end toward his palm to shelter it from the rain.

Tereus descended onto the pitted tarmac of the yard. He seemed composed, almost distant.

'My name's Charlie Parker,' I said. 'I'm a private detective.'

I reached out my hand but he didn't take it. In explanation he pointed to the mop. 'You don't want to shake hands with me, suh, not now.'

I gestured to his feet. 'Where'd you do your time?'

There were marks around his ankles, circular abrasions as if the skin had been rubbed away to such a degree that it could never be restored to its former smoothness. I knew what those marks were. Only leg irons could leave them.

'Limestone,' he said. His voice was soft.

'Alabama. Bad place to do time.'

Ron Jones, Alabama's commissioner of corrections, had reintroduced chain gangs in 1996: ten hours breaking limestone in one hundred degree heat, five days each week, the nights spent with four hundred other inmates in Dorm 16, an overcrowded cattle shed originally built for two hundred. The first thing an inmate on the chain gang did was to remove his laces from his boots and tie them around the irons to prevent the metal from rubbing against his ankles. But somebody had taken Tereus's laces and kept them from him for a long time, long enough to leave permanent scarring on his flesh.

'Why'd they take away your laces?'

He gazed down at his feet. 'I refused to work the gang,' he said. 'I'll be a prisoner, do prisoner's work, but I won't be no slave. They tied me to a hitching post in the sun from five A.M. to sunset. They had to drag me back to Sixteen. I lasted five days. After that, I couldn't take no more. To remind me of what I'd done, gunbull took away my laces. That was in ninety-six. I got paroled a few weeks back. I spent a lot of time without laces.'

He spoke matter-of-factly, but he fingered the cross around his neck as he spoke. It was a replica of the one that he had given to Atys Jones. I wondered if his cross contained a blade as well.

'I've been employed by a lawyer. His name is Elliot Norton. He's representing a young man you met in Richland: Atys Jones.'

At the mention of Atys, Tereus's attitude changed. It reminded me of the woman in the club when it became clear that I wasn't going to pay for her services. Seemed like I had ended up paying anyway.

'You know Elliot Norton?' I asked.

'Know of him. You're not from around here?'

'No, I've come from Maine.'

'That's a long way to travel. How come you ended up working way down here?'

'Elliot Norton is a friend of mine, and nobody else seemed keen to get involved in this case.'

'You know where the boy at?'

'He's safe.'

'No, he's not.'

'You gave him a cross, just like the one you wear around your neck.'

'You must have faith in the Lord. The Lord will protect you.'

'I've seen the cross. Seems like you decided to help the Lord along.'

'Jail is a dangerous place for a young man.'

'That's why we got him out.'

'You should have left him there.'

'We couldn't protect him there.'

'You can't protect him anywhere.'

'So what do you suggest?'

'Give him to me.'

I kicked at a pebble on the ground and watched as it bounced into a puddle. I could see my reflection, already distorted by the rain, ripple even more, and for a moment I disappeared in the dark waters, fragments of myself carried away to its farthest edges.

'I think you know that's not going to happen, but I'd like to know why you went to Richland. Did you go there specifically to contact Atys Jones?'

'I knew his momma, and his sister. Lived close by them, down by the Congaree.'

'They disappeared.'

'That's right.'

'You know what might have happened to them?'

He didn't reply. Instead, he released his grip on the cross and walked toward me. I didn't step back. There was no threat to me from this man.

'You ask questions for a living, don't you, suh?'

'I guess so.'

'What questions you been asking Mr. Norton?'

I waited. There was something going on here that I didn't understand, some gap in my knowledge that Tereus was trying to fill.

'What questions should I ask?'

'You should ask him what happened to that boy's momma and aunt.'

'They disappeared. He showed me the cuttings.'

'Maybe.'

'You think they're dead?'

'You got this the wrong way round, suh. Maybe they dead, but they ain't disappeared.'

'I don't understand.'

'Maybe they dead,' he repeated, 'but they ain't gone from Congaree.'

I shook my head. This was the second time in less than twenty-four hours that somebody had spoken to me of ghosts in the Congaree. But ghosts didn't take rocks and use them to beat in the heads of young women. Around us, the rain had stopped and the air seemed cooler. To my left, I saw Handy Andy approaching from the road. He took one look at me, shrugged resignedly, then lit another cigarette and started back the way he had come.

'You know about the White Road, suh?'

Distracted momentarily by Andy, I now found Tereus almost face-to-face with me. I could smell cinnamon on his breath. Instinctively, I moved away from him.

'No. What is it?'

He looked once again at his feet, and the marks on his ankles.

'On the fifth day,' he said, 'after they tied me to the hitching post, I saw the White Road. The blacktop shimmered and then it was like somebody had turned the world inside out. Dark became light, black became white. And I saw the road before me, and the men working, breaking rocks, and the gunbulls spitting chewing tobacco on the dirt.'

He was talking now like an Old Testament preacher, his mind filled with the vision he had seen, near crazy beneath the burning sun, his body sagging against the wood, the ropes tearing into his skin.

'And I saw the others too. I saw figures moving between them, women and children, old and young, and men with nooses around their necks and gunshots to the body. I saw soldiers, and the night riders, and women in fine, fine dresses. I saw them all, suh, the living and the dead, side by side together on the White Road. We think they gone, but they waiting. They beside us all the time, and they don't rest till justice come. That's the White Road, suh. It's the place where justice is made, where the living and the dead walk together.'

With that, he removed the tinted glasses that he wore, and I saw that his eyes had been altered, perhaps by their exposure to the sun, the bright blue of the pupils dulled, the irises overlaid with white, as if a spiderweb had been cast upon them.

'You don't know it yet,' he whispered, 'but you on the White Road now, and you best not step off it, because the things waiting in the woods, they worse than anything you can imagine.'

This wasn't getting me anywhere – I wanted to know more about the Jones sisters, and about Tereus's reasons for approaching Atys – but at least Tereus was talking.

'And did you see them too, the things in the woods?'

He seemed to consider me for a time. I thought he might be trying to figure out whether or not I was mocking him, but I was wrong.

'I saw them,' he said. 'They was like black angels.'

He wouldn't tell me anything more, at least nothing useful. He had known the Jones family, had watched the children grow up, watched as Addy was made pregnant at the age of sixteen by a drifter who was also screwing her mother, giving birth nine months later to a son, Atys. The drifter's name was Davis Smoot. His friends called him Boot on account of the leather cowboy boots he liked to wear. But I knew this already, because Randy Burris had told me all about it, just as he had told me how Tereus had served nearly twenty years in Limestone for killing Davis Smoot in a bar in Gadsden.

Handy Andy was coming back, and this time he didn't look like he was planning on taking another long walk. Tereus picked up his bucket and mop in preparation for a return to his labors.

'Why did you kill Davis Smoot, Tereus?'

I wondered if he was going to make some expression of regret, or tell me how he was no longer the man who had taken the life of another, but he made no attempt to explain away his crime as a mistake from his past.

'I asked him for his help. He turned me down. We got to arguing and he pulled a knife on me. Then I killed him.'

'What help did you ask from him?'

Tereus raised his hand, and shook it from side to side in the negative. 'That's between him and me and the good Lord. You ask Mr. Norton, and maybe he'll be able to tell you how come I was looking for old Boot.'

'Did you tell Atys that you were his father's killer?'

He shook his head. 'Now why would I do somethin' dumb as that?'

With that, he replaced his glasses on the bridge of his nose, hiding those damaged eyes, and left me standing in the rain.

15

I called Elliot from my hotel room later that afternoon. He sounded tired. He wasn't going to get too much sympathy from me.

'Bad day at the office?'

'I got the justice blues. You?'

'Just a bad day.' I didn't mention Tereus to Elliot, mainly because I hadn't learned anything useful from him as yet, but I had checked two more of the witness statements after I left LapLand. One was a second cousin of Atys Jones, a God-fearing man who didn't approve of the lifestyles of Atys or of his missing mother and aunt, but who liked to hang around dive bars to give himself something to get offended by. A neighbor told me he was most likely back at the Swamp Rat, and that was where I found him. He recalled Atys and Marianne Larousse leaving and was still at the bar, praying for all sinners over a double, when Atys reappeared with blood and dust on his face and hands.

The Swamp Rat stood at the end of Cedar Creek Road, close to the edge of the Congaree. It wasn't much to look at, inside or out, an eyesore of cinder blocks and corrugated iron, but it had a good jukebox and was the kind of place that rich kids went to when they wanted to flirt a little with danger. I walked through the trees surrounding it and found the small clearing where Marianne Larousse had died. There was still crime scene tape dangling from the trees, but there was no other sign that she had lost her life here. I could hear Cedar Creek flowing close by. I followed it west for a time, then headed back north, hoping to intersect with the trail that led back to the bar. Instead, I found myself at a rusted fence, dotted at intervals with 'Private Property' signs announcing that the land was owned by Larousse Mining Inc. Through the mesh I could see fallen trees, sunken ground, and patches of what looked like limestone. This section of the coastal plain was littered with limestone deposits; in places, the acidic groundwater had percolated through the limestone, reacting with it and dissolving it. The result was the kind of karst landscape visible through the mesh, riddled with sinkholes, small caves, and underground rivers.

I followed the fence for a time, but found no gap. It began to rain again, and I was soaked through once more by the time I got back to the bar. The bartender didn't know much about the Larousse land, except that he thought it might once have been the site of a proposed limestone quarry that had never been developed. The government had made offers on it to the Larousses in an effort to extend the state park, but they'd never been taken up.

The other witness was a woman named Euna Schillega, who had been shooting pool in the Swamp Rat when Atys and Marianne had entered the bar. She recalled the racist abuse directed at Atys and confirmed the times that they had arrived and left. She knew because, well, because the man she was shooting pool with was the man she was seeing behind her husband's back, you know what I mean, hon, and she was keeping a close eye on the time so that she'd be home before he finished his evening shift. Euna had long red hair, tinted to the color of strawberry jelly, and a small tongue of fat jutted over the lip of her faded jeans. She was saying good-bye to her forties, but in her mind she was only half as old and twice as pretty.

Euna worked part-time as a waitress in a bar near Horrel Hill. A couple of servicemen from Fort Jackson were sitting in a corner sipping beers and sweating gently in the afternoon heat. They were sitting as close as they could to the AC but it was nearly as old as Euna. The army boys would have been better off blowing air at each other over the edges of their cold bottles.

Euna was about the most cooperative of the witnesses to whom I'd spoken so far. Maybe she was bored and I was providing a distraction. I didn't know her, and I didn't imagine that I was going to, but I guessed that the pool player was probably a distraction too, the latest in a long line of distractions. There was something restless about Euna, a kind of roving hunger fueled by frustration and disappointment. It was there in the way she held herself as she spoke, the way her eyes wandered lazily across my face and body as if she were figuring out which parts to use and which to discard.

'Did you see Marianne Larousse in the bar before that night?' I asked her.

'Couple of times. Seen her in here too. She was a rich girl, but she liked to slum it some.'

'Who was she with?'

'Other rich girls. Rich boys, sometimes.'

She gave a little shudder. It might have been distaste, or perhaps something more pleasurable.

'You got to watch their hands. Those boys, they think their money buys them beer but their tip buys them mining rights, you get my meaning.'

'I take it that it doesn't.'

Remembered hunger flashed in her eyes, then was softened by the memory of her appetite's satiation. She took a long drag on her cigarette.

'Not every time.'

'You ever see her with Atys Jones before that night?'

'Once, but not in here. It ain't that kind of place. It was back at the Swamp Rat. Like I said, I go there some.'

'How did they look to you?'

'They weren't touching or nothing, but I could tell they was together. I guess other folks could too.'

She let her last words hang.

'There was trouble?'

'Not then. Next night she was back in here and her brother came looking for her.' Again there was a shudder, but this time her feelings were clear.

'You don't like him?'

'I don't know him.'

'But?'

She looked around casually, then leaned in slightly closer across the bar. The action forced her shirt open a little, exposing the sweep of her breasts and their dusting of freckles.

'The Larousses keep a lot of folks in jobs around here, but that don't mean we got to like them, Earl Jr. least of all. There's something about him, like . . . like he's a faggot but not a faggot? Don't get me wrong, I like all men, even the ones that don't like me, you know, physically and all, but not Earl Jr. There's just something about him.'

She took another drag on her cigarette. It was almost gone after three puffs.

'So Earl Jr. came into the bar looking for Marianne?'

'That's right. Took her by the arm and tried to drag her out. She slapped him, then this other fella came forward and together they managed to get her out.'

'Do you remember when this happened?'

'About a week before she was killed.'

'You think they knew about her relationship with Atys Jones?'

'Like I said, other folks knew about it. If they knew, it would get back to her family in the end.'

The door behind me opened, and a group of men entered, shouting and laughing. It was the start of the evening rush.

'I got to go, hon,' said Euna. She had already declined to sign a written statement.

'Just one more question: did you recognize the man with Earl Jr. that night?'

She thought for a moment. 'Sure. He's been in here once or twice before. He's a piece of shit. His name is Landron Mobley.'

I thanked her, and left a twenty on the bar to cover my OJ and her time. She gave me her best smile.

'Don't take this wrong, hon,' said Euna as I stood to leave, 'but that boy you're trying to help deserves what he got coming.'

'Lot of people seem to think that way.'

She blew a steady stream of smoke from her cigarette into the air, pushing out her lower lip as she did so. It was swollen slightly, like it had been bitten recently. The smoke dissipated. I watched it go.

'He raped and killed that girl,' continued Euna. 'I know you got to do what you're doing, asking questions and all, but I hope you don't find out nothing to get that boy off.'

'Even if I find out that he's innocent?'

She lifted her breasts from the bar and stabbed her cigarette out in the ashtray.

'Hon, there ain't nobody innocent in this world except little babies, and sometimes I ain't even sure about them.'

I told all of this to Elliot over the phone.

'Maybe you should talk to your client Mobley when you find him, see what he knows.'

'*If* I can find him.'

'You think he's skipped?'

There was a pause.

'I hope he's skipped,' said Elliot, but when I asked him to explain what he meant he laughed it off. 'I mean, I think Landron's facing serious jail time if it goes to trial. In legal terms, Landron's fucked.'

But that wasn't what he meant.

That wasn't what he meant at all.

I showered, then ate in my room. I called Rachel and we spoke for a while. MacArthur had been true to his word in calling by regularly, and Klan Killer was staying out of sight when the cops came by. If Rachel hadn't quite forgiven me for springing him on her, she seemed to be finding something vaguely reassuring in his presence. He was also clean and didn't leave the toilet seat up, factors that tended to weigh heavily in Rachel's formation of opinions about people. Mac Arthur was due to go out with Mary Mason that evening, and MacArthur had promised to keep Rachel posted. I told her that I loved her, and she told me that if I loved her I'd bring her back chocolates. Sometimes, Rachel was a simple girl.

After we had talked, I called to check on Atys. The woman answered and told me, best that I could understand, that he was a 'spile chile. Uh yent hab no mo' pashun wid'um.' Clearly, she was less sympathetic to Atys's plight than her husband. I asked her to put Atys on the line. Seconds later, I heard footsteps and he answered.

'How you doing?' I asked.

'Okay, I guess.' He lowered his voice. 'The old woman is killin' me. She's *hard*.'

'Just be nice to her. You got anything more you want to tell me?'

'No. I done tole you all I can.'

'And all you know?'

He didn't speak for so long I thought that he had simply put the phone down and walked away. Then he spoke.

'You ever feel like you been shadowed all your life, like there's always someone there with you, someone you can't see most of the time, but you know, you just know that they's there?'

I thought of my wife and my daughter, of their presence in my life even after they had gone, of shapes and shadows glimpsed in darkness.

'I think so,' I said.

'The woman, she's like that. I been seein' her all my life, so's I don't know if I dream her or not, but she's there. I know she is, even if there ain't nobody else sees her. That's all I know. Don't ask me no more.'

I changed the subject.

'You ever have a run-in with Earl Larousse Jr.?'

'No, never.'

'Landron Mobley?'

'I heard he was looking for me, but he didn't find me.'

'You know why he was looking for you?'

'To kick the shit out of me. Why you think Earl Jr.'s dog be lookin' for me?'

'Mobley worked for Larousse?'

'He didn't work for him, but when they needed dirty work done for them they went to Mobley. Mobley had friends, too, people worse than him.'

'Like?'

I heard him swallow.

'Like that guy on TV,' he said. 'The Klan guy. Bowen.'

That night, far to the north, the preacher, Faulkner, lay awake in his cell, his hands clasped behind his head, and listened to the night sounds of the prison: the snores, the cries from troubled sleepers, the footsteps of the guards, the sobbing. It no longer kept him awake as it had once done. He had quickly learned how to ignore it, reducing it, at worst, to the level of background noise. He could now sleep at will, but this night his thoughts were elsewhere, as they had been since the release of the man named Cyrus Nairn. And so he lay unmoving on his bunk, and waited.

'Get them off me! Get them off me!'

The prison guard Dwight Anson awoke in his bed, kicking and wrenching at the sheets, the pillow beneath his head soaked with sweat. He leaped from the bed and brushed at his bare skin, trying to remove the creatures that he felt crawling across his chest. Beside him, his wife, Aileen, reached out and switched on the bedside lamp.

'Jeez, Dwight, you're dreaming again,' she said. 'It's just a dream.'

Anson swallowed hard and tried to slow down the beating of his heart, but he still found himself shuddering and brushing aimlessly at his hair and arms.

It was the same dream, for the second night running: a dream of spiders crawling across his skin, biting him while he lay constrained in a filthy bathtub in the center of a forest. As the spiders bit him his skin began to rot, the flesh falling from his body in small clumps that left gray hollows in their wake. And all the time he was being watched from the shadows by a strange, emaciated man with red hair and thin white fingers. The man was dead, though: Anson could see his ruined skull illuminated by the moonlight, could pick out the blood on his face. Still, his eyes were alive with pleasure as he watched his pets feeding on the trapped man.

Anson placed his hands on his hips and shook his head.

'Come back to bed, Dwight,' said his wife, but he didn't move, and after a few seconds had elapsed, the disappointment showed in her eyes and she turned over and pretended to go back to sleep. Anson almost reached over to touch her, then decided against it. He didn't want to touch her. The girl he wanted to touch was missing.

Marie Blair had disappeared on the way home from her job at the Dairy Queen the night before, and had not been seen or heard from since. For a time, Anson half expected the police to come looking for him. Nobody knew about his thing with Marie, or nobody was supposed to know, but there was always the possibility that she had shot off her mouth to one of her dumb-ass friends and that, when the police came calling, they might have mentioned his name. But so far there had been nothing. Anson's wife had sensed his unease and knew that there was something bothering him, but she hadn't brought it up and that suited him fine. Still, he was worried for the girl. He wanted her back, as much for his own selfish reasons as for her own sake.

Anson left his unmoving wife and headed down the stairs to the kitchen. It was only when he opened the door of the refrigerator and reached for the milk that he felt the blast of cool air at his back and heard, almost simultaneously, the banging of the screen door against the frame.

The kitchen door was wide open. He supposed that the wind could have blown it open, but he didn't think it was likely. Aileen had come to bed after him, and she usually made sure that all the doors were locked. It wasn't like her to forget. He wondered too why they had not heard it banging before now, for even the slightest noise in the house was normally enough to wake him from his sleep. Carefully, he laid down the carton of milk and listened, but he could hear no sound in the house. From out in the yard came the whispering of the wind in the trees, and the sound of distant cars.

Anson kept a Smith & Wesson 60 in his night table. He briefly considered heading back upstairs to retrieve it before deciding against it. Instead, he took the carving knife from its block and padded to the door. He glanced first right, then left, to make sure there was nobody waiting for him outside, then pushed it open. He stood on the porch and looked out on the empty yard. Ahead of him was an expanse of tidy lawn with trees planted at its verge, shielding the house from the road beyond. The moon shone behind him, sending the clean lines of the house racing ahead of him.

Anson stepped out onto the grass.

A figure detached itself from where it had lain beneath the porch steps, the sound of its approach masked by the wind, its shape devoured by the black mass of the house's shade. Anson was not even aware of its presence until something gripped his arm and he felt a pressure across his throat, followed by a surge of pain as he watched the blood shoot up into the night. The knife fell from his grip and he turned, his left hand pressed uselessly against the wound in his neck. His legs weakened and he fell to his knees, the blood coming less freely now as he began to die.

Anson looked up into the eyes of Cyrus Nairn, and at the ring Nairn was holding in the palm of his hand. It was the garnet ring that Anson had given Marie Blair for her fifteenth birthday. He would have known it anywhere, he thought, even if it hadn't been circling Marie's severed forefinger. Then Cyrus Nairn turned away as Anson's legs began to shake uncontrollably, the moonlight gleaming on the killer's knife as he made his way to the house, Anson shaking and, at last, dying as Nairn turned his thoughts to the now slumbering Aileen Anson and the place he had prepared for her.

And in his cell at Thomaston, Faulkner closed his eyes and fell into a deep, dreamless sleep.

16

Magnolia Cemetery lies at the end of Cunnington Street, east of Meeting. Cunnington Street is a virtual cemetery row: here can be found the Old Methodist, the Friendly Union Society, the Brown Fellowship, the Humane and Friendly, the Unity and Friendship. Some are better kept than others but each serves to hold the dead with equal ease; the poor are as well-off as the wealthy, and all make the worms fat.

The dead lie scattered around Charleston, their remains resting beneath the feet of tourists and revelers. The bodies of slaves are now covered by parking lots and convenience stores, and the junction of Meeting and Water marks the site of the old cemetery where the Carolina pirates were buried after their execution. The place in which they were interred was once the low-water mark in the marsh but the city has expanded since then and the hanged men have long since been forgotten, their bones crushed by the foundations of mansions and the streets that run beside them.

But in the cemeteries of Cunnington Street the dead are remembered, in however small a way, and the greatest of these cemeteries is Magnolia. Fish jump in the waters of its lake, watched from the rushes by lazy herons and gray-white wood storks, and a sign warns of a $200 fine for feeding the alligators. Flocks of curious geese throng the narrow road to the offices of the Magnolia Cemetery Trust. Evergreens and wax myrtle shade the stones, and laurel oaks dotted with blood-spot lichen hide crying birds.

The man named Hubert has been coming here for two years. Sometimes, he chooses to sleep among the monuments with rye bread for sustenance and a bottle for comfort. He has learned the ways of the cemetery, the movements of the mourners and the staff. He does not know if his presence is tolerated or merely unnoticed, and he does not care. Hubert keeps himself to himself and he tries to bother others as little as possible in the hope that his quiet existence may continue undisturbed. There have been one or two scares with gators but nothing worse than that, although the gators were bad enough to be getting along with, if you asked Hubert.

Hubert once had a job, and a house, and a wife, until Hubert lost his job and then, in quick succession, lost his house and his wife too. For a time he even lost himself, until he came to in a hospital bed with his legs in plaster casts after a truck sideswiped him out on Route 1 somewhere north of Killian. Since then he has tried to be more careful but he will never return to his former life, despite the efforts of the social workers to establish him in a permanent home. Hubert doesn't want a permanent home because he is wise enough to understand that there is no such thing as permanency. In the end, Hubert is just waiting, and it doesn't matter where a man waits as long as he knows what he is waiting for. The thing that is coming for Hubert will find him, wherever he is. It will draw him to itself, and wrap him in its cold, dark blanket, and his name will be added to the roll call of paupers and indigents buried in cheap plots by chain-link fences. That much Hubert knows, and of that alone he is certain.

When the weather grows cold or wet, Hubert walks to the men's shelter of the Charleston Interfaith Crisis Ministry at 573 Meeting, and if there is a bed available, he fishes in the purse he keeps around his neck and hands over three crumpled dollar bills for a night's lodging. No one is ever turned away empty-handed from the shelter; at the very least they are given a full supper, toiletries if needed, even clothing. The shelter takes messages and passes on mail, although no one has sent mail to Hubert in a very long time.

It has been many weeks since Hubert last took a bed in the shelter. There have been wet nights since then, nights when the rain soaked him through and left him sneezing for days, but he has not returned to the beds at 573 Meeting, not since the night that he saw the olive-skinned man with the damaged eyes, the strange light that danced before him, and the shape that it assumed.

He had noticed him for the first time in the showers. Hubert doesn't look at the other men in the showers as a rule. That is a way of attracting attention and maybe trouble to himself, and Hubert doesn't want that. Hubert isn't very tall or very strong and he has lost possessions in the past to men more violent than he. He has learned to stay out of their way and not to meet their eyes, which is why he always looks down in the shower, and why the other man first came to his notice.

It was his ankles, and the scarring around them. Hubert had never seen anything like it before. It was as if the man's feet had been severed from his legs and then crudely reattached, leaving the marks of the stitches as a reminder of what had occurred. It was then that Hubert broke his own rule and glanced up at the man beside him, at his stringy muscles, his frizzy hair, and his strange haunted eyes, semibleached of color and obscured by clouds. He was humming something to himself, and Hubert thought that it might have been a hymn or one of those old Negro spirituals. The words were unclear, but Hubert picked up on some of them.

Walk with me, brother,
Come walk with me, sister,
And we'll walk, and we'll walk
On the White Road to—

The man caught Hubert looking at him, and fixed him with a stare.

'You ready to walk, brother?' he asked.

And Hubert found himself answering, his voice sounding strange to him as it echoed hollowly from the tiles: 'Walk where?'

'On the White Road. Are you ready to walk on the White Road? She's waiting for you there, brother. She's watching you.'

'I don't know what you're talking about,' said Hubert.

'Sure you do, Hubert. Sure you do.'

Hubert turned off the shower and stood back, grabbing his towel from the rail. He didn't say anything more, even when the man began to laugh and called to him: 'Hey, brother, you mind your step, now, y'hear? You don't go stumbling, you don't go falling. You don't want to fall down on the White Road, because they folks waiting for you, waiting for you to fall. And when you fall, they going to take you. They going to take you and they going to tear you apart!'

And as Hubert hurried from the showers, the song began again:

Walk with me, brother.
Come walk with me, sister.
And we'll walk, and we'll walk
On the White Road together.

That night, Hubert was assigned a cot by the rest rooms. Hubert didn't mind. His bladder played up sometimes, and he often had to get up two or three times a night to take a leak. But it wasn't his bladder that caused him to wake that night.

It was the sound of a female voice, crying.

Hubert knew that couldn't be right. The family shelter was down at 49 Walnut, and that was where the women and children slept. There was no cause for a woman to be in the men's shelter, but there were men among the homeless whose ways nobody could know, and Hubert didn't want to think of a woman or, worse, a child being hurt by anybody.

He rose from his bed and followed the noise. It came from the showers, he thought. He recognized the way the voice echoed, recalling the sound of his own voice and the man's song earlier in the evening. Hubert padded to the entrance and stood there, transfixed. The olive-skinned man was standing before the silent showers, dressed in cotton shorts and an old black T-shirt, his back to the doorway. There was a light shining before him, bathing his face and body in light, although the showers themselves were dark and the fluorescents were off. Hubert found himself moving to catch a better sight of the light source, sliding softly to his right in his bare feet, his eyes straining.

There was a pillar of light before the man, maybe five feet in height. It shifted, flickering like a candle flame, and it seemed to Hubert that there was a figure behind or within it, cocooned in its glow.

It was a little blonde girl. Her face was contorted in pain, her head shaking from side to side in a blur of movement, faster than was humanly possible, and he could hear the sound of her cries, a steady *nuh-nuh-nuh-nuh-nuh* filled with fear and agony and rage. Her clothes were shredded and she was naked from the waist down, her body torn and marked where she had been dragged along the road beneath the wheels of the car.

Hubert knew who she was. Oh yes, Hubert knew. Ruby Blanton, that was her name. Pretty little Ruby Blanton, killed when a guy distracted by his pager hit her as she was crossing the street to her house and dragged her sixty feet beneath the wheels of his car. Hubert recalled her head turning at the last moment, the impact of the hood against her body, the final sight of her eyes before she disappeared under his wheels.

Oh, Hubert knew who she was. He knew for sure.

The man standing before her made no attempt to reach for her, or to console her. Instead, he hummed the song that Hubert had heard for the first time that day.

Walk with me, brother.
Come walk with me, sister.
And we'll walk, and we'll walk—

He turned, and something shone behind those blighted eyes as they regarded Hubert.

'You on the White Road now, brother,' he whispered. 'You come see what's been waiting for you on the White Road.'

He moved aside, and the light advanced toward Hubert, the girl's head shaking, her eyes closed and the sound pouring from her lips like the steady drip of water.

Nuh-nuh-nuh-nuh-nuh.

Her eyes opened and Hubert stared into them, his guilt reflected deep within, and he felt himself falling, falling to the clean tiles, falling toward his own reflection.

Falling, falling, to the White Road.

They found him there later, blood pooling from the wound he had opened in his head on impact. A doctor was called, and he asked Hubert about dizzy spells and alcohol consumption and suggested that Hubert should maybe take up the offer of a proper home. Hubert thanked him, then collected his things and left the shelter. The olive-skinned man was already gone and Hubert didn't see him again, although he found himself looking over his shoulder, and for a time he didn't sleep in Magnolia, preferring instead to sleep in streets and alleys, among the living.

But now he has returned to the cemetery. It is his place, and the memory of the vision in the showers is almost forgotten, the stain of its recalling papered over with the excuse of alcohol and tiredness and the temperature he had been running since before that night at the shelter.

Hubert sometimes sleeps close to the Stolle grave, marked by the figure of a woman weeping at the foot of a cross. It is sheltered by trees, and from here he can see the road and the lake. Nearby is a flat granite stone covering the resting place of a man named Bennet Spree, a comparatively recent addition to the old cemetery. The plot had been in the ownership of the Spree family for a very long time but Bennet Spree was the last of his line and he had finally claimed the plot as his own when he died in July 1981.

There is a shape lying on Bennet Spree's stone as Hubert approaches. For a moment he almost turns away, not wanting to argue with another wanderer over territory and not trusting a stranger enough to want to sleep beside him in the cemetery, but something about the form draws him closer. As he nears it a light breeze stirs the trees, dappling the figure with moonlight, and Hubert can see that it is naked and that the shadows that lie on the body are unaltered by the movement of the trees.

There is a ragged wound at the man's throat, a strange hole, as if something has been inserted into his mouth through the soft flesh beneath his chin. The torso and legs are almost black with blood.

But there are two other things that Hubert notices before he turns and runs.

The first is that the man has been castrated.

The second is the implement that has been thrust into his chest. It is rusted and T-shaped and a note is impaled upon it, the blood from the man's chest staining it slightly. There is something written on the note in neatly drawn letters.

It reads: DIG HERE.

And they will dig. A judge will be sought and an exhumation order signed, for Bennet Spree has no living relatives to give their consent to the further desecration of his resting place. It will be a day or two before the rotting coffin is lifted from the ground, carefully bound with ropes and plastic so that it does not fall apart and spill Bennet Spree's mortal remains upon the dark, exposed earth.

And where the coffin had rested for so long they will find a thin sprinkling of earth, and as they move it carefully away bones will be revealed: first the ribs, then the skull, its jawbone shattered, the cranium itself broken, cracks radiating from the ragged holes gouged in it by the blows that killed her.

It is all that is left of a girl on the verge of becoming a woman.

It is all that is left of Addy, the mother of Atys Jones.

And her son will die without ever knowing the final resting place of the woman who brought him into this world.

PART FOUR

When [the angels] descend, they put on the garment of this
world.
If they did not put on a garment befitting this world
they could not endure in this world and the world could not
endure them.

The Zohar

17

It was almost sunrise.

Cyrus Nairn crouched naked in the dark womb of the hollow. Soon, he would have to leave this place. They would come looking for him, suspecting immediately some form of vendetta against the guard Anson and turning their attention toward those who had most recently been released from Thomaston. Cyrus would be sorry to go. He had spent so long dreaming of being back here, surrounded by the smell of damp earth, root ends caressing his bare back and shoulders. Still, there would be other rewards. He had been promised so much. In return, sacrifices were to be expected.

From outside there came the calling of the first birds, the gentle lapping of the water upon the banks, the buzzing of the last night insects as they fled the approaching light, but Cyrus was deaf to the sounds of life beyond the hole. Instead he remained motionless, conscious only of the noises coming from the loose earth under his feet, both watching and feeling the slight shifting as Aileen Anson struggled beneath the dirt and, finally, grew still.

I was woken up by the telephone ringing in my room. It was 8:15 A.M.

'Charlie Parker?' said a male voice that I didn't recognize.

'Yeah. Who is this?'

'You got a breakfast appointment in ten minutes. You don't want to keep Mr. Wyman waiting.' He hung up.

Mr. Wyman.

Willie Wyman.

The boss of the Dixie Mafia's Charleston branch wanted to have breakfast with me.

This was not a good way to start the day.

The Dixie Mafia had existed, in one form or another, since Prohibition, a conglomeration of loosely associated criminals with bases in most of the big Southern cities but particularly Atlanta, Georgia, and Biloxi, Mississippi. They recruited one another for out-of-state jobs: an arson attack in Mississippi might be the work of a firefly from Georgia, or a hit in South Carolina could be farmed out to a contract killer from Maryland. The Dixies were pretty unsophisticated, dealing in drugs, gambling, murder, extortion, robbery, arson. The closest they ever got to white-collar crime was robbing a laundry, but that didn't mean that they weren't a force to be reckoned with. In September 1987, the Dixie Mafia had murdered a judge, Vincent Sherry, and his wife, Margaret, at their home in Biloxi. It was never made clear why Sherry and his wife had been shot – there were allegations that Vincent Sherry had been involved in criminal operations through the law offices of Halat and Sherry, and Sherry's law partner, Peter Halat, was later convicted on charges of racketeering and murder connected to the deaths of the Sherrys – but the reasons behind the murders were largely inconsequential. Men who kill judges are dangerous because they will act before they think. They don't weigh up the consequence of their actions until after the fact.

In 1983 Paul Mazzell, the then boss of the Charleston branch, was convicted with Eddie Merriman of the murder of Ricky Lee Seagreaves, who had robbed one of Mazzell's drug deals. Since then, Willie Wyman had been the king in Charleston. He was five four in height and weighed about one hundred pounds in wet clothes, but he was mean and cunning and capable of doing just about anything to maintain his position. At 8:30 A.M., he was sitting at a table by the wall in Charleston Place's main dining room, eating bacon and eggs. There was one other empty chair at the table. Nearby, four men sat in two pairs at separate tables, keeping watch over Willie, the door, and me.

Willie had short, very dark hair, deeply tanned skin, and was wearing a bright blue shirt and blue chinos. The shirt was decorated with small white clouds. He looked up at me as I approached the table and waved his fork to indicate that I should join him. One of his men seemed about to frisk me but Willie, conscious of operating in a public place, waved him away.

'We don't need to frisk you, do we?'

'I'm not armed.'

'Good. I don't think the people at Charleston Place would appreciate their breakfast tables being all shot up. You want to order? It's on you.' He grinned humorlessly.

I ordered coffee, juice, and toast from the waitress. Willie finished devouring his food and wiped his mouth on a napkin.

'Now,' he said, 'to business. I hear you kicked Andy Dalitz's nuts so far up his tubes that he can scratch them by sticking his fingers in his mouth.'

He waited for a reply. Under the circumstances, it seemed wise to oblige.

'LapLand's your place?' I said.

'One of them. Look, I know Andy Dalitz is a moron. Hell, I've wanted to kick him in the nuts for as long as I've known him, but the guy's got three fucking Adam's apples now because of you. Maybe he had it coming, I don't know. All I'm saying is that if you want to visit one of our clubs, then you should ask, and ask nice. Kicking the manager so hard that he can taste his balls in his mouth is not asking nice.

'And I got to tell you: if you'd done that in public, in front of customers or the girls, then we'd be having a very different conversation now. Because if you make Andy look bad, then you make me look bad, and the next thing you know I have guys thinking maybe my time has come and I should make way for somebody new. Then I have two choices: I either convince them that they're wrong, and then I got to find somewhere to put them and we waste a day driving around with them stinking up the trunk until we find a place, or else I'm the one stinking up the trunk and between you and me, that's not gonna happen. We clear?'

My coffee, OJ, and toast arrived. I poured the coffee and offered Willie the option of a fresh refill. He accepted, and thanked me. He was nothing if not polite.

'We're clear,' I assured him.

'I know all about you,' he said. 'You could screw up paradise. The only reason you're still alive is that even God doesn't want you near Him. I hear you're working with Elliot Norton on the Jones case. Is there something I need to know here, because that case stinks like my kid's diapers? Andy told me you wanted to speak to the half-breed, Tereus.'

'Is that what he is?'

'The fuck am I, his cousin?' He relented a little. 'His people came from Kentucky way back, is all I know. Who knows who they were fucking out there? There are people in those mountains who are maybe half fucking goat because their daddies got an itch at a bad time. Even the blacks don't want nothing to do with Tereus or his kind. Lesson over. Give me something.'

I didn't have any choice but to tell him something of what I knew.

'Tereus visited Atys Jones in jail. I wanted to know why.'

'You find out?'

'I think Tereus knew the family. Plus he's found Jesus.'

Willie looked unhappy, although not terminally so.

'That's what he told Andy. I figure Jesus should be more careful about who finds Him. I know you're not telling me everything, but I'm not going to make an issue of it, not this time. I'd prefer it if you didn't go back to the club, but if you do have to go, keep it discreet and don't kick Andy Dalitz in the balls again. In return, I expect you to let me know if there's anything that I should be worried about, you understand?'

'I understand.'

He nodded, seemingly content, then sipped his coffee.

'You tracked down that preacher, right? Faulk ner?'

'That's right.'

He watched me carefully. He seemed amused.

'I hear Roger Bowen is trying to get him out.'

I hadn't called Elliot since Atys Jones had told me of Mobley's connection to Bowen. I wasn't sure how it fitted into what I already knew. Now, as Willie Wyman mentioned Bowen's name, I tried to block out the noise from the adjoining tables and listen only to him.

'You curious about why that might be?' Willie continued.

'Very.'

He leaned back and stretched, exposing the sprinkling of sweat under his arms.

'Roger and me go way back, and not in a good way. He's a fanatic and he has no respect. I've thought about maybe sending him away on a cruise: a long cruise, strictly one-way to the bottom, but then the crazies would come knocking on my door and it would be cruises for everyone. I don't know what Bowen wants with the preacher: a figurehead, maybe, or could be the old man has something stashed away that Bowen wants to get hold of. Like I said, I don't know, but you want to ask him, I can tell you where he'll be later today.'

I waited.

'There's a rally in Antioch. Rumor is that Bowen is going to talk at it. There'll be press there, maybe some TV. Bowen didn't use to make public appearances too often, but this Faulkner thing has brought him out from under his rock. You go along, you might get to say hi.'

'Why are you telling me this?'

He stood, and the other four men rose at the same time.

'I figure why should it just be me who has his day fucked up by you, you know? If you've got shit on your shoe, you spread it around. And Bowen's already having a bad day. I like the idea of you making it worse.'

'What's so bad about today for Bowen?'

'You should watch the news. They found his pit bull Mobley up at Magnolia cemetery last night. He was castrated. I gotta go tell Andy Dalitz, maybe make him see how lucky he was just to get his nuts bruised instead of cut off completely. Thanks for breakfast.'

He left me, his blue shirt billowing, his four goons in tow like big children following a little piece of fallen sky.

Elliot did not turn up for our scheduled meeting that morning. The answering machine was picking up calls at his office and at his home. His cell phones – both his own and the clean one we were using for day-to-day contact – were off. Meanwhile, the papers were full of the discovery of Landron Mobley's body at the Magnolia cemetery, but hard details were scarce. According to the reports, Elliot Norton had been uncontactable for comment on his client's death.

I spent the morning confirming the details of more witness statements, knocking on trailer doors and fighting off dogs in overgrown yards. By midday I was worried. I checked on Atys by phone, and the old man told me he was doing okay, although he was becoming a little stir-crazy. I spoke to Atys for a couple of minutes, but his replies were surly at best.

'When can I leave here, man?' he asked me.

'Soon,' I replied. It was only a half truth. If Elliot's fears about his safety were real, my guess was that we'd be moving him soon enough, but only to another safe house. Until his trial, Atys was going to have to get used to staring at TVs in unfamiliar rooms. Pretty soon, though, he wouldn't be my concern. I was getting nowhere fast with the witnesses.

'You know Mobley's dead?'

'Yeah, I heard. I'm all cut up.'

'Not as cut up as he is. You got any idea who might have done a thing like that to him?'

'No I ain't, but you find out, you let me know. I want to shake the man's hand, m'sayin?'

He hung up. I looked at my watch. It was just after twelve. It would take me more than an hour to get to Antioch. I tossed a mental coin and decided to go.

The Carolina Klans, in common with klaverns across the country, had been in decline for the best part of twenty years. In the case of the Carolinas the decline could be dated back to November 1979, when five Communist Workers died in a shoot-out with Klansmen and neo-Nazis up in Greensboro, North Carolina. The anti-Klan movements assumed a new momentum in the aftermath while Klan membership continued to drop, and on those occasions when Klansmen took to the streets, they were vastly outnumbered by protesters. Most of the recent Klan rallies in South Carolina had been the work of the Indiana-based American Knights of the Ku Klux Klan, since the local Carolina Knights had demonstrated a reluctance to become involved.

But against their decline had to be set the fact that over thirty black churches had been burned in South Carolina since 1991 and Klansmen had been linked to at least two of those burnings, in Williamsburg and Clarendon counties. In other words, the Klan may have been dying on its feet, but the hatred that it represented was still alive and well. Now Bowen was trying to give that hatred a new momentum, and a new focus. If the news reports were to be believed, he was succeeding.

Antioch didn't look like it had too much to recommend it at the best of times. It resembled the suburb of a town that didn't exist: there were houses, and streets that somebody had taken the trouble to name, but none of the larger malls or town centers that might have been expected to grow up alongside them. Instead, the section of 119 that passed through Antioch had sprouted small strip malls like clumps of mushrooms, boasting between them little more than a couple of gas stations, a video store, a pair of convenience stores, a bar and, a laundromat.

It looked like I had missed the parade, but midway along the strip was a green square surrounded by a wire fence and untended trees. Cars were parked nearby, maybe sixty in all, and a makeshift stage had been created on the back of a flatbed truck, from which a man was addressing the crowd. A group of about eighty or ninety, consisting mostly of men but with some women scattered throughout, stood before the stage listening to the speaker. A handful wore white robes but most of them were dressed in their usual T-shirts and jeans. The men in the robes were sweating visibly beneath the cheap polyester. A crowd of fifty or sixty protesters stood some distance away, kept back from Bowen's people by a line of police. Some were chanting and catcalling, but the man speaking from the stage never broke his stride.

Roger Bowen had a thick brown mustache and wavy brown hair, and he looked like he kept himself in good condition. He wore a red shirt and blue jeans, but despite the heat his shirt appeared to be unsullied by sweat. He was flanked by two men who led the occasional bursts of applause when he said something particularly important, which seemed to be about every three minutes, judging by his aides. Each time they applauded, Bowen looked to his feet and shook his head, as if embarrassed by their enthusiasm yet unwilling to curb it. I spotted the cameraman from the Richland County lockup close by the stage with a pretty blond reporter close by. He was still wearing his fatigues, but this time nobody was giving him a hard time over them.

I had a CD playing in the car at top volume as I cruised in. I'd chosen it especially for the occasion. My timing was pretty good. Joey Ramone's girl had gone to L.A. and never come back, and Joey was blaming the KKK for taking his baby away just as I swung into the parking lot.

Bowen paused in his speech and stared over in my direction. A considerable portion of the crowd followed his gaze. A guy with a shaven head and wearing a black 'Blitzkrieg' T-shirt approached the car and asked politely but firmly if I would turn the music down. I killed the engine, cutting the music off, then stepped from the car. Bowen kept looking in my direction for about another ten seconds, then continued his speech.

Perhaps he was conscious of the media presence, but Bowen appeared to be keeping the invective to a minimum. True, he tossed in references to Jews and coloreds, talked of how non-Christians had seized control of the government at the expense of white people, and spoke of AIDS as a visitation from God, but he steered away from the worst racial slurs. It was only as his speech reached its close that he got to his main point.

'There is a man, my friends, a good man, a Christian man, a man of God, who is being persecuted for daring to say that homosexuality and abortion and the mixing of races is against the will of the Lord. A show trial is being organized in the state of Maine to bring this man down and we have evidence, my friends, *hard* evidence, that his capture was funded by Jews.' Bowen waved some papers that looked vaguely legal in form. 'His name, and I hope you know it already, is Aaron Faulkner. Now they've said some things about him. They've called him a murderer and a sadist. They have tried to smear his name, to drag him down before his trial has even begun. They are doing this because they have no proof against him and are trying to poison the minds of the weak so that he will be found guilty before he even has the chance to defend himself. The Reverend Faulkner's message is one that we should all take to heart, because we know it is right and true. Homosexuality is against God's law. Baby killing is against God's law. The mixing of bloods, the undermining of the institutions of marriage and the family, the elevation of non-Christian worship above the one true religion of Jesus Christ, our Lord and Savior, all are against God's law, and this man, the Reverend Faulkner, has taken a stand against it. Now his only hope for a fair trial is if he can assemble himself the best defense possible, and to do that he needs funds to get himself out of jail and pay the finest attorneys that money can buy. And that's where you folks come in: you give what you can. I count maybe one hundred here. You give twenty bucks each, and I know that's a lot for some of you people, and we got two thousand dollars. If those of you that can afford it give a little more, well, then that's all for the better.

'Because you mark my words: It is not just one man who is facing a false trial. It is a way of life. It is *our* way of life, *our* beliefs, *our* faith, our *futures* that will be on trial in that courtroom. The Reverend Aaron Faulkner represents us all, and if he falls, then we fall with him. God is with us. God will give us strength. Hail victory! Hail victory!'

The chant was taken up by the crowd as men moved among them with buckets, collecting donations. I saw the odd ten or five slipped in, but most gave twenties, even fifties or hundreds. At a conservative estimate, I reckoned Bowen's work this afternoon had probably made three thousand dollars. According to that day's paper, which had carried some advance coverage of the rally, Bowen's people had been working flat out since shortly after Faulk ner's arrest, encouraging everything from yard sales and bake-offs to a draw for a new Dodge truck donated by a sympathetic auto dealer, with thousands of tickets already sold at $20 a pop. Bowen had even succeeded in galvanizing into action those who would not usually have been drawn to his cause, the vast constituency of the faithful who saw in Faulkner a man of God being persecuted for beliefs that were similar, if not identical, to their own. Bowen had taken Faulkner's arrest and approaching trial and made it a matter of faith and goodness, a battle between those who feared and loved the Lord and those who had turned their backs on Him. When the subject of violence was raised Bowen usually skirted the issue, arguing that Faulkner's message was pure and that he could not be held accountable for the actions of others, even if those actions were justified in many cases. Racist insults would be kept for the old guard and for those occasions where TV cameras and microphones were absent or forbidden. Today, he was preaching to the new converts and those who had yet to be converted.

Bowen stepped from the stage and people moved forward to shake his hand. Just inside the gate, two trestle tables had been set up so that the women behind them could display the items they had brought for sale: Johnny Reb flags, Nazi battle flags decorated with eagles and swastikas, bumper stickers announcing that the driver was 'White by Birth, Southern by Grace.' There were also cassettes and CDs of country and western music, although I figured that they weren't the kind Louis would have wanted in his collection. Pretty soon, the two women were doing steady business.

A man appeared at my side. He wore a dark suit over a white shirt, with a baseball cap perched incongruously on his head. His skin was reddish purple, and peeling badly. Clumps of fair hair hung on grimly to his skull like sparse vegetation on a hostile landscape. Shades concealed his eyes. I could see an earpiece in his left ear, connected to a unit at his belt. Immediately, I felt uneasy. Maybe it was the strangeness of his appearance, but there was a sense of unreality about him. There was also a smell emanating from him, like the odor left after an oil fire has been extinguished.

He smelled of slow burning.

'Mr. Bowen would like to talk to you,' he said.

'It was the Ramones,' I said. 'On the CD player. I'll make him a copy if he'd like it.'

He didn't blink.

'Like I said, Mr. Bowen wants to talk to you.'

I shrugged and followed him through the crowd. Bowen had almost finished glad-handing the troops, and as I watched, he stepped behind the truck to a small area enclosed by a white tarp that stretched from the bed of the truck. Beneath it were chairs, a portable AC unit, and a table with a cooler on top. I was shown through to Bowen, who sat in one of the chairs sipping from a can of Pepsi. The cap-wearing man stayed but the other people bustling outside moved away to give us some privacy. Bowen offered me a drink. I declined.

'We didn't expect to see you down here today, Mr. Parker,' he said. 'You considering joining our cause?'

'I don't see much of a cause,' I said, 'unless you call hustling rednecks for dimes a cause.'

Bowen exchanged a look of mock disappointment with the other man. There was blood in Bowen's eyes. Although he was ostensibly in charge, he appeared to defer to the man in the suit. Even his posture suggested that he was somehow afraid of him, his body turned slightly away from the other man, his head lowered. He looked like a cowering dog.

'I should have introduced you,' he said. 'Mr. Parker, this is Mr. Kittim. Sooner or later, Mr. Kittim is going to teach you a harsh lesson.'

Kittim removed his sunglasses. The eyes revealed were empty and green, like raw, flawed emeralds.

'Forgive me if I don't shake hands,' I said to him. 'You look like bits of you might start to drop off.'

Kittim didn't react, but the smell of oil grew stronger. Even Bowen's nose wrinkled slightly.

Bowen finished his cola and tossed it in the garbage bag.

'Why are you here, Mr. Parker? If I was to get up on that stage and announce to the crowd who you are, I think your chances of getting back to Charleston unscathed would be very slim.'

Maybe I should have been surprised that Bowen knew that I was staying in Charleston, but I wasn't.

'Keeping track of my movements, Bowen? I'm flattered. By the way, it's not a stage. It's a truck. Don't get above yourself. You want to tell the morons who I am, go right ahead. The TV cameras will eat it up. As for why I'm here, I wanted to take a look at you, see if you're really as dumb as you seem to be.'

'Why am I dumb?'

'Because you're aligning yourself with Faulkner, and if you were smart you'd see that he's crazy, even crazier than your friend here.'

Bowen's eyes flicked toward the other man. 'I don't think Mr. Kittim is crazy,' he said. The words left a sour taste in his mouth. I could see it in the curl of his lips.

I followed his glance. There were flakes of dried skin caught in Kittim's remaining hair and his face almost throbbed with the pain of his condition. He seemed to be slowly disintegrating. His was a Catch-22 situation: looking and feeling the way he did, he'd have to be crazy not to be crazy.

'The Reverend Faulkner is a man unjustly persecuted,' resumed Bowen. 'All I want to see is justice done, and justice will result in his vindication and release.'

'Justice is blind, not stupid, Bowen.'

'Sometimes it's both.' He stood up. We were almost the same height but he was broader than I was. 'The Reverend Faulkner is about to become a figurehead for a new movement, a unifying force. We're bringing more people into our fold day by day. With people come money and power and influence. This isn't complex, Mr. Parker. It's very simple. Faulkner is the means. I am the end. Now, I'd advise you to go and take in some of the sights of South Carolina while you still can. I have a feeling it may be the last chance that you have. Mr. Kittim will escort you back to your car.'

With Kittim at my side, I walked through the crowd. The TV crews had packed up and left. Children had joined the celebrations, running in between the legs of their parents. Music was playing from the trestle tables, country music that spoke of war and vengeance. Barbecues had been set up, and the smell of burning meat filled the air. Close by one of them, a man with slicked-back hair bit greedily into a hot dog. I looked away before he could see me staring at him. I recognized him as the man who had followed me from the airport to Charleston Place and who had then pointed me out to Earl Larousse Jr. Both Atys Jones and Willie Wyman had confirmed to me that the late Landron Mobley, in addition to being a client of Elliot's, had been one of Bowen's attack dogs. Mobley, it seemed, had also been helping the Larousses hunt down Atys before Marianne's death. Now another link between the Larousses and Bowen had been revealed.

At my car I turned to Kittim. He had replaced his sunglasses, obscuring his eyes. An object lay on the ground between us. He pointed his finger at it.

'You dropped something,' said Kittim.

It was a black skullcap, ringed with a red and gold band. Blood had soaked into it. It hadn't been there when I'd parked.

'I don't think so,' I said.

'I suggest you take it with you. I'm sure you know some old kikes who'd be glad to receive it. It might answer some questions that they have.'

He backed away from me, made a pistol from the finger and thumb of his right hand, then fired it at me as a farewell.

'I'll be seeing you,' he said.

I picked up the skullcap from the ground and wiped the dirt from it. There was no name inside it, but I knew that it could only have come from one source. I drove as far as the nearest strip mall and made a call to New York.

When the end of the working day came with no contact from Elliot, I decided to go looking for him. I drove out to his house, but the workmen hadn't seen him since the day before, and as far as they could tell, he hadn't slept in the house the previous night. I headed back to Charleston and decided to check the tag number of Elliot's dining companion from earlier in the week. I took out my laptop and, ignoring the e-mail notifications, went straight to the Web. I entered the license plate on three databases, the huge NCI and CDB Infotek services as well as SubTrace, which flirted with illegality and was more expensive than regular searches but was faster too. I red-flagged the SubTrace request and got a response less than an hour later. Elliot had been arguing with one Adele Foster of 1200 Bees Tree Drive, Charleston. I found Bees Tree on my DeLorme street atlas and headed out.

Number 1200 was an impressive classical revival tabby manse that must have been more than a century old, its facade constructed from a mixture of oyster shell and lime mortar and dominated by a two-tiered entry porch supported by slender white columns. The SUV was parked to the right of the house. I walked slowly up the central staircase, stood in the shade of the porch, and rang the doorbell. The sound of it echoed in the hallway beyond, eventually losing itself in the sound of firm footsteps on the boards before the door opened. I half expected Hattie McDaniel to be standing before me in a pinafore, but instead it was the woman I had seen arguing with Elliot Norton on my first night in town. Behind her, dark wood extended through the empty white hallway like muddy water through snow.

'Yes?'

And suddenly I didn't know what to say. I wasn't even sure why I had come here, except that I couldn't find Elliot and something told me that the argument I had witnessed went beyond any professional issue, that there was more between them than a typical client-lawyer relationship. Also, seeing her up close for the first time, I was confirmed in another suspicion that I had: she was wearing widow's weeds. All she needed was a hat and a veil and the look would have been complete.

'I'm sorry to disturb you,' I said. 'My name is Charlie Parker. I'm a private investigator.'

I was about to reach into my pocket for ID but a movement on her face stopped me. Her expression didn't soften, exactly, but something flashed across it, like a tree moving in the wind that briefly allows moonlight to flash through its branches and illuminate the bare ground beneath.

'You're him, aren't you?' she said softly. 'You're the one that he hired.'

'If you mean Elliot Norton, then yes, I'm the one.'

'Did he send you here?' There was no hostility in the question. Instead, I thought there something almost plaintive in it.

'No, I saw you . . . talking to him in a restaurant two nights ago.'

Briefly, she smiled. 'I'm not sure that "talking" was what we were doing. Did he tell you who I was?'

'To be honest, I didn't tell him that I'd seen you together, but I made a note of your license plate.'

She pursed her lips. 'How very farsighted of you. Is that how you usually behave: making notes on women you've never met?'

If she was expecting me to act embarrassed, she was disappointed.

'Sometimes,' I said. 'I'm trying to give it up, but the flesh is weak.'

'So why are you here?'

'I was wondering if you might have seen Elliot.'

Instantly, there was worry on her face.

'Not since that night. Is something wrong?'

'I don't know. Can I come in, Ms. Foster?'

She blinked. 'How do you know my name? No, let me guess, the same way you found out where I lived, right? Jesus, nothing's private anymore.'

I waited, anticipating the closing of the door in my face. Instead, she stepped to one side and gestured for me to enter. I followed her into the hallway and the door closed softly behind me.

There was no furniture in the hall, not even a hat stand. Before me, a staircase swept up to the second floor and the bedrooms. To my right was a dining room, a bare table surrounded by ten chairs at its center. To my left was a living room. I followed her into it. She took a seat at one end of a pale gold couch, and I eased myself into an armchair close by. Somewhere, a clock ticked, but otherwise the house was silent.

'Elliot's missing?'

'I didn't say that. I've left messages. So far, he hasn't replied.'

She digested the information. It seemed to disagree with her.

'And you thought that I might know where he is?'

'You met him for dinner. I figured that you might be friends.'

'What kind of friends?'

'The kind that have dinner together. What do you want me to say, Ms. Foster?'

'I don't know, and it's *Mrs.* Foster.'

I started to apologize but she waved it away. 'It's not important,' she said. 'I suppose you want to know about Elliot and me?'

I didn't reply. I wasn't going to pry into her affairs any more than was necessary, but if she felt the need to talk, then I'd listen in the hope that I might learn something from her.

'Hell, you saw us fighting, you can probably guess the rest. Elliot was a friend of my husband. My late husband.' She was smoothing her skirt with her hand, the only indication she gave that she might be nervous.

'I'm sorry.'

She nodded. 'We all are.'

'Can I ask what happened?'

She looked up from her skirt and stared directly at me. 'He killed himself.' She coughed once, then seemed to have trouble continuing. The coughing grew in intensity. I stood and followed the living room through to where a bright modern kitchen had been added to the rear of the house. I found a glass, filled it with water from the tap, and brought it back to her. She sipped at it, then placed it on the low table before her.

'Thank you,' she said. 'I don't know why that happened. I guess I still find it hard to talk about. My husband, James, killed himself one month ago. He asphyxiated himself in his car by attaching a pipe to the exhaust and feeding it through the window. It's not uncommon, I'm told.'

She could have been talking about a minor ailment, like a cold or a rash. Her voice was studiedly matter-of-fact. She took another sip from the glass of water.

'Elliot was my husband's lawyer, as well as his friend.'

I waited.

'I shouldn't be telling you this,' she said. 'But if Elliot's gone . . .'

The way that she said the word 'gone' made my stomach lurch, but still I didn't interrupt.

'Elliot was my lover,' she said at last.

'Was?'

'It ended shortly before my husband's death.'

'When did it begin?'

'Why do these things ever begin?' she answered, mishearing the question. She wanted to tell and she would tell it in her own way and at her own pace. 'Boredom, discontent, a husband too tied up with his work to notice that his wife was going crazy. Take your pick.'

'Did your husband know?'

She paused before she answered, as if she were thinking about it for only the first time. 'If he did, then he didn't say anything. At least, not to me.'

'To Elliot?'

'He made comments. They were open to more than one interpretation.'

'How did Elliot choose to interpret them?'

'That James knew. It was Elliot who decided to end things between us. I didn't care enough about him to disagree.'

'So why were you arguing with him at dinner?'

She resumed the rhythmic stroking of her skirt, picking at pieces of lint too small to be of real concern.

'Something is happening. Elliot knows, but he pretends that he doesn't. They're all pretending.'

The stillness in the house suddenly seemed terribly oppressive. There should have been children in this house, I thought. It was too big for two people, and far too large for one. It was the kind of house bought by wealthy people in the hope of populating it with a family, but I could see no trace of any family here. Instead there was only this woman in her widow's black picking methodically at the tiny flaws in her skirt, as if by doing so she could make the greater wrongs right again.

'What do you mean by "them all"?'

'Elliot. Landron Mobley. Grady Truett. Phil Poveda. My husband. And Earl Larousse. Earl Jr., that is.'

'Larousse?' I couldn't keep the surprise from my voice.

Once again, there was the trace of a smile on Adele Foster's face. 'They all grew up together, all six of them. Now something has started to happen. My husband's death was the beginning. Grady Truett's was the continuation.'

'What happened to Grady Truett?'

'Somebody broke into his home about a week after James died. He was tied to a chair in his den, then his throat was cut.'

'And you think the two deaths are connected?'

'Here's what I think: Marianne Larousse was killed ten weeks ago. James died six weeks later. Grady Truett was killed one week after that. Now Landron Mobley has been found dead, and Elliot is missing.'

'Were any of them close to Marianne Larousse?'

'No, not if you mean intimate with her, but like I said, they grew up with her brother and would have known her socially. Well, maybe not Landron Mobley but certainly the others.'

'And what do you believe is happening, Mrs. Foster?'

She took a deep breath, her nostrils flaring, her head rising, then released it slowly. In the gesture there was a trace of a spirit that had been subdued by the black clothes and it was possible to see what had attracted Elliot to her.

'My husband killed himself because he was afraid, Mr. Parker. Something he had done had come back to haunt him. He told Elliot, but Elliot wouldn't believe him. He wouldn't tell me what it was. Instead, he pretended that everything was normal, right up until the day he went into the garage with a length of yellow hose and killed himself. Elliot is also trying to pretend that things are normal, but I think he knows better.'

'What do you think your husband was afraid of?'

'Not what. I think he was afraid of someone.'

'Do you have any idea who that person might have been?'

Adele Foster rose and, with a movement of her hand, indicated that I should follow her. We ascended the staircase, past what, in the house's former days, would have been used as a receiving room for visitors but was now a large and very luxurious bedroom. We paused in front of a closed door, in its keyhole a key that she now turned to unlock the door. Then, keeping her back to the room, she pushed the door open and revealed its contents.

The room had once been a small bedroom or dressing room, but James Foster had transformed it into an office. There was a computer desk and chair, a drafting board, and a set of shelves against one wall lined with books and files. A window looked out onto the front yard, the top of the flowering dogwood below the window visible above the bottom of the frame, the last of its white blooms now fading and dying. A blue jay stood on its topmost branch, but our movement behind the glass must have disturbed him because he disappeared suddenly with a flash of his blue rounded tail.

Yet, in truth, the bird was only a momentary distraction, because it was the walls that drew the eye. I couldn't tell what color they had been painted because no paint showed through the blizzard of paper that seemed to have adhered to them, as if the room was in a constant state of motion and they had been propelled there and held in place by centrifugal force. The sheets were of varying sizes, some little more than Post-it notes, others larger than the surface of Foster's drafting board. Some were yellow, others dark, some plain, a few lined. The detail varied from drawing to drawing, from hurried sketches executed with a flurry of pencil strokes to ornate, intricate depictions of their subject. James Foster had been quite an artist, but he seemed to have only one main theme.

Almost every drawing depicted a woman, her face concealed, her body swathed in a cloak of white from the top of her head to the soles of her feet. The cloak spread out behind her like water pooling from an ice sculpture. It was not a false impression, for

Foster had drawn her as if the material that covered her was wet. It clung to the muscles in her legs and buttocks, to the sweep of her breasts and the thin blades of her fingers, the bones of the knuckles clearly visible where she gripped the cloak tightly from beneath.

But there was something wrong with her skin, something flawed and ugly. Her veins appeared to be above rather than beneath the epidermis, creating a tracery of raised pathways across her body like the levees over a flooded rice field. The result was that the woman under the veil seemed almost to be plated, her skin armored like that of an alligator. Unconsciously, instead of drawing closer I took a single step back from the wall, and felt Adele Foster's hand come to rest gently on my arm.

'Her,' she said. 'He was afraid of her.'

We sat over coffee, some of the drawings spread on the coffee table before us.

'Did you show these to the police?'

She shook her head. 'Elliot told me not to.'

'Did he tell you why?'

'No. He just said that it would be best not to show them the drawings.'

I rearranged the papers, setting the depictions of the woman aside and revealing a set of five landscapes. Each depicted the same scene: a huge pit in the ground, surrounded by skeletal trees. In one of the drawings a pillar of fire emerged from the pit, but it was still possible to pick out, even there, the shape of the hooded woman now clothed in flame.

'Is this a real place?'

She took the picture from me and studied it, then handed it back to me with a shrug.

'I don't know. You'd have to ask Elliot. He might know.'

'I can't do that until I find him.'

'I think something has happened to him, maybe the same thing that happened to Landron Mobley.'

This time, I heard the disgust in her voice when she said Mobley's name.

'You didn't like him?'

She scowled. 'He was a pig. I don't know why they let him stay with them. No' – she corrected herself – 'I do know why. He could get things for them: drugs, booze when they were younger, maybe even women. He knew the places to go. He wasn't like Elliot and the others. He didn't have money, or looks, or a college education, but he was prepared to go places that they were afraid to go, at least at first.'

And Elliot Norton had still seen fit, after all those years, to represent Mobley in the impending case against him, despite the fact that it could bring no credit to Elliot. This was the same Elliot Norton who had grown up with Earl Larousse Jr. and was now representing the young man accused of killing his sister. None of this made me feel good.

'You said that they did something, when they were younger, something that had come back to haunt them. Do you have any idea what that might be?'

'No. James would never talk about it. We weren't close before his death. His behavior had altered. He wasn't the man I married. He began to hang out with Mobley again. They went hunting together up at Congaree. Then James started going to strip clubs. I think he might have been seeing prostitutes.'

I laid the drawings down carefully on the table.

'You know where he might have gone?'

'I followed him, two or three times. He always went to the same place, because it was where Mobley liked to go when he was in town. It's called LapLand.'

And while I sat talking to Adele Foster, surrounded by images of spectral women, a disheveled man wearing a bright red shirt, blue jeans and battered sneakers strolled up Norfolk Street on the Lower East Side of New York and stood in the shadow of the Orensanz Center, the oldest surviving synagogue in New

York. It was a warm evening and he had taken a cab down here, electing not to endure the heat and discomfort of the subway. A daisy chain of children floated by, suspended between two women wearing T-shirts identifying them as members of a Jewish community group. One of the children, a little girl with dark curls, smiled up at him as she passed and he smiled back at her, watching her as she was carried around the corner and out of his sight.

He walked up the steps, opened the door, and moved into the neo-Gothic main hall. He heard footsteps approach from behind and turned to see an old man with a sweeping brush in his hand.

'Can I help you?' said the cleaner.

The visitor spoke.

'I'm looking for Ben Epstein,' he said.

'He is not here,' came the reply.

'But he does come here?'

'Sometimes,' the old man conceded.

'You expecting him this evening?'

'Maybe. He comes, he goes.'

The visitor found a chair in the shadows, turned it so that its back was facing the door, and sat down carefully upon it, wincing slightly as he lowered himself down. He rested his chin on his forearms and regarded the old man.

'I'll wait. I'm very patient.'

The old man shrugged, and began sweeping.

Five minutes went by.

'Hey,' said the visitor. 'I said I was patient, not made of fucking stone. Go call Epstein.'

The old man flinched but kept sweeping.

'I can't help you.'

'I think you can,' said the visitor, and his tone made the old man freeze. The visitor had not moved, but the geniality and passivity that had made the little girl smile at him was now entirely gone from him. 'You tell him it's about Faulkner. He'll come.'

He closed his eyes, and when he opened them again there was only spiraling dust where the old man had stood.

Angel closed his eyes again, and waited.

It was almost seven when Epstein arrived, accompanied by two men whose loose shirts did not quite manage to hide the weapons they carried. When he saw the man seated on the chair, Epstein relaxed and indicated to his companions that they could leave him be. Then he pulled up a chair and sat opposite Angel.

'You know who I am?' asked Angel.

'I know,' said Epstein. 'You are called Angel. A strange name, I think, for I see nothing angelic about you.'

'There's nothing angelic to see. Why the guns?'

'We are under threat. We believe we have already lost a young man to our enemies. Now we may have found the man responsible for his death. Did Parker send you?'

'No, I came here alone. Why would you think Parker sent me?'

Epstein looked surprised. 'We spoke with him, not long before we learned of your presence here. We assumed that the two occurrences were related.'

'Great minds thinking alike, I guess.'

Epstein sighed. 'He quoted Torah to me once. I was impressed. You, I think, even with your great mind, will not be quoting Torah. Or Kaballah.'

'No,' admitted Angel.

'I was reading, before I came to you: the *Sefer ha-Bahir*, the Book of Brightness. I have long been considering its significance, more often now since the death of my own son. I had hoped to find meaning in his sufferings, but I am not wise enough to understand what is written.'

'You think suffering has to have meaning?'

'Everything has meaning. All things are the work of the Divine.'

'In that case, I got some harsh words to say to the Divine when I see Him.'

Epstein spread his hands. 'Say them. He is always listening, always watching.'

'I don't think so. You think He was listening and watching when your son died? Or worse: maybe He was and just decided not to do anything about it.'

The old man winced involuntarily at the pain that Angel's words caused him, but the younger man did not appear to notice. Epstein took in the rage and grief on his face. 'Are you talking about my son, or yourself?' he asked gently.

'You didn't answer the question.'

'He is the Creator: all things come from Him. I do not pretend to know the ways of the Divine. That is why I read Kaballah. I do not yet understand all that it says, but I am beginning to comprehend a little.'

'And what does it say to explain the torture and death of your son?'

This time, even Angel recognized the pain that he had caused.

'I'm sorry,' he said, reddening. 'Sometimes, I get angry,'

Epstein nodded – 'I too get angry' – then resumed.

'I think it speaks of harmony between the upper and lower worlds, between the visible and the unseen, between good and evil. World above, world below, with angels moving in between. Real angels, not nominal ones.'

He smiled.

'And because of what I have read I wonder, sometimes, about the nature of your friend Parker. It is written in the Zohar that angels must put on the garment of this world when they walk upon it. I wonder now if this is true of angels both good and evil, that both hosts must walk this world in disguise. It is said of the dark angels that they will be consumed by another manifestation, the destroying angels, armed with plagues and the avenging wrath of the fury of the Divine, two hosts of His servants fighting against one another, for the Almighty created evil to serve His purposes, just as He created good. I must believe that or else the death of my son has no meaning. I must believe that his suffering is part of a larger pattern that I cannot comprehend, a sacrifice in the name of the greater, ultimate good.'

He leaned forward on his chair.

'Perhaps your friend is such an angel,' he concluded. 'An agent of the Divine: a destroyer, yet a restorer of the harmony between worlds. Perhaps, just as his true nature is hidden from us, so too it may be hidden even from himself.'

'I don't think Parker is an angel,' said Angel. 'I don't think he does either. If he starts saying he is, his girlfriend will have him committed.'

'You think these are an old man's fancies? Perhaps they are. An old man's fancies, then.' He dismissed them with a graceful sweep of his hand. 'So why are you here, Mr. Angel?'

'To ask for something.'

'I will give you all that I can. You punished the one who took my son from me.' For it was Angel who had killed Pudd, who had in turn killed Epstein's son Yossi; Pudd, or Leonard, the son of Aaron Faulkner.

'That's right,' said Angel. 'Now I'm going to kill the one who sent him.'

Epstein blinked once.

'He is in jail.'

'He's going to be released.'

'If they let him go, men will come. They will protect him, and they will take him out of your reach. He is important to them.'

Angel found himself distracted by the old man's words. 'I don't understand. Why is he so important?'

'Because of what he represents,' replied Epstein. 'Do you know what evil is? It is the absence of empathy: from that, all evil springs. Faulkner is a void, a being completely without empathy, and that is as close to absolute evil as this world can bear. But Faulkner is worse still, for he has the capacity to drain empathy from others. He is like a spiritual vampire, spreading his infection. And such evil draws evil to itself, both men and angels, and that is why they seek to protect him.

'But your friend Parker is tormented by empathy, by his capacity to feel. He is all that Faulkner is not. He is destructive, and angry, but it is a righteous anger, not merely wrath, which is sinful and works against the Divine. I look to your friend and I see a greater purpose in action. If evil and good are both creations of the Almighty, then the evil visited on Parker, the loss of his wife and child, was an instrument of the greater good, just like Yossi's death. Look at the men that he has hunted down as a result, the peace that he has brought to others, living and dead, the balance that he has restored, all born of the sorrow that he has endured, that he continues to endure. In his response to all that he has suffered, I, for one, see the work of the Divine.'

Angel shook his head in disbelief.

'So this is some kind of test for him, for all of us?'

'No, not a test: an opportunity to prove ourselves worthy of salvation, to create that salvation for ourselves, maybe even to become salvation itself.'

'I'm more concerned with this world than the next.'

'There is no difference. They are not separate, but linked. Heaven and hell begin here.'

'Well, one of them sure does.'

'You are a wrathful man, are you not?'

'I'm getting there. I hear another sermon and I'll arrive.'

Epstein raised his hands in surrender.

'So you are here because you want our help? Our help with what?'

'Roger Bowen.'

Epstein's smile widened.

'That,' he said, 'will be a pleasure.'

18

I left Adele Foster and headed back into Charleston. Her husband had begun visiting LapLand prior to his death, and LapLand was where Tereus worked. Tereus had hinted to me that Elliot knew more than he was telling me about the disappearances of Atys Jones's mother and aunt, and from what Adele Foster had told me Elliot and a group of his former boyhood friends were now under active threat from some outside force. That group included Earl Larousse Jr. and three men now deceased: Landron Mobley, Grady Truett, and James Foster. I tried Elliot's phones again, with no result, then swung by his office close by the intersection of Broad and Meeting, what the locals called the Corners of Four Laws since St. Michael's Church, the federal court, the state courthouse and City Hall each stood on a corner of the intersection. Elliot occupied a building with two other law firms, all three sharing a single, street-level entrance. I headed straight for the third floor but there was no sign of life behind the frosted glass door. I took off my jacket, placed it against the door, then used the butt of my gun to break the glass. I reached in through the hole and opened the door.

A small reception area with a secretary's desk and shelves of files led into Elliot's office. The door was unlocked. Inside, filing cabinet drawers were open and files lay scattered across the desk and chairs. Whoever had gone through the files knew what he or she was looking for. There was no Rolodex or address book that I could find, and when I tried to access the computer I found that it was password locked. I spent a few minutes going through the alphabetically ordered files, but could find nothing on Landron Mobley and nothing on Atys Jones that I did not already have in my possession. I turned out the lights, stepped over the broken glass at the door, and closed it softly behind me.

Adele had given me an address in Hampton for Phil Poveda, one of the by now rapidly dwindling group of friends. I drove out there in time to find a tall man with long gray-black hair and a flecked beard closing his garage door from the inside. As I approached him he paused. He looked nervous and skittish.

'Mr. Poveda?'

He didn't reply.

I reached for my ID. 'My name is Charlie Parker. I'm a private investigator. I wondered if I could have a few minutes of your time.'

He still didn't reply, but at least the garage door remained open. I took it as a positive sign. I was wrong. Phil Poveda, who looked like a hippy computer geek, pulled a gun on me. It was a .38, and it shook in his hand like unset Jell-O, but it was still a gun.

'Get out of here,' he said. His hand was still shaking, but compared to his voice it was steady as a rock. Poveda was falling apart. I could see it in his eyes, in the lines around his mouth, in the sores that had opened on his face and neck. On my way to his house, I had wondered if he might be responsible in some way for what was occurring. Now, faced with the reality of his disintegration and the fear he exuded, I knew that he was a potential victim, not a possible killer.

'Mr. Poveda, I can help you. I know something is happening. People are dying, people to whom you were once close: Grady Truett, James Foster, Landron Mobley. I think Marianne Larousse's death may also be linked. Now Elliot Norton is missing.'

He blinked. 'Elliot?' he said. Another little shard of hope seemed to fall away from him and shatter on the ground.

'You have to talk to somebody. I think that sometime in the past, you and your friends did something, and now the consequences of that act have come back to haunt you. A snub-nose thirty-eight in a shaky hand isn't going to save you from what's coming.'

I took a step forward, and the garage door slammed down in front of me before I could get to it. I hammered hard on it.

'Mr. Poveda!' I shouted. 'Talk to me.'

There was no reply, but I sensed him there, waiting, at the other side of the metal, trapped in a darkness of his own devising. I took a card from my wallet, inserted it partly into the gap between the door and the ground, then left him there with his sins.

When I looked back, the card was gone.

Tereus wasn't at LapLand when I called by, and Handy Andy, his courage now boosted by the presence of a bar-tender and a couple of doormen in black jackets, wasn't in any mood to be helpful. I also failed to get a reply from Tereus's apartment: according to the old guy with the permanent residency on the front steps, he had left for work that morning and hadn't returned since. I seemed to be having a lot of trouble finding the people with whom I needed to talk.

I walked across King and entered Janet's Southern Kitchen. Janet's was a relic of times past, where folks took a tray and queued up to receive fried chicken, rice and pork chops over the counter. I was the only white person eating, but nobody paid me much attention. I picked at my chicken and rice, but my appetite had still not returned. Instead, I drank glass after glass of lemonade in an effort to cool myself down, but it did me no good. I was still parched, and my temperature was still way above normal. Louis would be here soon, I told myself. Things would become clearer then. I pushed my plate to one side and headed back to the hotel.

Once again, as darkness fell, my desk was covered in depictions of a woman. The folder containing the Larousse crime scene photographs and reports lay closed by my left hand. All other available space was taken up by James Foster's drawings. In one picture, the woman had been captured in the act of looking over her shoulder, the place where her face should have been shaded in tones of gray and black, the bones in her fingers visible beneath the thin material that enveloped her body and what seemed like the tracery of raised veins or scales shrouding her skin. There was also, I thought, something almost sexual about her depiction, a combination of loathing and desire expressed in artistic form. The shape of her buttocks and legs was carefully etched, as if sunlight were shining between her legs, and her nipples were erect. She was like the lamia of myth, a beautiful woman from the waist up but a serpent from the waist down, beguiling travelers with the sound of her voice, only to devour them when they came within reach. Except, in this case, the scales of the serpent appeared to have spread across her entire body; the myth's origins in a male fear of aggressive female sexuality had clearly found fertile ground in Foster's imagination.

And then there was the second subject of his endeavors, the pit surrounded by stone and rugged, barren ground, the shapes of thin trees in the background like mourners around a grave. In the first drawing, the pit was simply a dark hole, seemingly deliberately reminiscent of the woman's hooded face, the shelving of the ground at its lip like the folds of cloth around her head. But in the second drawing, the column of fire roared up from deep within, as if a channel had been opened straight to the earth's core or to hell itself. The woman at its heart was consumed by flames, her body wreathed in fingers of orange and red, her legs wide, her head thrown back in pain or ecstasy. It might have been dime-store psychological analysis, but my guess was that Foster had been a very disturbed man. That'll be $100. You can pay my secretary on the way out.

The final item that his widow had allowed me to remove from his office was a photograph, a picture of six young men standing together before a bar, a neon Miller sign visible behind the figure at the far left of the group. Elliot Norton was smiling, a bottle of

Bud raised in his right hand, his left arm curled around the waist of Earl Larousse Jr. Beside him was Phil Poveda, taller than the rest, leaning back against a car, his legs crossed at the ankles, his white shirt open to his chest, his arms folded before him, a beer bottle poking out close to his left breast. Next in line was the smallest member of the company, a dough-faced, curly-haired boy-man with a starter-kit beard and legs that seemed too short for his body. He had been caught in a dancer's pose, his left leg and left arm outstretched before him, his right raised high behind him, tequila glistening in the flash of the bulb as the last of it spilled from the bottle in his hand: the late Grady Truett. Beside him, a boyish face peered bashfully into the camera, its chin lowered to its chest. This was James Foster.

The last young man was not smiling as widely as the rest. His grin seemed awkward, his clothes somehow cheaper. He wore jeans and a check shirt, and he stood awkward and straight upon the gravel and dirt of the parking lot, like one who was not used to having his picture taken. Landron Mobley, the poorest of the six, the only one who did not go on to college, who did not progress to greater things, the only one never to leave the state of South Carolina to advance himself. But Landron had his own uses: Landron could score drugs; Landron could find cheap, slutty women who would go down for the price of a beer; Landron's big fists could pummel anyone who decided to take issue with a bunch of wealthy young men intruding on territory that was not their own, taking women that were not theirs to take, drinking in bars that held no welcome for them. Landron was the point of entry for a world that these five men wanted to use and abuse, but of which they wanted no lasting part. Landron was the gatekeeper. Landron knew things.

Now Landron was dead.

According to Adele Foster, the allegations of improper relationships made against Mobley had come as no surprise to her. She knew what Landron Mobley was like, knew what he liked to do to girls even while he was systematically flunking high school. And though her husband claimed to have cut off all ties with him, she had seen him talking to Landron a couple of weeks before his death, had seen Landron pat him on the arm as he leaned into the car, and had watched as James had passed him a small wad of bills from his wallet. She had confronted him that evening, only to be told that Landron was down on his luck since he'd lost his job, and he had only given him the money so that he would go away and leave James alone. She hadn't believed him, though, and his patronage of LapLand had only confirmed her suspicions. By that time the distance between husband and wife was growing ever greater, and she told me that it was to Elliot Norton, not James, that she had confessed her fears about Landron Mobley as she lay beside him in the small room above his office, the room in which he sometimes slept when working on a particularly demanding case but which now, increasingly, he used to satisfy other, more pressing demands.

'Has he approached you for money?' she asked Elliot.

Elliot looked away. 'Landron always needs money.'

'That's not an answer.'

'I've known Landron for a long time, and yes, I've helped him out from time to time.'

'Why?'

'What do you mean, why?'

'I don't understand, that's all. He wasn't like the rest of you. I can see why he might have been useful to you when you were young and wild—'

He reached for her then – 'I'm still wild' – but she forced him gently away.

'But now,' she continued, 'what part can somebody like Landron Mobley have to play in your lives? You should have left him in your past.'

Eliot pushed back the sheets to stand naked in the moonlight, his back to her, and it seemed that his shoulders dropped briefly, the way a man's shoulders will slump when exhaustion threatens to overcome him and he briefly accedes to it.

And then he said something strange.

'Some things you can't leave in the past,' he said. 'Some things follow you all through your life.'

That was all he said. Seconds later, she heard the sound of the shower from the bathroom and knew that it was time to leave.

It was the last time that she and Elliot had made love.

But Elliot's loyalty to Landron Mobley had gone beyond simply helping him out when he needed a few bucks. Elliot was representing his old friend in what could have turned out to be a very nasty rape case, a case now rendered null and void by Mobley's death. In addition, Elliot appeared willing to destroy a long-standing friendship with Earl Larousse Jr. in order to defend a young black man with whom Elliot had no apparent connection. I pulled out the notes I had made so far and went through them once again, hoping to find something that I might have missed. It was only when I laid the sheets of paper side by side that I noticed one curious correspondence: Davis Smoot had been killed in Alabama only a few days before the disappearance of the Jones sisters in South Carolina. I went back to the notes I had jotted down while talking to Randy Burris about the events surrounding Smoot's death and the hunt for, and subsequent arrest of, Tereus for the killing. According to what Tereus himself had told me, he had gone down to Alabama to seek the help of Smoot, who had fled South Carolina in February 1980, days after the alleged rape of Addy Jones, and had remained in hiding until at least July 1981, when he was confronted and killed by Tereus. He had denied to prosecutors that his confrontation with Smoot was in any way connected with rumors that Smoot had raped Addy. Addy Jones had subsequently given birth to her son Atys early in August 1980.

There had to be some mistake.

The sound of the cell phone pulled me away. I recognized the number on display immediately. The call was coming from the safe house. I picked it up on the second ring. There was no speech, just a tapping, as of somebody banging the phone gently on the ground. *Tap-tap-tap.*

'Hello?'

Tap-tap-tap.

I picked up my jacket and ran for the parking garage. The gaps between the taps were growing longer now and I knew for certain that the person at the other end was in trouble, that somebody's strength was fading and this was the only way that he or she could communicate.

'I'm on my way,' I said. 'Hold on. Just hold on.'

There were three young black guys standing outside the safe house when I arrived, shifting uncertainly from foot to foot. One of them was carrying a knife and he spun toward me as I ran from the car. He saw the gun in my hand and raised his hands in acquiescence.

'What happened?'

He didn't answer, but an older guy behind him did.

'We heard glass breaking. We didn't do nothin'.'

'Keep it that way. Just stay back.'

'Fuck you, man,' was the reply, but they made no further move toward the house.

The front door was locked so I made for the rear of the house. The back door was wide open but undamaged. The kitchen was empty but the ever-present lemonade jug now lay shattered on the floor. Flies buzzed around the liquid pooled upon the cheap linoleum.

I found the old man in the living room. There was a sucking hole in his chest and he lay like a black angel lost in his own blood, red wings spreading outward from behind. In his left hand he held the phone while the fingers of his right scraped at the wooden boards. He had scraped so hard that he had torn the nails and drawn blood from his fingers. He was reaching for his wife. I could see her foot in the doorway, the slipper pulled back from her heel by the pressure of her bent toes. There was blood on the back of her leg.

I knelt by the old man and clasped his head, looking for something with which to stem the flow of blood from the gunshot wound. I was shrugging off my jacket when he reached for my shirt, gripping it tightly in his fist.

'Uh ent gap me mout'!' he whispered. His teeth were pink with blood. 'Uh ent gap me mout'!'

I didn't tell.

'I know,' I said, and I felt my voice break. 'I know you didn't. Who did this, Albert?'

'Plateye,' he hissed. '*Plateye.*'

He eased his grip on my shirt and reached again for his dead wife.

'Ginnie,' he called.

His voice faded.

'Ginnie,' he repeated, and then he was gone.

I let his head rest on the floor, then stood and moved toward the woman. She lay facedown with two holes in the back of her dress: one low to the left of her spine, the other higher, close to her heart. There was no pulse.

I heard a noise on the floor behind me and turned to see one of the boys from outside the house standing in the kitchen doorway.

'Stay out!' I said. 'Call nine-one-one.'

He took one more look at me, his eyes falling to the body of the old man, then disappeared.

No noise came from upstairs. The couple's son, Samuel, who had driven Atys to the house earlier in the week, lay naked and dead in the bathtub, the shower curtain clenched in his hand and the water from the shower head still beating down upon his face and body. He had taken two shots in the chest. When I searched the four rooms above I could find no trace of Atys, but the window of his room was broken and tiles had been dislodged from the kitchen roof. It looked like he might have jumped, which meant that Atys might still be alive.

I went back downstairs and was standing in the yard when the police arrived. My gun was back in its holster and I was holding my license and permit. Naturally, the cops took my gun and my phone away and made me sit in a car until the detectives arrived. By now, a crowd had gathered and the uniforms were doing their best to keep them back, the lights on the Crown Vics casting firework glows across the faces and houses. There were a lot of cars because the Charleston PD assigned only one officer to a car, with the exception of the safe streets unit, two officers from which had arrived on the scene within minutes of the call. The mobile crime scene unit, an old converted bookmobile, had also pulled up by the time a pair of detectives from the violent crimes unit decided that they wanted to talk to me.

I had told them to find Atys Jones and they were already looking for him, although not as a potential victim but as a suspect in two further murders. They were wrong, of course. I knew that they were wrong.

At a gas station in South Portland, the hunched man stood over the Nissan and filled the car with twenty dollars' worth of gas. There was only one other vehicle at the pumps: an '86 Chevy C-10 with a busted right wing that had cost its new owner the grand total of $1,100, half down with the rest to pay by the end of the year. It was the first car Bear had owned in more than half a decade and he was hugely proud of it. Now, instead of bumming rides to the co-op, he was there waiting each morning when they opened up, music blaring from the Chevy's tinny stereo.

Bear hardly glanced at the other man close by. He had seen enough strange men in prison to know that the best thing to do in their presence was to mind his own business. He gassed the car with money borrowed from his sister, checked the pressure on every tire, then drove away.

Cyrus had paid the bored gas station attendant in advance and was aware that the young man was still watching him, mesmerized by Cyrus's crooked body. Although used to the revulsion of others, Cyrus still considered it bad manners to be too obvious about it. The boy was lucky that he was safe behind the glass and that Cyrus had other things to occupy him. Still, if he had time he might come back and teach him that it was rude to stare. Cyrus replaced the pump, got into the car, and took his notebook from beneath the seat. He had been keeping careful notes of all that he saw and did, because it was important that he did not forget anything useful.

The boy went into the notebook, along with Cyrus's other observations that evening: the movements of the redheaded woman in her house and the brief, troubling sighting of the large black man who now shared it with her. It made Cyrus unhappy.

Cyrus didn't like getting the blood of men upon him.

19

The headquarters of the Charleston PD occupied a redbrick structure on Lockwood Boulevard, opposite the Joe Riley Stadium and facing out over Brittlebank Park and the Ashley river. The interview room didn't have much of a view, though, unless you counted the faces of the two irate detectives currently sharing it with me.

To understand the Charleston Police Department, you had to understand Chief Reuben Greenberg. Greenberg had been chief since 1982 and was that contradiction in terms, a popular police chief. In his eighteen years in charge he had introduced a range of innovations that had contributed to containing, and in some cases reducing, the crime rate in Charleston: everything from Weed and Seed programs in poorer areas to issuing running shoes to officers to enable them to chase felons more effectively. Homicide rates had consistently dropped in that time, allowing Charleston to compare favorably with any Southern city of similar size.

Unfortunately, the deaths of Albert, Ginnie, and Samuel Singleton meant that any hopes of matching the previous year's figures were pretty much gone, and anybody even remotely connected with holing the good ship *Crime Statistics* below the waterline was likely to be very unpopular at 180 Lockwood Boulevard.

I was very unpopular at 180 Lockwood Boulevard.

After an hour spent waiting in a locked patrol car outside the East Side house, I was brought to a room painted in two shades of ugly and furnished by Functional-R-Us. A cup of coffee had since grown cold in front of me. The two detectives who questioned me weren't noticeably warmer.

'Elliot Norton,' the first repeated. 'You say you're working for Elliot Norton.'

His name was Adams, and there were patches of sweat beneath the arms of his blue shirt. His skin was blue-black and his eyes were bloodshot. I'd already told him twice that I was working for Elliot Norton, and we'd gone through Albert's final words half a dozen times, but Adams saw no reason why I shouldn't do it all again.

'He hired me to do some background work on the Jones case,' I said. 'We picked Atys up from the Richland County lockup and took him to the Singleton place. It was supposed to be a temporary safe house.'

'Mistake number two,' said Adams's partner. His last name was Addams, and he was as pale as his partner was dark. Somebody in the Charleston PD had a warped sense of humor. It was only the third time that he had spoken since the interview had begun.

'What was mistake number one?' I asked.

'Getting involved with the Jones case in the first place,' he replied. 'Or maybe stepping off the plane at Charleston International. See, now you got three mistakes.'

He smiled. I smiled back. It was only polite.

'Doesn't it get confusing, you being called Addams and him being called Adams?'

Addams scowled. 'No, see I'm A*dd*ams, with two *d*'s. He's A*d*ams, with one *d*. It's easy.'

He seemed serious about it. The Charleston PD offered an ascending scale of incentive pay based on educational achievement, from 7 percent for an associates' degree to 22 percent for a Ph.D. I knew this from reading and rereading the notices on the board behind Addams's head. I was guessing that the incentive box on Addams's pay slip was pretty empty, unless they gave him a nickel a month for his high school diploma.

'So,' his partner resumed, 'you pick him up, drop him at the safe house, go back to your hotel . . . ?'

'Clean my teeth, go to bed, get up, check on Atys, make some calls—'

'Who'd you call?'

'Elliot, some people back in Maine.'

'What did you say to Norton?'

'Nothing much. We just touched base. He asked me if I was making any progress and I told him that I was just getting started.'

'Then what did you do?'

We had reached the point, once again, where the paths of truth and untruth diverged. I opted for the middle ground, hoping to pick up the path of truth again later.

'I went to a strip joint.'

Adams's right eyebrow made an ecclesiastical arch of disapproval.

'Why'd you do that?'

'I was bored.'

'Norton pay you to go to strip joints?'

'It was my lunch break. I was on my own time.'

'And after?'

'Went back to the hotel. Had dinner. Bed. This morning: tried calling Elliot, had no luck, checked witness statements, went back to my hotel room. The call came about an hour later.'

Adams rose wearily from the table and exchanged a look with his partner.

'Doesn't sound to me like Norton was getting his money's worth,' he said.

For the first time, I picked up on his use of the past tense.

'What do you mean, "was"?'

The look passed between them again, but neither replied.

'Do you have any papers relating to the Jones case that might prove helpful to the course of this investigation?' asked Addams.

'I asked you a question.'

Addams's voice rose a notch. 'And I asked you a question: do you, or do you not, have material in your possession that might assist this investigation?'

'No,' I lied. 'Elliot had it all.'

I caught myself.

'Eliot *has* it all,' I corrected. 'Now tell me what happened.'

It was Adams who spoke.

'Highway Patrol found his car off 176, down by Sandy Road Creek. It was in the water. Looks like he swerved to avoid something on the road and ended up in the river. The body's missing, but there's blood in the car. A lot of blood. Blood type is B rhesus positive, which matches Norton's. We know he participates in the city's blood drives, so we're checking the samples from the car against a sample of his donated blood.'

I buried my head in my hands and took a deep breath. First Foster, then Truett and Mobley, and now Elliot. That left two names: Earl Larousse Jr. and Phil Poveda.

'Can I go now?' I wanted to return to my hotel room and get the material there out of harm's way. I just hoped that Adams and Addams hadn't gone looking for a search warrant while I was locked up.

Before either of the detectives could answer, the door to the interview room opened. The man who entered was two or three inches taller, and at least two decades older, than I was. He had buzz-cut gray hair, gray-blue eyes, and carried himself like he'd just stepped out of Parris Island to hunt down some AWOL marines. The military impression was enforced by his immaculate uniform and name badge. It read 'S. Stilwell.' Stilwell was the Lieutenant Colonel in charge of the Charleston PD's Operations Bureau, answerable only to the chief himself.

'Is this the man, detective?' he barked.

'Yes sir.' It was Addams. He shot me a look that told me my troubles had only just begun and that he was going to enjoy what came next.

'Why is he here? Why is he not currently occupying a holding cell with the worst filth, the most disgusting reprobates that this fine city can furnish?'

'We were questioning him, sir.'

'And did he answer your questions in a satisfactory manner, detective?

'No sir, he did not.'

'Did he not indeed?'

Stilwell turned to Adams. 'You, detective, you are a good man, are you not?'

'I try to be, sir.'

'I do not doubt that, detective. And do you not, to the best of your abilities, look favorably on your fellow man?'

'I do, sir.'

'I would expect no less of you. Do you read your Bible?'

'Not as much as I should, sir.'

'Damn right, detective. Nobody reads his Bible as much as he should. A man should be out living the word of God, not studying on it. Am I right?'

'You are, sir.'

'And does the Bible not tell us to think well of our fellow man, to give him every chance that he deserves?'

'I couldn't say for sure, sir.'

'Neither could I, but I feel certain that there is such an injunction. And if there is not such an injunction in the Bible, then it was an oversight, and the man responsible, if he could go back and correct his mistake, would most certainly return and include said injunction, would he not?'

'He most certainly would, sir.'

'Amen. So we are agreed, detective, that you have given Mr. Parker every chance to answer the questions put to him; that you, as a God-fearing man, have heeded the Bible's probable injunction to take all that Mr. Parker has said as the word of an honest man; and yet you still doubt his basic sincerity?'

'I guess so, sir.'

'Well that certainly is a most unfortunate turn of events.'

He gave me his full attention for the first time.

'Statistics, Mr. Parker. Let's talk about statistics. Do you know how many people were murdered in the fine city of Charleston in the year of our Lord, nineteen hundred and ninety-nine?'

I shook my head.

'I will tell you: three. It was the lowest murder rate in more than forty years. Now, what does that tell you about the police force in the fine city of Charleston?'

I didn't reply. He cupped his left hand around his left ear and leaned toward me.

'I can't hear you, son.'

I opened my mouth, which gave him his cue to continue before I could say anything.

'I will tell you what it says about this police force. It says that this fine body of men and women does not tolerate murder; that it actively discourages said form of antisocial activity; and that it will come down upon those who commit murder like two tons of shit from a trainload of elephants. But your arrival in our city appears to have coincided with a shocking increase in acts of homicide. That will affect our statistics. It will cause a blip on the screen, and Chief Greenberg, a fine, fine man, will have to go to the mayor and explain this unfortunate turn of events. And the mayor will ask him why this should be, and Chief Greenberg will then ask me, and I will say that it is because of you, Mr. Parker. And the chief will ask me where you are, and I will lead him to the deepest, darkest hole that the city of Charleston can provide for those of whom it most seriously disapproves. And under that hole will be another hole, and in that hole will be you, Mr. Parker, because I will have put you there. You will be so far below the ground that you will no longer officially be in the jurisdiction of the city of Charleston. You will not even officially be within the jurisdiction of the United States of America. You will be in the jurisdiction of the People's Republic of China, and you would be advised to hire yourself a Chinese lawyer in order to cut down on traveling expenses incurred by your legal representative. Do you think I am shitting you, Mr. Parker? Because I am not shitting you. I do not shit people like you, Mr. Parker, I shit *on* people like you, and I have been saving some of my nastiest shit for just such an occasion as this. Now, do you have anything further that you wish to share with us?'

I shook my head. 'I can't tell you any more.'

He stood. 'Then our business here is concluded. Detective, do we have a holding pen available for Mr. Parker?'

'I'm sure we do, sir.'

'And will he be sharing this holding pen with the dregs of this fine city, with drunks and whoremongers and men of low moral character?'

'That can be arranged, sir.'

'Then arrange it, detective.'

I made a vain attempt to assert my rights.

'Don't I get to call a lawyer?

'Mr. Parker, you do not need a lawyer. You need a travel agent to get you the hell out of this city. You need a priest to pray that you do not irritate me any more than you already have. And finally, you need to go back in time to get hold of your mother before your father impregnates her with his sorry seed and ask her not to let you be born because, if you continue to obstruct this investigation, you are going to regret the day she thrust you mewling and screaming into this world. Detective, get this man out of my sight.'

They put me in the drunk tank until 6 A.M., then when they felt I had stewed for long enough, Addams came down and had me released. As we headed for the main door, his partner stood in the hallway and watched us pass.

'I find out anything on Norton, I'll let you know,' he said.

I thanked him, and he nodded.

'I found out what "plateye" means too. Had to ask Mr. Alphonso Brown himself, man who guides folks round the old Gullah places. He said it was a kind of ghost: a changeling, one that could shift its form. Could be he was trying to say that your client turned on them.'

'Could be, except that Atys didn't have a gun.'

He didn't reply, and his partner hustled me on.

My possessions were handed back to me, minus my gun. I was given a slip and told that the gun was not being returned to me for the time being. Through the doors I could see prisoners in jail blues arriving to work on the lawns and clear garbage from the flower beds. I wondered how much trouble I'd have getting a cab.

'You planning on leaving Charleston in the near future?' asked Addams.

'No. Not after this.'

'Well, you make a move and you let us know, y'hear?'

I made for the door but found Addams's hand resting against my chest. 'You remember this, Mr. Parker: I got a bad feeling about you. I made some calls while you was in here and I didn't like one thing that I heard. I don't want you starting one of your crusades in Chief Greenberg's city, you understand me? So just to guard against that, and to make sure that you call on us again when you're leaving, we'll be holding on to that Smith 10 of yours until your plane starts heading down the runway. Then maybe we'll give you your cannon back.'

The hand dropped, and Addams opened the door for me.

'Be seeing you,' he said.

I stopped, frowned, and clicked my fingers.

'Which one were you again?'

'Addams.'

'With one *d*.'

'Two *d*s.'

I nodded. 'I'll try to remember.'

When I got back to my hotel I barely had enough energy to undress before I fell into my bed and slept soundly until after ten. I didn't dream. It was as if the deaths of the night before had never happened.

But Charleston had not yielded up the last of its bodies. While the cockroaches skittered across the cracked sidewalks to hide from the daylight and the last of the night owls made for their beds, a man named Cecil Exley was walking to the site of the small bakery and coffee shop that he owned over on East Bay. There was work to be done, fresh bread and croissants to be baked, and although the clock had not yet struck six, Cecil was already running late.

At the corner of Franklin and Magazine, he began to slow down slightly. The bulk of the old Charleston jail loomed over him, a testament to misery and grief. A low white wall surrounded a yard thick with long grass, at the center of which stood the jail itself. The red bricks that had formed its side-walks were missing in places, stolen, presumably, by those who felt their need was greater than the demands of history. Twin four-story towers topped with battlements and weeds stood at either side of the locked main gate, its bars and the bars of the windows around and above it stained red with oxidized rust. The concrete had crumbled and fallen from around the frames, exposing the brickwork beneath, as the old building succumbed to slow decay.

Denmark Vesey and his co-conspirators in the ill-fated slave revolt of 1822 had been chained up in the whipping house for blacks at the back of the jail before their execution, most of them led to the gallows still proclaiming their innocence and one of them, Bacchus Hammett, even laughing as they placed the noose around his neck. Many others had passed through its gates before and since. There was nowhere else in Charleston, Cecil Exley believed, where the past and the present were so closely linked, where it was possible to stand quietly on an early morning and feel the aftershocks of past violence still shuddering through new days. It was Cecil's habit to pause occasionally at the gates of the old jail and say a short, silent prayer for those who had languished there at a time when men with skin the color of Cecil's could not even arrive in Charleston as part of a ship's crew without being consigned to a cell for the duration of their visit.

To Cecil's right, as he stood at the gates, was the old paddy wagon known as Black Lucy. It had been many years since Lucy had thrown her arms open to receive a new guest, but as Cecil looked closer, he could see a shape standing against the bars at the rear of the wagon. For a moment, Cecil's heart seemed to pause in its beats, and he leaned a hand against the gate to guard against collapse. Cecil had already suffered two minor heart attacks in the previous five years, and he did not particularly want to leave this world in the event of a third. But instead of holding his weight, the gate opened inward with a creak.

'Hey,' said Cecil. He coughed. His voice sounded like it was about to break. 'Hey,' he repeated. 'You okay in there?'

The figure did not move. Cecil entered the grounds of the jail and walked warily toward Black Lucy. Dawn was lighting the city, the walls glowing dimly in the first rays of the early morning sun, but the figure in the wagon was still cast in shadow.

'Hey,' said Cecil, but his voice was already fading, the single syllable transformed into a descending cadence by the realization of what he was seeing.

Atys Jones had been tied to the bars of the wagon, his arms outstretched. His body was bruised, his face bloodied and almost unrecognizable, swollen by the blows. Blood had darkened and dried upon his chest. There was also blood – too much blood to have merely soaked down – on his white shorts, the only clothing that he retained. His chin rested on his chest, his knees bent, his feet curled slightly inward. The T-bar cross was missing from around his neck.

The old jail had just added a new ghost to its legions.

20

It was Adams who broke the news to me. His eyes were even more bloodshot than before from lack of sleep when he met me in the lobby of my hotel, and he had built up a sprinkling of gray-black stubble that had already begun to itch. He scratched at it constantly as we spoke, with a noise like bacon sizzling in a pan. A smell rose from him, the smell of sweat and spilled coffee, of grass and rust and blood. There were grass stains too on his trousers and on the sides of his shoes. Around his wrists, I could see the circular marks left by the disposable gloves he had worn at the scene as they had struggled to contain the great bulk of his hands.

'I'm sorry,' he said. 'I got nothing good to say to you about what happened to that boy. He died hard.'

I felt Atys's death as a weight on my chest, as if we had both fallen at the same time and his body had come to rest across my own. I had failed to protect him. We had all failed to protect him and now he had died for a crime that he had not committed.

'Do you have a time of death?' I asked him, as he drowned a piece of toast in thick butter.

'Coroner reckons he'd been dead for about two or three hours when he was found. Doesn't look like he was killed at the jail, either. There wasn't enough blood in the paddy wagon, and none that we've found so far on the walls or grounds of the jail itself, even under UV. The beating was systematic: started at his toes and fingers, then moved on to his vital organs. They castrated him before he died, but probably not too long before. Nobody saw a thing. My guess is they picked him up before he got too far from the house, then took him somewhere quiet to work on him.'

I thought of Landron Mobley, the cruelties visited upon his body, and almost spoke, but to give Adams more than he already had would be to give him everything and I was not ready to do that. There was too much here that I did not yet understand.

'You going to talk to the Larousses?'

Adams finished off his toast. 'My guess is they knew about it as soon as I did.'

'Or maybe even sooner.'

Adams waved a finger at me in warning. 'That's the kind of implication could get a man in trouble.' He gestured to a waitress for more coffee. 'But since you brought it up, why would the Larousses want Jones beaten in that way?'

I stayed silent.

'I mean,' he continued, 'the nature of the injuries he received seems to indicate that the people who killed him wanted him to reveal something before he died. You think they wanted him to confess?'

I almost spat in contempt.

'Why? For the good of his soul? I don't think so. If these people went to the trouble of killing his guardians and then hunting him down, then it doesn't seem to me like they were in any doubt about why they were doing it.'

There was, though, the possibility that Adams was at least partly right in his suggestion that a final confession was the motive. Suppose the men who found Atys were *almost* certain that he had killed Marianne Larousse, but almost certain wasn't good enough. They wanted it from his own lips because if he wasn't responsible, then the consequences were even more serious, and not simply because the real culprit might evade detection. No, the actions that had been taken in the last twenty-four hours indicated that some people were very concerned indeed about the possibility that someone might have targeted Marianne Larousse for very particular reasons. It seemed to me that it was about time to ask some hard questions of Earl Larousse Jr., but I wasn't about to do that alone. The Larousses were hosting their party the following day, and I was expecting some company to join me in Charleston. The Larousses would have two unwelcome guests crashing their big occasion.

That afternoon, I did some research in the Charleston Public Library. I pulled up the newspaper reports of Grady Truett's death, but there was little more than Adele Foster had already told me. Persons unknown had entered his house, tied him to a chair, and cut his throat. No prints had been lifted, but the crime scene squad had to have found *something*. No crime scene is entirely clean. I was tempted to call Adams, but, once again, to do so would be to risk blowing everything that I had. I also found out a little more about the plateye. According to a book called *Blue Roots*, the plateye was a permanent resident of the spirit world, the underworld, although it was capable of entering the mortal world to seek retribution. It also had the ability to alter its form. As Adams had said, the plateye was a changeling.

I left the library and headed onto Meeting. Tereus had still not returned to his apartment, and he now hadn't shown up for work in two days. Nobody would tell me anything about him, and the stripper who had taken the twenty and then sold me out to Handy Andy was nowhere to be seen.

Finally, I called the public defender's office and was told that Laird Rhine was defending a client over at the state courthouse that afternoon. I parked at my hotel and walked down to the Four Corners, where I found Rhine in court number three at the arraignment of a woman named Johanna Bell, who had been accused of stabbing her husband in the course of a domestic argument. Apparently, she and her husband had been separated for about three months when he had returned to the family home and a quarrel had broken out over the ownership of the couple's VCR. The quarrel had ended abruptly when she stabbed him with a carving knife. Her husband sat two rows behind her, looking sorry for himself.

Rhine handled himself pretty well as he asked the arraignment judge to convert her bail to O.R. release. He was probably in his early thirties but he put up a good argument, pointing out that Bell had never been in trouble before; that she had been forced to call the cops on a number of occasions during the dying months of her marriage following threats and actual physical assault by her husband; that she could not meet the bail set; and that no purpose could be served by keeping her in jail and away from her infant son. He made her husband sound like a creep who was lucky to get away with a punctured lung, and the judge agreed to her release on her own recognizance. Afterward, she hugged Rhine and took her son in her arms from an older woman who stood waiting for her at the back of the court.

I intercepted Rhine on the courthouse steps.

'Mr. Rhine?'

He paused, and something like worry flashed across his face. As a PD, he encountered some of the lowest forms of life and was sometimes forced to try to defend the indefensible. I didn't doubt that, on occasion, his clients' victims took things personally.

'Yes?' Up close he looked even younger. He hadn't started to gray yet and his blue eyes were shielded by long, soft lashes. I flashed him my license. He glanced at it and gave a nod.

'What can I do for you, Mr. Parker? You mind if we talk while we walk? I promised my wife I'd take her out to dinner tonight.'

I fell into step alongside him.

'I'm working with Elliot Norton on the Atys Jones case, Mr. Rhine.'

His steps faltered for a moment, as though he had briefly lost his bearings, then resumed at a slightly faster speed. I accelerated to keep up.

'I'm no longer involved in that case, Mr. Parker.'

'Since Atys is dead, there isn't much of a case, period.'

'I heard. I'm sorry.'

'I'm sure. I have some questions for you.'

'I'm not sure that I can answer any questions. Maybe you should ask Mr. Norton.'

'You know, I would, except Elliot isn't around, and my questions are kind of delicate.'

He stopped at the corner of Broad as the light changed to red. He gave the offending signal a look that suggested he was taking its interference in the course of his life kind of personally.

'Like I said, I don't know that I can help you.'

'I'd like to know why you gave up the case.'

'I have a lot of cases.'

'Not like this one.'

'My caseload doesn't allow me to pick and choose, Mr. Parker. I was handed the Jones case. It was going to take up a lot of my time. I could have cleared ten cases in the time it took me just to go through the files. I wasn't sorry to see it go.'

'I don't believe you.'

'Why not?'

'You're a young public defender. You're probably ambitious, and from what I saw of your work today you have good reason to be. A high-profile case like the murder of Marianne Larousse doesn't come along every day. If you had acquitted yourself well, even if you had ultimately lost, it would have opened doors for you. I don't think you wanted to give it up so easily.'

The lights had changed again, and we were jostled slightly as people crossed ahead of us. Still, Rhine didn't move.

'Whose side are you on in this, Mr. Parker?'

'I haven't decided yet. In the end, though, I guess I'm on the side of a dead woman and a dead man, for what it's worth.'

'And Elliot Norton?'

'A friend. He asked me to come down here. I came.'

Rhine turned to face me.

'I was asked to pass the case on to him,' he said.

'By Elliot?'

'No. He never approached me. It was another man.'

'You know who he was?'

'He said his name was Kittim. He had something wrong with his face. He came to my office and told me that I should let Elliot Norton defend Atys Jones.'

'What did you say?'

'I told him that I couldn't do that. There was no reason to. He made me an offer.'

I waited.

'We all have skeletons in our closet, Mr. Parker. Suffice it to say that he gave me a glimpse of mine. I have a wife and a young daughter. I made mistakes early in my marriage, but I haven't repeated them. I wasn't planning on having my family taken away from me for sins that I've tried to make up for. I told Jones that Elliot Norton would be better qualified to handle his case. He didn't object. I walked away. I haven't seen Kittim since then, and I hope I never see him again.'

'When were you approached?'

'Three weeks ago.'

Three weeks ago: about the time that Grady Truett had been killed. By then, James Foster and Marianne Larousse were also dead. As Adele Foster had said, something was happening, and whatever it was, it had reached a new level with the death of Marianne Larousse.

'Is that all, Mr. Parker?' asked Rhine. 'I'm not happy about what I did. I don't really want to go over it again.'

'That's pretty much it,' I said.

'I really am sorry about Atys,' he said.

'I'm sure that's a great comfort to him,' I replied.

I returned to my hotel. There was a message from Louis, confirming that he would be arriving the next morning, a little later than expected. My spirits lifted slightly.

That night, I stood at the window of my hotel, drawn by the steady, repeated hooting of a car horn. Across the street, in front of the cash machine, the black Coupe de Ville with the shattered windshield idled by the curb. As I watched, the rear driver's side door opened, and the child emerged. She stood by the open door and beckoned to me, her lips moving soundlessly.

I got a place we can go

Her hips moved, shimmying to music only she could hear. She lifted her skirt, and she was naked yet sexless beneath, the skin smooth as a child's doll. Her tongue moved over her lips.

Come down

Her hand moved over the smoothness of herself.

I got a place

She thrust herself at me once more before she climbed back into the car and it began to pull slowly away, spiders spilling from its half-closed door. I awoke rubbing gossamer from my face and hair and had to shower to banish the sensation of creatures moving across my body.

21

I was awakened by a knock at my door shortly after 9 A.M. Instinctively, I felt myself reaching for a gun that was no longer there. I wrapped a towel around my waist, then padded softly to the door and peered through the peephole.

Six feet six inches of attitude, razor-sharp dress sense, and gay Republican pride looked me square in the eye.

'I could see you looking out,' said Louis as I opened the door. 'Shit, don't you ever go to the movies? Guy knocks, skinny-ass character actor looks out, guy puts barrel of gun to glass and shoots skinny-ass in the eye.' He was dressed in a black linen suit, offset with a white collarless shirt. A wave of expensive eau de cologne followed him into the room.

'You smell like a French whore,' I told him.

'I was a French whore, you couldn't afford me. By the way, you maybe could use a little makeup yourself.'

I paused, saw myself in the mirror by the door, and looked away again. He was right. I was pale, and there were dark smudges under my eyes. My lips were cracked and dry, and I could taste something metallic in my mouth.

'I picked up something,' I said.

'No shit. The fuck you pick up, the plague? They bury people look better than you.'

'What have you got, Tourette's? You have to swear all the time?'

He raised his hands in a backing-off gesture. 'Hey, glad I came. Nice to be appreciated.'

I apologized. 'You checked in?'

'Uh-huh, 'cept some motherfucker – sorry, but, shit, he was a motherfucker – try to hand me his bags at the door.'

'What did you do?'

'Took them, put them in the trunk of a cab, gave the guy fifty bucks, and told him to take them to the charity store.'

'Classy.'

'I like to think so.'

I left him watching television while I showered and dressed, then we headed down to Diana's on Meeting for coffee and a bite to eat. I ate half a bagel, then pushed it away.

'You got to eat.'

I shook my head. 'It'll pass.'

'It'll pass and you'll be dead. So how we doin'?'

'Same as usual: dead people, a mystery, more dead people.'

'Who we lost?'

'The boy. His guardians. Maybe Elliot Norton.'

'Shit, don't sound like we got anybody left. Anyone hires you better leave you your fee in their will.'

I filled him in on all that had occurred, leaving out only the black car. That I didn't need to burden him with.

'So what you gonna do?'

'Push a stick into the beehive and rustle up some bees. The Larousses are hosting a party today. I think we should avail ourselves of their hospitality.'

'We got an invite?'

'Has not having one ever stopped us before?'

'No, but sometimes I just like to be invited to shit, you know what I'm sayin', instead of having to bust in, get threatened, irritate the nice white folks, put the fear of the black man on them.'

He paused, seemed to think for a while about what he had just said, then brightened.

'Sounds good, doesn't it?' I said.

'Real good,' he agreed.

We drove most of the way to the old Larousse plantation in separate vehicles, Louis parking his car about half a mile from the gates before joining me for the rest of the journey. I asked him about Angel.

'He workin' on a job.'

'Anything I should know about?'

He looked at me for a long time.

'I don't know. Maybe, but not now.'

'Uh-huh. I see you made the news.'

He didn't reply for a couple of seconds. 'Angel tell you somethin'?'

'Just gave me the name of the town. You waited a long time to settle that score.'

He shrugged. 'They was worth killin', they just wasn't worth travelin' too far to kill.'

'And since you were on your way down here anyway . . .'

'I figured I'd stop by,' he finished. 'Can I go now, Officer?'

I let it drop. At the entrance to the Larousse estate, a tall man in a flunky's suit waved us down.

'Can I see your invitations, gentlemen?'

'We didn't get invitations,' I said, 'but I'm pretty sure somebody is expecting us.'

'The names?'

'Parker. Charlie Parker.'

'By two,' added Louis, helpfully.

The guard spoke into his walkie-talkie, out of earshot from us. We waited, two or three cars lining up behind us, until the guard finished talking.

'You can go ahead. Mr. Kittim will meet you at the parking area.'

'Surprise, surprise,' said Louis. I had told him about my encounter with Bowen and Kittim at the Antioch rally.

'Told you this would work,' I said. 'That's why I'm a detective.' It struck me then, my worries about the consequences of the Caina incident aside, that I was already feeling better since Louis had arrived. That wasn't too surprising, since I now had a pistol, thanks to him, and I was pretty certain that Louis had at least one more on his person.

We followed half a mile of live oaks, palmettos, and palms, much of it overhung with Spanish moss. Cicadas chirped in the trees and droplets from the morning's now departed rain kept up a steady rhythmic patter on the roof and road until we emerged from the trees and onto an expanse of green lawn. Another white-gloved flunky directed us to park the car beneath one of a number of tarpaulins erected to shelter the vehicles from the sunlight, the canvas shifting slightly in the currents of cold air cast by one of a number of huge industrial air conditioners arrayed on the grass. Long tables had been arranged along three sides of a square and covered by starched linen tablecloths. Huge amounts of food had been arrayed upon them, while black servants in pristine white shirts and dark trousers hovered anxiously, waiting to serve guests. Others moved through the crowds already gathered on the lawn, offering champagne and cocktails. I looked at Louis. He looked at me. Apart from the servants, he was the only person of color present. He was also the only guest dressed in black.

'You should have worn a white jacket,' I said. 'You look like an exclamation mark. Plus, you might have picked up a few bucks in tips.'

'Look at them brothers.' He despaired. 'Ain't nobody here heard of Denmark Vesey?'

A dragonfly glided across the grass by my feet, hunting for prey among the blades. There were no birds to prey on him in turn, at least none that I could see or hear. The only sign of life came from a single heron standing in a patch of marshland to the northeast of the house, the waters around it seemingly stilled by a carpet of algae. Beside it, amid rows of oak and pecans, stood the remains of small dwellings, equidistantly spaced, their tiled roofs now gone and the miscast and broken bricks used in their construction weathered by the elements over the century and a half that had probably passed since their original establishment. Even I could guess what it represented: the remains of a slave street.

'You'd think they'd have knocked them down,' I said.

'That's heritage,' said Louis. 'Right up there with flying the Confederate flag and keeping one pillowcase clean at all times. Y'know, for special wear.'

The Larousses' old plantation house was pre-Revolutionary redbrick, a Georgian-Palladian villa dating back to the mid–eighteenth century. Limestone steps led up a set of twin staircases to a marble–floored portico. Four Doric pillars supported the gallery that ran across the front of the house, four windows on either side over two levels. Elegantly dressed couples crowded in the shade of the porch.

Our attention was distracted by a party of men moving quickly across the lawn. They were all white, all had earpieces, and all were sweating beneath their dark suits, despite the efforts of the air conditioners. The only exception was the man at the center of the group. Kittim wore a blue blazer over tan trousers and penny loafers, his white shirt buttoned to the neck. His head and face were largely concealed by the baseball cap and sunglasses, but they couldn't conceal the blade wound that had been torn in his right cheek.

Atys. That was why the T-bar cross had not been on his body when he was found.

Kittim stopped about five feet away from us and raised his hand. Instantly, the men around him paused, then spread out in a semicircle surrounding us. No words were spoken for a moment. His attention shifted from Louis to me, then back again. His smile remained fixed in place, even when Louis spoke to him for the first time.

'What. The fuck. Are you?' asked Louis.

Kittim didn't respond to him.

'This is Kittim,' I explained.

'Ain't he the pretty one?'

'Mr. Parker,' said Kittim, still ignoring Louis. 'We weren't expecting you.'

'It was a last-minute decision,' I replied. 'Some sudden deaths cleared my schedule.'

'Mm-hmm,' said Kittim. 'I can't help but notice that you and your colleague appear to be armed.'

'Armed.' I looked disapprovingly at Louis. 'Told you it wasn't that kind of party.'

'Never hurts to come prepared. Folks don't take us seriously otherwise,' said Louis.

'Oh, I take you very seriously,' said Kittim, acknowledging him properly for the first time. 'So seriously that I'd be grateful if you would come with us to the basement, where we can dispose of your weapons without alarming the other guests.'

Already I could see people casting curious looks in our direction. As if on cue, a string quartet struck up from the far side of the lawn. They were playing a Strauss waltz. How quaint.

'No offense, man, but we ain't goin' to no basement with you.' It was Louis.

'Then you'll force us to take action.'

Louis's eyebrow rose about half an inch. 'Yeah, what you gonna do, kill us on the lawn? That's gonna be some party, you do that. People be talkin' about it for a *loooong* time. "Hey, you remember Earl's party, when those sweaty guys and the fucker with leprosy tried to take the guns away from those fellas that arrived late, and they drew down on them and Bessie Bluechip got all that blood on her dress? Man, how we laughed . . ."'

The tension was perceptibly rising. The men around Kittim were waiting for an indication from him on how to proceed, but he wasn't moving. His smile remained fixed in place as if he'd died with it and then been stuffed and mounted on the lawn. I felt something roll down my back and pool at the base of my spine, and realized that the security guards weren't the only ones who were sweating.

The tension was broken by a voice from the porch.

'Mr. Kittim,' it said. 'Don't keep our guests on the grass. Bring them up here.'

The voice came from Earl Jr., looking elegantly wasted in a blue double-breasted jacket and jeans pressed with the crease along the knee. His light hair was brushed forward to disguise his widow's peak, and his lips seemed even fuller and more feminine than when last I saw him. Kittim inclined his head slightly, indicating we should do as requested, then he and his men fell into place behind and around us. It was obvious to anyone with half a brain that we were about as welcome as bugs in the buffet, but the guests around us studiously pretended to ignore us. Even the servants didn't look our way. We were led through the main doors and into a great hall floored with loblolly pine. Two drawing rooms opened up on either side, and a graceful double stairway led to the upper floor. The doors closed behind us and we were disarmed within seconds. They got two guns and a knife out of Louis. They seemed impressed.

'Look at you,' I said. 'Two guns.'

'And a knife. I had to get the trousers cut special.'

Kittim moved around until he was standing by Earl Jr.'s side. Kittim had a shiny blue Taurus in his hand.

'Why are you here, Mr. Parker?' said Larousse. 'This is a private party, the first such occasion since the death of my sister.'

'Why break out the champagne now? You have something to celebrate?'

'Your presence is not welcome here.'

'Somebody killed Atys Jones.'

'I heard. You'll forgive me if I shed no tears.'

'He didn't murder your sister, Mr. Larousse, but I suspect you already know that.'

'Why would you suspect that?'

'Because I think Mr. Kittim here probably tortured Atys before he killed him in an effort to find out who did. Because you think, as I do, that the person responsible for your sister's death may also be responsible for the deaths of Landron Mobley, Grady Truett, the suicide of James Foster, and possibly the death of Elliot Norton.'

'I don't know what you're talking about.' He didn't look surprised at the mention of Elliot's name.

'I also think that Elliot Norton might have been trying to find out who was responsible as well, which was why he took on the Jones case, and I'm starting to think that he may have taken it on with your approval, maybe even your cooperation. Except he wasn't making enough progress, so you took matters into your own hands after Mobley's body was found.'

I turned to Kittim.

'Did you enjoy killing Atys Jones, Kittim? Did you enjoy shooting an old woman in the back?'

I saw the blow coming too late to react. His fist caught me in the hollow of my left temple and sent me sprawling to the ground. Louis twitched slightly, on the verge of movement, but froze with the sound of hammers cocking.

'You need to work on your manners, Mr. Parker,' said Kittim. 'You can't come in here and make accusations of that kind without incurring the consequences.'

I raised myself slowly onto my hands and knees. The punch had rattled me, and I felt bile rising into my throat. I gagged, then vomited.

'Oh dear,' said Larousse. 'Now look what you've done. Toby, get somebody to clean that up.'

Kittim's feet appeared beside me. 'You're a mess, Mr. Parker.' He squatted down so I could see his face. 'Mr. Bowen doesn't like you. Now I can see why. Don't think that we've finished with you yet. Me, I'd be very surprised if you make it home alive out of South Carolina. In fact, I'd say the odds against it would be quite attractive, if I were a gambling man.'

The door in front of me opened, and a manservant entered. He didn't appear to register the guns or the tension in the room. He simply knelt down as I stood unsteadily, and began to scrub the floorboards clean. He was followed by Earl Sr.

'What's going on here?' he asked.

'Some uninvited guests, Mr. Larousse,' replied Kittim. 'They're about to leave.'

The old man barely glanced at him. It was clear that Larousse didn't like Kittim and resented his presence in his house, yet still Kittim was here. Larousse said nothing to him and instead diverted his attention to his son, whose confidence immediately began to dissipate in his father's presence.

'Who are they?' he asked.

'This is the investigator I spoke to at the hotel, the one hired by Elliot Norton to get Marianne's nigger murderer off the hook,' stammered Earl Jr.

'Is that true?' asked the older man.

I wiped the back of my hand over my mouth.

'No,' I said. 'I don't believe that Atys Jones killed your daughter, but I will find out who did.'

'It's not your business.'

'Atys is dead. So are the people who gave him sanctuary in their home. You're right: finding out what happened isn't my business. It's more than that. It's my moral obligation.'

'I would advise you to take your moral obligations elsewhere, sir. This one will lead you to ruin.' He turned to his son. 'Have them escorted off my property.'

Earl Jr. looked to Kittim. The decision was clearly his to make. After a pause to assert his authority, Kittim nodded to his men and they moved forward, their guns held discreetly by their sides so as not to alarm the guests when we left the house.

'And Mr. Kittim,' added Earl Sr.

Kittim turned to look at him.

'In future, conduct your beatings elsewhere. This is my house and you are not a member of my staff.'

He shot a final harsh look at his son, then went out onto the lawn to rejoin his guests.

We were placed at the center of a circle of men and escorted to the car. Our weapons were placed in the trunk, minus their ammunition. Kittim leaned on the driver's side window as I prepared to drive away. The smell of burning was so strong that I almost gagged again.

'Next time I see you will be the last,' he said. 'Now take your porch monkey and get out of here.' He winked at Louis, then he patted the roof of the car and watched us drive away.

I touched my temple where Kittim's punch had landed, and winced at the contact.

'You okay to drive?' asked Louis.

'I think so.'

'Looked like Kittim was makin' himself at home back there.'

'He's there because Bowen wants him there.'

'Means Bowen got something on the Larousses, if his boy has the run of the house.'

'He called you a bad name.'

'I heard.'

'You seem to be taking it pretty calmly, all things considered.'

'Wasn't worth dyin' over. Least, not worth my dyin' over. Kittim's another matter. Like the man said, we be seein' him again. It'll wait.'

'You think you can stay with him?'

'Sure. Where you goin'?'

'To get a history lesson. I'm tired of being nice to people.'

Louis looked mildly surprised.

'Just how exactly you been definin' "nice" up to now?'

22

There was a message waiting for me when I got back to my hotel. It was from Phil Poveda. He wanted me to call him. He didn't sound panicked or fearful. In fact, I thought I detected a note of relief in his voice. First, though, I called Rachel. Bruce Taylor, one of the patrolmen out of Scarborough, was in the kitchen when she answered, drinking coffee and eating a cookie. It made me feel better knowing that the cops were dropping by as MacArthur had promised and that somewhere the Klan Killer was being intolerant of lactose, among other things.

'Wallace has been by a few times as well,' said Rachel.

'How is Mr. Lonelyheart?'

'He went shopping in Freeport. He bought himself a couple of jackets in Ralph's, some new shirts and ties. He's a work in progress, but there's potential there. And Mary really seems to be his type.'

'Desperate?'

'The word you're looking for is "easygoing". Now go away. I have an attractive man in uniform to take care of.'

I hung up and dialed Phil Poveda's number.

'It's Parker,' I said when he picked up the phone.

'Hey,' he replied. 'Thanks for calling.' He sounded upbeat, almost cheerful. This was a far cry from the Phil Poveda who had threatened me with a gun two days before. 'I've just been putting my affairs in order. You know, wills and shit. I'm a pretty wealthy man, I just never knew it. Admittedly, I'll have to die to capitalize on it, but that's cool.'

'Mr. Poveda, are you feeling okay?' It was kind of a redundant question. Phil Poveda appeared to be feeling better than okay. Unfortunately, I figured Phil Poveda felt that way because his sanity was falling down around his ears.

'Yeah,' he said, and for the first time a twinge of doubt crept into his voice. 'Yeah, I think so. You were right: Elliot's dead. They found his car. It was on the news.'

I didn't reply.

'Like you said, that leaves just me and Earl, and unlike Earl, I don't have my daddy and my Nazi friends to protect me.'

'You mean Bowen.'

'Uh-huh, Bowen and that Aryan freak of his. But they won't be able to protect him forever. Someday, he'll find himself alone, and then . . .'

He let himself trail off before resuming.

'I just want it all to be over.'

'You want what to be over?'

'Everything: the killing, the guilt. Hell, the guilt most of all. You got time, we can talk about it. I got time. Not much, though, not much. Time's running out for me. Time's running out for all of us.'

I told him I'd be right over. I also wanted to tell him to stay away from the medicine cabinet and any sharp objects, but by then the glimmer of sanity that had briefly shone through had been swallowed up by the dark clouds in his brain. He just said, 'Cool!' and put down the phone.

I packed my bags and checked out of the hotel. Whatever happened next, I wouldn't be back in Charleston for a while.

Phil Poveda answered his door wearing shorts, deck shoes, and a white T-shirt depicting Jesus Christ pulling back his robes to reveal the thorn-enclosed heart within.

'Jesus is my Savior,' explained Phil. 'Every time I look in the mirror, I'm reminded of that fact. He is ready to forgive me.'

Poveda's pupils had shrunk to the size of pinheads. Whatever he was on was strong stuff. You could have given it to the folks on the *Titanic* and watched them descend beneath the waves with beatific smiles on their faces. He shepherded me into his neat oak kitchen and made decaf coffee for both of us. For the next hour, his coffee sat untouched beside him. Pretty soon, I'd laid mine aside as well.

After hearing Phil Poveda's tale, I didn't think I'd ever want to eat or drink again.

The bar, Obee's, is gone now. It was a roadhouse dive off Bluff Road, a place where clean-cut college boys could get five-dollar blow jobs from poor blacks and poorer whites out among the trees that descended in dark conclave down to the banks of the Congaree, then return to their buddies, high-fiving and grinning, while the women washed their mouth out from the tap in the yard. But close to where it once stood is a new structure: the Swamp Rat, where Atys Jones and Marianne Larousse spent their last hours together before her death.

The Jones sisters used to drink in Obee's, though one of them, Addy, was barely seventeen and the older sister, Melia, by a quirk of nature, looked younger still. By then, Addy had already given birth to her son, Atys: the fruit, it appeared, of an ill-fated liaison with one of her momma's passing boyfriends, the late Davis 'Boot' Smoot, a liaison that might have been classified as rape had she seen fit to report it. So Addy had begun to raise the boy with her grandma, for her mother couldn't bear to look at her. Pretty soon, she wouldn't be there for her mother to ignore, for on this night all traces of Addy and her sister were about to be erased from this earth.

They were drunk and swaying slightly as they emerged from the bar, a chorus of whistles and catcalls sending them on their way, a boozy wind in their sails. Addy tripped and landed on her ass, and her sister doubled over with laughter. She hauled the younger girl up, her skirt rising to reveal her nakedness, and as they stood swaying they saw the young men packed into the car, the ones in the back climbing over one another to catch a glimpse. Embarrassed and not a little afraid, even in their drunkenness, the laughter of the young women faded and they aimed for the road, their heads down.

They had walked only a few yards when they heard the sound of the car behind them and the headlights picked them out among the stones and fallen pine needles on the road. They looked behind them. The huge twin eyes were almost upon them, and then the car was alongside and one of the rear doors had opened. A hand reached out for Addy, grasping. It tore her dress and drew ragged parallel cuts along her arm.

The girls started running into the undergrowth toward the smell of water and rotting vegetation. The car pulled in by the side of the road, the lights died, and with whoops and war cries, the chase was on.

'We used to call them whores,' said Poveda. His eyes were still unnaturally bright. 'And they were, or as good as. Landron knew all about them. That was why we let him hang out with us, because Landron knew all the whores, the girls who'd let you fuck them for a six-pack of beer, the girls who wouldn't talk if you maybe had to force them a little. It was Landron who told us about the Jones sisters. One of them had a child, and she couldn't have been but sixteen when it was born. And the other one, Landron said she was just crying out for it, took it anyway she could. Hell, they didn't even wear panties. Landron said that was so the men could get in and out easier. I mean, what kind of girls were they, drinking in bars like that, going around buck naked under their skirts? They were advertising it, so why not sell? They might even have enjoyed it, if they'd heard us out. And we'd have paid them. We had money. We didn't want it for nothing.'

He was in his own place now, no longer Phil Poveda, a late thirty-something software engineer with a paunch and a mortgage. Instead, he was a boy again. He was back with the others, running through the long grass, his breath catching in his throat, feeling the ache at his crotch.

'Hey, hold up!' he cried. 'Hold up, we got money!'

And around him, the others cracked up laughing, because it was Phil, and Phil knew how to have a good time. Phil always made them laugh. Phil was a funny guy.

They chased the girls into the Congaree and along Cedar Creek, Truett stumbling and falling into the water, James Foster helping him to his feet again. They caught up with them where the waters began to grow deeper, close by the first of the big cypress trees with their swollen boles. Melia fell, tripping on an exposed root, and before her sister could pull her to her feet they were on them. Addy struck out at the man nearest her, her small fist impacting above his eye, and Landron Mobley hit her so hard in response that he broke her jaw and she fell back, dazed.

'You fucking bitch,' Landron said. 'You fucking, *fucking* bitch.' And there was something in his voice, the low menace, that made the others pause; even Phil, who was struggling to hold on to Melia. And they knew then that it was going down, that there was no turning back. Earl Larousse and Grady Truett held Addy down for Landron while the others stripped her sister. Elliot Norton, Phil, and James Foster looked at one another, then Phil pushed Melia to the ground and soon he, like Landron, was moving inside, the two men falling into a rhythm beside each other while the night insects buzzed around them, attracted by the scent of them, feeding on the men and on the women, and probing at the blood that began to seep into the ground.

It was Phil's fault, in the end. He was getting off the girl, breathing hard, his face turned away from her, looking toward her sister and her sister's ruined face, the import of what they were doing gradually dawning on him now that he had spent himself, when suddenly he felt the impact at his groin and he tumbled sideways, the shock already transforming itself into a burning at the pit of his stomach. Then Melia was on her feet and running away from the swamp, heading east toward the Larousse tract and the main road beyond.

Mobley was the first to head after her, then Foster. Elliot, torn between taking his turn with the girl on the ground or stopping her sister, stood unmoving for a time before running after his friends. Grady and Earl were already pushing at each other, joshing as they fought for their turn with Addy.

The purchase of the karst had been an expensive mistake for the Larousse family. The land was honeycombed by underwater streams and caves, and they had almost lost a truck down a sinkhole following a collapse before they discovered that the limestone deposits weren't even big enough to justify quarrying. Meanwhile, successful mines were being dug in Cayce, about twenty miles upriver, and Wynnsboro, up 77 toward Charlotte, and then there were the tree huggers protesting at the potential threat to the swamp. The Larousses turned their attentions in other directions, leaving the land as a reminder to themselves never to be caught out like that again.

Melia passed some fallen, rusted fencing, and a bullet-riddled 'No Trespassing' sign. Her feet were torn and bleeding, but she kept moving. There were houses beyond the karst, she knew. There would be help for her there, help for her sister. They would come for them and take them to safety and—

She heard the men behind her, closing rapidly. She looked back, still running, and suddenly her toes were no longer on solid ground but were suspended over some deep, dark place. She teetered on the brink of the sinkhole, smelling the filthy, polluted water below, then her balance failed her and she plummeted over the edge. She landed with a splash far below, emerging seconds later choking and coughing, the water burning her eyes, her skin, her privates. She peered up and saw the three men silhouetted against the stars. With slow strokes, she swam for the edges of the hole. She tried to find a handhold, but the stone kept slipping beneath her fingers. She heard the men talking, and one of them disappeared. Her arms and legs moved slowly as she kept herself afloat in the dank, viscous waters. The burning was getting worse now, and she had trouble keeping her eyes open. From above, there came a new light. She stared up in time to see the rag flare and then the gasoline can was falling, falling . . .

The sinkholes had, over the years, become a dumping ground for poisons and chemicals, the waste infecting the water supply and slowly, over time, entering the Congaree itself, for all of these hidden streams ultimately connected with the great river. Many of the substances dumped in the hole were dangerous. Some were corrosives, others weed killers. Most, though, had one thing in common.

They were highly inflammable.

The three men stepped back hurriedly as a pillar of flame shot up from the depths of the hole, illuminating the trees, the broken ground, the abandoned machinery, and their faces, shocked and secretly delighted at the effect they had achieved.

One of them wiped his hands on the remains of the old sheet he had torn for use as a wick, trying to rid himself of the worst of the gasoline.

'Fuck her,' said Elliot Norton. He wrapped the rag around a stone and tossed it into the inferno. 'Let's go.'

I said nothing for a time. Poveda was tracing unknowable patterns on the tabletop with his index finger. Elliot Norton, a man whom I had considered a friend, had participated in the rape and burning of a young girl. I stared at Poveda, but he was intent upon his finger patterns. Something had broken inside Phil Poveda, the thing that had allowed him to continue living after what they had done, and now Phil Poveda was drowning in the tide of his recollection.

I was watching a man go insane.

'Go on,' I said. 'Finish it.'

'Finish her,' said Mobley. He was looking down at Earl Larousse, who was kneeling beside the prone woman, buttoning his pants. Earl's brow furrowed.

'What?'

'Finish her,' repeated Mobley. 'Kill her.'

'I can't do that,' said Earl. He sounded like a little boy.

'You fucked her quick enough,' said Mobley. 'You leave her here and somebody finds her, then she'll talk. We let her go, she'll talk. Here.' He picked up a rock and tossed it at Earl. It struck him painfully on the knee and he winced, then rubbed at the spot.

'Why me?' he whined.

'Why any of us?' asked Mobley.

'I'm not doing it,' said Earl.

Then Mobley pulled a knife from beneath the folds of his shirt. 'Do it,' said Mobley, 'or I'll kill you instead.'

Suddenly, the power in the group shifted and they understood. It had been Mobley all along: Mobley who had led them; Mobley who had found the pot, the LSD; Mobley who had brought them to the women; and Mobley who had ultimately damned them. Maybe that had been his intention all along, thought Phil later: to damn a group of rich, white boys who had patronized him, insulted him, then taken him under their wing when they saw what he could procure for them just as they would surely abandon him when his usefulness came to an end. And of them all, it was Larousse who was the most spoiled, the most cosseted, the weakest, the most untrustworthy; and so it would fall to him to kill the girl.

Larousse began to cry. 'Please,' he said. 'Please don't make me do this.'

Mobley, unspeaking, lifted the blade and watched it gleam in the moonlight. Slowly, with trembling hands, Larousse picked up the rock.

'Please,' he said, one last time. To his right, Phil turned away, only to feel Mobley's hand wrench him around.

'No, you watch. You're part of it, you watch it end. Now—' He turned his attention back to Larousse. 'Finish her, you chicken-shit fuck. Finish her, you fucking pretty boy, unless you want to go back to your daddy and have to tell him what you've done, cry on his shoulder like the little fucking faggot that you are, beg him to make it go away. Finish her. *Finish her!*'

Larousse's whole body was shaking as he raised the rock then brought it down, with minimal force, on the girl's face. Still there came a cracking sound, and she moaned. Larousse was howling now, his face convulsed with fear, the tears rolling down his cheeks, streaking through the dirt that had accumulated on them during the rape of the girl. He raised the rock a second time, then brought it down harder. This time, the crack was louder. The rock came up once more, then down, faster now, and Larousse was making a high-pitched mewling sound as he struck at the girl again and again and again, lost in the frenzy of it, blood-spattered, until hands reached out for him and they dragged him from her body, the rock still grasped between his fingers, his eyes huge and white in his red face.

The girl on the ground was long dead.

'You did good,' said Mobley. The knife was gone. 'You're a regular killer, Earl.' He patted the sobbing man on the shoulder. 'A regular killer.'

'Mobley took her away,' said Poveda. 'People were coming, drawn by the fire, and we had to leave. Landron's old man was a grave digger in Charleston. He'd opened a grave in Magnolia the day before, so Landron and Elliot dumped her there and used some of the earth to cover her. They buried the guy on top of her the next day. He was the last in his family. Nobody was ever going to be digging up the plot again.' He swallowed. 'At least, they weren't until Landron's body got dumped there.'

'And Melia?' I asked.

'She was burned alive. Nothing could have survived that blaze.'

'And nobody knew about this? You told no one else about what you'd done?'

He shook his head. 'It was just us. They looked for the girls, but they never found them. Rains came and washed everything away. As far as anybody knew, they'd just disappeared off the face of the earth.

'But somebody found out,' he concluded. 'Somebody's making us pay. Marianne was killed. James took his own life. Grady got his throat cut. Mobley was murdered, then Elliot. Someone is hunting us down, punishing us. I'm next. That's why I had to get my affairs in order.'

He smiled.

'I'm leaving it all to charity. You think that's a good thing to do? I think so. I think it's a good thing.'

'You could go to the police. You could tell them what you did.'

'No, that's not the way. I have to wait.'

'I could go to the police.'

He shrugged. 'You could, but I'll just say you made it all up. My lawyer will have me out in a matter of hours, if they even bother to take me in at all, then I'll be back here, waiting.'

I stood.

'Jesus will forgive me,' said Poveda. 'He forgives us all. Doesn't He?'

Something flickered in his eyes, the last dying thrashing of his sanity before it sank beneath the waves.

'I don't know,' I said. 'I don't know if there's that much forgiveness in the universe.'

Then I left him.

The Congaree. The spate of recent deaths. The link between Elliot and Atys Jones. The T-bar in Landron Mobley's chest, and the smaller version of it that hung from the neck of the man with the damaged eyes.

Tereus. I had to find Tereus.

The old man still sat on the worn steps of the house smoking his pipe and watching the traffic go by. I asked him for the number of Tereus's room.

'Number eight, but he ain't there,' he told me.

'You know, I think you may be bad luck for me,' I said. 'Whenever I come here, Tereus is gone but you're taking up porch space.'

'Thought you'd be glad to see a familiar face.'

'Yeah, Tereus's.'

I walked past him and headed up the stairs. He watched me go.

I knocked on the door to eight, but there was no reply. From the rooms at either side I could hear competing radios playing, and stale cooking smells clung to the carpets and the walls. I tried the handle and it turned easily, the door opening onto a room with a single unmade bed, a punch-drunk couch, and a gas stove in one corner. There was barely enough room between the stove and the bed for a thin man to squeeze by and look out of the small, grime-caked window. To my left was a toilet and shower stall, both reasonably clean. In fact, the room might have been threadbare, but it wasn't dirty. Tereus had done his best to make something of it: new drapes hung from the plastic rod at the window, and a cheap framed print of roses in a vase hung on the wall. There was no TV, no radio, no books. The mattress had been torn from the bed and thrown in a corner, and clothes were scattered around the room, but I guessed that whoever had trashed the place had found nothing. Anything of value Tereus owned he kept elsewhere, in his true home.

I was about to leave when the door opened behind me. I turned to find a big, overweight black man in a bright shirt blocking my way out. He had a cigarette in one hand and a baseball bat in the other. Behind him, I could see the old man puffing on his pipe.

'Can I help you with something?' asked the man with the bat.

'You the super?'

'I'm the owner, and you're trespassing.'

'I was looking for somebody.'

'Well, he ain't here, and you got no right to be in his place.'

'I'm a private detective. My name is—'

'I don't give a good goddamn what your name is. You just get out of here now before I have to defend myself against an unprovoked assault.'

The old man with the pipe chuckled. 'Unprovoked assault,' he echoed. 'Thass good.' He shook his head in merriment and blew out a puff of smoke.

I walked to the door and the big man stood to one side to let me pass. He still filled most of the doorway and I had to breathe in deeply to squeeze by. He smelled of drain cleaner and Old Spice. I paused at the stairs.

'Can I ask you something?'

'What?'

'How come his door was unlocked?'

The man's face creased in puzzlement. 'You didn't open it?'

'No, it was open when I got here, and somebody had gone through his things.'

The owner turned to the man with the pipe. 'Anybody else asking after Tereus?'

'No sir, just this man.'

'Look, I'm not trying to make any trouble,' I continued. 'I just need to talk to Tereus. When was the last time that you saw him?'

'Few days ago,' said the owner, relenting. 'Round about eight, after he finished over at the club. He had a pack with him, said he wouldn't be back for a couple of days.'

'And the door was locked then?'

'Watched him lock it myself.'

Which meant that somebody had entered the building since the death of Atys Jones and had probably done what I had just done: gone into the apartment, either to find Tereus himself or something connected with him.

'Thanks,' I said.

'Yeah, don't mention it.'

'Unprovoked assault,' said the pipe smoker again. 'Thass funny.'

The late-afternoon deviants were already assembled in LapLand by the time I arrived, among them an elderly man in a torn shirt who rubbed his hand up and down his beer bottle in a manner that suggested he spent too much time alone thinking about women, and a middle-aged guy in a tatty business suit, his tie already at half-mast, and a shot glass before him. His briefcase lay at his feet. It had fallen open and now stood, slack-jawed, on the floor. It was empty. I wondered when he would pluck up the courage to tell his wife that he'd lost his job, that he'd been spending his days watching pole dancers or low-priced afternoon movies, that she didn't have to iron his shirts anymore because, hell, he didn't have to wear a shirt. In fact, he didn't even have to get out of bed in the mornings if he didn't feel like it, and hey, you got a problem with that, then don't let the door hit your ass on the way out.

I found Lorelei sitting at the bar, waiting for her turn to dance. She didn't look too happy to see me, but I was used to that. The bartender made a move to intercept me, but I lifted a finger.

'My name's Parker. You got a problem, you call Willie. Otherwise, back off.'

He backed off.

'Slow afternoon,' I said to Lorelei.

'They're always slow,' she said, her head turning away from me to signal her lack of interest in engaging me in conversation. I figured that she'd taken an earful from her boss for talking too much the last time I visited, and didn't want to be seen to repeat her mistake. 'The only cash these guys got are nickels and dimes.'

'Well then, I guess you'll be dancing for the love of your art.'

She shook her head and stared back at me over her shoulder. It wasn't a friendly stare.

'You think you're funny? Maybe even think you got "charm"? Well, let me tell you something: you don't. What you got I see here every night, in every guy who sticks a dollar bill in the crack of my ass. They come in, they think they're better than me, they maybe even got some fantasy that I'll look at them and I won't want to take their money, I'll just want to take them home and fuck them till their lights go out. Well, that just ain't gonna happen, and if I don't put out for free for them, I sure ain't gonna put out for free for you, so if you want something from me, you show me green.'

She had a point. I put a fifty on the bar but kept my finger firmly fixed on the nose.

'Call me cautious,' I said. 'Last time, I think you reneged on our agreement.'

'You got to talk to Tereus, didn't you?'

'Yeah, but I had to go through your boss to get to him. Literally. Where is Tereus?'

Her lips thinned. 'You really got it in for that guy, don't you? You ever get tired of pressuring people?'

'Listen to me,' I said. 'I'd prefer not to be here. I'd prefer not to be talking to you in this way. I don't think I'm better than you, but I'm certainly no worse than you, so save the speeches. You don't want my money? That's fine.' The music came to a close, and the customers clapped desultorily as the dancer gathered up her clothes and headed for the dressing room.

'You're up,' I said. I began to pull the fifty back, but her hand slapped down upon the edge.

'He didn't come in this morning. Last couple of mornings neither.'

'So I gather. Where is he?'

'He has a place in town.'

'He hasn't been back there in days. I need more than that.'

The bartender announced her name, and she grimaced. She slipped from her chair, the fifty still trapped between us.

'He got hisself a place up by the Congaree. There's some private land in the reserve. That's where he's at.'

'Where exactly?'

'You want me to draw you a map? I can't tell you, but there ain't but one stretch of private left in the park.'

I released the fifty.

'Next time, I don't care how much money you bring, I ain't talking to you. I'd be better earning two dollars from those sorry motherfuckers than a thousand selling out good people to you. But you can take this for free: you ain't the only one bein' askin' about Tereus. Couple of guys came in yesterday, but Willie gave them the bum's rush, called them "fucking Nazis."'

I nodded my thanks.

'And I still liked them better than you,' she added.

With that she walked to the stage, the CD player behind the bar knocking out the first bars of 'Love Child.' She had palmed the fifty.

Obviously, she planned to turn over her new leaf tomorrow.

Phil Poveda was sitting at his kitchen table that night, two cups of cold coffee still lying untouched close by, when the door opened behind him and he heard the padding of feet. He raised his head, and the lights danced in his eyes. He turned around in his chair.

'I'm sorry,' he said.

The hook was poised above his head, and he recalled, in his final moments, Christ's words to Peter and Andrew by the Sea of Galilee:

I will make you fishers of men.

Poveda's lips trembled as he spoke.

'This won't hurt, will it?'

And the hook descended.

23

I drove in silence to Columbia. There was no music in the car. I seemed to drift along I-26, northwest through Dorchester, Orangeburg and Calhoun counties, the lights of the cars that passed me in the darkness like flights of fireflies moving in parallel, slowly fading into the distance or lost to the twists and bends of the road.

And everywhere there were trees, and in the blackness beyond their margins the land brooded. How could it not? It had been tainted by its own history, enriched by the bodies of the dead that lay beneath the leaves and the rocks: British and Colonial, Confederate and Union, slave and freeman, the possessor and the possessed. Go north, to York and Lancaster Counties, and there were trails once traversed by the night riders, their horses galloping through dirt and water, white-draped, mud-speckled, the riders urging them on, terrorizing, annihilating, stamping the first shoots of a new future into the dirt beneath the horses' hooves.

And the blood of the dead ran into the earth and clouded the rivers, flowing from the mountain forests of poplar, red maple, and flowering dogwood, the sculpin and dace absorbing it into their system as it passed through their gills; and the river otters that plucked them from the water gulped them down, and the blood with them. It was in the mayflies and stoneflies that darkened the air of the Piedmont Shoals, in the black-sided darters that anchored themselves to the bottom of ponds to avoid being eaten, in the sunfish that hovered near the safety of the spider lilies, the beauty of their white flowers masking their ugly, arachnoid underparts.

Here, on these silt-loaded waters, the sunlight moves in strange patterns, independent of the flow of the river or the demands of the breeze. These are the shiners, the small, silvery fish that blend with the light reflecting off the surface of the stream, dazzling predators into seeing the shoal as one single entity, one enormous, threatening life-form. These swamps are their safe haven, although the old blood had found its way even into them.

(And is that why you stayed here, Tereus? Is that why the little apartment contained so few traces of your existence? For you don't exist in the city, not as you truly are. In the city you're just another ex-con, another poor man cleaning up after those wealthier than himself, witnessing their appetites while quietly praying to your God for their salvation. But that's just a front, isn't it? The reality of you is very different. The reality of you is out here, in the swamps, with whatever you've been hiding for all these years. It's you. You're hunting them down, aren't you, punishing them for what they did so long ago? This is your place. You discovered what they did and you decided to make them pay. But then jail got in the way – although, even in that, you were making somebody pay for his sins – and you had to wait to continue your work. I don't blame you. I don't think any man could look upon what those creatures had done and not want to punish them in any way possible. But that's not true justice, Tereus, because by doing what you're doing, the truth of what they did – Mobley and Poveda, Larousse and Truett, Elliot and Foster – will never be revealed, and without that truth, without that revelation, there can be no justice achieved.

And what of Marianne Larousse? Her misfortune was to be born into that family and to be marked by her brother's crime. Unknowingly, she took his sins upon herself and was punished for them. She should not have been. With her death, a step was taken into another place, where justice and vengeance were without distinction.

So you have to be stopped, and the story of what took place in the Congaree told at last, because otherwise the woman with the scaled skin will continue wandering through the cypress and holly, a figure glimpsed in the shadows but never truly seen, hoping to find at last her lost sister and hold her close, cleansing the blood and filth from her, the misery and humiliation, the shame and the pain and the hurt.)

The swamps: I was passing close by them now. I drifted for a moment and felt the car cleave to one side, crossing the hard shoulder, jolting against the uneven ground, until I found myself back on the road. The swamps are a safety valve: they soak up the floodwater, keep the rains and the sediment from affecting the coastal plains. But the rivers still flow through them and the traces of the blood still linger. They are with them when the waters reach the coastal plain, there when they enter the black water, there when the flow of the salt marshes begins to slow, and there at last when they disappear into the sea: a whole land, a whole ocean, tainted by blood. One single act, its ramifications felt throughout all of nature; and so a world can be changed, ineffably altered, by a single death.

Flames: the light of the fires set by the night riders; the burning houses, the smoldering crops. The sound of the horses as they begin to smell the smoke and panic, their riders wrenching at the reins to hold them, to keep their eyes from the flames. But when they turn there are pits set in the ground before them, dark holes with black water in their depths, and more flames emerge, pillars of fire shooting up from the interconnected caverns, and the screams of the woman are lost in their roar.

Richland County: the Congaree River flowed to the north, and I was floating above the road, carried ever onward, my momentum determined by my surroundings. I was moving toward Columbia, toward the northwest, toward a reckoning, but I could think of nothing but the girl on the ground, her jaw detached, her eyes already emptying of consciousness.

Finish her.

She blinks.

Finish her.

I am no longer of myself.

Finish her.

Her eyes roll. She sees the rock descend.

Finish her.

She is gone.

I had booked a room at Claussen's Inn on Greene Street, a converted bakery in the Five Points neighborhood close to the University of South Carolina. I showered and changed, then called Rachel again. I just needed to hear her voice. When she answered the phone she sounded a little drunk. She'd had a glass of Guinness – the pregnant woman's friend – with one of her Audubon colleagues in Portland and it had gone straight to her head.

'It's the iron,' she said. 'It's good for me.'

'They say that about a lot of things. It's usually not true.'

'What's happening down there?'

'Same old same old.'

'I'm worried about you,' she said, but her voice had changed. This time there was no slurring, no tipsiness, and I realized that the hint of drunkenness in her voice was a disguise, like a quickly executed artwork painted onto an old master to hide it and protect it from recognition. Rachel wanted to be drunk. She wanted to be happy and merry and unconcerned, drifting slightly on a glass of beer, but it was not to be. She was pregnant, the father of her child was far to the south, and people around him were dying. Meanwhile, a man who hated us both was trying to free himself from the state prison, and his promises of bargains and truces echoed dully in my head.

'I mean it,' I lied. 'I'm okay. It's coming to a close. I understand now. I think I know what happened.'

'Tell me,' she said. I closed my eyes, and it was as if we were lying side by side in the darkness. I caught the faint scent of her, and thought I felt the weight of her against me.

'I can't.'

'Please. Share it, whatever it is. I need you to share something important with me, to reach out to me in some way.'

And so I told her.

'They raped two young women, Rachel, two sisters. One of them was the mother of Atys Jones. They beat her to death with a rock, then burned the other one alive.'

She didn't respond, but I could hear her breathing deeply.

'Elliot was one of the men.'

'But he brought you down there. He asked you to help.'

'That's right, he did.'

'It was all lies.'

'No, not entirely.' For the truth was always close to the surface.

'You have to get away from there. You have to leave.'

'I can't.'

'Please.'

'I can't. Rachel, you know I can't.'

'Please!'

I ate a burger at Yesterday's on Devine. Emmylou Harris was playing over the sound system. She was singing 'Wrecking Ball,' Neil Young's cracked voice harmonizing with Emmylou's on his own song. In an age of Britneys and Christinas, there was something reassuring and strangely affecting about two older voices, both perhaps past their peak but weathered and mature, singing about love and desire and the possibility of one last dance. Rachel had hung up in tears. I could feel nothing but guilt for what I was putting her through but I couldn't walk away, not now.

I ate in the dining area then moved into the bar and sat in a booth. Beneath the plexiglass of the table lay photographs and old advertisements, all fading to yellow. A fat man in diapers mugged for the camera. A woman held a puppy. Couples hugged and kissed. I wondered if anyone remembered their names.

At the bar, a man in his late twenties, his head shaved, glanced at me in the mirror, then looked back down at his beer. Our eyes had barely met, but he couldn't hide the recognition. I kept my eyes on the back of his head, taking in the strong muscles at his neck and shoulders, the bulge of his lats, his narrow waist. To a casual observer, he might have looked small, almost feminine, but he was wiry and he would be hard to knock down, and when he was knocked down he would get right back up again. There were tattoos on his triceps – I could see the ends of them below the sleeves of his T-shirt – but his forearms were clear, the bundles of muscle and tendon bunching then relaxing again as he clenched and unclenched his fists. I watched him as he flicked his glance at the mirror for a second time, then a third. Finally, he reached into the pocket of his faded, too-tight jeans, and dumped some ones on the bar before springing from his stool. He advanced on me, his fists still pumping, even as the older man beside him at last understood what was happening and tried to reach out to stop him.

'You got a problem with me?' he asked. In the booths at either side of mine the conversation faded, then died. His left ear was pierced, the hole contained within an Indian ink clenched fist. His brow was high, and his blue eyes shone in his pale face.

'I thought you might have been coming on to me, way you were looking at me in the mirror,' I said. To my right, I heard a male voice snicker. The skinhead heard it too because his head jerked in that direction. The snickering ceased. He turned his attention back to me. By now, he was bouncing on the balls of his feet with suppressed aggression.

'Are you fucking with me?' he said.

'No,' I replied innocently. 'Would you like me to?'

I gave him my most endearing smile. His face grew redder and he seemed about to make a move toward me when there came a low whistle from behind him. The older man materialized, his long dark hair slicked back against his head, and grasped the younger man firmly by the upper arm.

'Let it go,' he advised.

'He called me a fag,' protested the skinhead.

'He's just trying to rile you. Walk away.'

For a moment, the skinhead tugged ineffectually at the older man's grip, then spit noisily on the floor and stormed toward the door.

'I got to apologize for my young friend. He's sensitive about these things.'

I nodded but gave no hint that I recalled the man before me. It was Earl Jr.'s messenger from Charleston Place, the man I had seen eating a hot dog at Roger Bowen's rally. This man knew who I was, had followed me here. That meant that he knew where I was staying, maybe even suspected why I was here.

'We'll be on our way,' he said.

He dipped his chin once in farewell, then turned to go.

'Be seeing you,' I said.

His back stiffened.

'Now why would you think that?' he asked, his head inclined slightly so that I could see his profile: the flattened nose, the elongated chin.

'I'm sensitive about these things,' I told him.

He scratched at his temple with the forefinger of his right hand. 'You're a funny man,' he said, giving up the pretence. 'I'll be sorry when you're gone.'

Then he followed the skinhead from the bar.

I left twenty minutes later with a crowd of students, and stayed with them until I reached the corner of Greene and Devine. I could see no trace of the two men, but I had no doubt that they were close by. In the lobby of Claussen's, jazz was playing over the speakers at low volume. I nodded a good night to the young guy behind the desk. He returned the gesture from over the top of a psychology textbook.

I called Louis from the room. He answered cautiously, not recognizing the number displayed.

'It's me,' I said.

'How you doin'?'

'Not so good. I think I picked up a tail.'

'How many?'

'Two.' I told him about the scene in the bar.

'They out there now?'

'I'd guess they are.'

'You want me to come up there?'

'No, stay with Kittim and Larousse. Anything I should know?'

'Our friend Bowen came through this evening, spent some time with Earl Jr. and then a whole lot longer with Kittim. They must figure they got you where they want you. It was a trap, man, right from the start.'

No, not just a trap. There was more to it than that. Marianne Larousse, Atys, his mother and her sister: what happened to them was real and terrible and unconnected to anything that had to do with Faulkner or Bowen. It was the real reason that I was down here, the reason that I had stayed. The rest was unimportant.

'I'll be in touch,' I said, then hung up.

My room was at the front of the inn, facing out onto Greene Street. I took the mattress from the bed and laid it on the floor, arranging the sheets loosely on top of it. I undressed, then lay close to the wall beneath the window. The chain was on the door, there was a chair in front of it, and my gun lay on the floor beyond my pillow.

She was moving out there, somewhere, a white blur among the trees, illuminated by bleak moonlight. Behind her, it bedecked the river with glittering stars as it flowed beneath the overhanging trees.

The White Road is everywhere. It is everything. We are on it, and we are of it.

Go to sleep. Go to sleep dreaming of shadows moving along the White Road. Go to sleep watching falling girls crush lilies beneath them as they die. Go to sleep with Cassie Blythe's torn hand emerging from the darkness.

Go to sleep without knowing if you are among the lost or the found, the living or the dead.

24

I had set my alarm for 4 A.M. and was still bleary-eyed as I made my way across the lobby to the back door of the inn. The night clerk looked at me curiously, saw that I wasn't carrying my bags, then went back to his books.

If I was being watched, then the two men were divided between the front and back doors. The back door led to the parking areas, with exits onto both Greene and Devine, but I doubted if I could drive away without being picked up. I took a handkerchief from my pocket and unscrewed the light inside the door. I'd already taken the precaution of busting the outside light with the sole of my shoe when I had come in the night before. I opened the door a fraction, waited, then slipped out into the darkness. I used the ranks of parked cars to hide my progress until I reached Devine, then called a cab from a pay phone outside a gas station. Five minutes later, I was on my way to the Hertz desk at Columbia International Airport; from there, I drove back in a loop toward Congaree.

The Congaree Swamp is still comparatively inaccessible by road. The main route, along Old Bluff and Caroline Sims, takes visitors to the ranger station, and from there sections of the swamp can be explored on foot using a system of boardwalks. But to venture deeper into the Congaree requires a boat, so I'd arranged to hire a ten footer with a small outboard. The old guy who hired them out was waiting for me at the Highway 601 landing when I arrived, traffic rumbling across the Bates Bridge overhead. We exchanged cash and he took my car keys as security, and then I was on the river, the early morning sun already shining on the brown waters and on the huge cypress and water oak that overshadowed the banks.

In wet weather, the Congaree swells and floods the swamp, dumping nutrients on the plain. The result was the enormous trees that lined the river, their boles monstrous and swollen, their foliage so wide that at times it created a canopy over the flow, darkening and shading the waters beneath. Hurricane Hugo might have claimed some of the largest trees as casualties when it tore through the swamp, but this was still a place to make a man catch his breath at the size and scale of the great forest through which he was passing.

The Congaree marks the borders of Richland and Calhoun Counties, its meanderings determining the limits of local political power, police jurisdictions, ordinances, and a hundred other tiny factors that influence the day-to-day lives of those who live within its reach. I had traveled some twelve miles along it when I came to a huge fallen cypress that jutted about halfway into the river. This, the old boatman had told me, marked the end of the state land and the beginning of the private tract, a section of swamp just under two miles long. Somewhere in there, probably close to the river, was Tereus's home. I only hoped that it wouldn't be too hard to find.

I tied up the boat at the cypress, then jumped for the bank. The chorus of crickets nearby grew suddenly silent, then picked up again as I began to move away. I stayed with the bank, looking for signs of a trail, but could find nothing. Tereus had kept his presence here as low-key as possible. Even if trails had once existed before he was jailed, they were long overgrown by now and he had made no effort to clear them again. I stood at the bank and tried to find landmarks that would allow me to get my bearings when I made my way back to the river, then headed into the swamp.

I sniffed the air, hoping to detect wood smoke or cooking, but I could smell only damp and vegetation. I passed through a forest of sweet gums and water oaks, and water tupelos thick with dark purple fruit. Lower on the ground there was pawpaw and alder and great American holly bushes, the earth so thick with shrubs that all I could see was green and brown, the ground wet and slippery with decaying leaves and vegetation. At one point I almost walked into the web of a spiny orb weaver, the spider hanging like a small dark star in the center of its own galaxy of influence. It wasn't dangerous, but there were other spiders here that were and I had endured enough of spiders in recent months to last me a lifetime. I picked up a branch about eighteen inches long and used it to strike out in front of me when I passed through stands of higher shrubs and trees.

I had been walking for about twenty minutes when I saw the house. It was an old cottage, based around a simple hall-and-parlor plan, two rooms wide and one room deep, but it had been expanded by the addition of an enclosed front porch and a long, narrow extension at the rear. There were signs of recent repairs to its heavy timber framing, and the central chimney had recently been repointed, but from the front the house still looked virtually the same as it had when it was first constructed, probably during the last century when the slaves who built the levees chose to stay on in the Congaree. There were no signs of life: the washing line that hung between two trees was bare and no sounds came from within. At the back of the house was a small shed, which probably housed the generator.

I climbed the rough-hewn stairs to the porch and knocked on the door. There was no reply. I walked to the window and put my face close to the glass. Inside, I could see a table and four chairs, an old couch and easy chair, and a small kitchen area. An open doorway led into the main bedroom, and a second doorway had been created at the back of the house leading into the rear extension. That door was closed. I knocked one last time, then walked around to the back of the house. From somewhere in the swamp, I heard the sound of gunshots, their noise muffled by the damp air. Hunters, I guessed.

The windows to the extension had been blacked out. I thought for a moment that there were dark drapes obscuring them, but when I drew closer I saw the lines that the brush had drawn through the paint. There was a door at the end. For the final time, I knocked and called before trying the knob. The door opened and I stepped into the room.

The first thing that I noticed was the smell. It was strong and faintly medicinal, although I detected something herbal and grassy to it rather than the sterile scent of pharmaceutical products. It seemed to fill the long room, which was furnished with a cot, a TV, and a set of cheap bookshelves uncluttered by any books. Instead, there were piles of out-of-date soap opera magazines and wrinkled, much-read copies of *People* and *Celebrity*.

Every bare space on the walls had been covered by photographs culled from the magazines. There were models and actresses and, in one corner, what looked like a shrine to Oprah. Most of the women in the photos were black: I recognized Halle Berry, Angela Bassett, the R&B group TLC, Jada Pinkett Smith, even Tina Turner. Over by the TV were three or four photographs from the society pages of local newspapers. Each showed the same person: Marianne Larousse. There was a thin coating of wood dust on the photos, but the blacking on the windows had prevented any fading. In one, Marianne was smiling in the middle of a group of pretty young women at her graduation. Another had been taken at a charity auction, a third at a party held by the Larousses to raise funds for the Republican Party. In every photo, Marianne Larousse's beauty made her stand out like a beacon.

I stepped closer to the cot. The medicinal smell was stronger here and the sheets were stained with brown patches like spilt coffee. There were also lighter blotches, some of them veined with blood. I gently touched the bedsheet. The stains felt moist beneath my fingers. I moved away and found the small bathroom, and the source of the smell. A basin was filled with a thick brown substance that had the consistency of wallpaper paste and dripped viscously from my fingers as I held them up before me. The bathroom itself had a free-standing bath, with a handrail attached to the wall and a second support rail screwed into the floor beside it. There was a clean toilet and the floor had been expertly, if cheaply, tiled.

There was no mirror.

I stepped back into the bedroom and checked the single closet. What looked like white and brown sheets lay piled on the floor and shelves, but once again I could find no mirror.

From outside, I heard the shots come again, closer now. I made a cursory search of the rest of the house, registering the man's clothing in the closet in the main bedroom and the woman's clothing, cheap and dated, that had been packed into an old sea chest; the tinned foods in the kitchen area; the scrubbed pots and pans. In a corner behind the couch I found a camp bed, but it was covered in dust and had clearly not been used in many years. Everything else was clean, spotlessly so. There was no telephone, and when I tried the light switch the lights came on low, bathing the room in a faint orange glow. I switched them off again, opened the front door, and stepped out onto the porch.

There were three men moving through the trees. Two of them I recognized as the men from the bar the night before, both the skinhead and the older man still wearing the same clothes. They had probably slept in them. The third was the overweight man who had been at the airport with his hunting partner on the day that I had first arrived in Charleston. He wore a brown shirt with his rifle slung over his right shoulder. He spotted me first, raised his right hand, and then all three paused at the tree line. None of us spoke for a moment. It seemed it was up to me to break the silence.

'I think you boys may be hunting out of season,' I said.

The oldest of the three, the man who had restrained the skinhead in the bar, smiled almost sadly.

'What we're hunting is always in season,' he replied. 'Anybody in there?'

I shook my head.

'Figured you'd say that, even if there was,' he said. 'You ought to be more careful who you hire your boats from, Mr. Parker. That, or you ought to pay them a little extra to keep their mouths shut.'

He held his rifle at port arms, but I saw his finger move from outside to inside the trigger guard.

'Come on down here,' he said. 'We got some business with you.'

I was already moving into the cottage when the first shot hit the door frame. I raced straight through, pulling my gun from its holster, and cleared the side of the generator hut as the second shot blew a chunk of bark from an oak tree to my right.

And then I was in the forest, the canopy rising above me until it was about a hundred feet above my head. I brushed through alders and holly, my head down. I slipped once on the slick leaves and landed hard on my side. I paused for a moment, but could hear no sounds of pursuit from behind me. I saw something brown about one hundred yards behind me, moving slowly through the trees: the fat man. He stood out only because he was stealing across the green of a holly bush. The others would be close by, listening for me. They would try to encircle me, then close in. I took a deep breath, drew a bead on the brown shirt, then squeezed the trigger slowly.

A red jet erupted from the fat man's chest. His body twisted and he slumped back heavily into the bushes behind him, the branches bending and cracking beneath his weight. Twin booms came from my left and right, followed by more shots, and suddenly the air was filled with splinters and falling leaves.

I ran.

I ran to the high ground, where the red maples and ironwoods grew, trying to avoid the open areas of the understory and sticking instead to places thick with bush and vines. I closed my jacket despite the warmth in order to hide my white T-shirt and stopped from time to time, trying to detect signs of my pursuers, but wherever they were, they were staying quiet and low. I smelled urine – a deer maybe, or even a bobcat – and found traces of an animal trail. I didn't know where I was going: if I could find one of the boardwalk trails it would lead me back to the ranger station, but it would also leave me dangerously exposed to the men behind me. That was assuming that I could even find the boardwalk this far in. The wind had been blowing northeast across the Congaree when I was making my way to the cottage, and now blew lightly at my back. I stayed with the animal trail, hoping to trace my way back to the river. If I got lost in the Congaree, I would become easy prey for these men.

I tried to disguise the signs of my passage, but the ground was soft and I seemed to leave sunken footprints and flattened shrubbery as I went. After about fifteen minutes, I came to an old fallen cypress, its trunk blasted in two by lightning and a huge crater beneath its overhanging roots. Shrubs had already begun to grow around it and in the depths of the crater, rising to meet the roots and creating a kind of barred hollow. I leaned against it to catch my breath, then unzipped my jacket, tossed it on the trunk, then stripped off my T-shirt. I leaned into the hollow, scaring the beetles, and draped my T-shirt midway down, snagging it among the twisted roots. Then I put my jacket back on and retreated into the undergrowth. I lay flat on the ground, and waited.

It was the skinhead who appeared first. I caught a glimpse of the egglike pallor of his skull behind a loblolly pine as he peered out, then ducked back in again. He had spotted the shirt. I wondered how dumb he was.

Dumb, but not dumb enough. He let out a low whistle and I saw a stand of alder twitch slightly, although I could see no sign of the man who had caused the movement. I wiped the sweat from my brow against the sleeve of my jacket to stop the worst of it from dropping into my eyes. Again, the movement came from behind the pine. I aimed and blinked the last of my sweat as the skinhead burst from cover, then stopped dead, seemingly distracted by something nearby.

Instantly, he was pulled off his feet and yanked backward into the undergrowth. It happened so quickly that I was unsure of what I had seen. I thought for a moment that he might have slipped, and was half expecting to see him rise again, but he didn't reappear. From near the alders came a whistle, but there was no response. The skinhead's companion whistled again. All was quiet. By then I was already retreating, crawling backward on my belly, desperate to get away from here, from the last of the hunters and from whatever was now pursuing us both through the sun-dappled green of the Congaree.

I had belly-crawled about fifty feet before I felt confident enough to rise. From somewhere ahead of me came the sound of water. From behind me I heard gunshots, but they were not aimed in my direction. I didn't stop, even when the stump of a broken branch ripped through my sleeve and drew a ragged line of blood across my upper arm. My head was up and I was breathing hard, a stitch building in my side, when I saw the flash of white to my right. Part of me tried to reassure myself that it was a bird of some kind: an egret, perhaps, or an immature heron. But there had been something about the way that it moved, a halting, loping progress, that was partly an attempt at concealment and partly a physical disability. When I tried to find it again among the undergrowth I could not, but I knew it was there. I could feel it watching me.

I moved on.

I could see the water gleaming through the trees, could hear it flowing. Lying about thirty feet to my left was a boat: it wasn't my boat, but at least two of the men who had brought it here were already dead and the third was somewhere behind me, running for his life. I stepped into a clearing dominated by cypress knees, the strange, vaguely conical shapes bursting from the soil like some miniature landscape from another world. I threaded my way through them and was almost at the boat when the dark-haired man emerged from the trees to my left. He no longer had his rifle, but he did have a knife, and he was already springing for me when I raised my gun and fired. I was off balance and the shot struck him in the side, breaking his stride but not stopping him. Before I could get off a second shot he was on top of me, his left arm forcing my gun hand away from him while I tried to arrest the progress of the knife. I aimed my knee at his injured side, but he anticipated the movement and used it against me, spinning me around and striking out at my left foot. I toppled and fell down as his boot connected with my hand, knocking the gun painfully from my fingers. I kicked out at him again as he descended on me, this time connecting with his wounded side. Spittle shot from his mouth and his eyes opened wide in surprise and pain, but by then his knee was on my chest and I was once again trying to keep that knife away from me. Still, I could see that he was dazed, and the wound in his side was bleeding freely. I suddenly eased some of the pressure on his arms and, as he fell forward, my head came up hard and connected with his nose. He cried out and I forced him off me, then rose up, knocked his feet out from under him, and slammed him back to the ground with all of the force that I could muster.

There was a wet crunching sound when he hit the earth and something exploded from his chest, as if one of his ribs had broken free and blasted through the skin. I stepped back and watched the blood running off the cypress knee as the man pinned upon it struggled to rise. He reached out and touched the wood, his fingers coming back red. He held them up to me, as if to show me what I had done, and then his head fell back and he died.

I wiped my sleeve against my face. It came back damp with sweat and filth. I turned to get my gun and saw the shrouded figure watching me from the trees.

It was a woman. I could see the shape of her breasts beneath the material, although her face remained covered. I called her name.

'Melia,' I said. 'Don't be afraid.'

I advanced toward her just as the shadow fell over me. I looked behind me. Tereus had a hook in his left hand. I just had time to register the crude sap in his right as it flew at me through the air, and then all was dark.

25

It was the smell that brought me back, the smell of the medicinal herbs that had been used to make the unguent for the woman's skin. I was lying in the kitchen area of the cottage, my hands and legs bound tightly with rope. I raised my head and the back of my skull nudged the wall. The pain was bad. My shoulders and back ached, and my jacket was gone. I guessed that I had lost it as Tereus dragged me back to the cabin. I had vague memories of passing beneath tall trees, the sunlight spearing me through the canopy. My cell phone and gun were both missing. I lay on the floor for what seemed like hours.

In time, there was movement from the doorway and Tereus appeared, surrounded by fading sunlight. He had a spade in his hands, which he rested against the doorjamb before entering the cabin and squatting down before me. I could see no trace of the woman, but I sensed her nearby and guessed that she was back in her own darkened room, surrounded by images of a physical beauty she would never again be able to claim as her own.

'Welcome back, brother,' said Tereus. He removed his dark glasses. Up close, the membrane that coated his eyes was clearer. It reminded me of tapetum, the reflective surface that some nocturnal animals develop to magnify low light and improve their night vision. He filled a water bottle from the faucet, then brought it to me and tilted it to my mouth. I drank until the water ran down my chin. I coughed, and winced at the pain it caused in my head.

'I'm not your brother.'

'You weren't my brother, you'd be dead by now.'

'You killed them all, didn't you?'

He leaned in close to me. 'These people got to learn. This is a world of balances. They took a life, destroyed another. They got to learn about the White Road, got to see what's waiting for them there, got to pass over and become part of it.'

I looked away from him toward the window, and saw that the light was failing. Soon, it would be dark.

'You rescued her,' I said.

He nodded. 'I couldn't save her sister, but I could save her.'

I saw regret, and more: I saw love.

'She was burned bad, but stayed under the surface, and the underground streams carried her out. I found her stretched over a rock, then I took her home and me and my momma, we took care of her. And when my momma died, she took care of herself for a year until I got released from jail. Now I'm back.'

'Why didn't you just go to the police, tell them what happened?'

'That ain't the way these things is done. Anyhow, her sister's body was gone. It was a dark night, and she was suffering. She can't even talk – she had to write their names for me – and even if she could tell who they was, who would believe it of young, rich white men like that? I ain't even sure what she thinks no more. The pain drove her crazy.'

But that didn't answer it. That wasn't enough to explain what had happened, what he had endured and what he had forced others to endure.

'It was Addy, wasn't it?'

He didn't reply.

'You loved her, maybe before Davis Smoot ever appeared. Was he your child, Tereus? Was Atys Jones your child? Was she afraid to tell others because of what you were, because even the blacks looked down on you, because you were an outcast from the swamps? That's why you went looking for Smoot, why you didn't tell Atys what landed you in jail: you didn't tell him you'd killed Smoot because it wasn't important. You didn't believe Smoot was his father, and you were right. The dates didn't match. You killed Smoot for what he did to Addy, then fled back here in time to discover another violation being visited on the woman you loved. But before you could avenge yourself on Larousse and his friends, the cops came for you and sent you back to Alabama for trial, and you were lucky just to get twenty years because there were enough witnesses to back up your claim of self-defense. I reckon that once old Davis caught sight of you he went straight for the nearest weapon, and you had an excuse to kill him. Now you're back, making up for lost time.'

Tereus did not respond. There would be no confirmation from him, and no denial. One of his big hands gripped my shoulder and dragged me to my feet. 'That time is now, brother. Rise up, rise up.'

A blade cut the ropes at my feet. I felt the pain begin as the blood began to circulate properly at last.

'Where are we going?'

He looked surprised, and I knew then just how crazy he was, crazy even before they chained him to a post in the blazing sun, crazy enough to keep an injured woman out here for years, protected by an old woman, in order to serve some strange messianic purpose of his own.

'Back to the pit,' he said. 'We going back to the pit. It's time.'

'Time for what?'

He drew me gently toward him.

'Time to show them the White Road.'

Although his small boat had an engine, he untied my hands and made me row. He was afraid: afraid that the noise might draw the men to him before he was ready, afraid that I might turn on him if he did not find some way to occupy me. Once or twice I considered striking out at him, but the revolver he now carried was unwavering in his grip. He would nod and smile at me in warning if I even paused in my strokes, as if we were two old friends on a boating trip together as the day descended softly into night and the dark gathered around us.

I didn't know where the woman was. I knew only that she had left the house before us.

'You didn't kill Marianne Larousse,' I said as we came in sight of a house set back from the bank and a dog barked at our passing, his chain jangling softly in the evening air. A light went on in the porch of the house, and I saw the form of a man emerge and heard him hush the dog. His voice was not angry, and I felt a rush of affection for him. I saw him tousle the dog's fur, and the silhouette of its dark tail flicked back and forth in response. I was tired. I felt as if I were approaching the very end of things, as if this river was a kind of Styx across which I was being forced to row myself in the absence of the boatman, and as soon as the boat struck the bank I would descend into the underworld and become lost in the honeycomb.

I repeated the comment.

'What does it matter?' he replied.

'It matters to me. It probably mattered to Marianne while she was dying. But you didn't kill her. You were still in jail.'

'They say the boy killed her, and he ain't about to contradict them now.'

I stopped rowing, and heard the click of the hammer cocking a moment later.

'Don't make me shoot you, Mr. Parker.'

I rested the oars and raised my hands.

'She did it, didn't she? Melia killed Marianne Larousse, and her own nephew, your son, died as a result.'

He regarded me silently for a time before he spoke.

'She knows this river,' he said. 'Knows the swamps. She wanders in them. Sometimes, she likes to watch the folks drinkin' and whorin'. I guess it reminds her of what she lost, of what they took away from her. It was just pure dumb luck that she saw Marianne Larousse running among the trees that night, nothing more. She recognized her face from the society pages of the newspapers – she likes to look at the pictures of the beautiful ladies – and she took her chance.

'Dumb luck,' he intoned again. 'That's all it was.'

But it wasn't, of course. The history of these two families, the Larousses and the Joneses, the blood spilled and lives destroyed, meant that it could never be anything as pure as luck or coincidence that drew them together. Over more than two centuries they had bound themselves, each to the other, in a pact of mutual destructiveness only partly acknowledged on either side, fueled by a past that allowed one man to own and abuse another and fanned into continuous flame by remembered injuries and violent responses. Their paths through this world were interweaved, crisscrossing at crucial moments in the history of this state and in the lives of their families.

'Did she know that the boy with Marianne was her own nephew?'

'She didn't see him until the girl was dead. I—'

He stopped.

'Like I said, I don't know what she thinks, but she can read some. She saw the newspapers, and I think she used to watch the jailhouse some, late at night.'

'You could have saved him,' I said. 'By coming forward with her, you could have saved Atys. No court would convict her of murder. She's insane.'

'No, I couldn't do that.'

He couldn't do it because then he would not have been able to continue punishing the rapists and killers of the woman he had loved. Ultimately, he was prepared to sacrifice his own son for revenge.

'You killed the others?'

'We did, the two of us together.'

He had rescued her and kept her safe, then killed for her and the memory of her sister. In a way, he had given up his life for them.

'It was how it had to be,' he said, as if guessing the direction of my thoughts. 'And that's all I got to say.'

I started to row again, drawing deep arcs through the water, the droplets falling back to the river in what seemed like impossibly languid descents, as if somehow I were slowing down the passage of time, drawing each moment out, longer and longer again, until at last the world would stop, the oars frozen at the moment they broke the water, the birds trapped in midflight, the insects caught like motes of dust in a picture frame, and we would never have to go forward again. We would never have to find ourselves by the lip of that dark pit, with its smells of engine oil and effluent, and the memory of the burning marked with black tongues along the grooves of its stone.

'There's just two left,' said Tereus at one point. 'Just two more, and it will all be over.'

And I could not tell if he was talking to himself, or to me, or to some unseen other. I looked to the bank and expected to see her shadowing our progress, a figure consumed by pain. Or to see her sister, her jaw hanging loose, her head ruined but her eyes wild and bright, burning with a rage fierce as the flames that had engulfed her sister.

But there was only tree shade and the darkening sky, and waters glittering with the fragmented ghosts of early moonlight.

'This is where we get off,' he whispered.

I steered the boat toward the left bank. When it struck land I heard a soft splash behind me and saw that Tereus was already out of the boat. He gestured for me to move toward the trees, and I began to walk. My trousers were wet and swamp water squelched in my shoes. I was covered in bites; my face felt swollen from them, and the exposed skin of my back and chest itched furiously.

'How do you know that they'll be here?' I asked.

'Oh, they'll be here,' he said. 'I promised them the two things they wanted the most: the answer to who killed Marianne Larousse.'

'And?'

'And you, Mr. Parker. They've decided that you've outlived your usefulness. That Mr. Kittim, I reckon he's gonna bury you.'

I knew that it was true, that the part Kittim was to play represented the last act in the drama they had planned. Elliot had brought me down here, ostensibly to find out about the circumstances of Marianne Larousse's murder in an effort to clear Atys Jones, but in reality, and in collusion with Larousse, to find out if her murder was linked to what was happening to the six men who had raped the Jones sisters, then killed one of them and left the other to burn. Mobley had worked for Bowen and I guessed that at some point Bowen had learned through him of what he and the others had done, which gave him the leverage he required to use Elliot and probably Earl Jr. too. Elliot would draw me down, and Kittim would destroy me. If I discovered the truth about who was behind the killings before I died, then so much the better. If I didn't, then I still wasn't going to live long enough to collect my fee.

'But you're not going to hand Melia over to them,' I said.

'No, I'm going to kill them.'

'Alone.'

His white teeth gleamed.

'No,' he said. 'I told you. Not alone. Never alone.'

It was still as Poveda had described it after all these years. There was the broken fence that I had skirted days earlier and the pockmarked 'No Trespassing' sign. I could see the sinkholes, some of them small and masked by vegetation, others so large that whole trees had fallen into them. We had walked for just five minutes when I smelled an acrid chemical stink in the air that at first was merely unpleasant but, as we drew closer to the hole, began to scorch the nostrils and cause the eyes to water. Discarded trash lay unmoving upon the ground without a breeze to stir it, and the skeletons of decayed trees, their trunks gray and lifeless, stretched thin shadows across the limestone. The hole itself was about twenty feet in circumference, and so deep that its base was lost in darkness. Roots and grasses overhung the verge, trailing down into the shadows.

Two men stood at the far side of the hole, looking down into its depths. One was Earl Jr. The second man was Kittim. He was without his trademark shades now that it was growing dark and he was the first to sense our approach. His face remained blank even as we stood and faced them across the expanse of the pit, Kittim's eyes briefly resting on me before he gave his full attention to Tereus.

'Do you recognize him?' he asked Earl Jr.

Earl Jr. shook his head. Kittim seemed dissatisfied with the answer, with the fact that he did not have the information he required to make an accurate assessment of the situation.

'Who are you?' he asked.

'My name is Tereus.'

'Did you kill Marianne Larousse?'

'No, I did not. I killed the others, and I watched Foster attach a hose to the exhaust pipe of his car and feed it in through his window. But I didn't kill the Larousse girl.'

'Then who did?'

She was nearby. I knew she was. I could feel her. It seemed to me that Larousse did too, because I watched his head flick back suddenly like a startled deer, his eyes roving across the trees, looking for the source of his unease.

'I asked you a question,' Kittim persisted. 'Who killed her?'

Three armed men emerged from the trees at either side of us. Instantly, Tereus dropped his gun to the ground and I knew that he had never planned to walk away from this.

Two of the men beside us I did not recognize.

The third was Elliot Norton.

'You don't seem surprised to see me, Charlie,' he said.

'It takes a lot to surprise me, Elliot.'

'Even the return of an old friend from the dead?'

'I have a feeling you'll be making a more permanent return in the near future.' I was too tired even to show my anger. 'The blood in the car was a nice touch. How were you going to explain your resurrection? A miracle?'

'We were under threat from some crazy Negro, so I did what I had to do to hide myself. What are they going to charge me with? Wasting police time? False suicide?'

'You killed, Elliot. You led people to their deaths. You bailed Atys just so your friends could torture him and find out what he knew.'

He shrugged. 'Your fault, Charlie. If you'd been better at your job and got him to tell all, he might still be alive.'

I winced. He'd struck close to the bone, but I wasn't going to bear the responsibility for Atys Jones's death alone.

'And the Singletons. What did you do, Elliot? Sit with them in the kitchen drinking their lemonade, waiting for your friends to come and kill them while the only person who could have protected them was in the shower. The old man said it was a changeling that attacked them, and the police thought that he was talking about Atys until he turned up tortured to death, but it was you. You were the changeling. Look at what they've reduced you to, Elliot, what you've reduced yourself to. Look at what you've become.'

Elliot shrugged. 'I had no choice. Mobley told Bowen everything, once when he was drunk. Landron never admitted it, but it was him. So Bowen had something on all of us and he used it to make me bring you down here. But by then all of this' – he made an all-encompassing gesture with his free hand, taking in the hole, the swamp, dead men, and the memory of raped girls – 'had started happening, so we used you. You're good, Charlie, I'll give you that. In a way, you've brought us all to this point. You should go to your grave a satisfied man.'

'Enough.' It was Kittim. 'Make the Negro tell us what he knows and we can finish this for good.'

Elliot raised his gun, pointing it first at Tereus, then at me.

'You shouldn't have come to the swamp alone, Charlie.'

I smiled at him.

'I didn't.'

The bullet hit him on the bridge of the nose and knocked his head back so hard I could hear the vertebrae in his neck crack. The men at either side of him barely had a chance to react before they too fell. Larousse stood confused and then Kittim was raising his weapon and I felt Tereus push me to the ground. There were shots, and warm blood splashed my eyes. I looked up to catch the look of surprise in Tereus's face before he tumbled into the pit and landed with a splash in the water far below.

I picked up his fallen revolver and ran for the woods, expecting to feel one of Kittim's shots tear into me at any moment, but he was already fleeing. I caught a glimpse of Larousse disappearing into the trees, and then he also disappeared from sight.

But only for a moment.

He reemerged seconds later, backing slowly away from something in the trees. I saw her moving toward him, draped in the light material, the only cloth that she could wear without paining her ruined body. Her head was uncovered. The skull was hairless, the features beneath it melting into one another, a blur of disfigurement and remembered beauty. Only her eyes appeared intact, glittering beneath her swollen eyelids. She extended a hand to Larousse and there was almost a tenderness to the gesture, like a rejected lover reaching out one last time to the man who had turned his back upon her. Larousse released a small cry, then struck out at her arm, breaking the skin. Instinctively, he rubbed his hand with disgust against his jacket, then moved quickly to his right in an effort to get by her and make for the safety of the forest.

Louis stepped from the shadows and pointed his gun at Larousse's face.

'Now where you goin?' he asked.

He stopped, caught between the woman and the gun.

Then she sprang at him, the force of her propelling them both backward, and she wrapped herself around him as they fell, he screaming, she silent, into the black water below. For a moment, I thought I saw a whiteness spread upon the surface, and then they were gone.

26

We walked back to Louis's car, but could find no trace of Kittim along the way.

'You understand now?' asked Louis. 'You understand why we can't let them go, can't let none of them go?'

I nodded.

'The bail hearing is in three days' time,' he said. 'The preacher's gonna walk, and then none of us will be safe again.'

'I'm in,' I said.

'You sure?'

I barely paused.

'I'm sure. What about Kittim?'

'What about him?'

'He got away.'

Louis almost smiled.

'Did he?'

Kittim drove at speed into the Blue Ridge, arriving at his destination in the early hours. There would be other chances for him, other opportunities. For the present, it was time to rest up and wait for the preacher to be brought to safety. After that, there would be a new momentum achieved.

He pulled into the clearing before the cabin, then walked to the door and unlocked it. The moonlight streamed through the windows, illuminating the cheap furniture, the unadorned walls. It shone too on the man who sat facing the door, and on the silenced pistol in his hand. He wore sneakers and faded jeans, and a loud silk shirt that he'd bought at final markdown in Filene's Basement. His face was unshaven and very pale. He didn't even blink as the shot hit Kittim in the belly. Kittim fell and tried to wrench his gun from his belt, but the man was already upon him. His gun dug into Kittim's right temple as Kittim eased his hand away from his belt and his weapon was taken from him.

'Who are you?' he shouted. 'The fuck are you?'

'I'm an angel,' said the man. 'What the fuck are you?'

Now there were other figures around him. Kittim's hands were pulled behind his back and cuffed before he was turned onto his back to face his captors: the small man in the mismatched shirt, two younger men armed with pistols who came in from the yard, and an older man who emerged from the shadows at the back of Kittim's cabin.

'Kittim,' said Epstein, as he examined the man on the ground. 'An unusual name, a scholarly name.'

Kittim did not move. There was a watchfulness about him now, despite the agony of his wound. He kept his eyes fixed on the older man.

'I recall that the Kittim were the tribe destined to lead the final assault against the sons of light, the earthly agents of the powers of darkness,' continued Epstein. He leaned forward, so close that he could smell the breath of the injured man. 'You should have read your scrolls more closely, my friend: they tell us that the dominion of the Kittim is short-lived, and for the sons of darkness there shall be no escape.'

Epstein's hands had been clasped behind his back. Now they emerged, and the light caught the metal case in their grasp.

'We have questions for you,' said Epstein, removing the syringe and sending a jet of clear liquid into the air. The needle descended toward Kittim, as the thing that lived inside him began the fruitless struggle to escape its host.

I left Charleston late the following evening. I told the SLED agents in Columbia, Adams and Addams beside them in the interview room, almost everything that I knew, lying only to leave out the involvement of Louis and the part I had played in the deaths of the two men in Congaree. Tereus had disposed of their bodies while I was tied up in his shack, and the swamp had a long history of swallowing up the remains of the dead. They would not be found.

As for those who had been killed by the old sinkhole, I said that they had died at the hands of Tereus and the woman, taken by surprise before they even had a chance to react. Tereus's body had floated to the surface, but there was no sign as yet of the woman or Earl Jr. As I sat in the interrogation room, I saw them falling once again, disappearing into the dark pool, sinking, the woman dragging the man down with her into the streams that lay beneath the stone, holding him until he drowned, the two united unto death and beyond.

At the Charleston airport terminal, a limousine waited, the tinted windows up so that no one could see the occupants. As I walked to the doorway, my baggage in my hand, one window rolled slowly down and Earl Larousse looked at me, waiting for me to approach.

'My son,' he said.

'Dead, like I told the police.'

His lips trembled, and he blinked away tears. I felt nothing for him.

'You knew,' I said. 'You must have known all along what your son did. When he came home that night, covered in her blood, didn't he tell you everything that he had done? Didn't he beg for your help? And you gave it to him, to save him and to save your family name, and you held on to that piece of worthless land in the hope that what had happened there would remain hidden. But then Bowen came along and got his hooks into you, and suddenly you weren't in control anymore. His people were in your house, and my guess is he was bleeding you for money. How much did you give him, Mr. Larousse? Enough to bail Faulkner, and then some?'

He didn't look at me. Instead, he retreated into the past, descending into the grief and madness that would finally consume him.

'We were like royalty in this city,' he whispered. 'We've been here since its birth. We are part of its history, and our name has lived for centuries.'

'Your name is going to die with you now, and they can bury your history with you.'

I walked away. When I reached the doors the car was no longer reflected in the glass.

And in a shack on the outskirts of Caina, Georgia, Virgil Gossard awoke to a feeling of pressure on his lips. He opened his eyes as the gun forced itself into his mouth.

The figure before him was dressed entirely in black, its face concealed beneath a ski mask.

'Up,' it said, and Virgil recognized the voice from the night at Little Tom's. His hair was gripped and he was dragged from his bed, the gun trailing spittle and blood as it was pulled from his mouth. Virgil, wearing only his tattered briefs, was pushed toward the kitchen of his pitiful home, and the back door leading to the fields beyond.

'Open it.'

Virgil began to cry.

'Open it!'

He opened the door and a hand at his back forced him out into the night. Barefoot, he walked through the yard, feeling the coldness of the ground beneath his feet, the long blades of overgrown grass slicing at his skin. He could hear the man breathing behind him as he walked toward the woods at the verge of his land. A low wall, barely three bricks high, came into view. A sheet of corrugated iron had been laid across it. It was the old well.

'Take the cover off.'

Virgil shook his head. 'No, don't,' he said. 'Please.'

'Do it!'

Virgil squatted down and dragged the sheet away, exposing the hole beneath.

'Kneel down on the wall.'

Virgil's face was contorted with fear and the force of his tears. He could taste snot and salt in his mouth as he eased himself down and stared into the darkness of the well.

'I'm sorry,' he said. 'Whatever I've done, I'm sorry.'

He felt the pressure of the gun in the hollow at the base of his skull.

'What did you see?' said the man.

'I saw a man,' said Virgil. He was beyond lying now. 'I looked up, I saw a man, a black man. There was another man with him. He was white. I didn't get a good look at him. I shouldn't have looked. *I shouldn't have looked.*'

'What did you see?'

'I told you. I saw—'

The gun cocked.

'What did you see?'

And Virgil at last understood.

'Nothing,' he said. 'I saw nothing. I wouldn't know the guys if I saw them again. Nothing. That's all. Nothing.'

The gun moved away from his head.

'Don't make me come back here, Virgil,' said the man.

Virgil's whole body shook with the force of his sobs.

'I won't,' he said. 'I promise.'

'Now you stay there, Virgil. You keep kneeling.'

'I will,' said Virgil. 'Thank you. Thank you.'

'You're welcome,' said the man.

Virgil didn't hear him moving away. He just stayed kneeling until at last the sun began to rise and, shivering, he rose and walked back to his little house.

PART FIVE

There is no hope of death for these souls,
And their lost life is so low,
That they are envious of any other kind.

Dante Alighieri, 'Inferno', Canto III

27

They began to drift into the state over the next two days, in groups and alone, always by road, never by plane. There were the couple that checked into the small motel outside Sangerville, who kissed and cooed like the young lovers they appeared to be yet slept in separate beds in their twin room. There were the four men who ate a hurried breakfast in the Miss Portland Diner on Marginal Way, their eyes always returning to the black van in which they had arrived, tensing whenever anyone approached it and relaxing only slightly when they had passed by.

And there was the man who drove a truck north from Boston, avoiding the interstate whenever possible, until at last he found himself among forests of pine, a lake gleaming in the distance before him. He checked his watch – too early – and headed back toward Dolby Pond and the La Casa Exotic Dancing Club. There were, he figured, worse ways to kill a few hours.

The worst case scenario came to pass: Supreme Judicial Court Justice Wilton Cooper carried out the review of the decision to deny bail to Aaron Faulkner. In the hour preceding the decision, Bobby Andrus and his team had presented their arguments against bail to Wilton Cooper in his chambers, pointing out that they believed Faulkner to be a substantial flight risk and that potential witnesses could be open to intimidation. When he asked them if they had any new evidence to hand, they had to admit that they had not.

In his submission, Jim Grimes argued that the prosecution had not presented sufficient evidence to suggest that Faulkner might have committed formerly capital crimes. He also offered medical evidence from three separate authorities that Faulkner's health was deteriorating seriously in prison (evidence that the state itself was unable to contest, since its own doctors had found that Faulkner appeared to be suffering from some illness, although they were unable to say from what, precisely, except that he was losing weight rapidly, his temperature was consistently higher than normal, and both blood pressure and heart rate were abnormally high); that the stresses of incarceration were endangering the life of his client, against whom the prosecution had not yet been able to establish a substantial case; and that it was both unjust and inhumane to keep his client in prison while the prosecution attempted to amass enough evidence to shore up said case. Since his client would require medical supervision of the highest order, there was no real risk of flight, and bail should be set accordingly.

Announcing his decision, Cooper dismissed most of my testimony on the basis of the unreliability of my character and determined that the decision by the lower court not to grant bail had been erroneous, since the prosecution had not demonstrated sufficient probable cause that Faulkner had himself committed a formerly capital offense. In addition, he accepted Jim Grimes's submission that his client's poor health meant that he was not a danger to the integrity of the judicial progress and that his need for regular medical treatment meant that he did not constitute a flight risk. He set bail at $1.5 million. Grimes announced that the cash was to hand. Faulkner, chained in an adjoining room under the guard of U.S. marshals, was to be released immediately.

To his credit, Andrus had foreseen the possibility that Cooper would set bail and, reluctantly, had approached the F.B.I. and requested that they serve a warrant for Faulkner's arrest on federal charges should he be released. It was not Andrus's fault that the warrant had been improperly presented: a secretary had misspelt Faulkner's name, rendering it null and void. When

Faulkner left the courthouse, there was no warrant waiting to be served.

Outside Courtroom Number One, a man in a brown Timberland jacket sat on an empty bench and made a call. Ten miles away, the cell phone in Cyrus Nairn's hand buzzed.

'You're good to go,' said the voice on the other end of the line.

Cyrus killed the phone and tossed it into the bushes by the side of the road, then started his car and drove toward Scarborough.

Flashbulbs opened fire as soon as Grimes appeared on the courthouse steps, but Faulkner was not with him. Instead, a Nissan Terrano, with Faulkner hidden beneath a blanket in the rear, turned right from the courthouse and headed toward the Public Market parking garage on Elm. Above it, a helicopter buzzed. Behind it, two cars shadowed. The AG's office was not about to let Faulkner disappear into the depths of the honeycomb world.

A battered yellow Buick pulled in behind the Terrano as it reached the entrance to the garage, causing the following traffic to brake suddenly. There was no need for the big jeep to pause for a ticket because its arrival had been prepared for well in advance: the ticket dispenser had been disabled by the simple application of industrial adhesive while the security guard was distracted by a fire in a garbage can, and the garage had been forced to leave both the entrance and exit barriers permanently raised while the damage was being repaired.

The Terrano passed through quickly, but the Buick following it ground to a halt, blocking the entrance. Crucial seconds passed before the police in the tracking cars realized what was happening. The first car reversed, then headed at speed up the exit ramp, while two detectives from a second car rushed to the Buick, pulled the driver from his seat, and cleared the entrance.

By the time the agents got to the abandoned Terrano, Faulkner was long gone.

* * *

At 7 P.M. Mary Mason left her house at the end of Seavey Landing for her date with Sergeant Mac Arthur. Beyond her house, she could see the marsh and the waters of the Scarborough River as they wended their way around the pointed finger of None such Point and into the sea at Saco Bay. MacArthur was her first real date since her divorce had come through three months earlier, and she was hopeful about a relationship with him. She had known the policeman by sight and, despite his rumpled appearance, thought him kind of cute in a hangdog way. Nothing in their first date had caused her to revise her estimate downward. In fact, he had been quite charming and when he had called her the night before to confirm that a second date was still on, they had talked for almost an hour, surprising him, she suspected, as much as she had surprised herself.

She was almost at the car door when the man approached her. He came from the trees that hid her property from the view of her neighbors. He was small and hunched, with long dark hair that trailed his shoulders and eyes that were almost black, like those of some underground, nocturnal creature. She was already reaching for the Mace in her bag when he struck her backhanded across the face and she fell. He knelt on her legs before she could react again and she felt the pain in her side, an immense burning as the blade entered below her ribs and began to tear its way across her stomach. She tried to scream but his hand was over her mouth and all she could do was wriggle impotently as the blade continued its progress.

And then, just as she felt that she could take no more, that she must surely die from the pain, she heard a voice and saw, over the man's shoulder, a huge hulking figure approach, a beaten-up Chevy idling behind him. He had a beard and wore a leather vest over his T-shirt. She could see the tattoo of a woman on his forearm.

'Hey!' said Bear. 'The fuck you doing, man?'

Cyrus had not wanted to use the gun. He had wanted this done as quietly as possible, but the big and strangely familiar man now racing up the driveway left him with no choice. He rose from the woman before he could finish his cut, took the gun from his belt, and fired.

Two white vans took the Medway exit off I-95 and followed 11 through East Millinocket toward Dolby Pond. In the first van were three men and one woman, all armed. In the second sat another man and woman, also armed, and the Reverend Aaron Faulkner, who was silently reading his Bible on a bench in the back of the van. Had one of the state's medical experts been on hand to check on the preacher, he would have found that the old man's temperature was virtually normal and that all signs of his apparent ill health had already begun to fade.

A cell phone disturbed the silence of the second van. One of the men answered, spoke briefly, then turned back to Faulkner.

'He's coming in to land now,' he told the old man. 'He'll be waiting for us when we get there. We're right on schedule.'

Faulkner nodded, but did not respond. Instead, his eyes remained fixed on his Bible and the account of the trials of Job.

Cyrus Nairn sat behind the wheel of his car at the Black Point Market and sipped a Coke. It was a warm evening and he desperately needed to cool down. The car's AC was busted. It didn't matter much to Cyrus anyway: once the woman was dead he would ditch the car and head south, and that would be the end of it. He could suffer a little discomfort; after all, it was nothing compared to what the woman was about to endure.

He finished the Coke, then drove toward the bridge and dumped the can from the window into the waters below. Things had not gone according to plan over at Pine Point. First, the woman was already leaving the house when he arrived, and had gone for the spray in her bag, causing him to take her outside. Then the big man had come along and he had no choice but to use his gun. He had been afraid, for a moment, that people would hear but there had been no immediate fuss, no clamor.

Still, Cyrus had been forced to leave hurriedly, and he did not like rushing his work.

He checked his watch and, his lips moving silently, counted down from ten. When he reached one, he thought he heard the muffled explosion from Pine Point. When he looked out of his window, smoke was already rising from Mary Mason's burning car. The police would arrive soon, maybe the fire department, and they would find the woman and the dead man. He had preferred to leave the woman dying, not dead. He wanted the noise of the ambulance, the distraction to the policeman MacArthur, even at the risk of her being able to provide a description of him. He suspected that he might not have cut her enough, that she might even survive her injuries. He wondered if he had left her too close to the car, if she might not already be burning. He didn't want there to be any doubt about her identity. They were minor issues, but they troubled Cyrus. The prospect of capture, though, did not: Cyrus would die before he would go back to prison. Cyrus had been promised salvation, and the saved fear nothing.

To his right, a road curved up into a copse of trees. Cyrus parked his car out of sight, then, his stomach tense with excitement, proceeded up the hill. He cleared the trees and passed a ruined shed to his left, the white house now glowing before him, the dying sunlight reflecting from its glass. Soon, the marsh too would be aflame, the waters running orange and red.

Red, mostly.

Mary Mason lay on her back on the grass, staring at the sky. She had seen the hunched man toss the device into her car, the slow fuse burning, and had guessed what it was, but she felt paralyzed, unable to move her hands to stem the bleeding, let alone pull herself away from the car.

She was weakening.

She was dying.

She felt something brush her leg, and managed to move her head slightly. A long trail of blood marked the big man's painful progress toward her. He was almost beside her now, hauling himself along by his ragged and bloodied fingernails. He reached out to her and grasped her hand, then pressed it against the wound in her side. She gasped in pain, but he forced her to maintain the pressure.

Then, slowly, he began to drag her by the collar of her shirt toward the grass. She screamed aloud once, but still she tried to keep her hand pressed to the wound until at last he could pull her no farther. He lay against the old tree in her yard, her head resting on his legs and his hand upon her hand, keeping the pressure on, the expanse of its trunk shielding them both from the car when the device exploded moments later, shattering the glass in the automobile and the windows in her house and sending a blast of heat rolling over the lawn and the tips of her toes.

'Hold on,' said Bear. His breath rattled in his throat. 'Hold on now. They'll be coming soon.'

Roger Bowen sat in a corner of Tommy Condon's pub on Charleston's Church Street, sipping on a beer. On the table before him lay his cell phone. He was waiting for the call to confirm that the preacher was safe and on his way north to Canada. Bowen checked his watch as two men in their late twenties passed by, joshing and pushing each other. The one nearest stumbled against Bowen's table, sending his cell phone tumbling to the floor. Bowen rose up in fury as the young man apologized and replaced the phone on the table.

'You fucking asshole,' hissed Bowen.

'Hey, take it easy,' said the guy. 'I said I was sorry.'

They left shaking their heads. Bowen watched them climb into a car outside and drive away.

Two minutes later, the phone on his table rang.

In the seconds before he pressed Receive, it might have struck him that the phone was a little heavier than he remembered, and that the fall to the floor had maybe scuffed it some.

He hit the green button and put the phone to his ear, just in time for the explosion to tear the side of his head off.

Cyrus Nairn stood in front of the house, clutching a map and looking puzzled. Cyrus wasn't much of an actor, but he figured that he didn't have to be. There was no movement from the house. He walked to the screen door and stared into the hallway beyond. The door was well oiled, and opened silently. He moved slowly inside, checking the rooms as he went, ensuring that each one was empty, wary of the dog, until at last he reached the kitchen.

The big man stood at the kitchen table, drinking soya milk from a carton. He wore a T-shirt that read 'Klan Killer.' He looked at Cyrus in surprise. His hand was already moving to the gun on the table when Cyrus fired and the carton exploded in a shower of milk and blood and the big man tumbled backward, breaking a chair as he fell. Cyrus stood over him and watched as the emptiness entered his eyes.

From behind the house, he heard the barking of a dog. It was young and stupid, and Cyrus's only concern about it was that, in the house, its barking might have given the woman warning. Carefully, he glanced out of the kitchen window and saw the woman strolling in her yard close by the edge of the marsh, the dog beside her. He walked to the back door and slipped out as soon as he was certain that the woman was out of sight. Then, skirting the side of the house and staying close to the walls, he found her once again. She was in the long grass, moving away from the house, picking wildflowers. He could see the swelling at her belly, and some of his desire cooled. Cyrus liked to play with them before he finished them off. He had never tried playing with a pregnant woman before and something told him that he wouldn't enjoy it, but Cyrus was always open to new experiences. The woman rose and stretched, holding her hand to her back, and Cyrus retreated back into the shadows. She was pretty, he thought, her face very pale, accentuated by her red hair. He drew a breath and tried to calm himself. When he looked again, she was strolling farther into the long grass and the evening shimmering of the waters, the dog racing ahead of her. Cyrus debated waiting for her to return to the house but he was afraid that somebody might come up that curving road and see his car, and then he would be trapped. No, there was cover out there, trees and long grass, and the rushes would hide him when he took her.

Cyrus unsheathed the knife at his waist and, holding it close to his thigh, moved after the woman.

The Cessna banked, then made a slow descent toward the Ambajejus Lake. It bounced a little on the water when it landed before drawing to a gradual halt, its wings tilting slightly as it approached the old jetty. The man at the controls of the Cessna was called Gerry Szelog and the only thing he had been paid for this flight was fuel money. That was okay, though, because Gerry was a believer, and believers did as they were asked and wanted nothing in return. In the past Szelog's Cessna had transported guns, fugitives, and in one case, the body of a woman reporter who had poked her nose where she had no business poking it and who now lay at the bottom of the Carolina Shoals. Szelog had scouted out the lake a couple of days earlier by taking a flight with the Katahdin Air Service that operated out of Spencer Cove. He'd also checked their hours to ensure that the pilots from Katahdin would not be around to ask questions when he came in to land.

The Cessna stopped and a man appeared from behind one of the trees on the shore. Szelog could see that he wore blue overalls that billowed slightly as he ran toward the plane. This would be Farren, the man responsible for the arrangements at this end. Szelog climbed out of the little cockpit, then hopped down onto the jetty to meet the advancing man.

'Right on schedule,' said Szelog, removing his shades.

He stopped.

The man standing before him wasn't Farren, because Farren was supposed to be white. This man was black. He also had a gun in his hand.

'Yeah,' said the man. 'You could say you're dead on time.'

It took a few moments for Cyrus to figure out why the woman appeared to be in a world of her own, for otherwise she would surely have heard the gunshot. She paused at the edge of a stream and reached into a small pouch at her waist, withdrawing the Discman and forwarding through the tracks. When she found the tune she was looking for, she replaced the device and continued on her way, skirting the trees, the dog racing ahead of her. The dog had paused once or twice and looked back toward Cyrus as he made his way, hunched, through the long grass, but Cyrus was moving slowly and the young dog's eyesight was not good enough to pick him out from the swaying grass. Cyrus's feet, and the ends of his jeans, were soaking wet. It felt uncomfortable to him but then he thought of the prison, and the stale stench of his cell, and decided that being wet wasn't so bad after all. The woman rounded the edge of the copse and almost disappeared from sight, but Cyrus could still see her pale blue dress moving between the trunks and the low branches. The trees would provide him with the cover he needed.

Close now, thought Cyrus.

Almost time.

And Leonard's voice echoed his words.

Almost time.

The only traffic encountered by Faulkner's small convoy as it headed up Golden Road was a big container truck that was signaling right from the Ambajejus Parkway. The man behind the wheel lifted three fingers in greeting as they passed, then began to make his turn onto the road. He checked his rearview mirror and watched as the vans turned onto Fire Road 17 and headed for the lake.

He stopped his turn and started to reverse.

Cyrus moved faster, his short legs struggling to eat up the distance as he tried to draw closer to the woman. He could see her clearly now. She had left the shelter of the trees and moved into the open, her head low, the long grass parting as she went, then reforming itself behind her. The dog, he noticed, was now on its leash. It didn't matter much to Cyrus either way. The dog was unlikely to respond quickly to the threat posed by Cyrus, if he responded at all. The blade on Cyrus's knife was five inches long. It would cut the dog's throat as easily as it would cut the woman's.

Cyrus left the shade of the trees and entered the marsh.

The fire road was strewn with brown and yellow leaves. Huge rocks lined its edges, and the trees grew thickly beyond them. Faulkner's people were within sight of the lakeshore when the driver's side window of the lead van disintegrated in a shower of glass and plastic, the impact of the bullets throwing the driver sideways and sending the van hurtling toward the trees. The woman beside him tried to wrench the wheel to the right but more shots came, tearing a ribbon of holes across the windshield and through the sides of the van. The rear door opened as the others inside tried to run for cover, but they were dead before they hit the road.

The driver of the second van responded quickly. He kept his head low and put his foot down hard, screeching around the disabled lead vehicle in a cloud of leaves and sending the front wheels and hood of the van straight into one of the rocks by the side of the road. Dazed, he reached beneath the dashboard, released the sawn-off, and rose up in time to take Louis's first bullet in his chest. The shotgun fell from his hands and he slumped forward.

Meanwhile, the woman was in the back of the van and preparing to respond. She took Faulkner by the arm and told him to start running for the lake as soon as she opened the doors. In her hands she held an H&K G11 automatic rifle set to fire bursts of three rounds, each round a special caseless cartridge that was simply a block of explosive with a bullet buried at its center. She counted down from three, then hit the release handle on the door and began firing. In front of her, a small fat man was punched backward by the impact of the rounds and lay twitching on the road. Behind the woman, Faulkner began to run for the trees and the waters beyond as she sprayed bursts toward the roadside and then turned to follow him. She was almost level with the old man when she felt the impact at her left thigh felling her instantly. She turned on her back, flipped the catch to fully automatic, and kept firing toward the approaching men as they dove for cover. When the gun locked empty, she tossed it to one side and drew her pistol. She had almost raised it when a hand touched her arm gently. Her head turned, her arm moving milliseconds slower. She barely had time to register the gaping hole of the gun leveled at her face before her life ended.

Mary Mason heard the sirens and the raised voices of her neighbors. She reached out her hand to let the big man know, and felt his stillness.

She began to cry.

Out on the road, the truck had reversed down and had already reached the scene of the trap. Its rear doors were opened, and a ramp was lowered to enable the two disabled vans to be pushed into its interior. The bodies of the dead were placed inside, while two men with back-mounted vacuums scoured the blood and broken glass from the road.

But the old man was still running hard, despite the briars that pulled at his feet and the branches of the trees that tugged at his clothes. He slipped on the damp leaves and sensed movement to either side of him as he struggled to rise, a gun clutched in his right hand. He got to his feet just as one of the figures detached itself from the trees and moved to intercept him. He tried to turn, to make for a gap in the woods to the north, but a second figure appeared, and the old man stopped.

Faulkner's face wrinkled in recognition.

'Remember me?' asked Angel. He had a gun in his hand, hanging loosely by his side.

To Faulkner's right, Louis walked slowly across the earth and stone. He too carried a gun by his side. Faulkner tried to back away, then turned to see my face. He raised his gun. It swung first toward me, then Angel, and finally Louis.

'Go ahead, Reverend,' said Louis. His gun was now pointing at Faulkner, one eye closed as he sighted down the barrel. 'You choose.'

'They'll know,' said Faulkner. 'You'll make me a martyr.'

'They ain't never gonna find you, Reverend,' said Louis. 'Far as people gonna know, you just disappeared off the face of the earth.'

I lifted my gun. So did Angel.

'But we'll know,' Angel said. 'We'll always know.'

Faulkner tried to turn his gun on himself as the three shots came simultaneously and the old man bucked and fell. He lay on his back, looking at the sky. Thin streams of blood trailed from the corners of his mouth, then the sky disappeared as we stared down upon him. His mouth opened and closed as he tried to say something. He swallowed and licked at the blood with his tongue. The fingers of his right hand moved feebly as he looked at me.

Slowly, carefully, I knelt down.

'Your bitch is dead,' he whispered, as his eyes closed for the last time.

And when I looked up, the trees were filled with ravens.

Cyrus's mouth was dry. He was so close to her now – thirty, maybe thirty-five feet away. He ran his finger along the blade and watched the dog tugging at the leash, straining to get ahead of its mistress, its attention distracted by the presence of the birds and small rodents it could hear moving through the grass. Cyrus couldn't understand why she had leashed the dog. Let it run, he thought. The hell harm can it do?

Twenty feet now. Just a few more steps. The woman stepped into a copse of trees above a small pool of water, an outpost of the larger forest that shadowed the marsh to the north, and was suddenly out of his sight. Ahead of him, Cyrus heard the ringing of a cell phone. He ran, his legs aching as he reached the trees. The first thing he saw was the dog. It was tied by its leash to the rotting trunk of a fallen tree. It looked at Cyrus in puzzlement, then yapped happily at what it saw behind.

Cyrus turned and the log caught him full in the face, breaking his nose and sending him stumbling backward out of the trees. He tried to raise his knife and was hit again in the same spot, the pain blinding him. He felt empty space beneath his heels and lifted his arms to try to stop himself from falling even as he tumbled and landed with a splash in the water. He broke back to the surface and began to struggle toward the bank, but Cyrus was not built for swimming. In fact, he could barely swim a stroke and panic had almost immediately set in as he sensed the depth of the water. Water levels in the Scarborough marshes were usually six to eight feet, but the monthly flood had raised them to fourteen and sixteen feet in places. Cyrus couldn't touch the bottom with his feet.

And then there was another impact on his skull and he felt something break in his head. The energy seemed to leach from his body, his hands and legs refusing to move. Slowly, he began to sink, descending until his lower body was surrounded by weeds and fallen branches, his feet deep in the mud. Air bubbled from his lips and the sight of it seemed to force one final effort from him. His whole body jerked and his hands and arms began to beat at the water, the surface drawing closer as he started to rise.

Cyrus's ascent was arrested as something pulled at his feet. He looked down but could see only weeds and grass. He tried kicking, but his feet were held fast in the murk and vegetation below, the branches like fingers wrapped around his ankles.

Hands. There were hands upon him. The voices in his head were shrieking, sending out contradictory messages as his air supply dwindled.

Hands.

Branches.

They're just branches.

But he could *feel* the hands down there. He could feel the fingers pulling at him, dragging him deeper, forcing him to join them, and he knew that they were waiting down there for him. The women from the hollow were waiting for him.

A shadow fell across him. Blood was flowing freely from the wound in his head and from his ears and nose. He looked up and the woman was staring down at him from the bank, the dog's head to one side as it peered at the water in puzzlement. The headphones were no longer at the woman's ears but lay curled around her neck, and something told Cyrus that they had been silent from the moment she had spotted him and began to draw him deeper into the marsh. He stared up at the woman imploringly and opened his mouth as if to beg her to save him, but instead the last of his air floated away and the water coursed into his body. He raised his hands to the woman, but the only move she made was to take her right hand and rub it slowly and rhythmically against the slight swell of her belly, so that it seemed that she was soothing the child within, that it was aware of what was occurring outside its world and was distressed by the action. The woman's face was empty. There was no pity, no shame, no guilt, no regret. There was not even anger, just a blankness that was worse than any fury Cyrus had ever seen or felt.

Cyrus felt a final tug at his legs as he began to drown, the water filling his lungs, the pain in his head growing as he was starved of oxygen, the voices in his mind rising to a last crescendo, then, slowly, fading away, his final vision that of a pale, pitiless woman rubbing gently at her womb, calming her unborn child.

EPILOGUE

The rivers flow.

The tide is receding, the waters returning to the sea. The shorebirds are gathering. The marsh is their resting stop on the way to the Arctic tundras in which they will nest, and the departing tides provide rich pickings for them. They flit over the streams, their shadows like melting ore in the runnels of molten silver.

It is only now, looking back, that I realize the part that water has played in all that has occurred. The bodies dumped in Louisiana, entombed in oil barrels, mute and undiscovered while the waters flowed around them. A family slain and their remains placed beneath leaves in an empty swimming pool. The Aroostook Baptists, buried by a lake, waiting for decades to be found and released. Addy and Melia Jones, the one slain within earshot of a river, the other twice dead in a polluted pit of foul water.

And one more: Cassie Blythe, found curled beneath the earth in a hollow by a riverbank, surrounded by the bodies of five others, the bones on her hands marked by the passage of Cyrus Nairn's blade.

Water, flowing endlessly to the sea; each of them in their way denied the promise offered by it, unable to answer the call until, at last, they were brought forth and allowed to follow its course to the final peace that comes to all.

Cyrus Nairn stood among the long stems of a cattail patch, the road visible before him. All around him they moved, their passage like silk against his skin, their presence felt and sensed as much as seen, a great mass of them descending ever onward to the sea, where at last they were absorbed into its waiting surf, the paleness of them joining with it until they disappeared from view. He remained still, like a bulwark against their flow, for his back was to the sea and it did not call to him as it did to the others that followed the white roads through the marsh and into the ocean. Instead, Cyrus watched the old car that idled on the black highway that wound its way toward the coast, its star-shattered windscreen reflecting the night sky above, until the door opened and he knew that it was time.

He climbed from the marsh, hauling himself upward on rocks and metal, and walked toward the waiting Coupe de Ville, its tinted windows revealing only the barest shadows of the figures that lay within. As he stepped around the hood, the driver's window rolled slowly down and he saw the man who sat with his hands on the wheel, a bald man with a too-wide mouth, a ragged red hole torn in the front of his filthy raincoat, as if his death had come about through impalement upon some great stake, a death that continued to be visited upon him for eternity, for as Cyrus watched the wound appeared to heal and then erupt forth again, and the man's eyes rolled in his agony. Yet he smiled at Cyrus, and beckoned him on. Behind him, barely visible, was a child dressed in black. She was singing, and Cyrus thought that her voice was one of the most beautiful sounds that he had ever heard, a gift from God. Then the child shifted and became a woman with a bullet wound in her throat, and the singing stopped.

Muriel, thought Cyrus. Her name is Muriel.

He was at the open door. He placed his hand upon its upper edge and peered inside.

The man who sat on the back seat was surrounded by cobwebs. Small brown spiders busied themselves around him, endlessly spinning the cocoon that anchored him in place. His head was ruined, torn apart by the shot that had killed him, but Cyrus could still see the remains of his red hair. The man's eyes were barely visible beneath the cobwebs and the folds of skin that surrounded the sockets, but Cyrus saw the pain within them, renewed over and over again as the spiders bit him.

And Cyrus understood at last that by our actions in this life, we make our own hell in which to exist in the next, and that his place was now here, and so it would always be.

'I'm sorry, Leonard,' he said, and for the first time since he was very young he heard his own voice, and thought how querulous it sounded, how uncertain. And he noticed that there was but one voice, that all the others had been silenced; and he knew that this voice had always been among those that he had heard but that he had chosen not to listen to it. It was the voice that had counseled reason and pity and remorse, the voice to which he had remained deaf throughout his adult life.

'I'm sorry,' he said again. 'I failed.'

And Pudd's mouth opened, and spiders tumbled forth.

'Come,' he said. 'We have a long way to go.'

Cyrus climbed into the car, and instantly felt the spiders move upon him, and the construction of a new web beginning.

And the car turned on the road, its back to the sea, and headed away, over mud and marsh grass, until it was lost in the darkness to the north.

There is long grass growing at the base of the stone and weeds have found their sparse anchorage in the dirt. They come away easily in my hand. I have not been here since before the summer. The caretaker of the small cemetery has been ill, so while the pathways have been tended the individual graves have not. I tear the grass out in clumps, the dirt hanging from the roots, and toss them to one side.

The little one's name had almost been obscured, but now it is clearly visible once again. For a moment, I run my fingers along the indentations of the letters, distracted by the sight, then return to the clearing of the grave.

A shadow falls across me, and the woman lowers herself down by my side, her legs apart to accommodate the swelling at her belly. I do not look at her. I am crying now and I do not understand why because I do not feel that terrible crushing sadness inside that has brought me to tears at other times. Instead I feel relief, and gratitude that she is here now beside me in this place for the first time, because it is good and necessary that she be here, that this should at last be revealed to her. But still the tears come and I find myself unable even to see the weeds and the grass clearly, until at last she reaches down and her hand guides mine, and together we work, discarding that which is ugly and unsightly, keeping that which is beautiful and enriching, our hands touching, brushing against each other, their presence with us in the breeze on our faces and the water flowing beside us: children gone and children yet to come; love remembered, love remaining; the lost and the found, the living and the dead, side by side together.

On the White Road.

ACKNOWLEDGEMENTS

In researching this book I relied greatly upon the work and knowledge of others, including *Before Freedom* by Belinda Hurmence (Mentor, 1990); *Rice and Slaves: Ethnicity and the Slave Trade in Colonial South Carolina* by Daniel C. Littlefield (Illini Books, 1991); *The Great South Carolina Ku Klux Klan Trials 1871–1872* by Lou Falkner Williams (University of Georgia Press, 1996); *Gullah Fuh Oonah* by Virginia Mixon Geraty (Sandlapper Publishing, 1997); *Blue Roots* by Roger Pinckney (Llewellyn Publications, 2000); *A Short History of Charleston* by Roger Rosen (University of South Carolina Press, 1992); *Kaballah* by Kenneth Hanson Ph.D (Council Oak Books, 1998); *American Extremists* by John George and Laird Wilcox (Prometheus Books, 1996); and *The Racist Mind* by Raphael S. Ezekiel (Penguin, 1995).

In addition, a number of individuals gave generously of their time and knowledge. I am especially grateful to deputy attorney general Bill Stokes and assistant attorney general Chuck Dow at the Maine Attorney General's office; Jeffrey D. Merrill, Warden of Maine State Prison, Thomaston, and his staff, especially Colonel Douglas Starbird and Sergeant Elwin Weeks; Hugh E. Munn, South Carolina Law Enforcement Division; Lieutenant Stephen D. Wright, City of Charleston Police Department; Janice Kahn, my guide to Charleston; Sarah Yeates, formerly of the Museum of Natural History in New York; and the National Park Service staff of the Congaree Swamp National Monument.

On a personal note, I want to thank Sue Fletcher, Kerry Hood and all at Hodder & Stoughton; my agent Darley

Anderson and his staff; my family; Ruth, for many kindnesses; and, belatedly, Dr Ian Ross, who introduced me to Ross Macdonald; and Ella Shanahan, who kept me in funds when few others would.

John Connolly on the Parker novels:

'Since about the second book I've thought of the Parker novels as a sequence rather than a series, in that each book develops themes, ideas and plots from the preceding books.'

Although each novel is self-contained, and can be enjoyed as a compelling thriller, collectively the Parker novels form a rich and involving epic sequence in which characters reappear and clues laid down in earlier stories are solved in later ones. Below is a précis of key events in each of the Charlie Parker novels.

Former NYPD Charlie Parker first appears (in **Every Dead Thing**) on a quest for the killer of his wife and daughter. He is a man consumed by violence, guilt and the desire for revenge. When his ex-partner asks him to track down a missing girl, Parker embarks on a grim odyssey through the bowels of organised crime; to cellars of torture and death; and to a unique serial killer, an artist who uses the human body as his canvas: The Travelling Man. By the end of the novel, Parker realises he is at the beginning of another dark journey – to avenge the voiceless victims of crime: the poor, women and children. It is a journey on which his dead wife and child will be constant ghostly companions.

In **Dark Hollow,** Parker returns to the wintry Maine landscape where he grew up and becomes embroiled in another murder hunt. The chief suspect is Billy Purdue, the ex-husband of the dead woman, and Parker is not the only one on his trail. Aided by his friends, hitmen Angel and Louis (first encountered in **Every Dead Thing**), Parker must go back thirty years into his own grandfather's troubled past and into the violent origins of a mythical killer, the monster Caleb Kyle. Parker's personal life seems to take an upward turn in the attractive form of psychologist Rachel Wolfe.

Parker's empathy with the powerless victims of crime is growing ever stronger. It makes him a natural choice to investigate the death of Grace Peltier in **The Killing Kind** – a death that appears to be a suicide. The discovery of a mass grave – the final resting place of a religious community that had disappeared forty years earlier – convinces Parker that there is a link between Grace and these deaths: a shadowy organisation called The Fellowship. His investigation draws him into increasingly violent confrontations with the Fellowship's enforcer, the demonic arachnophile, Mr Pudd. Genial killers Angel and Louis join Parker again as he descends into a honeycomb world populated by dark angels and lost souls.

Parker's relationship with Rachel reaches a new level in **The White Road**, but he is still driven to solve the most challenging of cases. A black youth faces the death penalty for rape and murder; his victim, the daughter of one of the wealthiest men in South Carolina. It is a case with its roots in old evil, and old evil is Charlie Parker's speciality. But this turns out not to be an investigation, but rather a descent into the abyss, a confrontation with dark forces that threaten all Parker holds dear.

Evil men from his past unite to exact a terrible revenge on the private detective. Seemingly unconnected events turn out to be part of a complex and intricate pattern.

The Killing Kind and **The White Road** effectively form two halves of a single, larger narrative and are probably best read in order.

In "The Reflecting Eye", a long novella featured in the **Nocturnes** collection, Parker becomes involved in a curious investigation into a former killer's abandoned house, and learns that someone, or something, seems be using its empty rooms as a base from which to hunt for victims. This novella introduces us for the first time to the character known as the Collector, an individual who will come to play an important, and sinister, role in the books that follow, most particularly in **The Unquiet** and **The Lovers**.

The Black Angel is not an object; it is not a myth. The Black Angel lives. And it is a prize sought for centuries by evil men. Not that Charlie Parker's latest case starts this way; it starts with the disappearance of a young woman in New York. Her abductors believe that no one will come looking for her, but they are wrong. For Alice is 'blood' to Parker's sidekick, the assassin Louis, and Louis will tear apart anyone who attempts to stop him finding her.

The hunt turns into an epic quest that will take Parker and his team to an ornate church of bones in Eastern Europe and a cataclysmic battle between good and evil. It marks a dawning realisation in Parker that there is another dimension to his crusade, a dangerous dimension that Rachel finds herself increasingly unable to live with.

The Unquiet begins with a missing man, a once respected psychiatrist who went absent following revelations about harm done to children in his care. His daughter believes him dead, but is not allowed to come to terms with her father's legacy. For someone is asking questions about Daniel Clay: the revenger Merrick, a father and a killer obsessed with discovering the truth about his own daughter's disappearance. Living apart from Rachel and their child, Charlie Parker is hired to make Merrick go away, but finds strange bonds with the revenger, who has drawn from the shadows pale wraiths drifting through the ranks of the unquiet dead. At the end of the novel comes a tantalising reference to Parker's own parentage that will inform events in **The Lovers.**

But first Angel and Louis take centre stage in **The Reapers,** where the elite killers themselves become targets. A wealthy recluse sends them north to a town that no longer exists on a map. A town ruled by a man with very personal reasons for wanting Louis's blood spilt. There they find themselves trapped, isolated and at the mercy of a killer feared above all others: the assassin of assassins, Bliss. Thanks to Parker, help is on its way. But can Angel and Louis stay alive long enough for it to reach them?

The bloody events in **The Unquiet** result in Parker losing his PI licence, so he returns to Maine and takes a job in a Portland bar while the fuss dies down. But **The Lovers** shows Parker engaged on his most personal case yet: an investigation into his own origins and the circumstances surrounding the death of his father. When he was a boy, Parker's father, himself a cop, killed a pair of teenagers then took his own life. His actions were never explained. Parker's quest for that explanation reveals lies, secrets and betrayal. Haunting it – as they have done all his life – are two figures in the shadows, an unidentified man and woman with one purpose: to bring an end to Parker's existence.

In **The Whisperers**, Parker is asked to investigate the apparent suicide of Damian Patchett, a former soldier. But this is not an isolated death; former combatants are dying in epidemic quantities, driven by someone or something to take their own lives.

Parker cannot defeat this evil on this own. To combat it, he is forced into an uneasy alliance with a man he fears more than any other. The Collector first appeared in the novella The Reflecting Eye and remains a sinister presence in Parker's consciousness. It is as though the two men are twin moons orbiting a dark, unknown planet. Now he steps out of the shadows and as their eyes meet, Parker sees for the first time that he himself inspires fear in the Collector.

In **The Burning Soul**, Charlie Parker becomes reluctantly involved in investigating the abduction of a fourteen-year-old girl

The small Maine town of Pastor's Bay is the home of Randall Haight, a man with a secret. When he was a teenager, he and his friend killed a girl. He did his time and has built a life for himself, not sharing details of his past with anyone. But someone has found out, and is sending anonymous threatening messages. And Anna Kore – the missing girl – lived in Pastor's Bay, not two miles away from Haight.

Randall Haight is not the kind of man Charlie Parker wants to help. But he is already drawn to the case of Anna Kore and cannot turn away from the chance to find her.
In the course of the investigation he comes up against the police, the FBI and a doomed mobster, Tommy Morris.

The Wrath of Angels, the eleventh Parker novel, is a sequel of sorts to **The Black Angel**, and returns to some of the themes and characters in that earlier novel.

Parker hears tales of a plane lost in the Maine woods, the mystery of its vanished pilots, and the possibility that it contained a living cargo. What draws Parker's interest is the possibility that the plane was also carrying a list of those who had struck deals with the Antichrist himself, a record of individuals who had committed acts of evil, or were yet capable of committing them. But the list's existence also draws others, both those interested in protecting it and also individuals who want to secure it for their own ends, among them Parker's nemesis, the serial killer known as the Collector. Yet it soon becomes clear that someone, or something, has survived the crash, and is waiting in the woods. **The Wrath of Angels** brings to an end certain elements in the Parker series, while also containing events that lead directly into the novel that follows it, **The Wolf in Winter**.

JOHN CONNOLLY

BAD MEN

'With BAD MEN, there's no chance of indifference. This . . . will knock your socks off' *Daily Mirror*

In 1693, the settlers on the small Maine island of Sanctuary were betrayed to their enemies and slaughtered. Since then, the island has known three hundred years of peace.

Until now. For men are descending on Sanctuary, their purpose to hunt down and kill the wife of their leader and retrieve the money that she stole from him. All that stands in their way are a young rookie officer, Sharon Macy, and the island's strange, troubled policeman, the giant known as Melancholy Joe Dupree. But Joe Dupree is no ordinary policeman. He is the guardian of the island's secrets, the repository of its memories. He knows that Sanctuary has been steeped in blood once; it will tolerate the shedding of innocent blood no longer. Now a band of killers is set to desecrate Sanctuary and unleash the fury of its ghosts upon themselves and all who stand by them.

On Sanctuary, evil is about to meet its match . . .

'Five-star chill with enough menace to keep the pages turning well into the wee small hours.' *Irish Times*

JOHN CONNOLLY

NOCTURNES

'Terrifying and delightful.' *Time Out*

Take his hand and follow him into the darkness.

John Connolly, bestselling author of Charlie Parker thrillers, turns his pen to the short story to give us a volume of chilling tales of the supernatural. In this macabre collection, echoing masters of the genre from M.R. James to Stephen King, Connolly delves into our darkest fears – lost lovers, missing children, subterranean creatures, and predatory demons.

Framing the collection are two substantial novellas: *The Cancer Cowboy Rides* charts the fatal progress of a modern-day grim reaper, while *The Reflecting Eye* is a haunted house tale with a twist and marks the return of private detective Charlie Parker, the troubled hero of Connolly's crime novels.

Nocturnes is a masterly volume to be read with the lights on – menace has never been so seductive . . .

'Twists the classic ghost story in a modern macabre way' *Radio Times*

JOHN CONNOLLY

THE BOOK OF LOST THINGS

'A moving fable, brilliantly imagined' *The Times*

'Everything you can imagine is real'

High in his attic bedroom, twelve-year-old David mourns the loss of his mother. He is angry and he is alone, with only the books on his shelf for company.

But those books have begun to whisper to him in the darkness and as he takes refuge in the myths and fairytales, so beloved by his dead mother, he finds that the real world and the fantasy world have begun to meld. The Crooked Man has come, with his mocking smile and his enigmatic words: 'Welcome, you majesty. All hail the new king.'

And as war rages across Europe, David is violently propelled into a land that is both a construct of his imagination yet frighteningly real, a strange reflection of his own world composed of myths and stories, populated by wolves and worse-than-wolves, and ruled over by a faded king who keeps his secrets in a mysterious book . . .

THE BOOK OF LOST THINGS.

'Written in the clear, evocative manner of the best British fairy tales from J.M. Barrie to C.S. Lewis, *The Book of Lost Things* is an engaging, magical, thoughtful read' *Independent*

BOOKS TO DIE FOR

Edited by
JOHN CONNOLLY
and
DECLAN BURKE

'Indispensable' *Sunday Telegraph*

Winner of the 2013 Agatha, Anthony and the Macavity Awards for Best Crime Non-Fiction.

With so many mystery novels to choose from and so many new titles appearing each year, where should the reader start? What are the classics of the genre? Which are the hidden gems?

In the most ambitious anthology of its kind yet attempted, the world's leading mystery writers have come together to champion the greatest mystery novels ever written. In a series of personal essays that often reveal as much about themselves and their work as they do about the books that they love, more than 120 authors from twenty countries have created a guide that will be indispensable for generations of readers and writers.

From Christie to Child and Poe to P.D. James, from Sherlock Holmes to Hannibal Lecter and Philip Marlowe to Peter Wimsey, *Books to Die For* brings together the cream of the mystery world for a feast of reading pleasure, a treasure trove for those new to the genre and those who believe that there is nothing new left to discover.

This is the one essential book for every reader who has ever finished a mystery novel and thought . . . 'I want more!'

'This volume challenges a few myths and is worth reading for that pleasure alone.' *Sunday Times*

JOHN CONNOLLY

THE WANDERER IN UNKNOWN REALMS

A short story in digital form

Lionel Maulding, a rare-book collector, has gone missing from his country home in Norfolk. Word War I veteran-turned detective, Soter investigates into the matter at Maulding's solicitor's behest.

From the nature of books in Lionel Maulding's impressive library at Bromdun Hall, it is clear that he was greatly interested in the occult. But how far did that take him? There is evidence of the withdrawal of £10,000, an extraordinary sum of money for the purchase of a single book.

As Soter's investigations take him from the slowly decaying Bromdun Hall to the sinister bookseller in Chelsea and the book scout in Whitechapel, he enters a nightmare world where his horrific experiences in the trenches echo the fearful reality unleashed by his search.

JOHN CONNOLLY

THE GATES:

A Samuel Johnson Adventure – 1

'Demonic, darkly comic'
Daily Telegraph

A brilliant new departure for bestselling author John Connolly.

Young Samuel Johnson and his dachshund Boswell are trying to show initiative by trick-or-treating a full three days before Hallowe'en. Which is how they come to witness strange goings-on at 666 Crowley Avenue.

The Abernathys don't mean any harm by their flirtation with Satanism. But it just happens to coincide with a malfunction in the Large Hadron Collider that creates a gap in the universe. A gap in which there is a pair of enormous gates. The gates to Hell. And there are some pretty terrifying beings just itching to get out . . .

Can Samuel persuade anyone to take this seriously? Can he harness the power of science to save the world as we know it?

'Destined to be another runaway success appealing to both young adults and their parent alike.'
Sunday Independent

JOHN CONNOLLY

HELL'S BELLS:

A Samuel Johnson Adventure – 2

'Demonic, darkly comic'
Daily Telegraph

Samuel Johnson is in trouble. The demon Mrs Abernathy is seeking revenge on him for his part in foiling the invasion of Earth by the forces of Darkness. She wants Samuel, and when a scientific experiment goes wrong, she gets her chance: Samuel and his faithful dachshund, Boswell, are pulled through a portal into Hell.

But catching Samuel is not going to be easy. Mrs Abernathy has reckoned without the bravery and cleverness of one boy and his dog, or the loyalty of Samuel's friend, the hapless demon Nurd. Most of all, she hasn't planned on the intervention of an unexpected band of little men, for Samuel and Boswell are not the only inhabitants of Earth who have found themselves in Hell.

If you thought demons were frightening, just wait until you meet Mr Merryweather's Elves . . .

'Hilarious, intelligent and fun. I loved it.'
Derek Landy

JOHN CONNOLLY

THE CREEPS:

A Samuel Johnson Adventure – 3

'Funny and a great read for teens'
Sun

Samuel Johnson is not in a happy place. He is dating the wrong girl, demons are occupying his spare room, and the town in which he lives appears to be cursed.

But there is some good news on the horizon. After years of neglect, the grand old building that once housed Wreckit & Sons is about to reopen as the greatest toyshop that Biddlecombe has ever seen, and Samuel and his faithful dachshund Boswell are to be guests of honour at the big event. A splendid time will be had by all, as long as they can ignore the sinister statue that keeps moving around the town, the Shadows that are slowly blocking out the stars, the murderous Christmas elves, and the fact that somewhere in Biddlecombe a rotten black heart is beating a rhythm of revenge.

A trap has been set. The Earth is doomed. The last hope for humanity lies with one young boy and the girl who's secretly in love with him. Oh, and a dog, two demons, four dwarfs and a very polite monster.

We Wish You a Merry Christmas and a Happy End of the World.

'Comedy is never far away'
Sunday Express